A Dangerous Mind

(Consciousness Belongs to God)

Also by Golam Maula

Darkness turns to Dawn turns to Daylight
(Love is no Stranger to Me)

A Dangerous Mind
(Consciousness Belongs to God)
by
Golam Maula

Published in the United Kingdom by Jem Authors Agency

First printed February 2022

Content copyright © Golam Maula 2022

Design copyright © Jem Authors Agency 2022

All rights reserved

No part of this publication maybe reproduced, distributed, stored in a retrieval system or transmitted in any form and at any time or by any means mechanical, electronic, photocopying or otherwise, without the prior, written permission of the publisher.

The right of Golam Maula to be identified as the author of this work has been asserted by him in accordance with the Copyright, Design and Patents Act 1988.

A CIP record of this book is available from the British Library.

ISBN: 979-842-468-6023

www.jemauthorsagency.com

preface

As the author of this work I offer the reader the opportunity to redeem a cash award for acting as my agent introducing this work to a publisher. On the signing of an acceptable contract, I promise to pay that person £1,000. Why am I offering this reward to my readers? Because I know it will work. Readers understand a good book. I offer the same award to anyone who can help in obtaining a done deal film contract, whether Hollywood or Bollywood. I am now asking for your assistance to help me find a publisher, someone who will translate and publish this novel, and a film producer.

Please send any leads as well as feedback on the novel to golammaula77@gmail.com.

Thank you in advance for your help and for reading this book.

Golam Maula

February 2022

contents

john	7
anjali	87
zoë	137
john	192
anjali	265
epilogue	333

part i
john

one

the colour of buttercup

2002

It was hot. Ferociously so. John Locke had never experienced heat like this before. It didn't burn the skin as much as scrape it, like the tines of a fork scratching down his arms, his face, the back of his neck. Death Valley had nothing on this; he had gone there as a boy with Mom and Dad and brother Joe Jr, just to say they had been. Their real destination was Las Vegas, but they detoured to pass through on their way. In Death Valley you melted, but it was somehow easier than what he was faced with right now; Delhi at noon.

He removed his hat, a Panama which he felt made him look mature, more *British,* and wafted it in front of his face. Street children crowded around him, their hands out for anything he could give them. He had loved his experiences in India but one thing that really bothered him was the poverty. He had seen poverty in his own country of America and the same in the UK where he lived; homelessness and low income families. But never on this scale. He considered himself poor, relying on handouts from his parents, but he felt ashamed when he saw this true and grinding poverty.

On his first day he had given out money and he soon realised his mistake; the crowd around him surged and he was physically stuck amidst the throng before a baton-wielding policeman came to his rescue. The man thought nothing of hitting the children. Locke was incensed and wanted to hit the policeman instead.

On his second day he smiled at the street kids and they never left his side. He raised one in his arms and embraced the rest. He'd been in India almost two weeks now and he was flying back home tomorrow. He had learned the only thing to do was ignore the children altogether.

He didn't like it, but he didn't have much choice. There were just so many of them and he was living on a budget. But they looked at this white man in the east of India and knew he had money to burn. That was their thinking.

The sun clawed at the top of his head and he put the Panama back on. He got to his feet and immediately looked like a beacon of white in the glare and dust of the Delhi street he found himself in. He had gone for the colonial look; white suit, white hat, smart brown shoes. He didn't know why, but he loved the British and increasingly sought to look and dress like them. His version of them at any rate. So much more class than Americans, he felt.

He hadn't worn a baseball cap in years and even when he had done so as a boy, he was always the odd one on his street in San Jose. Somehow never cool. Integrating into his community was never easy for him. There was just too much daft fashion around him all the time. The whooping and the cheers, the blind adoration of your school, or your local sports team. There wasn't much to choose from: football, ice hockey, baseball, basketball. As long as you supported locally in one of those sports you were okay.

He didn't get it. He was much more interested in diversity and colour. And when he watched *Indiana Jones and Raiders of the Lost Ark* he loved Denholm Elliott's Englishman abroad. The image never really left him, then Anthony Hopkins turned up in the same outfit at the end of *Silence of the Lambs.* He was twenty-two now and travelling around India looking like the English gentleman he aspired to be. He heard locals say he was English; he would never correct them; it was his own little joke. But Jesus, it was hot.

Across the street a four-storey building rose awkwardly amongst the street vendors, hawkers and rickshaws. From his viewpoint, the front was ornately decorated with white plaster, but Locke thought it looked cheap. It was attempting to look classy and refined when really its red brick side walls told the truth of it. It was a fake. He laughed to himself. He was doing exactly the same thing with his white suit.

Camera in hand, he crossed the road carefully, avoiding anything moving faster than he was, for Indian drivers did not seem to respect pedestrians or crossings, and started to take some pictures. He had been to some amazing places and packed in a lot in his two weeks. At first he headed north, to Shimla, where the British had had their summer capital. He knew it to be mountainous and wanted to look out at the Himalayas beyond. He had chosen to drive there and hired a car. There seemed to be no rules of the road anywhere in the country and his journey had been one of serene beauty puckered by sheer terror. He wondered often about the number of road deaths there must be. He arranged to leave his car in Shimla and headed back by train. That had been even worse, but he felt he was getting the real Indian experience of overcrowded trains, riding on the roof of the carriages. He had got the best view from up there, and took his camera out to snap happily away. The people seemed genuine and friendly towards him. He felt a little godlike in his own world where everyone seemed to smile.

Next he headed south to Agra for the Taj Mahal, and had tears in his eyes as he read the history and finally looked upon that stunning façade he had seen so many times in pictures. He had heard it from people and read it in books. All of them said the same thing, that people who fall in love don't fear the world, and that people who are afraid don't fall in love. He often asked himself if he could do something equivalent for the women he would love. But reality has struck him, there is not such love in our generation today. Sex was far more advanced than being a pious wife. From there east to Cawnpore and Lucknow, which had been at the centre of the Indian Mutiny of 1857. He loved history; it was probably the reason why he liked the British so much, because they seemed to have more history than anyone else. Certainly more than his own country, which was barely two hundred years old.

He had photographed everywhere he went. Fabulous views of mountains, of garishly and beautifully coloured buses, of poverty-stricken street children and glorious sunsets. And of cows simply sitting in the road. A sacred cow to the locals. There had been a lot of them.

Then he had returned to Delhi for his last few days and on his last full day decided to go somewhere unfashionable, where typical tourists wouldn't venture. That morning he had risen early to take a rickshaw to the Red Fort before the camera-toting hordes arrived, and got some stunning pictures on his digital camera. He would have needed an extra suitcase if he had been using film. To him at least, digital was the future and he had managed to convince his father to buy him a new Minolta for his twenty-first birthday. He spent a couple of hours at the Red Fort then decided to walk although he had no idea where. He crossed the Yamuna River and headed in roughly the same direction waiting for something to catch his eye. It wasn't long before he had lost the tourist trail completely and he was looking at the real India.

And the smells were incredible. He wretched at the open sewer one canal seemed to be then basked in the stunning wafts of cooking spices. It was not quite lunch, but the street food stalls were churning out their amazing dishes. Many had queues thirty or forty people long. He wondered if it was because they were good or because they were cheap. Probably both.

Two smaller streets formed a crossroads with a busier road and he chose to go down one of them. Very quickly a gaggle of different kids surrounded him as others that had followed him for miles started to slouch off back to their normal stamping grounds. It was here that he had sat down and here that he first noticed the white-faced building across the street. As he looked closer, the sweat pouring down his back, he realised it was some sort of temple. He suspected it would be much cooler inside and made his way towards its entrance, snapping every angle of the building as he did so. He spied the sandals left outside and took off his own brown leather brogues, putting them neatly next to the other shoes, his Panama hat placed on top.

When he first arrived in India and visited a temple in Shimla, he had not expected his shoes to be where he left them when he came out. But they hadn't moved, and they hadn't moved the several times he had left his shoes outside other temples. He saw the grinding poverty in the form of the street kids who didn't follow him into the temple, yet not one chose to steal his shoes and sell them for a chapatti. India was a country of contradictions.

He washed his hands in the basin and walked in to be met with a riot of purple and blue hews, with gold ornaments everywhere. He saw the now familiar sight of the statues of Hindu gods and the intricate paintings on the walls. He loved how colourful it all was and tried to convince himself he wasn't there just because he knew it would be much cooler inside. An elderly man in flowing robes walked silently towards him. Locke knew the score by now. If the temple was photographer-friendly, there would be a small fee to pay. If it wasn't, no amount of money would allow you to snap away. This was the first back street temple he had been to; the rest had been unbelievable works of engineering and art, none more so than the Taj Mahal, and the rules around photography varied.

He looked at the elderly man, then held up his camera. The elderly man smiled back and opened his hand, gesturing for Locke make his donation in a small bowl. He donated plenty; he was trying to get rid of his remaining Indian rupees, emptying his pockets of any coins and a good number of the smaller notes in his wallet. He felt better for giving the money to an unassuming temple such as this rather than one of the huge tourist sites. The elderly man put his hands together and bowed graciously and blessed him in Hindi. Locke didn't realise the man had blessed him to find the girl of his dreams. And the bell rang at the perfect moment. He didn't understand the language. He returned the bow and the two parted, leaving Locke to look at his surroundings in peace.

The temple was eerily quiet for somewhere so brilliantly colourful. It didn't seem quite right. He studied the scene around him and tried to guess the age of the building. It was probably quite old, he reasoned, history being the one subject that fascinated him. He thought about the many streets in the surrounding area which were narrow and twisty as though little thought had gone into their design. Locke noticed the American in him coming out and repressed the thought; he had decided long ago that narrow and twisty was far better than the US grid system.

Occasionally a sound would emanate from somewhere in the temple. A woman's sari might swish along the ground or a man's bare feet might slap sweatily on the temple's ceramic floor. Locke ignored them, or occasionally bowed slightly when he caught someone's eye. They always seemed to bow and smile back. The Indian people had been so welcoming and he had long since lost his cynicism that it was because he might give them some money.

He was looking upwards, at the temple's central dome and its amazing richness and riot of colour, when he heard the cough. It had been delicate and he had no idea where it came from, but still he looked around. He saw no one, but then he heard another cough and this time he seemed able to place it somewhere to his right. For some reason he moved in that direction, his bright red socks masking any sound as he walked.

A young woman in a buttercup yellow sari knelt in a side room before a shrine to a Hindu god. Locke watched transfixed as the woman went through her worship. She would raise her hands to her god, then lean forwards in supplication, her arms now outstretched. There was a fluidity to her movement, a grace that he found beautiful. Her eyes were closed, as if there were no other people in the world but herself and her god. She had her back to him, a gentle breeze blowing her sari, the end of which flew into the air like a sail as if it was dancing; as if the wind was giving her a sign of what was to come. He decided to photograph her. He wanted to keep the moment pure, so that she wasn't aware that he was there or that he was taking her picture. He had done the same thing many times during his visit. Usually he would tell the person he had photographed and ask them for a posed picture. Most were fine with what he had done and only a couple demanded payment of a few rupees before letting him take another of them. He didn't mind. The temple bell struck three times, not that he knew the significance.

He crept along the side of the room, using the pillars to mask his presence. The picture was forming in his mind; he would take it on an angle, from behind her left ear, as she raised he hands upwards and her rich black hair cascaded down her shoulders and back. He leant against a pillar and brought the camera up, waiting for her to look skywards once more. *It was as if her eyes didn't come from this world,* he thought. It seemed to him that someone had brought these eyes from heaven and given them to this woman. She wore the heavy eye makeup he had found out was called *Kajal* and he saw then how *Kajal* enhanced her beauty. She looked up and he clicked away, taking picture after picture while she was oblivious to his presence. He felt drugged. *Those eyes are the home of my eyes, my eyes are meant to be seen through your eyes.* They were both lost in the moment; she in spiritual reverie, he smitten by her incredible beauty.

He continued to take pictures and she continued to almost dance in front of the shrine. She remained kneeling but her body swayed rhythmically like bulrushes in a gentle breeze. Locke was captivated. His senses swam and coursed through his body until he was confused as to whether he could touch colours or see flavours. She was mesmeric and the camera continued to click until at last he stopped pressing the button and just watched in delirious wonder. His eyes felt heavy as if he was being hypnotised by the stunning creation before him. She had an audience of one and she didn't know it. Or she didn't care. He watched on as she twisted her wrists, her lithe fingers forming shapes as if she was caressing the air, stroking it with infinite gentleness. He noticed her nails; perfect and painted a pale silver. She wore a large gold ring on one finger and diamond bell earrings that seemed to fall from her lobes like glistening rain. Her lips a pale dusky pink. And her eyes remained closed.

John Locke was infatuated. *You can construct a wall between us, or apply as many guards as you wish. You can put mountains and clouds or deep oceans and waves between us, but nothing can keep me from coming for you.*

Then she got up. She rose to her full height and bowed one final time to her god. She looked over her left shoulder, right at Locke who felt as though her gaze had pierced his heart. Her eyes the colour of the deepest onyx flashed at him as they caught a single beam of sunlight slicing through the room. He instinctively took a picture, but still she held his gaze and he lowered the camera to look straight back at her. And just when he thought he couldn't take anymore, she smiled coyly. Then she gazed downwards, as if the sky rushed down upon her, and walked away.

He almost fell to his knees, but managed to stop himself. The spell broken he looked to where she had been but there was no one there. She had vanished, and he had not even spoken to her. He rushed in the direction he thought she must have gone and realised it was a different way back to the front entrance to the temple. He hurried out and was blinded by the fierce afternoon sun and brought his hand up to create a visor.

Where is she? Locked scanned the throngs in front of him as street children spied the foreigner and started to gather.

There!

He caught a glimpse of her yellow sari as it flowed around a corner she had taken. There was a tug at his sleeve and one of the children held Locke's shoes in one hand and his Panama hat in the other. He snatched them off the boy who looked both eager at the prospect of reward and hurt that his efforts had gone unacknowledged. Afterwards Locke felt ashamed that he had not given the boy anything, but he had to catch up with the woman who had stolen his heart. She would be his muse and he would photograph her anywhere and everywhere. He had fallen in love with her and they had not even spoken.

He put the hat on, but didn't tie his shoelaces. He was down the dozen or so steps of the temple in two strides then rushed across the bustling street. People tried to get out of his way although he still collided with some. The street children chased after him. He ran a short way along the pavement then reached the corner where he had watched the yellow fabric recede. This street was much narrower, with barely room for a car, and it bent gently to the right so that he could not see that far ahead. It wasn't crowded, and he set off in pursuit of the woman.

He ignored the sweat pouring down the back of his shirt, or the fact that he might lose his shoes at any moment, and shimmied his way through what people there were, always looking ahead for that glimpse of bright yellow, the colour of buttercup, softly waving as the woman walked on. But he couldn't see her. The yellow never appeared. He burst into a wider area, a market square of some kind, and the heavenly smells of spice fought with the noise of many more people. Locke could not see what had suddenly become the most precious desire of his life. She had disappeared, swallowed up by the crowd in front of him. He looked as hard as he could through the haze and the rising smoke of the street stalls. Nothing. Maybe she hadn't reached this far, but had gone into one of the houses lining the curved street? Or perhaps he was further behind her than he thought and she had already passed through the market square. He scanned above the heads of the crowd and his heart sank. There were two exits.

John Locke removed his hat and mopped his brow with his sleeve. The white linen darkened with his sweat. He had lost sight of the most beautiful woman he had ever seen in a heady mix of noise and spice and wondered suddenly whether it had all been a dream.

two

he had captured eternity

His mind was blown with the images in his head of that beautiful woman in the yellow sari and the shapes she made as she worshipped her god. They had been alone in that Hindu temple. The two of them had been alone in that moment. He didn't think she had known, but she had. She was aware of her surroundings. She was a conscious woman. Locke had been mesmerised. It made the moment ever more powerful. And then that look right before she left his life forever. Reimagining that look sent a physical pain through his heart. He kicked himself for not approaching her. He almost cried.

It was one of the few remaining street children that brought him out of his trance-like state. A young boy, no more than six or seven years old, was tugging at his camera. Locke pulled back. He knew the boy was just trying to look at it, rather than steal it, but he didn't like that. The boy looked hurt, deep brown eyes showing confusion and apology. But Locke's mind was still on the shock of losing the woman. *His woman?* He ruffled the boy's hair, a non-verbal gesture that received a smile in return.

The camera. Until now he had largely forgotten about it, as the images in his mind swirled. But the images he had captured in that Hindu temple remained on his camera. The realisation hit him and he leapt up, startling the little throng of children. He retraced his steps until he was back on the street with the temple and looked for a rickshaw to take him to his hotel. One appeared almost immediately.

He rushed up to his room. Cleaners were making their way along his corridor and he hoped that they had already been through his. They had. He got his laptop computer out and plugged it in, then connected his camera and scrolled through the dozens of photographs he had taken that day.

There she was. He was beginning to wonder if it was his imagination, but she was real.

She was kneeling, the yellow sari almost gold in his composition. Her hands were raised to the heavens, her eyes closed deep in worship and her long black hair cascaded down her back. He had taken the photo in such a way that everything around her blended into the background. Only she was in focus, the rest a blur of rich brown, making the sari stand out even more. He sighed and touched the screen, and said aloud, "Will I ever see you again?"

His fingertips were seeking something he knew he could never find. This time a tear did prick at his eye, then fell down his cheek, as he realised it was his final day in India. He knew he could take a good photograph, but his subject, this model of India, took the composition way beyond that. He had captured eternity. He clicked on the next image. And the next. In all he had taken close to fifty pictures of his unknown muse and each one hurt him as much as the next.

"Sort it out, John," he said aloud as he struggled to understand why he was reacting like a lovelorn teenager. Outside it was dark. He hadn't noticed the time, and he found it got very dark very quickly in India, but it meant he had been staring at the pictures of the mystery woman for at least three hours.

He usually ate in the hotel's restaurant, but tonight he called room service, then quickly jumped in the shower. There was a knock at his door as he dried himself off and the waiter smiled professionally and bowed slightly as Locke gave him a five hundred-rupee tip. He returned to the desk where his laptop whirred quietly and pored again over the images of the woman in the sari as he slowly ate his food.

"Well done, John," he said. "You've just lost the most beautiful woman in the world."

*

His flight left at two in the afternoon. He was flying with Air India and it was direct. No annoying connections. He had packed his bags as soon as he had woken up then did his usual sweep of the room. He liked to travel light, but with a bulky laptop and his camera, that seemed to be a thing of the past. He was at the airport well before the recommended two hours and had to wait for a short while for the check-in desk to open. He was third in the queue and sailed through immigration and security.

He wasn't normally like this; but staring at his computer screen until well past midnight at the same images, over and over, he had thought about his future, the possibilities, about Life itself. He thought about what he would say to his *Miss India* should he ever see her again, then gave serious thought to extending his holiday to try to find her, before he shook the nonsense away.

He wanted to be busy next morning to try to forget about the woman, the *mystery woman* he had photographed. That, he knew, would take time, but he didn't want to allow himself to be reduced to some kind of vacant idiot thinking about her. He had deliberately packed his laptop in his main suitcase, so he wouldn't be tempted to get it out and look at the images again. His camera was in there as well, not that he could see the pictures on it.

He walked past the various statues of elephants and took up a seat in a bar that offered a view of the runway as well as a television screen detailing the flights. He loved flying and always marvelled at how a thing so huge could get off the ground. He knew it was to do with drag, or was it thrust? He realised long ago that he was a creative not a scientist. He didn't understand numbers beyond being able to count and so watching an enormous Air India 747 take off was nothing to do with the science and all to do with the beauty of that magnificent white beast roaring down the runway, it's black mask beguiling below the cockpit and the passionate red paint of its logo proudly telling the world where it was from.

The aircraft's nose lifted then the great white and silver bird left the ground and soared away towards whatever destination it was going to. Locke wished he'd had his camera with him. Flight was a thing of beauty, just like the mysterious girl from yesterday. He turned to his drink, a refreshing gin and tonic, and spied the TV screens for his flight.

*

He noticed her as he struggled in the squashed crowd of hundreds of fellow passengers trying to pack overhead lockers and take their seats. It was the one place he felt people tolerated being knocked about as others wielded their hand luggage at eye level and frequently made contact. Locke stood a little back from a large Indian man in front of him trying to navigate luggage and seats for two. An elderly Indian lady, perhaps the man's mother, was chirping away at him. Evidently he wasn't quick enough to avoid the woman's rebuke.

Locke turned slightly in the aisle and looked in the direction of the three seats next to him. He saw the man nearest the aisle and the woman in the middle of the three. They seemed to be a married couple, not that Locke was looking that closely. There was another woman, seemingly younger not that he could tell because she was looking out of the aircraft's window, in the furthest seat. She turned and John Locke's world caved in itself. It was as if his mind imploded at that instant and he was rendered mute. It was the woman he had seen in the temple, the woman he had spent all night pouring out his heart to because he thought he would never see her again. She was without doubt the most beautiful thing he had ever seen and his mouth dropped open. She smiled and Locke nearly collapsed. He wasn't aware of it, but the woman next to his muse was looking disapprovingly at the man who was so clearly staring at her daughter.

Locke tried to say something but nothing came out. His mind tried for reality; why was she on the plane? Was she a tourist just like him and not from India? The woman by the window winked and smiled and he felt like he was drowning. He knew at once he had to talk to her, but then she shook her head ever so slightly and her eyes looked to her right. He realised she was telling him not to say hello because of her parents.

A man behind him tapped his shoulder and said something, he thought it might have been Hindi, but Locke didn't understand the words. He managed to tear his gaze away from the woman by the window and looked into the eyes of an irate white man. The man said something else, this time it was heavily accented English and Locke wondered if he was actually German. The large man with the irate mother had managed to sort themselves out and it was now Locke who was blocking the aisle.

He looked back at the woman by the window. She laughed, silently, then peered out at the activity on the airport's apron. Locke looked at his plane ticket, then at the overhead seating numbers and made his way in a daze to his seat. He found he was about twenty rows back but was next to the aisle in the middle row of four seats.

He could not believe what had happened. Yesterday was surreal and it already felt like a dream; the kind you tell yourself everyday but only half believe it. He had his pictures, though. He had his *proof*. But now, to see her again? He head was a maelstrom of different thoughts and feelings. He had to talk to her. He had to know her. He wondered if he loved her.

"Shut up, John!" and the woman sat next to him looked at him quizzically.

Shit! I said that out loud. Get a grip!

Locke stared at where his mystery woman was seated. He couldn't see her; the back of her chair too high. How he longed to go up to her and tell her who he was. Stupid scenarios flashed across his eyes; whether he should ask him if he had the right seat number, or whether she could help him with his luggage.

My God! I think she recognised me!

Every possible thought went through Locke's mind as the realisation dawned. That she had recognised him sent him into further tumult. Did she really know who he was? She had only looked at him briefly the day before, then she disappeared into the crowds. He was certain she was unaware of him the whole time he was taking pictures, but the fact she turned to look straight at him after she had finished her worship was proof enough that she had known he was there.

An air stewardess blocked his view to where his muse sat. She was beginning the safety announcement that no one ever listened to. He tried to move about in his seat the better to try to catch a glimpse of his woman should she get up.

A thought entered his head and he looked around for the bathrooms, then remembered there would be an aircraft plan in the back of the seat in front of him. It took him moments to work out there was a block of four toilets in the centre of the aircraft and about ten rows in front of him. He also realised there was one right in front of the object of his desire.

He relaxed and felt his heart slow down. He hadn't noticed, but it had been racing and he realised there was a thin sheen of sweat on his brow, even though the aircraft cabin was cool. He knew then he was going to go down the aisle and, if her parents, assuming that was what they were, were asleep, he was going to try to talk to her. If they were awake, she had already made it clear that he couldn't talk to her. In that case, he would simply pretend to use the toilet in front of her. He decided to give it a couple of hours into the flight, after food was served, then make his way down. His heart rate picked up once more as he tried to formulate what he might say.

*

John Locke made his move at over thirty-five thousand feet. The on-board screens said as much as he tracked the aircraft's path across southern Asia. They were passing over Afghanistan when he stood up. He walked down his aisle and crossed over to the other side when he reached the block of toilets. His thinking was simple enough; he would approach her from the front by going past her row then crossing back to head towards her seat. He found himself in the galley area of the aircraft, the air crew clearing away the early evening meal they had served. He received one or two curious glances and one steward asked if he was lost. Locke said he was fine and crossed the aircraft's cabin back to the side he had seen her seated.

He had noticed on his little wander around the aircraft that many people were already asleep and he hoped her parents would be as well. When he turned the corner and walked the short distance to her seat, his heart was, once again, crushed. The man he took to be her father was asleep, but the mother was not. And she seemed to recognise him instantly as he walked towards her, looking as though he was intent on attacking her daughter.

Worse still, the woman he had fallen headlong in love with was wearing a sleep mask. He didn't break stride, aware the mother's gaze remained fixed on him, but walked slowly enough to take in more of his muse's beauty. Her dusky brown lips were slightly parted below a small nose, her chest rose and fell as she breathed, her hands clasped in her lap. She was leaning against the aircraft's fuselage, a blow-up pillow making things more comfortable. Then he passed her row and the mother's frown ceased, as if he was no longer attacking her daughter.

He made his way back to his seat wondering if he was ever to get a chance to talk to Miss India.

three

he heard the sigh

John Locke looked again at the vast print hanging on the wall. It was of the woman in the temple and he had had it blown up, printed and framed. When friends came round they marvelled at the beauty it showed. Many said he should take up photography professionally, but since his return from India, his heart hadn't been in it. His friends had no idea who the woman in the picture was or what she meant to him. He hadn't told anyone that she had been on his flight back to Manchester. He thought some might ridicule him because he couldn't stop thinking about her. He knew it was pointless; Manchester was a city of a couple of million people. He would never find her, so he didn't look. But she was in his head and it seemed like she wasn't going to leave.

His friends would stare for a moment or two at the picture, then get back to their drinks and their party conversations. He had always held gatherings in his flat, initially to ingratiate himself with people he knew at college. But then he had dropped out. He loved doing photography, but he found his course dull. He didn't want to take sterile pictures of urban Manchester; he wanted light and colour and vibrancy. But concrete was on the curriculum and he left.

His father, already pissed off that he was not doing an academic course, hit the roof, threatened to stop funding his lifestyle and even suggested he might fly over from the US to drag him back to San Jose. His father believed that he would never become anything or that he would find it difficult to be anything. That worried him. But none of it happened. Instead he got a job with an agency who found him a crap role as an office clerk in the centre of Manchester. Locke didn't mind. The work was tedious, but it allowed his mind to wander and he was popular with the other staff. He started going out with some of them to bars and pubs that were everywhere in the city centre.

But he was in a bad place now. He had managed to lose the love of his life twice. He couldn't help but think that was more than a little careless and that there was nothing he could do about it. He clenched his fist as he thought back to the flight once more. After he had tried and failed to make contact with her on the plane, he had gone back to his seat and fallen asleep. He woke up just as the aircraft was making its final descent into Manchester airport and the seatbelt signs were on. In his hand a note, in a beautifully neat scrawl. He knew instantly who had written it, but he couldn't understand what it said.

Tere naseeb mein main hoo ke nahee

Ham kisee din phir milenge.

He found out later that it translated as *Am I there in your destiny or not? We will meet again.*

But by the time he got off the aircraft, Miss India and her parents had already gone. He hurried to catch up with them, but somehow couldn't. There were too many people in front of him and he just couldn't see them. Even at immigration control, where the airport had created barriers to make passengers walk back and forth as they got nearer to showing their passports, Locke could not see them. It was as if they and, more importantly *she,* had vanished. He couldn't work it out. They were nowhere to be seen at the luggage carousel either, although there had been three of them operating and, on the off chance they had been somehow delayed, Locke waited in the arrivals lounge for another hour, just in case he had overtaken her, in the hope she would come out behind him. She didn't.

He took the train into Manchester Piccadilly station and a taxi across town to his flat in Castlefield. He cried that night and most of the following day as well. He didn't normally struggle much with jet lag, but this time he just couldn't shake it. It was just as well he wasn't working for another week – he had forgotten to put in his request for work before he went away or and only hoped that his job would remain when he got back.

As it was his manager at the office said he was much more reliable than the other people put forward in his absence, and requested his return. It meant three weeks without wages, but then he hadn't spent all of his father's money in India. As always he would be okay.

*

Three weeks had passed and Manchester was showing unusual signs of having a good summer. It had been high teens and low twenties pretty much daily, although Locke still wore a light jacket. He had grown up in San Jose, California, and the climate there was much warmer than Manchester. It was a lot drier as well, so he was usually a bit more covered up than the locals, whatever season it was.

He still thought about that day in the temple. He dropped the 'Miss' and had taken to calling the woman in his picture simply 'India'. A friend told him that that was the name a mutual acquaintance had given to his new-born daughter. Locke thought it beautiful. When people looked at his picture he would say it was called India and they would figure he was talking about the symbolism not the woman. He would say goodbye to her every time he left his flat, as if she was there at the apartment or talking to him while he entertained himself. As if she was going to respond. He thought she had turned his life around.

He was sporting Ray-Bans as he made his way down Deansgate. The sun was still high, but there was a light breeze funnelling down the chasm of Manchester's busiest shopping street. The locals were in tee-shirts, a number of the men in shorts. Locke thought them a bit giddy; it was like a pleasant spring day to him, certainly not worthy of holiday gear. His phone buzzed as he neared Waterstones.

'Moon Under Water' the text said. Locke was almost there. He crossed Deansgate and headed into a cacophony of noise as the doors to the pub opened to reveal a vast clientele enjoying their drinks in the smog. He coughed a couple of times as he got used to the smoke then peered ahead to see if he could see any of his friends. There were meant to be five of them going out and he knew at least Tony was there because it had been his text.

He found Tony, Pete, Tom and Rich in a booth near the back of the massive pub. Tony stood up when he saw Locke. He clearly had had a few beers already.

"Oi, Oi!" Tony shouted, cigarette in one hand and a pint in the other. "Here he is!" Tony spread his arms wide and waited for Locke to go in and embrace him. He duly obliged and looked down at the table. His friends all had nearly full pints. His timing had been impeccable.

"Get the lad a lager, Rich," Tony said. "He looks thirsty to me." Rich stood up and rolled his eyes. Clearly it had been his round and they had barely touched their drinks. Locke shook hands with Pete and Tom and sat down.

"Gonner be a biggun, this," Tony said, taking a drag of his cigarette. "I'm reckoning a bird or a curry. Or both." He laughed at his own joke. Pete shook his head. It was always like this; Tony was a bit older than the rest of them and the self-appointed leader of the group. They always seemed to go where he chose to go, but that was because they let him. If he took them somewhere shit, then he got the piss ripped out of him. It was a strange group dynamic and one that Locke found fascinating.

It just wasn't the same as America where the drinking culture was very different. Apart from the smoking, which he hated because he went home stinking of cigarettes all the time, he loved just sitting in a pub spouting nonsense with four other like-minded mates. The Brits called it 'putting the world to rights', and he liked that. Everyone was correct in what they said until someone pointed out how wrong they were. No one took offence and all of them had a bloody good laugh in the meantime.

Rich returned with Locke's beer. He hadn't asked him what he wanted; it was Stella, the only permissible drink. Locke held it up and his companions did the same.

"Cheers," they said as one and then took a large draught.

"What you been up to, Lockesley?" Pete's question. He was the thoughtful one in that he actually seemed interested in others.

"Not much. Just chillin'."

Tony laughed. "Still love the accent." Locke grimaced. He was conscious of his American accent and was deliberately trying to suppress it. He saw it as important if he was going to fit completely in with the Brits. His life was to be here, and he didn't want to sound too much of an outsider.

Tony pointed a finger across the table. "Rich here's got himself a new bird. She's coming along later. I asked her to bring a couple of mates."

"Dick!" said Rich.

"No, you're the dick," Tony retorted looking at Locke. "Shouldn't have left his phone on the table, should he?"

"He texted her on my phone," Rich said by way of explanation. "As you can imagine it wasn't the most graceful of texts."

"I asked for a couple of proper scrubbers and she replied yes." Tony laughed again. He could barely contain himself. Locke laughed at him rather than with him. After a couple of pints he would be laughing with him. He just needed to catch up.

As it was, Rich's new girlfriend Siobhan brought three friends with her. Two of them were very pretty, the third, Tanya, was on the big side with a considerable amount of flesh on show. Tony was immediately drawn to her and she seemed to like it.

The table was big enough to accommodate them all and the conversation flowed easily. One of the other girls, Sue, seemed to have paired up pretty quickly with Tom and the last, Marie, sat happily between Locke and Pete. They started talking about jobs but then Pete mentioned Locke's trip India and he was delighted to find Marie had gone there as part of a year out from university. They went to different parts of the country, but the stories were similar; street kids, death trap roads, temples and lovely locals.

Pete had a girlfriend and Locke realised he had mentioned India so that Marie would find him interesting. Pete was trying to match him up, not that Locke minded. Marie was nice, but she wasn't his muse. He would chat away to her all night and it seemed as though the girls were his equal at that. The conversation was never strained. They moved from bar to bar before Tony made good his suggestion of a curry and they found a small place just off Albert Square in the centre of the city.

Tony and Tanya had given up on flirting and started kissing at the end of the table in the curry house. There were a few shouts of "get a room," but they were ignored until the waiter appeared shortly afterwards with their starters. Locke, as always, had gone for the tandoori chicken. It was his first curry since he had returned from holiday, and he realised how bland it was. Much of the food he ate in India was clean and fresh tasting, with a heat that made you hiccup, but you could still eat more.

He ate his chicken all the same and then failed to finish a vindaloo; even though he had eaten hotter in India, there was something about the way the curry in front of him had been made that meant the heat got too much. He tried to work out why, but his head was foggy with beer. Outside, the air hit him like a freight train and he was immediately sick. Behind him, somewhere, Tony cheered and Tanya cackled. He heard Marie tell them to shut up.

It was the last thing he could remember.

*

He blinked as the sun streamed in through the window. He clearly hadn't closed his curtains before he had gone to bed. But he'd managed to get undressed. In fact, he was naked, which was a bit odd as he usually slept in his boxers. Then he heard the sigh and realised he wasn't alone. Marie rolled over and looked contentedly at Locke.

"Hi," she breathed, propping herself up on an elbow.

"Hello," he said, feeling awkward. He couldn't remember how he had got home and certainly couldn't remember whether anything had happened between them. Then he had a vision of being outside the restaurant in Albert Square. "I was sick."

Marie laughed. "Nice. I see you're the romantic sort, then." She brought her free hand up and caressed his cheek. It made Locke more uncomfortable.

"I'll get us a cup of tea," he said, hurriedly getting up from his bed and keeping his back to Marie while he put his dressing gown on. He turned back. "How do you like it?"

There was a look of total incredulity on Marie's face. Locke blinked back at her.

"Are you being serious?" she asked. He nodded and she flopped back onto the bed, staring up at the ceiling. "You couldn't do it last night and you don't want to do it now? Have you got a girlfriend or something?"

"No."

"Then what's up?"

Locke didn't know what to say. He silently walked out of the room and glanced at the picture of 'India' as he went into the kitchen. He knew exactly what was up, and he was beginning to hate himself for it. He could hear rustling in the bedroom and realised Marie was getting dressed. He breathed a sigh of relief and hoped the sound of the kettle had masked it.

He had poured the hot water and was waiting for the tea to brew when Marie appeared at the kitchen door.

"Don't bother with mine. I only drink coffee."

Locke looked at the space where Marie had been, long after he heard his front door slam shut. He stopped momentarily to look again at the picture of India, then went back to bed. This time he closed the curtains.

four
the shapes that so mesmerised

"How long are you going to keep this up?"

"How do you mean?"

It was lunchtime and Locke was in Subway with Tony. The sandwiches didn't compare to back home in the States. In fact the food was the one thing Locke really missed about America; in Britain it was on the small side and overpriced.

"That bird on Friday. She was beautiful. All over you." A thin sliver of tomato sauce dribbled down Tony's chin. He wiped it away. "Just like that one when I first met Tanya. What was her name? Mary?"

"Marie," Locke corrected.

"That's it," Tony said with a mouthful of meatball. "She's gorgeous as well. Seen her since when me and Tan have gone out. She doesn't talk highly of you. Reckons you must be gay."

Locke looked down at his sandwich. It was a month since he had not had sex with Marie, despite having it offered to him on a plate.

"You're not are you?" Tony had stopped chewing, as if he had suddenly realised something.

"Not what?"

"Gay!" Tony said loudly. A couple of young women on the table next to them looked across.

"No!" Locke insisted, but he could tell Tony was trying to join the dots. "I simply want a woman, not someone vulgar. She's a woman, yes, and a daughter. And one day she'll become a wife, a mother, a grandmother and a friend. But when she is no-one, she could become a whore."

Tony raised his eyebrows, surprised. "Okay, then what's with the celibacy? I don't reckon you've had a shag since, oooh, since before India. Why do you keep turning these belters down?"

"I don't," Locke said, feeling very uncomfortable. He took a bite of his sandwich to gain a bit of time. "I just haven't fancied anyone lately. I know Marie was beautiful, but she went to bed with me having watched me being sick in the street. I don't even remember brushing my teeth. What sort of woman tries to have sex with someone like that?"

"I would."

"I know you would, but luckily I'm not like you." Locke saw Tony about to come back at him. "I don't mean anything by it. I'm not having a pop. Just for me... I don't know. It's like I have to be really into someone to take it further. Same as with Jen. Beautiful and I was offered it on a plate, but that's what turned me off. She was too easy. Imagine how many times she has done that."

Tony took the comment literally and started to guess. He hadn't thought about Jen's promiscuity, real or imagined. Suddenly he found himself thinking quite high numbers.

"Gotta be ten at least. Twenty even."

"It doesn't matter and we will never find out. What I am saying is I will know it when I see it and when I do, I'll act. But not before."

"You're not going to stay young and handsome for long, though..."

"Sure you're not gay?" Locke shot back. Tony saw it for what it was and laughed, spitting a bit of meatball onto the table. They both looked at it.

"I'm photographing a wedding at the weekend," Locke said. "Old mate of mine from uni. He has asked me if I can take the unposed pics for him as a kind of favour. Actually, I offered."

"You getting paid?"

"No. It's more like a wedding present from me. I dropped out because I didn't want to take pictures of wet tarmac. But what's a wedding if it's not going to be colourful? Maybe I'll meet someone there."

*

David's wedding was in a country house just outside Rochdale, a few miles north of Manchester. Locke got a lift from Jack, another friend from university, and they reminisced on the half hour journey to the venue. They were leaving earlier than was necessary so Locke could get some pictures of guests arriving and of the venue and its surrounds.

"Like bloody Wuthering Heights," Jack said as the two of them gazed out over the sweeping moorland scene in front of them. "It's a book," Jack clarified when he saw Locke's confusion. "Got lots of moors in it. Not that I've read it."

Locke started to snap away. It wasn't the Himalayas, but there was something striking in the bleak views and the way the sun kissed the wet ground after the morning's light rain. As the sun rose higher, the rain that had fallen turned to steam and disappeared. He spent a lot of time trying to capture the wisp of the steam and got creative as he took a picture along the length of a low drystone wall. The unevenness of the stones created just the right effect to show that what he was capturing was the rain evaporating, and not someone's cigarette smoke as he feared many pictures might look like.

Jack wandered around the front of the venue, getting in the way of some of Locke's shots. He moved when he realised. And then the first of the guests arrived. Locke was there to photograph them unawares. The real photographer was with Hannah, the bride. Locke hadn't met her yet, but Jack said she was a real stunner.

"David's way above his paygrade there," Jack had said. "And she's minted, I believe. Lucky bastard."

Locke was looking forward to being introduced. David was one of the good guys and he wished him well, but he couldn't help feeling it was too early to be getting married. Locke's year had only just graduated the September before and one of his best mates was tying the knot already. Still, if it was true love, why wait?

From seemingly nowhere, the increasing numbers of guests were being served champagne and canapes. David had arrived looking frankly terrified and just about everyone was trying to relax him. Locke snapped away. He had made sure he had charged the battery and that he had a spare as well. He also had a wallet full of memory cards. He expected to take a lot of pictures and already knew he had taken some great ones.

The guests started to move into the room where the ceremony would take place and Locke looked for a vantage point, aware the real photographer would be focusing on the bride and groom. He took up station behind where the registrar would state the blessings and ask for the David and Hannah to say their vows. He would get shots of the bride and groom and the happy and expectant faces of the guests.

The tension mounted in the room. It was a midday wedding and Locke checked his watch. Hannah was due any minute. David stood at the front nervously facing forwards. His best man, a friend from school that Locke didn't know, periodically whispered encouragement in the groom's ear. Then the music began; *My Heart Will Go On* by Celine Dion. Locke hated it. He had the image in his head of Jack and Rose at the front of the *Titanic,* then an image of the ship sinking. He wasn't sure David and Hannah had chosen the best theme tune for the bride to walk down the aisle.

The assembled guests stood up as one when asked, then the bridesmaids walked in. Locke had chosen a position which was slightly elevated and so that when he was standing, he could see over the heads of the guests. There were four bridesmaids and the first thing that struck Locke was that they did not look like bridesmaids. Each dress was a different brilliant colour; red came first, then blue, then green and finally gold. Each of the bridesmaids wore a veil. The look was striking.

The look was India, Locke realised with a gasp. He snapped away as the four women slowly made their way down the aisle towards an expectant David. As each arrived they removed their veil and smiled at the groom. It was a beautiful bit of theatre Locke thought as he moved slightly to try to capture the moment each bridesmaid revealed herself. Gold brought up the rear and there was something familiar about her. Locke looked up from his camera and watched as she gracefully walked forwards. She somehow seemed to have more poise about her, more elegance. Locke was enchanted. So was the rest of the audience.

She reached the table and turned to face David. The camera dangled loosely in Locke's hands as he sat entranced by what he was looking at. The woman removed her veil and he gasped.

"India!" he said, quietly, his heart trying to burst from his chest. He didn't care that the nearest few guests heard him. He was looking at the woman in the temple. There was no doubt; he had stared at his pictures of her for hour after hour.

He knew every contour of her exquisite face; her deep brown eyes, the narrow nose and full mouth. He stared so hard at the delicate make up that made her eyes seem bigger and her mouth richer. Yet it was, again, so understated. She just sought to accentuate her features. She didn't need to do any more.

'India' stepped back and sat down next to the other bridesmaids, a look of joy and excitement on her face. Locke could not stop looking at her, even as Hannah walked down the aisle. All eyes were on the bride except his. The camera remained useless in his hands as he stared at his muse.

When he thought back, Locke had no idea what he was thinking at that moment. The guests broke into applause; Hannah really was indescribably beautiful. A woman sobbed and others laughed. It was enough to break Locke's trance.

Shit! he thought. *I've missed the bride.* Locke remembered his purpose and clicked away as the ceremony went on. Later, when he was looking back over what he had produced, he realised he had taken pictures of just one subject; his India.

The ceremony by went in a blur. He hardly noticed the cheers and applause, and he got frustrated when his view was blocked. David and Hannah walked back down the aisle and out through the doors. The guests filed out after them and, almost immediately, India was lost but for the gold headdress she wore.

He followed it like a beacon of light slowly receding. She walked through the doors and her gold disappeared. Locke blinked. His heart hammered away in his chest. He had to speak to her, but when? Instinct took over; he knew he couldn't walk straight up to her. The camera weighed heavy in his hands and he realised he had to get back to taking pictures. He checked the battery; plenty of juice left. He changed the memory card and joined with other guests to file out of one stunning room and into another, larger hall where the wedding tables were arranged. To one side there was a large dancefloor and what looked like a stage complete with a curtain pulled across.

Locke could not see his India. In fact he could see none of the bridesmaids or the bride. David, oddly, walked around on his own. The groom couldn't hide his joy, but it appeared he could hide his bride. He talked animatedly and Locke saw him playing with the ring newly placed on his wedding finger. Then the curtains were drawn, plunging the room into an eerie dusk. Disco lights lit the stage, then the music started. It wasn't a familiar tune, but it was undeniably Indian.

Out of the corner of his eye, Locke saw the curtain on the stage begin to move. The audience, almost as one, turned to see what was happening. The curtain revealed the red, then the blue and then the green bridesmaids. Locke suddenly realised they were wearing saris, which is why they didn't quite look like bridesmaids. The music was still quiet at this moment. Delicate, almost, and the three women waved and weaved their hands in exquisite shapes to the soft notes playing over the speakers.

Then the beat kicked in and the three formed a circle as they shuffled around. Some of the guests started to rhythmically clap in tune with the music, which suddenly picked up speed and urgency. The circle of three spread out to reveal India! Locke gasped again. He had not seen how she had managed to get into the circle but now red, blue and green stood to the side and swayed to the rhythm as gold took centre stage. Locke was transfixed. He was instantly taken back to the temple in Delhi where she had almost danced through her prayers to her god. Now she was dancing once again and it almost seemed as though it was just for him. He began to sweat as if the very image of her had taken him back to the heat of Delhi.

The rest of the audience watched in wonder at the beauty of this graceful, exotic woman as her arms seemed to spin and intertwine and loop with effortless grace. Her hands, her fingers always twisting and rolling to create the shapes that so mesmerised Locke. The clapping had stopped. She had captivated the entire audience, yet she seemed almost oblivious. Locke considered briefly that she was the only non-white person in the room. And she had everyone in rapture.

A sudden change of musical pace and India danced aside to reveal Hannah, her white dress flowing, as she started to move towards the front of the stage. The crowd whooped and whistled. David looked on with untold pride in his face as his bride pushed her hands skyward in tune to the music and others in her audience joined in.

Locke never took his eyes off his India. She was on the far side of the stage, with red beside her. Blue and green were this side of the bride and together the four bridesmaids formed a square around Hannah. Slowly they inched their way forwards, shrinking the square and eventually hiding the bride, briefly, before the square broke and the bridesmaids formed a line with two either side of Hannah, her brilliant ivory dress shining out against the darker hues of red, gold, blue and green.

The music was quickening and so were the dancers. They shimmied to one side, then back to the other. They must have practiced for hours as they were so in sync with each other. They formed a pattern as their hands pulsed upwards as if to push away the air above them. Faster and faster. And then stop. The music ended on a single hard drumbeat.

Hannah stood side on to the audience, one hand on her hip, the other pointing up. Her chest heaved as she smiled, knowing the surprise had gone perfectly. Each of the bridesmaids took a different pose, but all were less extravagant than Hannah. But then it was her day. Locke looked at India. She was now the furthest dancer from him but again she struck a pose that had him melting. She leant slightly to her left, her right leg straight, her left leg bent at the knee so she had to tiptoe. Her left hand pointed to the floor, her right arm was bent at the elbow, her right hand near her face. Her eyes were closed and she didn't seem to be breathing at all, certainly nothing like as heavily as Hannah or the other bridesmaids. She was grace personified.

After a moment of silence, the audience erupted into wave after wave of applause. David walked forward and held his hands out to Hannah so that he could lower his bride to dancefloor level. They embraced and he whispered something in her ear. The bridesmaids took that as their cue to leave the stage as well, using the steps down to one side. India, as furthest away, was last to descend. Locke watched her all the way. The curtains were opened, the disco lights turned off. Suddenly they were back in an English country house on a bright summer's day and everyone seemed to want to talk to the dancers. Locke stood on his tiptoes, but couldn't see what he was searching for.

India had disappeared. Again.

five

"Would you like to ask me to dance?"

How did she do it? Was she even real? Locke could not understand how, yet again, his India had given him the slip and vanished. She had been right there in front of him and suddenly he couldn't see her. It was not as though she was camouflaged; she was wearing a sari of the deepest gold and she the only person in the entire room that wasn't white skinned. Was she a figment of his imagination? Locke genuinely wondered if he was going mad.

"Hope you've got some crackers, mate."

The comment brought Locke out of his trance-like state. David was standing next to him, the gorgeous Hannah on his arm. Both of them had seemingly impossibly wide smiles.

"Hannah," David began, "this is John Locke. He's the one I was talking to you about; we only saw him for a few months before he dropped off our course, but we've kept in touch."

Hannah offered her hand and Locke shook it.

"You look absolutely stunning," he managed to say to Hannah. "He's incredibly lucky to have you."

"Thank you," Hannah replied. "And I think we're both very lucky."

David nodded to Locke as if to say, *touché*. "Can't wait to see the pics, mate," he said as the newlyweds moved on to other guests.

"Wait," Locke said. David and Hannah turned back to him. "The girl in the gold sari…"

"Oh, we've been best friends for years," Hannah said. "The dancing was her idea. I've danced loads with her, but it's the other bridesmaids' first time."

"They were all brilliant," Locke offered and Hannah beamed.

"Hang on, didn't you tell me John's just been to India?" Hannah looked at David, who nodded.

"A few months back," Locke said. "I Loved it."

"Really?" Hannah said. "Then I must introduce you." The bride studied her guests and Locke scanned the room as well. His India was still nowhere to be seen and he felt the air rush out of him.

"She must have wandered off. She'll be around, though," Hannah insisted, smiling as she turned away to talk to an elderly lady who had touched her arm. The two kissed cheeks. Locke figured she was Hannah's grandmother. David gave him a gentle punch on the arm and smiled. He faked a smile back and looked around the room again. She was still nowhere to be seen. Suddenly the idea of taking pictures of happy people seemed the least important thing for him to be doing. He turned to walk out of the room and headed to a bar that he had noticed in a small room next to where the wedding had taken place. There were a number of people, mostly men, in there already.

Locke leant on the bar and waited patiently to be served. He ordered a sparkling water. Alcohol didn't seem the best idea this early in the day. Drinking in the middle of the afternoon was one thing he didn't try to copy the Brits in doing. He'd be asleep far too soon.

"And I'll have a prosecco," a voice said close to him. Locke initially didn't think the comment was aimed at him, but something made him turn.

"India!" he said aloud and immediately rose out of his slouch on the bar. 'India' gave him a perplexed look, then the barman returned with his sparkling water. Locke asked for the prosecco. It was all he could say as he looked down upon the woman he had fantasised about for months now.

Her soft, deep brown eyes studied him closely. She saw how he reacted to her and was fascinated. She realised she had rendered him mute and smiled gratefully as the flute of prosecco appeared at her elbow. She raised her glass and Locke reciprocated. They sipped their drinks.

"Should we find a seat?" she said, heading towards a vacant table by a window that looked out onto the rugged hills in the distance.

Locke's mind was in overdrive and he could think of nothing rational to say. This was the woman in the temple, the woman he had lost in the crowds then found again on the plane. It was the woman whose parents would not let her speak to him, and the woman who had disappeared from view at the airport. It was the woman who adorned his wall at home. She was his fantasy and she was sitting opposite him. No, he could not think of anything to say.

"So that's your name?" he asked after a pause. She nodded almost playfully. "I've always known you as 'India'."

"It's Anjali," she said, taking another sip of prosecco. Locke repeated it back to her, but it came out wrong.

"It's Anjali," she persisted. "It means putting your palms together." Gently she moved one graceful hand across the other and watched Locke mimicked the movement. She smiled then looked at him quizzically. "You saw me in the temple in India. And then again on the plane. Tell me, are the pictures you took of me any good?"

Locke looked down at the floor, suddenly feeling ashamed that he had taken the photographs without her permission. "Erm, yeah, I think they are," he stammered. "I'm sorry I didn't ask you first."

Anjali laughed. "Don't be daft. I saw you photographing the temple. You looked like you were showing proper respect and I thought that was nice. I knew it was you when I heard you clicking away as I prayed. I didn't mind. I thought it was all a bit romantic, really, a bit exciting."

Locke shifted uncomfortably in his seat. She had said *romantic*. That was exactly as he saw it. For an instant he thought she meant it, but then he realised how ridiculous that was. He needed to say something. Anything.

"I liked the dancing," he said and inwardly kicked himself. Why was he being so tongue tied and shy? He never was with anyone else. *You've got it bad, John. Get a grip.*

"Thank you," Anjali said. "I love it. I love anything to do with Bollywood. We all sit down together on a Sunday afternoon and watch one."

"I've never really been interested," Locke said, feeling a bit more confident. "They've always seemed a bit daft to me with all that dancing in the streets and the not quite kissing."

"Would you want anything more than kissing if you were watching it with your grandmother?"

"I didn't realise it was such a family event," Locke said, again wanting to kick himself. "I thought your dance routine just now was amazing. It must have taken a lot of practice."

"Not for me," Anjali laughed. "And Hannah's good because we've danced together for years. But Becky, Sam and Clare, the other bridesmaids, took some teaching. I thought they did well. We've only had a couple of run throughs." She looked at his camera. "Hannah told me one of David's friends was coming to take pictures. I had no idea it was my mystery man from Delhi. Shouldn't you get back in there and take some more?"

Locke knew she was playing with him. Her eyes danced with mischief as she took another sip of her now nearly finished prosecco. He took the suggestion as an invitation. He was still stammering but she had given him an opportunity to wander off and sort his head out a bit. He gulped the last of his water.

"Maybe I could get some pictures of you and the other bridesmaids in your saris?" he offered.

"Oh, no," Anjali replied rising from her seat, "the official photographer snapped us before the dance. I meant you should do more of the reportage-type photos. Hannah has been really excited about getting pictures from a different source. Sounds like David really bigged you up."

Locke smiled weakly. She had somehow done him again. He stood up as well, which emphasised the differences in their respective heights. She looked up into his eyes, studying him and put a hand on his arm.

"You never told me your name. I do love a bit of mystery." Anjali turned away as the beginnings of a cheeky smile developed at the corners of her mouth. Locke watched her leave and stared at the door long after she had walked through it.

"It's John," he said quietly.

*

Locke got to work and started snapping away. It had taken a few minutes to compose himself since he had finally spoken to Anjali although he kept catching himself refer to her as 'India'. After he had stared at the door for however long, he went to one of the mansion's many windows and looked out over the darkening moors.

He had not been here before and the rolling hills with their unkempt grass and frequent breaks and cliffs looked sombre, even in the continuing sunshine. He had seen mountains all over America and of course those in India, but the low undulating hulks before him seemed menacing rather than magnificent, cold rather than celebratory. He found them fascinating and a little eerie as the sun began to set and the landscape seemed to settle into a louring darkness.

The main hall played host to the meal and Locke took surreptitious pictures of fellow guests between courses. The guests on his table found his constant wandering off amusing and seemed a little more drunk each time he came back to eat his own meal. He didn't mind. He had started drinking himself and just hoped his pictures would be okay despite feeling the effects of the alcohol. The speeches came and went and then came the first dance. Hannah and David waltzed their way around the dancefloor to wild whoops and laughter from their guests. They had obviously practiced. Soon other guests took to the floor and danced their way around to the sound of *She* by Elvis Costello.

"Stunning, isn't she?"

Locke startled as he turned to see the amused features of Anjali looking up at him. She had whispered the words and her breath had titillated his ear. He was in no doubt at what was suddenly happening. During the wedding breakfast and the speeches, he had made a point of not going too near to Anjali, to try to keep his distance and allow her the time to enjoy the party with her friends. She had noticed and played along. She knew he had still taken a couple of sneaky shots of her though and loved it.

"She is," he said, looking at Hannah. "David is a very lucky man." Anjali watched the happy couple and waited. Locke knew this was his moment. "But I think there is another more stunning still," he said. He watched as Anjali smiled, and then laughed happily. He could have melted at that very moment as she turned to face him.

"Is that what you think of me, mystery man? You think I'm stunning?"

Locke struggled to keep his composure. "Yes, and I thought it the moment I saw you in the temple."

"Does it happen often, you falling in love with girls you don't know?" Her lips parted slightly and eased into a mischievous smile. He was being played and he wasn't quite sure whether to play along.

"It doesn't, no," he said. "And as beauty is sometimes only skin deep, I need to know someone properly before I truly fall in love."

Anjali nodded thoughtfully. "I like that," she said. "You have a depth, mystery man. Clearly not just some perv walking around taking pictures of women." Locke made to complain, but Anjali stopped him with a gently placed hand on his forearm. "I joke, of course. And you know it."

Locke could have dived into her eyes at that moment as she flashed her gorgeous smile and threw her head back laughing.

"It's John Locke," he said.

"What is? Your name?" Locke nodded. "Well John Locke, would you like to ask me to dance?" she said. He steeled himself against blowing his chance and tried to make himself seem as confident as possible. He decided against words and merely offered his hand for her to take. The camera bounced gently against his back as they walked onto the dancefloor and joined the others. It was over too quickly. *She* ended and the DJ started with the party tunes.

Locke took his camera back to his table and returned immediately to the dancefloor. Anjali smiled once more as she danced happily. She was in her element and he realised that she was mixing club moves with Indian expressions of grace and beauty. She was now part of a group containing Hannah and David, a couple of the bridesmaids and a couple of younger lads Locke didn't know. Anjali saw him and beckoned him. Locke was comfortable dancing; if there was one thing he could feel confident in right at that moment it was that he would not look like an idiot waving his arms about.

A couple of younger lads started to dance nearer to Anjali. She didn't seem fazed, but Locke was immediately concerned. One tried to catch her glance and hold her hand. Locke leaned in and whispered. "She's not that kind of girl, mate."

The young lad turned to see who had spoken to him and saw Locke towering above him. Drunk, the lad beerily raised a hand in supplication and started dancing in a different direction. His wing man followed.

Anjali nodded her approval and he finally relaxed. She moved closer to him and Locke's arm slid around her waist. David noticed this and winked. They swayed together often that night, broken only by occasional trips to the bar. Locke's head was swimming. Alcohol and lust mingled and left him with a gorgeous sense of ecstasy, all driven by Anjali's closeness and wonder.

*

"Oh," she said, staring at the picture hanging on Locke's wall.

After what seemed like hours of dancing, she had suggested they go back to his place because she still lived with her parents in Oldham. He knew they were strict but she explained anyway. They thought she was staying in Manchester with another friend who was at the wedding. But after Hannah and David left the party, Anjali suggested they go to his flat in Manchester. Locke needed no second invite and collected his camera.

The taxi ride took them just under an hour and Anjali settled comfortably into Locke as the car made its way through mostly deserted streets. He was a little uncomfortable, but thought she had fallen asleep so stayed as still as he could so as not to wake her. From how things had gone so far, he was sure that she would sleep with him tonight. There was a nagging doubt that she would want to do that on what was, in effect, their first date, but he had wanted this moment for months.

He had never expected it would happen, and now that it might, he was conflicted. He decided he was being stupid; he had no business being such a prude. He had slept with others on the first night, just none recently. If Anjali did the same, who was he to pass judgement?

The car swept through Salford and turned right towards Castlefield and home. Locke moved a little to alleviate a gathering pain in his lower back. Anjali murmured and moved, twisting her neck to reach up and kiss him delicately on his neck. The cab driver glanced at his backseat and thought she was with the wrong crowd. She settled back down and he listened to her soft breathing as the sodium glow of streetlights flashed past.

"Coffee or something stronger?" Locke asked from his kitchen. He had opened the door to his flat and took Anjali's coat to reveal the stunning hues of the golden sari.

"Coffee, please, just milk," she said as he walked ahead of her. Anjali followed slowly behind, taking in her new surroundings. In the entrance hall there were pictures of mountains and of an older couple she took to be Locke's parents. There was a coat stand and, somewhat out of place, a surfboard.

She could hear the kettle boiling and the sound of crockery clinking as her host busied himself making their drinks. She walked ahead and peered into the gloom of an unlit room where she could just make out a television and a sofa so assumed it to be the living room. Her hand felt for the switch on the wall and the room was suddenly bathed in light. She stepped forward, and that was when she saw it.

Locke came into the room and realised what had happened. Anjali was staring at the picture he had taken of her in the temple in Delhi. He stood stock still wondering what to say or whether to say anything at all. She studied the picture intently. Locke wondered if she wanted to run away, thinking that she was looking at some kind of freaky shrine. Anjali looked at him.

"Do you see God in me?" she asked, but Locke didn't understand her question. "The person we love, adore or worship, we see God in them. Love is bestowed upon us by God as a gift. There are many forms of love in our society; a brother's love, a sister's, parents love us, a husband and wife love each other. But a love sets itself apart from the rest of forbidden love. It means falling in love."

Locke had never considered this before. He realised then that their cultures were different. He thought himself a cut above the average Tony when it came to love and sex. He realised he wasn't.

"Oh," she said and Locke tried to read meaning in her exquisite face. "What do you tell the women you bring back here when they see this?"

Locke could hardly breathe. "There have been women, but I've slept with none since I came back from India. And none that have been here have had the grace to ask."

Anjali nodded thoughtfully. "Then you mean what you say; it's not just the outer beauty you need to see." She took her gaze away from the image and crossed to the kitchen doorway where Locke remained holding two steaming mugs of coffee. He looked down at her and she reached up to kiss him fully on the lips.

six
a gentle, tender kiss

Anjali stayed at Locke's flat often. Under no circumstances did he ever stay with her at her parents' house; they would never allow it. But for one awful moment weeks ago now, he never thought he would get to this stage.

He thought over the scene often; she staring up at the large picture of herself praying to her god, and him standing there, a coffee in each hand, wondering what to do or say. After she kissed him passionately for the first time, she had returned to look at the image again.

"*Subhanallah, mashallah,* which means marvellous. I think it's beautiful, you really captured my consciousness," she had said. "I knew you had taken pictures of me, but it never crossed my mind you might do something like this."

She had left Locke hanging as she continued to stare at herself in the throes of her most personal worship, arms raised, eyes closed in silent devotion.

And the breeze blows her hair, as if there was somebody else in that temple; they wouldn't let you take a picture of a stranger. Locke often questioned that in his mind. He was so grateful it was Anjali and not somebody else. *What were you praying or wishing for? Peace, asking for blessings for the society. I want the world to be in a better place.*

There was no denying the composition's intense beauty and feeling, and she wondered whether he had done much work on it or it had just come out like that.

"I think, one day, you will explain this to me." Anjali turned to Locke and her eyes bore deep into him. He had no idea which way she was going to go. He trembled, and felt hot coffee wet his right hand where he had spilled a little over the rim. He railed at the scorching heat and Anjali felt a sudden burning sensation on her skin, which soon appeared red. But both of these phenomena were unknown to them.

She walked to the window and opened it to let the air in. The moon was full. She stood there, taking in the scene.

"Veil yourself from the moon," Locke said. "Perhaps the moon may steal your *noor?* Your beauty?" He walked towards her and could smell the fragrance of her hair. He noticed her lips and thought they looked like a bud from a rose garden.

Anjali walked away because he was too close. She walked towards a vase of flowers and began to rearrange them.

"Veil yourself from the flowers," he said. "Perhaps they might steal your beauty?"

Locke walked towards her again. Anjali stepped in front of mirror and saw her reflection. He stood behind her.

"Veil yourself from yourself, Anjali. Perhaps you may steal your own beauty?"

Anjali smiled shyly and walked away to the emptiness of the room. He followed her again.

"When you smile it becomes a written history." She could no longer look into his eyes. "When you look down the sky falls down with you."

Anjali slowly walked towards the sofa.

"Veil yourself from your God. Perhaps he will steal your *noor?*"

Anjali turned to Locke. "Try to understand the situation John, I can't explain it to you. I have some limits." She sat down on his sofa. He felt the sweat collect at the base of his spine and he tried to put her coffee down on the table next to her without spilling any more.

His picture had taken on a different meaning. Whenever he looked at it previously he had only ever felt heartache at her beauty and his loss. He worried that he was becoming obsessed by it and comments such as those from Tony deepened his own concerns. Tony had been right; he did not go for those other women, not because he was turned off by their eagerness to sleep with him, but because he could not get 'India' out of his mind. Now that she was actually in his flat, the picture seemed somehow sinister. As if it was not an image that signified beauty in prayer, but that rather it showed a man's unhealthy obsession with a woman he never expected to see again.

They sat in silence. Locke wondered about putting some late night music on, but felt the moment had gone. He drank some coffee and the hot liquid burned his throat. In the end, Anjali studied Locke one more time, as she drank her coffee and wondered what to make of the man who worshipped her image. She placed her cup down. There was a table lamp next to her and she turned it on, then got up and turned off the main light. The room was suddenly dimly lit as she walked slowly towards Locke and kneeled down next to him. The gas fire's flames jumped and danced bathing the room in a golden glow. Locke lit a candle on the table beside the sofa, giving the atmosphere another lease of life. She sat gracefully, head down slightly and then gazed toward Locke. Her jewellery completed the look. He thought she looked like a poem for she had grace and piety as if she represented every woman in society.

She said softly, "You know what the hardest job on Earth is?" Locke guessed at a few, but Anjali shook her head. "It's being a wife."

"If that's the hardest, why do people marry on a daily basis?"

"We're all getting married, but not all of us understand what marriage means. It is easy to be a woman, to be a sister or a daughter, but it is much harder to accomplish our duties as a wife, which is why a lot of us don't succeed. This is why women are regarded as devout. It's the ultimate test of a relationship."

Softly she pulled him towards her and they kissed.

He was in rapture.

*

They fell into a passionate relationship. Locke had felt the relief wash over him when he finally came to the conclusion that he was actually in love with Anjali the person, and not 'India' the photographic composition that he had so worshipped.

It was a few weeks before he dared introduce her to any of his work colleagues and then he chose a night when Tony would not be there. He and Tanya had split up, but strangely they often met up in town and sometimes Marie was with her friend. She always gave Locke daggers or ignored him completely. It was so unnecessary.

So instead she just met Pete and his girlfriend Cath initially. The four of them had gone into Manchester and tried out an Italian restaurant in Exchange Square. The evening had been a great success. Cath loved dancing and Anjali promised to show her how to dance in the same way she had started to show Locke.

At first it was just in his living room, and their shared love of dancing brought them closer but he progressed quickly and they decided to hire out a dance studio with a full length mirror so they could really see how good they were becoming. Anjali put together a routine and she wore a sari; crimson red. She even told Locke how to dress and he turned up to the dance studio on Great Ancoats Street dressed in a white shirt, the three top buttons undone, white jeans and black boots.

David had been in touch with Locke to thank him for the unofficial pictures he had taken at the wedding. Hannah in particular was said to be utterly delighted with the photographs, which she preferred to the official prints they had received. It was then that Locke had his idea and the dance in the studio suddenly took on greater meaning. He and Anjali had practised to near perfection and Locke thought it would be amazing to film the routine. When he heard, David offered to do it as he'd loved the film module on his university course and promised he was quite handy with a video camera.

When it came to the day, David turned up with four expensive looking cameras; three to be on tripods and another with which he would move around the studio as Locke and Anjali danced. The dance studio was a room ten metres squared, with mirrors making up the whole of one wall. It took the best part of an hour for David to set up his cameras, with one taking in the whole of the mirrored wall, and the other tripods facing inwards from either side. Every angle was catered for, and the cameras were synced so that they would all be filming at the same time. The handheld worked separately, but David would be able to edit that footage in later.

Anjali and Locke did a walk through of their routine as David watched on intently. He was looking for opportunities to get close ups, or make sure he caught the key moments Anjali had told him had special meaning. Then she went to get changed into her outfit and Locke and David gawped when she returned in a deep crimson sari, folds of silk flowing behind as she entered the room. David was shocked; Locke was transported back to the temple in India. He nearly feinted at the sight of her beauty. She laughed as she saw the looks on the two men's faces, then told them to behave; she wanted this video, *this moment,* to be magical.

*

Anjali and Locke took up their positions at opposites ends of the room. David took a few close-up shots of each of them. Locke played the dark determined stranger, exuding masculinity and strength. Anjali was demure, she didn't look at Locke, but hid her gaze beneath her crimson veil. Anjali nodded that she was ready and Locke did the same. David first turned on his synchronised cameras, then the fan and finally the music. A few syncopated bells chimed and Anjali spread her arms wide to make the sari catch the air from the fan, sending its train sprawling behind her, fluttering on the breeze. She had her back to Locke who started to sway as the first of utterances of a male singer breathed across the room. David focused on Locke as his movements became more exaggerated. He arched his back and pointed an arm skyward, the fingers of his hand spread wide.

The beat kicked in. Anjali began to twirl and spin on the spot, her sari fluttering and twisting as she slowed then stopped to look across at Locke. Her eyes studied his and he returned the stare, opening his arms wide as if to invite her in. Anjali stayed where she was and resumed her graceful spinning, her arms shaping and sliding about her body in time to the rhythm of the music. Locke continued to move and slowly began to walk towards Anjali. Her eyes were closed, as if in rhapsody with the music, then a woman's voice began to sing with the man and so she, also, slowly began to move in Locke's direction. She leant back, her black hair cascading downwards and her arms twirled as if she was trying not to fall. Locke neared her, ready to catch her if she did, but she remained as she was. He leaned over her. His face was inches from Anjali's and she raised one arm to hold the back of his head. They gazed at each other and Locke found himself lost in the moment. He no longer heard the music, or the fan, the sound of David shuffling about with his camera. He no longer saw the mirrors or the tripods; he saw only Anjali and she was lost in Locke's eyes. His heart felt like it would explode with passion. Anjali stood up and twisted. She passed across Locke's front and made to fall, but Locke caught her with his left hand and together they leant towards the ground, her hair again flowed like a dark waterfall towards the floor.

He lowered her further and further until her hair touched the wooden boards, then he lowered her again and made to kiss her neck. But the dance told him not to. It was touch without touching. The dance was not erotic, but sensual. It was about love, but one which was forbidden. Locke, almost broke with the dance at that moment, but instead did as he had trained and kept his face close to Anjali's, raising her back up so they were standing upright. She raised a hand and caressed his face, then brought her eyes up to look at his. They were inches apart. She could smell his aftershave and he her perfume. He made to kiss her, as she had taught him to do, but the act was mischievous. Anjali released herself from his grasp and ran a few steps away, pretending to be insulted by the attempt. Locke followed, his steps rhythmic with the music. His faced was pained, haunted, and his arms were outstretched as if to ask *why?*

Anjali continued to look away, testing Locke to see if he would follow. She swayed her hips, the crimson sari draped over one arm, the female singer sounded tormented and upset. She was willing her man to return to her. Anjali took on the role and her expression was one of desolation. She raised the arm draped in the sari; the silk swaying with her movement, then her arm lowered and Locke stood behind her once more. He stared at her; it was a look of intensity and deep love, and of a man who is so desperate to kiss his woman. He took a stride forward and placed a hand on her shoulder. Anjali kept her gaze elsewhere, then closed her eyes at his touch.

Locke pulled on the shoulder, perhaps rougher than was necessary. Anjali spun around then stopped, their faces an inch apart once again. He looked deep into her eyes and she into his. He grabbed her hand and she fell backwards, hurtling towards a floor swept by hair and silk. Locke hauled her back and she spun as she returned to her full height. She leant into Locke who held her close and stroked her neck. He gently rubbed his face against her skin, his cheek caressing hers. Then embraced her fully.

This time she did not run away, this time she turned once more and gazed at him, stroking the side of his face and running her fingers through his soft hair. She smiled, pretended to walk away then rushed back to his embrace when he beckoned her. They held each other close, and swayed gently to the music. Then Anjali broke away, but Locke held on to her hand and she spun back into him. Her free arm came to rest on his shoulder. Locke's went around her waist and together they strode on twisting and returning after a few synchronised steps. At the end of each little run they faced one another. They were Locke's favourite moments as he almost melted into his partner time and again.

The male singer returned and they parted once more. Locke danced his heart out swaying and holding his head as he twisted and turned. It was hard to tell if he was in agony or rapture. He played his part well. Anjali watched on mesmerised, feeling his passion leave Locke in waves and make its way towards her. He finished his solo and looked intently at Anjali. The woman's voice returned and Anjali began to move, tracing shapes with her foot, her hands, her head and slowly, seductively, closing the gap to Locke. Her route took her towards the fan and her sari flowed behind, a deep crimson sheet fluttering in an otherwise colourless room. Locke saw her movement and ran towards her, once again catching her in his arms and spinning her so that he held her up with her silk sari gently touching the floor. Their faces were close; closer than they had been when they had the failed kiss. His head swam, a darkness almost took over his thoughts as he felt as though he might feint. Anjali's eyes never left his. The connection between their minds was almost physical as she came back into focus. She was willing him to say it. He thought he heard her say the words before he had but the moment remained. The music quietened then ceased altogether. They didn't move from their embrace. Neither dared breathe.

"Will you marry me," Locke said.

Anjali replied on the 'M' of marry. They kissed. Passionately they explored each other as they had many times before. But this time was different; this time they were betrothed. It was a kiss Locke thought he would remember for the rest of his life. Their lips parted and they gazed deep into one another's eyes again. The only sound that of the fan. Slowly Locke pulled Anjali upwards and kissed her once more. A gentle, tender kiss. In that kiss everything of Locke's had become Anjali's. He willed her to feel the sensations going through his head. When he looked at her, he realised she had felt everything. A tear formed at the corner of his eye whilst Anjali smiled and made his heart crumble. They held each other tight and revelled in the moment. Somewhere in the room David continued filming. He wasn't sure if he was supposed to, wasn't sure if it was part of the dance.

Anjali and Locke didn't know he was there.

seven

they became *ardhangini*

Anjali rested her head on Locke's bare chest, listening to the beating of his heart. Gently, rhythmically, his chest rose and fell and Anjali's eyes closed. They had just made love and lay quietly, intimately together in the darkness of his bedroom. A tear rolled down her cheek and made the tiniest sound as it fell onto Locke's chest. Not because she wanted to, but because she violated all the rules of her family law. Not because it felt wrong, but it felt right being with John. She hated the situation she had got herself into, but this was not the time, she thought, to be discussing it. She wanted to stay in a moment of pure love. *There are billions of us on Earth,* she thought, *every single one slightly different. So why do we have a connection to just one person? Why do our lives suddenly change?* She wanted to forget that the relationship had gone too far. Sex was sacred, just like it was mentioned in the Bible, the Torah or the Quran. But it had been playing on her mind for days. Locke felt the wetness on his chest more than he heard her little sobs.

"What's wrong?" he said, turning his head towards his fiancée. She didn't answer but struggled for composure. Locke leant to his right and turned on his bedside lamp. It was dim, deliberately so, and gave out just enough light for the two of them to see each other. The rest of the room remained in darkness. Anjali's tears glistened. Locke propped himself up on one arm and kissed her forehead, concern writ large across his face.

"Tell me," he said gently, and wiped a tear away with his hand.

"My parents," Anjali said. "Once a woman receives a stain it isn't easy to get rid of."

"Your parents? What about them?" Locke barely heard her. He was confused. She breathed deeply and tried to calm herself down.

"I think they know about us. Or at least they suspect something and as you know, they would not approve of my choice of boyfriend. Lying to your parents is a sin. They give us shelter, food, clothing and life until we are an adult. I know what you'll say, John, that's their primary duty. But we can't take privilege for granted. My mother has started asking questions about who I keep staying with when I am here. I couldn't say I was staying with Hannah, because she is newly married, so I invented someone, I called her Thea and said she was from work. Mother repeatedly asks me for information on Thea and I keep lying. I'm going to slip up at some point, I know I am."

Anjali rolled onto her back and looked up at Locke.

"I realised the other day that she isn't interested in Thea. I realised that she is trying to catch me out. Or get me to admit that I am seeing someone I shouldn't be. I am certain they know."

"Is that such a bad thing?" Locke instantly regretted saying it. Anjali had told him several times how her parents would not approve of her marrying outside of her religion or seeing other men. At first, he said that was racist, but she explained that it was neither race nor caste, but about constructing the right choice for their daughter. She won him round. Her parents were conservative and religious, modern yet traditional at the same time. They were of a generation that still clung on to the old ways of India. Marrying outside their religion was beyond their comprehension. Other cultures had no appreciation for marriage and they pointed at the statistics as self-explanatory. But Anjali hoped there was time still. It wasn't the fact that Locke was white. But things had changed the moment he proposed. They had been lost in love for weeks now, the world swimming in and out of focus as they were so wrapped up in each other's love and company. Locke ignored the fact that Anjali was taking riskier chances to see him as much as she could. For her, the lying hurt, but she could look beyond it. Just that week her mother had gone from mild curiosity in Anjali's life, to subjecting her to an almost interrogatory conversation. The cracks in the Thea cover story were blindingly obvious to Anjali. She thought they must be to her mother as well and she supposed that if her mother knew they were lies, then she would know why her daughter was lying to her.

"Yes," she said. "It is a bad thing. I would be a prisoner in my own house. I have told you why and I know you don't understand. Just imagine if your parents were white supremacists or something. It's really not the same thing, but the point is; would you ever let your parents know about me?"

Locke gritted his teeth. The rapture of just a few minutes ago had evaporated. In its place the anger he always felt when this conversation arose. Of course he understood; he wasn't stupid, he just didn't want to admit it.

"It's 2003, not 1903," he said. "I'm sorry, but your parents need to get with the programme. We can do whatever the fuck we want now. I know your religion means a lot to you, but it's bullshit that it means we can't be together."

"Time never changes for a woman, John. The world may be different, the technology may have shifted, but the formula for a woman never changes. There might be some examples, but those women are exceptional and we can't compare their lives with ours. No matter how modern we are in this century, the world can't change the fact a woman's first duty is to get married, then be a mother and raise our children. That is the line of descent of a woman and the world hasn't changed that much."

"We're in love," Locke said. "You show me a God that thinks that's a bad idea."

Anjali was always torn when this became the discussion. She understood why Locke was so angry, but it hurt her to hear him dismiss her religion and the views of her parents so readily. Religion was a force for good in her eyes. Love was a gift from God, but the world still hasn't understood what love truly means to humans. But she couldn't argue against the key point; her God would surely choose love over misery for her. It had become the single most important thing in her worship; she had asked the question a thousand times and never got the answer she craved.

The ceiling above was just discernible in a dim circle of faint light. For some reason, she didn't want to look at it. Locke turned off the bedside lamp when she asked him to and they lay on their backs staring up at nothing but darkness, each lost in their own thoughts. It was nearing midnight and it was Anjali's birthday tomorrow. He couldn't even wish her happy birthday properly.

*

Sunlight filtered through a gap in the curtains turning everything in the room grey. Anjali hadn't slept well. Her eyes had been closed, but she was wide awake. It was barely six o'clock when she got up, had a shower, brushed her teeth and got dressed. Dressed in her sky-blue sari she looked for teabags in the kitchen cupboards. Tea, she insisted, was the best tonic for headaches and she was desperate to end the continual fog of her mind. The hot liquid scorched her throat and she took a bite of the buttered toast she had also made.

Is this how life would be, if I got married? It was a glimpse into her future.

Locke appeared in the doorway, his eyes blood red. She knew he'd not slept either.

"Tea? Coffee?" she asked, beginning to wonder if he had forgotten her birthday.

"Tea, please."

She poured him a cup and put some bread in the toaster. Her eye was drawn to a sorry looking plant on the windowsill. Locke watched as she gave it some water and said a quiet prayer.

"Why would you worship a plant?" he asked.

"Because everything is energy. Humans and plants have a connection, that's why when we have plants it benefits our body. It heals us of cancer and clinical diseases. Everything is alive and moving. Plants can feel and cry and he was calling for water. The only difference is we can't hear them and simply because we can't hear it, doesn't mean it doesn't have feelings. Humans have a low hearing frequency."

"Okay," Locke said quietly. He wasn't convinced; science wasn't his strong subject, but he usually loved it when she said spiritual things like this. He agreed with Anjali if only to avoid any friction between them. "I've been thinking," he said, "why don't we get out of Manchester? Go for a drive somewhere? We could head out to Saddleworth; it's beautiful there. We can take a walk around the reservoir, drive over the tops, that kind of thing."

"Sounds wonderful."

"It is. Green everywhere and water and stunning cliffs and rocks. Might be a bit chilly, though. You might want to take a coat."

Anjali laughed. "We dwelled in the mountains, hillside and rivers, these are our friends. I've seen it in my life. The cold can't enter our physical structure."

"And happy birthday!" Locke added, feeling the warmth return between them. He walked over to the fridge and took out a small cupcake. She laughed at the gesture; she'd seen it in the fridge but not realised what it was for. She could have cried when he then presented her with a beautiful, delicate silver bracelet. It wasn't much, but he thought it was so pretty and simple. She did too as she put it on her wrist.

*

Locke had borrowed Pete's car. It had taken a bit of persuading, but he offered him a pint and a curry by way of compensation. They drove out of Manchester and the houses changed subtly before they reached any proper countryside. Red brick was replaced by sand-coloured stone and buildings started to look much older. Then came the hills and within half an hour they were winding their way up a steep road that took them to the top of Saddleworth Moor. Here John stopped and they looked back down on a glistening reservoir with the skyscrapers of Manchester just visible in the hazy distance.

Locke turned the car around and freewheeled back down the steep road, turning left at the bottom to head to the reservoir carpark. Anjali changed her shoes and they started walking, firstly through the gates by the sailing club and then around the far side of the reservoir. Across the water rose a formidable peak that looked as though the ground itself had been petrified in the middle of a hideous scream.

"It's called Aldermans," Locke said

Anjali drank in the atmosphere and listened as tiny brown birds twittered low above the ground. She heard the gurgling stream as she approached it.

"Sense the water, see life in the water," she said then playfully cupped some water and threw it Locke. She knew the environment; it might have been a hill in northern England, but it wasn't so different to the mountaintops of India. She could almost hear the hillside calling her.

"This is beautiful, John. Thank you." Locke smiled as she leaned in for a kiss.

"Better than shopping? I didn't know if you'd like it."

"I love it." She opened the backpack Locke had brought and took out his camera. "I think you should take some pictures so we will never forget this moment."

The images of Anjali in her flowing sky-blue sari against the green hues of the hillside or the dark tones of the Scots pine woodland were, as ever, stunning. She removed the clips and shook her head, releasing her raven-coloured hair to the winds. It fell either side of her shoulders and nestled to the front of her neck, highlighting the necklace there. He was captivated by her hair making her beauty come alive. She silently sat on a rock. Locke seemed to have a way of capturing her that enriched everything in the image. He asked her to pose with her right hand raised as she looked upwards at the tree canopy of the woods. He was trying to get an angle from below and slightly behind her. He shifted slightly to his right and crouched down. His camera clicked incessantly.

Something's wrong.

Anjali didn't know where the voice came from but it sounded as though someone was standing right beside. She looked to where the sound had emanated; nothing but the trunks of the tall trees, then at Locke who was now standing normally.

"What's up?" he asked, looking quizzically at Anjali.

He was about to take another step backwards, ready to take his next set of pictures when Anjali saw the danger. She screamed and rushed forwards, grabbing at John's arm, pulling him away from the edge of the cliff. He slipped as she did so, causing a small cascade of rocks to fall over the edge, and fell heavily on his side. Pain shot through his hip, but he managed to keep his camera aloft. They looked at each other. Awkwardly, Locke got to his feet and went towards the edge. There was a drop of thirty feet onto boulders.

Anjali joined him in looking down. "If you had died here, how would you get me home?"

"Why would you say that, Anjali?"

"You could have been killed. If you want to live, you should walk alongside me, not ahead of me. A voice warned me of the danger, but there is no-one else here."

"What are you saying?" Locke asked. "Who are you?"

"I am your life."

"Okay, I get it that I nearly fell, and that would not have been pretty, but why are you talking like this? Life and death don't give you notice, tell them you're coming."

"I don't expect you to understand, John, but I'm the same in your life. You needed to be salvaged. I am here to save you. At first, I thought it was the hill that was calling me. Then I thought it was the lake, which was addressing me. Only now I realised it was you who was calling me here."

"Of course it was. It was my idea. Are you trying to tell me that something made me bring you here today so that you could then save me from falling off a cliff?"

"Don't be like that, John. You know my spirituality is important to me. I believe in Nature, in mountains and rivers and lakes and forests. If you call someone from your core, they surely will come. They can hear you breathing. The voice echoes back to you."

"It sounds like you're waiting for someone."

"Someone in my essence, yes, but he isn't in front of me all the time. That is the person you call too."

Locke looked out across the reservoir towards the green and brown hues of the hillside opposite. "Only I am in front of you right now," he said.

"When the voice calls, the heart echoes the frequency and then it lives in you."

Anjali reached out and took Locke's hand, leading him away from the edge and further into the woods. "I recognise a lot more than you might think," she said. "For instance your clothing."

"What about it?"

"You told me to bring a coat. It was you that should have brought a coat. The deeper we go into these woods the colder you will get. You will shiver. But my ancestors were from the mountains. I won't feel the cold. You might become ill, because you are not used to the outside."

"What the hell are you talking about? You sound like you're in some kind of trance."

They came to a river, a waterfall just below them.

"I'll show you," Anjali said. She bent down and removed her shoes, then hitched up the sari to above the knee.

"Wait, we don't need to cross this river; we can go across a bridge further up."

Anjali turned. "I'll show you." And took a determined step into the freezing moorland water. Locke watched aghast as she reached the other side and turned to face him. "As I told you, you will feel the cold. I did not. Can you cross the river, John?"

Locke thought this ridiculous. He was beginning to feel cold and regretted not bringing a coat. But what the hell was she playing at?

"It's your turn," said Anjali, laughing. "Take off your shoes and cross over, it's fine. Is it too cold for you? Are you sure you want to take the bridge and prove me right?"

Locke sat down on a rock and took off his shoes, rolling his jeans up as high as they would go. He didn't find things at all funny, but it was her birthday and she did sometimes behave like this. Usually he marvelled at it, her spirituality something he couldn't understand, but it made her all the more alluring.

"Don't think about it, John, just walk across. Putting your feet in cold water will help your body's blood flow and you will feel warm again."

Locke took a deep breath and marched right across the stream, his feet suddenly felt like ice and complained as he stepped on some of the sharp stones in the riverbed. *How did she make it look so graceful?* He rushed out onto the other riverbank, hopping about to get more warmth in his feet.

Anjali laughed at him, but he wasn't amused.

"You are trembling," she said.

"It's bloody freezing and I can't feel my feet!"

"Calm down, John, it's only the shock. Haven't you felt ice on your feet before?"

"Of course I bloody haven't! Who in their right mind walks through a freezing mountain stream when there's a perfectly good bridge up there? I can't even feel my feet."

John began to shiver. Only afterwards did he think it strange that the shivering was so violent. Anjali led him gently down towards a rock which she asked him to sit on. She then took his right foot and blew on it, rubbing and massaging the warmth back into it.

"What are you doing?" But Anjali shushed him and continued to massage heat back into his foot. Satisfied she lowered it and picked up Locke's other foot.

"What's wrong with this?" Anjali asked.

"Well, you're touching my feet for a start. It's demeaning."

Anjali shook her head sadly. "In many cultures, people bow down on their mother's feet for blessing. Jesus Christ washed his disciples' feet. And I bow down to the one I fall in love with. Do you know who takes care like this? A wife. And did you notice when you get lost in life, who brings you back home? A lover helps you find your ways."

The warmth had returned and Locke felt amazing. What had been chill became like a slowly marauding heat rising up his legs and into his torso. He was sure he could feel it. He looked at Anjali as she gently lowered his left leg; her massage complete.

"I don't believe it. You made me walk through that river and suddenly I feel so much better."

"It's not about the water, John. It's about the trust that lives inside. The woman became the drop of pure water that flows in the river. And she becomes that drop of drinking water and lives in a woman's essence. Thus any man who drinks that drop of water will become my love. When someone looks at you deep beyond your soul, he then becomes a devotee. A man lives in a woman. He becomes her world. Lives in her essence. You know your woman, John."

Locke felt something change inside. He didn't know how he could love Anjali any more than he already did. But he felt the warmth still rising through his body and thought he loved her a little bit more.

"Nobody has ever experienced the purity of a woman," he said. "If they did, they would worship women. Even women don't understand their true nature."

"A woman would dance for you," Anjali replied. "She's going to sing for you. Twist and turn for you. She would ruin herself for you. She would kill herself for you. She's going to be expecting love from you. She is the woman of the river. She will be with you forever. She wishes this relationship would never end. While she lives, she will worship you. She will remain with you until she receives your shoulder. She would get lost in the river and then find you on the other side. This is the wife of the river. She saw the diamond and the pearl, enough, by the time she looked at you.

"She keeps someone secret in her heart. Match a symbol like that. She's a thirsty lover. She'll be a servant to you. She came for you into the world. She's the girl in the river."

"When someone looks at you deep beyond your soul, he then becomes a devotee," Locke added. "He Lives in her. He becomes her world. Lives in her essence."

Anjali shuffled slightly then looked up at the surrounding hills. "Before we leave here, do you want to hear the mountain speak to you?"

"How?" said John.

"Say something, say anything, speak with your heart, John."

Locke looked around at the jagged cliffs and mountaintops, at the green hill and the misty cloud. Words fell into place in his mind and he looked into her eyes.

"I love you Anjali!" Locke's voice echoed across the valley. "I can't live without you, Anjali!" he shouted, and the hillside shouted back.

That day Anjali knew he was the right man for her.

*

They returned home. The day had been incredible for Locke, for Anjali she knew she had got her man thinking. But she knew he was still troubled by the night before. How he couldn't get beyond the frustration of the unfairness of it all.

She could sense his anger. Although the day had been a success, and she had achieved all she had hoped, neither had forgotten the night before. She wanted to reach across and touch him again, to tell him it was okay and that he was what she wanted. It was true, but a vision of her parents flashed before her eyes. She didn't want to disrespect or humiliate her parents in the process and her hand stayed by her side.

"Tell me more about yourself, John."

"Well, as you know I love taking photographs, but I always wanted to be more intelligent. People always looked at me as the pretty boy, not the intelligent one. People always belittled me. So any knowledge I have feels less worthy. I want to help the world, people and society. If I had the skills or the knowledge, I would make the world a better place. Currently, any knowledge we hold is for sale, people want to make money when it should be shared. This world is not made for us, Anjali."

Their gaze lingered, then he led her to his sofa where they sat together for what seemed like hours, knowing the question was still floating in the air. Locke looked at the clock; it was a quarter to four in the afternoon.

"We could elope," he said.

The words seemed to hang in the air between them. It wasn't the first time they had been uttered, but Locke was increasingly thinking it was the only solution. Initially, he had joked about Las Vegas, or some place in Scotland called Gretna Green. Las Vegas sounded better, but he wasn't serious initially. He was getting more serious by the day. Anjali said nothing.

"Look," Locke said. "I've been thinking. Maybe not elope, although you know I'd do it in a heartbeat if you said yes, but how about we just move away? Like London or something. Somewhere neither of us knows anyone and yet we could build a life there and see where it takes us. You could get a job anywhere with your qualifications, and I've been thinking about working as a photographer."

"Sounds nice," Anjali said. Locke was getting animated.

"There are loads of opportunities to work down there. Just imagine me doing weddings or christenings or whatever? They'd pay big bucks down there."

Anjali listened but was not really convinced. She smiled, but it stopped Locke. He fell silent and the silence lingered. She didn't want to upset him as it had been such a good day. She couldn't remember a better birthday.

"Yes," she said, eventually. Locke looked at Anjali.

"What? You're serious?"

"I think so." She turned to face him. "You know how much I love you. I adore you. In my religion, there is a thing called *'ardhangini'*. It means I am one half of you. If I am not with you I am but half of me. I cannot live without you, John. I don't know why or how, but I have fallen for a man outside of my religion, yet I am still your *ardhangini*. I pray to my Gods, Radha and Krishna, and to Ardhanarishvara – the Lord of the Dance who is half-woman. I pray to my Gods daily that I will be allowed *ardhangini,* but I am still waiting for an answer. I think it is time for me to make my own decision."

Locke could say nothing. Every time they had this conversation, it had soured the moment. Suddenly Anjali had made this moment sweet. He had never expected her to say any different this time. His mind raced. As did his heart. She really wanted to take the next step. He tried to calm his breathing, tried to sound confident when his stomach was turning somersaults.

"It sounds like you've been thinking about London a lot," Anjali offered.

"I have," Locke said a little too high pitched. "I think about it all the time. We can do it. I've got enough saved from my folks to go without work for a bit, but I'd be able to find at least temp work to start with. And the same with you, do temping work until you get a proper job. Surely it would be easy to get an accountancy job down there? Could you just transfer?"

"I could," Anjali said. "But I'd probably need to work out my notice."

"And I could rent out this place; Castlefield is the next big thing in Manchester. All these buildings are going to be renovated, not just this one. It'll be the place to live and there's no doubt people will want to rent this flat. We could go tomorrow."

Anjali laughed. "No, we couldn't!" she said. "But we could go soon. Maybe the end of the month? Like I say, I'll probably have to give notice, and we don't need to make rash decisions. It's not certain I could get a transfer to London, but perhaps I should get a job first, then we can find a place to live? I'd be able to work for someone, definitely. I'll even do your accounts once you become a professional photographer."

Locke smiled. The response from his photographs at David and Hannah's wedding had been overwhelming. It had been the kick he had needed to stop thinking of photography as a hobby and start thinking of it as a career. He'd even started to build a website or, at least, had asked one of the IT guys at work to do it for him. It was a basic one, but it was still going to cost him over a hundred pounds. With pictures from David and Hannah's wedding on there, he was sure couples would jump at the chance of employing him.

Anjali got up from the sofa and walked to the bedroom door. She looked coquettishly at him then slipped inside. Locke knew that look and needed no second invitation.

"I really think I can do it," Locke said breathlessly as they lay on the bed

"I know," Anjali replied, laughing and reaching under the cover to hold Locke's hand. "I've got every faith in you. We just need to plan a little instead of dropping everything for tomorrow. You've got a bit carried away, I think. It feels like you want to leave this place, this world behind."

"It's not that. I'm happy here, but if I can't have you here, then I'll have you anywhere else," Locke said. "Seriously though, what will you tell your parents?"

Anjali pulled her hand away. She had been thinking about running away for so long and it tore her in two. She adored her parents. They had given her everything and she loved everything about them except the one single point on which she disagreed. She always thought she would marry conventionally, but John Locke stole her heart.

"I don't think I can tell them anything. They won't understand and they won't give their blessing. They will say I have brought shame on the family and they will beg me to change my mind. It's all psychological and I just don't know how hard I am going to find it to talk to them about this. I think that would be harder even than simply walking away. I've been dreading this moment for weeks. On the one hand they want happiness for their child, but on the other they don't permit their children to make the biggest decision of their own lives. But I am one half of you; *ardhangini*. I cannot be whole if I'm not with you."

Locke rolled back on to his side and reached across to stroke Anjali's face. It was wet again and he surprised himself when he realised he was crying too. "Whatever we need to do, we will. I am also ardyhanging, or whatever it is. I am nothing without you in my life."

Anjali giggled through her tears.

"What?" Locke said, surprised.

"*Ardhangini*."

"That's what I said," Locke insisted. Anjali laughed louder. It was infectious and Locke found himself laughing along with her. She turned to face him, still chuckling.

"It says something when we can have a conversation about me killing myself that ends with us both laughing." Anjali reached out into the darkness and rested her hand on Locke's bare, muscular shoulder. She stroked it, gave it a squeeze.

"You are my everything. You are my lover, my best friend, you are the one that makes me laugh and you are the one that makes me cry. You will see one day our love story will make history, our name will be everywhere, people will remember us for who we are for generations."

eight
the scene blurred and blackened

Locke took a sip of his coffee. The train was due to leave just after two but he was an hour early. Beside him a sports bag full of what he considered essential: his cameras, laptop, clock radio, toiletries and clothes. Beside the bag India leant up against a low wall. He had placed it the right way up, Anjali's lower half obscured by the bag, but he could see her face clearly, her eyes closed as she prayed.

      He thought back over the crazy changes in his life since he had taken that photograph mere months earlier. It didn't matter to him that he was moving cities. He had loved his time in Manchester, but the growing issue of his race and of his religion meant it was too difficult for them to stay. For him it was a bit of a wrench. For some reason he liked the Mancunians he met more than he did the 'southerners' as they were derogatorily called. There was a special dislike of anyone from London and it surprised him just how many people he had met since coming to Manchester that had told him what was wrong with the people from down South. Miserable was a common refrain, as was unsociable, tight with money, posh. He had to have the last one explained, but there were many phrases people used to describe what exactly was wrong with southerners. He found it bewildering, and now he was preparing to live amongst this 'enemy' of the north. Initially amused by the conflict, he now wondered how long it would be before he experienced this unfriendliness for himself.

      He looked at his watch; 13:22. He had arranged to meet Anjali at half one to leave plenty of time to get their tickets and make their train. He began to focus on the main entrance to Manchester's Piccadilly station where he expected Anjali to come striding through at any moment. He tried to curb his excitement. For him this move was the start of the rest of his perfect life because Anjali was to be in it. Nothing else mattered. But for her he knew it to be very different. Right now he supposed she was struggling to cope with the fact that she had left her parents, *her old life,* behind to start again with him. His heart went out to her and his first duty was to protect her from her pain. It was a strange sensation to know he had to hold back on his excitement because Anjali was likely to be devastated.

Life had not turned out as he planned. But then again he didn't really have a plan before Anjali. It had been months now, meeting in secret, the relationship a secret, their love a secret. Maybe that was why it had lasted as long as it had, he wondered airily as passengers passed by and announcements barked over the tannoy.

He thought back to all the times they had met in parks, cinemas, concerts, met for lunch or dinner, or both. How conversation was rarely stilted. Locke felt as though he was flying having met the girl, literally, of his dreams. All those months dreaming about her only for Anjali to appear at that wedding. It felt like heaven, but it felt real.

Will it last? A shadow crossed Locke's face. She still hadn't told her parents because it wasn't the 'norm' for her to do so. She was violating all the rules of her traditions, by even meeting him, having a relationship, going out, lying to her parents, and allowing a stranger to touch her body. Falling in love wasn't a sin, it was precautionary tale, in her religion. And he was no longer a stranger. He knew she feared her parents' reaction and how she would approach them.

Locke's fists tightened as he thought of the fear she was going through. How she needed consent even though she was an adult and he couldn't really understand the dilemma.

"Your life is yours, not your parents'," he said to her once. She agreed.

"Truth gun," was the reply that had surprised him. "Two fingers to make your hand look like a gun pointed at my head, then ask questions, quickly. If I falter, the guns goes off."

Locke didn't pick up the game quickly, so she did it to him first. He found it unsettling, but then got into the rhythm. Hs hand made the shape of a gun and he pointed it at her temple.

"Who do you live with?"

"My parents."

"Who is your best friend?"

"Hannah."

"What's your favourite TV series?"

"Friends."

"Who do you love the most, me or your parents?"

"My parents."

"Are you ready to run away with me?"

"Yes."

"Who do you fear the most?"

"My parents."

"Who do you love most in this world?"

"You."

He had lowered his 'truth gun'. He remembered the moment as though she had said it right there. Only she wasn't there. She had agreed to run away with him, but she wasn't there.

The station clock ticked on. The digital figures a luminous yellow against the black of the departure board. 13:42. There was no sign of Anjali. He resolved to only call her mobile at 13:45. He wanted to give her as much space as she needed at that moment. His coffee finished he slung the hefty bag over his shoulder and picked up his picture, making his way to the ticket office. He thought he would buy their tickets while he was waiting for her, but something stopped him.

Instead he took out his phone and rang her mobile. His heart skipped a beat as he heard Anjali speak, but it was her voicemail. He hung up; no point leaving a message as he expected here at any moment. 13:50 and still she hadn't walked through the entrance. *Is she still coming?* Locke shook the thought away and decided to be proactive. If they missed their planned train, there would be another within the hour.

Two o'clock came and went. So did the train. He took out his phone and called again, but again only voicemail. Locke felt the bile rise up. His mouth had gone dry and he had an overwhelming urge to run. *She's not coming. She's not coming!* He became frantic and looked about the other passengers.

This can't be happening. He hadn't even considered the possibility she might not turn up at all. His breathing became rapid, the sinking feeling in the pit of his stomach tearing at him as myriad thoughts went through his mind. At the forefront of all them, a single word; No! He heard himself shout it aloud and a nearby couple shrank a little from the strange man shrieking in a crowded train station. He called her a third time with the same response. He became aware of his palms sweating as his phone slipped. He wiped his brow on his jacket. *No!*

And there she was. Locke almost felt his legs give way. He smiled, almost cried, as the relief washed over him. But something was wrong; she looked upset as he knew she must be, but there was more. She was crying uncontrollably. When she spotted Locke she stopped, as if a barrier had come between them. *She's got no bag...* he thought, the significance beginning to dawn on him. Locke hurried towards her, catching her from falling as her grief overcame her and she wailed. She sounded like a wounded animal. A policeman heard her and started to walk towards them, but stopped a short distance away to see how things might develop.

"What's wrong?" Locke asked. "What's happened?"

She looked worried, frightened, even, the tears streaming down her face. Locke held her face in his hands. "I knew you would come," he said. "I knew you would entrust your family for me. I just had a feeling."

Locke held her tight as they walked towards the wall where he had left his bag and the picture of India. Anjali sat down on his bag, her back against the wall. Locke knelt next to her. Other passengers looked on curiously, but left a respectful gap around them as they formed a picture of despair. Slowly she managed to compose herself. He had said nothing, the fear that the lack of a bag meant only one thing; London was not happening.

His heart felt as though it was tearing in two at the sight of her tear-stricken face. Her eyes were red raw and she sobbed as she looked at him. Seeing India had made her sob again. And then laugh a little. The last thing she felt at that moment was beautiful. His eyes pleaded with her to tell him what had happened. Neither knew it, but the policeman had moved so that he remained a respectful distance away just in case he was needed.

"You're wrong, John. I have come here to tell you I can't do it. I can't leave my family, my parents. I'm sorry, but I am here to tell you I am leaving you. I'm so, so, sorry."

Every word a stab at his heart. The world seemed to turn black as his head swam.

"I came here with an ultimatum, you can either forget me or you can ask my father for my hand in marriage."

"But we've discussed this," he pleaded. "I'm not ready. We're not ready. We are going to London to see how it works out."

"Then, I guess you should forget me. I cannot leave my family without that proposal."

Locke stared at the floor, but saw nothing. "I can't come!" Anjali shouted finally and burst into tears once more. Locke felt as though his insides had been torn out. The words swam through his mind, over and over again; *I can't come... I can't come... I can't come,...* He said nothing, and struggled for breath. Anjali recovered, but the tears continued.

"They found out," she said. "They found the bag I had packed. It wasn't where I had put it. I came out of my bedroom and they were standing in the hallway. They came straight out with it. "You've got a boyfriend and you are running away with him." I didn't know what to say."

Locke heard the words, but they barely registered. *I can't come....* Anjali covered her face with her hands. She was aware of curious passers-by looking at her.

"Why didn't you just push past them?" Locke said, more to break the silence than anything else.

"My dad had a gun."

"What?" Locke looked at Anjali. He wasn't sure he had heard correctly.

"My dad pulled out a fucking gun!" she said, whispering. The policeman was still nearby. Locke stared blankly at her. *A gun?* Anjali took a deep breath. "He walked into the living room, leaving my mother to block the way and he came back with a fucking gun. He held it by the barrel and tried to hand it to me. I just looked at it. He told me to take it. He said that if I was to leave them to be with you that I would have to shoot them first. My mother nodded as he said it. He told me I would have to kill them to be with you."

"They can't have been serious—"

"They were totally fucking serious!" Anjali's shouted response again caused others to look in their direction. She was also keenly aware of the policeman who remained, hopefully, just out of earshot. "My parents are not the sort that would kill their own daughter. Some might have done. It has happened in India. But my parents are not like that. They hate the idea. But this shows just how important their faith is to them that they would rather die than have their daughter run off with someone else."

Locke looked blankly at the floor. Anjali reached out, place a gentle hand under his chin. He returned her gaze as fresh tears began to fall.

"They have done the one thing that could stop me from coming with you."

"They might have been faking it."

"Are you not listening, John? They are proud and honourable people. They simply do not understand you, us. They have known about it and I think they have let me continue. But they could not let me leave with you. They will never accept marriage outside our faith. And they know I could never kill them. Can you imagine trying to live a normal life after that? Apart from the fact I'd go to prison, how could we ever have what we have now knowing I had murdered my family?"

Locke could think of nothing to say.

"John," she said. "Before you came into my life, my parents were in my life. They were long before you were and I made a promise to them, one that a girl makes even before her birth, that I was to fulfil whatever their wishes were as my parents. Before I made a promise to you, before I made love to you, I made that promise to my parents. I will never put them to shame; I am going to choose the path they choose for me, even if it means I die daily from grief. If you genuinely love me, ask my parents for my hand. We can't start a life without their approval. One day we too will be parents, so imagine how we would feel if our children would do the same with us? Everything we do has a consequence."

Locke pinched the bridge of his nose and tried to stem the tears.

"I will wait for you," Anjali whispered. "Life isn't about how we plan it, it's about the unknown."

"There must be some other way?" Locke's voice was breaking. He saw his life disappearing before his eyes. *Ardhangini* he thought. "You must be able to talk them round. I can't live without my other half, *without you*. You're here now. Forget about your bag, you can get stuff in London."

Anjali's shook her head. His voice got more desperate the more he realised the relationship was over. "Please," he begged, but Anjali only sobbed, and shook her head more violently. Locke saw her face, her beautiful face and knew it was over. From somewhere deep within came a howl that rose up. The scream had the policeman rush over as Locke bent double, his forehead on the floor, his arms clutching at his stomach as if it might burst.

He cried out again, louder. Anjali covered her ears to the sound and made to move away. Locke's hand shot out and grabbed her by the ankle. He felt the policeman's strong grip on his shoulder, but wouldn't let go. Anjali pulled, distraught that she was leaving her lover, distraught that her parents had stopped her, distraught at the sight of what had become of her John Locke. She couldn't bear it. She pulled her leg back sharply, as the policeman yanked harder on Locke. His fingers lost their grasp on her ankle and he fell forwards as she scurried backwards on her haunches. The policeman looked at Anjali.

"Are you okay?" he asked, realising he no longer had to restrain Locke, who had curled up into a ball on the station concourse. Anjali nodded and looked at the huddled, sobbing mess that her lover had become.

"I'll stay with him," the policeman continued. "Maybe you should go?" She didn't need asking twice. Her heart was broken, but even that had been eclipsed by Locke's reaction. She had no doubt if they were on the platform, he would be jumping under the next train. She got up and ran. Locke got back to his knees, the policeman holding him back by his jacket.

"No!" Locke screamed as he watched Anjali run from him. The scene blurred and blackened as he screamed again and again. Anjali's eyes flooded with fresh tears as the cries went through her then lessened. She could still hear them as she ran out of the doors into the bright Manchester afternoon.

"Anjali!" Locke shrieked, shrugging off the policeman's grip and leaping to his feet. "Anjali," he wailed one last time, but he knew she wasn't coming back. The policeman had hold of him again, but Locke was oblivious. It was as though Piccadilly station was deserted. There was no one else there. No one else mattered. His throat was raw from his screams. His eyes stung from tears. His head splitting. He bent over and retched, but nothing came out. He slowly became aware of the policeman's grip and gave a little shrug, but the grip remained. Locke looked down to wear Anjali had been sitting. There was an in print in the material of his bag, a depression that said so much.

Then he saw it, leaning against the wall to the side of the bag. He stared at it, at the picture, at Anjali, at India. Then he glared at it, launched himself at it and swung a boot which ripped through the canvas. The force of the kick almost knocked him over as his foot went through the picture and met with the resistance of the wall behind. A searing pain shot up from his foot all the way up his leg.

The policeman was quick and pushed Locke against the wall, one of Locke's arms pinned behind his back. But it wasn't hard, merely firm. The policeman whispered for Locke to calm down, to not do anything stupid. He didn't; instead he became limp and allowed the policeman to turn him round and lower him onto his bag, which still felt warm from where Anjali had been just moments before. The policeman squatted down beside Locke and said a few words. Locke nodded, but wasn't listening. As he felt his life slipping by, there was just one thing on his mind. An image had formed. And it stayed there.

All Locke could think about was the gun.

nine
only their eyes were visible

The video whirred and the television made shadows and sent bursts of light around the room. The shades of colour altered as the scenes played out, lighter, dimmer, crimson, white. Then darkness. Locke's hand located the remote and he rewound the tape. When he heard the click, he pressed the play button again.

"Do you feel my pain, Anjali? Don't we have the right to fall in love?" He never knew how long he had been watching the video. The curtains in his living room were drawn and no light seeped through. The flickering images of Anjali dancing, and then of him, started up again.

"Don't mind me if you see me weeping."

He saw light bounce off the empty whisky bottles he had dropped on the floor. There were two of them. A third remained upright on his table, but it too contained no liquid. He had bought four bottles, smashed one and finished off the others. His mouth tasted sour and he was almost sick as he tried to swallow.

"I might be alive, Anjali, but my spirit is hurting me. I cannot face the world."

His eyes stung and his head pounded relentlessly. He had muted the sound as a result and the silent dance matched his mood; empty. He didn't even know what day it was. He looked at his watch, but it wasn't on his wrist. He screwed up his eyes against the light of the television and looked about him.

"Love isn't open to people like you and me, Anjali."

He picked up his phone which lay on the carpet by his feet. But when he pressed the 'on' button, the screen didn't light up. *Battery,* he thought.

Locke lay back on his sofa and cried out as the axe he felt was embedded in his head moved a little. He lay there for some time. He became aware the video had finished and this time did not search for the remote. He slowly opened his eyes and looked up. There was the faintest glow emanating from the television, enough that he could make out the patterns on his ceiling above.

"You said only God could recognise our love. Where is your lover? What have you done to me? When will you visit? When will you understand?"

He was hungry and knew he had to get up, but the pain in his head took over everything. It even hurt to think. He gently touched his forehead, then pinched the bridge of his nose. He sighed, tasted the sourness in his mouth and retched, rolling to his side in case he was going to be sick. He didn't. But he continued to roll and fell off the sofa cracking his knee on the floor and sending an empty bottle scurrying across the floor to clank against a skirting board.

"There's nothing more of me left! This is why I drink, Anjali, to see my pain away. Allow me to be drunk!" he shouted at the top of his voice, as he lay amongst the empty bottles, his head splitting and his knee throbbing.

Slowly he pulled himself up onto all fours, leaning against his sofa so as not to fall. The room was spinning and he had got up too quickly. He steadied himself, planted one foot flat on the carpet then heaved himself up. His hand clutched at the arm of his chair as he regained his senses and his balance. He stood up to his full height and winced as he put his weight on his right foot.

He remembered how much it had hurt when he kicked out at the canvas picture and then collided with the wall. He wondered if he had left Piccadilly station with a broken bone to go with his destroyed heart.

Locke slowly looked about him. The room was a mess; the contents of his sports bag were strewn about the floor where he had dug for the video of his dance with Anjali. A camera lay against the other chair. He hoped it wasn't broken.

Locke limped across the room and slowly opened his curtains. The room flooded a sodium orange and he blinked away the new brightness, his head complaining loudly. *Evening,* he thought and turned back into the room.

"When I drink I speak my heart's words."

Locke laughed at the sentiment. India lay in shreds on the chair. He looked away.

*

The inside of the Briton's Protection was warm and welcoming. But Locke had no need or wish for company. What he had was further need for whisky and the quaint little pub had that in spades. A booklet claimed there were over a hundred different whiskies to choose from. Locke had ordered five doubles.

"I'm doing a tasting session," he had said to the barmaid. "By myself," he added, making her more wary. She warned him he would have to leave if he got too drunk. Locke shrugged and threw a twenty-pound note on the bar, then walked around to the back of the pub where it was quieter.

The décor was scruffy; patterned red carpets faded at the edges. The benches and chairs suffering a similar fate. He didn't care and lit a cigarette. "And he she comes," he said aloud as another memory of Anjali came flooding back. He never usually smoked, in fact he usually hated it, but for some reason he liked the effect at that moment in his life. He coughed and the young couple in another corner of the room looked away when Locke glared at them. Drunk as he was, he reckoned the cigarettes reduced the need for food. His stomach gurgled away, but he didn't feel particularly hungry. The whiskies arrived.

"Bit quiet," he said, hoping to give the barmaid a sober-looking smile.

"It usually is on a Monday night," she replied flatly and walked away.

Locke knew he wasn't welcome tonight. He wondered how he must look and stared down at the sleeves of his jacket. They seemed clean enough. His jeans less so. He had been wearing the same clothes for three days and realised he must stink. But a three-day bender was what he needed. *Just one glimpse of you,* he thought. *Just one glimpse of your face.* Instead he tried to blot Anjali from his mind. He had just about succeeded when something would happen, a sound, an image, a sensation and he would be straight back in her arms with all the pain it caused him.

There had been low points in his life, but this was the lowest by far. He decided quickly that the only way to get through his pain was to forget. He decided to drink and drink because that was the only way to make the days go faster. *Monday? Shit!* It felt longer. He needed to drink a lot more and took a large gulp of the first of the whiskies.

Anjali in the temple, ringing the bell.

The back of his throat felt like fire as the alcohol hit it. He spluttered, then coughed, the phlegm from three days' smoking coming up and making him want to retch.

"How much more will you drink, John? I want to see you live not die."

The voice was in his head. He had heard it many times. The moment of being sick passed and he dared not look at the young couple across from him. If they were disgusted at the sight of him, then they would be right to. He took a long drag on his cigarette and wondered how it could be finished so quickly; he thought he had only just lit it.

I'm not crazy! I can picture her!

He looked at the murals on the wall. They depicted scenes from the Peterloo Massacre of 1819 when mounted soldiers broke up a rally in the centre of Manchester killing some and wounding many, many others. He thought it had happened quite near to where he was sitting. Locke looked closely at one soldier riding through the crowd, sabre raised. He wore a black shako and a uniform of a dark blue jacket with white shoulder belts forming a cross at his chest. The trousers were also white. As he often did, he wondered if the man depicted had served in India, just before the start of the Napoleonic wars. It wasn't impossible, given the dates.

He knew the history because he had been in the pub many times before as he felt it was the most British pub he had yet found in Manchester. It also wasn't too far from his apartment in Castlefield. Today, though, he was not enjoying himself. The whisky he was forcing down no longer seemed to numb the pain. The sight of a young couple having a quiet drink reminded him of Anjali as he had brought her to this pub several times, not that she never drank the whisky. Even the soldier in the picture was starting to turn his thoughts back to India.

"Bloody India!" he said out loud, then wondered whether he meant the country or his photograph.

He looked down at the table he was seated at; there were three full tumblers and the ashtray had four cigarette butts in it. Locke didn't think he had smoked four, but thought it probably true when he fished out the packet and looked inside. He took out a fifth and lit it, then gulped down his third whisky. He was getting better. He neither spluttered nor coughed, but instead smiled drunkenly to himself.

"There you are, John boy, there you are." The young couple stood up to leave. Locke realised he had also said this out loud and chuckled. He said it again, more quietly, just to himself, and found the joke funny. He didn't see the looks he got as the couple left. He was now alone in the room. *Alone.* The tears threatened once more as his face curled up and he almost sobbed. He stifled it and instead took another large drag on his cigarette. *Need a piss.*

Locke stood up unsteadily and immediately felt the pain in his right foot. Leaning against the wall he reached for his fourth tumbler, but overbalanced, fell forwards onto the table and crashed to the ground. Glass shattered and the barmaid shouted something. Locke tried to make sense of his surroundings.

A moment earlier he had been standing up, now he was staring at the ceiling. His crotch felt wet and he hoped it was whisky and that he'd not wet himself. His eyes started to close, but then he felt two large hands slip under his shoulders and lift him up. He was in a sitting position and then standing, but he wasn't sure how it happened. He could see people in front of him and thought they might be concerned, but he couldn't make out their faces or what they were saying. Everything felt blurred. He had to get out. He patted his pockets; his wallet was there and so was his phone, not that it was switched on. He also felt the cigarette packet and his keys.

"Fine," he said and took a step forwards. His foot complained and he could still feel a hand under his arm. He realised he was being led out of the pub and went with it. The night air was cool and there were few people about. He turned to wave at whoever it was that had led him out, but the door had already closed. He staggered to his left, got his balance properly back and started to limp in the direction of home.

Anjali appeared to him and beckoned him. He followed. "Hey, India!" he said, laughing to himself. His senses began to return a little and he just managed to avoid getting run over as he crossed the road. The blare of a horn sobered him up a bit.

In front of him a low wall. He leaned on it and looked down, realising he was standing on a bridge over a canal. He knew the canal ran near his apartment block and had walked along it many times.

He wondered if it might be a shortcut and decided to take it, even though somewhere in the depths of his mind he knew it was actually further to get home. He slowly made his way down the steps, stopping at the foot to look at the ink-black water and the many bits of rubbish floating on top.

"Time for you to go, John. Take the jump. End your life. Isn't that what you're trying to do?"

Locke looked up and down the towpath. The voice seemed real, but he saw no one. He reached in his pocket and pulled out his cigarettes, fumbling with the lighter. The cool air and smoke combined to rush against the back of his throat. It was a sensation he was beginning to like.

"Got a cig, lad?" Locke turned towards the voice. And saw two young lads in front of him. They were wearing dark clothing, their hoods were up and he noticed, but struggled to understand, that their faces were covered. Only their eyes were visible.

"Yeah," Locke said and held the open packet of cigarettes for the nearest boy to take one. He took the whole lot. "Hey, buddy!" he protested, slipping back into his American accent as he sometimes did.

"And your wallet." Locke looked down and saw a blade glinting in the harsh glare of a streetlight. He realised the other boy had moved and was now standing behind him. The punch to his kidney floored him immediately and he vainly waved his arms around trying to connect with either assailant. He felt a punch to the side of his head and curiously wondered what had happened to his cigarette. His head swam and he fell forwards, his skull cracking on a cobble stone with a sickening thud. Hands rifled through his pockets and he knew his wallet had gone. He reached up for the face of the nearest mugger and grabbed, pulling the scarf down. He didn't let go of the scarf and he barely got a look at the boy. But he heard him shout, "Fuck! He's seen me!"

The boot was aimed right at his face and crashed home with hideous accuracy. John Locke lay motionless on the cobbles next to the putrid Rochdale canal. His jaw broken, he didn't hear the boys talking to each other or feel them lift up his body. He never felt the splash or sensed the enveloping water, and he didn't realise he was sinking down into the canal's black depths. He settled on the silty bottom, his head resting against a discarded tyre on the canal floor, sightless eyes staring upwards.

Anjali, he thought, a last dying breath escaped him as the filthy water filled his lungs.

ten

a thousand moons will not lessen our shame

Anjali sat silently sobbing as she looked down at the broken body of John Locke. Tubes and monitors beeped, clicked and hissed and Locke's chest slowly rose and fell. He barely breathed; his survival was uncertain. He had been like this for two days.

A couple of days earlier she had been lying on her bed thinking about nothing but her John. Her tears were constant. He had gone and it was over. Prayer, fasting and talking to him were the only comforts she could give herself.

"I know there are many who no longer believe in this miracle. But where medicine fails, prayer is the answer. And we don't even have the evidence to prove it other than showing our gratitude. I have trust you will return."

Downstairs there had been the quiet sounds of her mother wandering about tidying her home, even though it was immaculate. Her parents had been so understanding since they forbade her to leave. Anjali's parents could imagine the devastation John's parents must have felt when they heard the news. No parent would like to see their child in a life or death situation such as this.

Anjali could not forgive them, but she recognised her parents took no pleasure in seeing their daughter so distraught. If only they could see the nonsense of aspects of their religion in the twenty-first century.

But children are often forgetful. When a relationship breaks, it is the children who return to their parents. And it is the parents that must rebuild their child, providing the courage, confidence and motivation for their child to live again. Then her phone had rung; it was John. He hadn't called since she had left him at Piccadilly station, and he hadn't answered any of her calls or texts. She snatched at the Nokia.

"John!"

"I'm sorry, no, I'm not John. My name is Neil Harries. I am a police officer." Anjali pulled the phone away from her ear and stared at its display. *John Locke,* it said.

"Hello? Hello? Who's speaking, please?" The voice was distant and tinny as Anjali continued to look at the screen. She brought it back to her ear. "Is that Anjali? Please could you answer? It is very important."

Anjali listened with increasing horror as the police officer on the other end of the phone asked who she was, what her relationship with John Locke was and whether she could come into Manchester. PC Harries would not tell exactly what had happened, but it was clear John had been hurt and she was needed. Her father drove her to Wythenshawe Hospital when he saw how frantic his daughter was. He didn't go in, initially, preferring to remain in the car park, but he relented after four hours and found Anjali sobbing by a bed that contained Locke's motionless body. His face was swollen, blackened and bruised. Myriad wires were attached to his body. Machines bleeped. Anjali still cried. He realised at that moment how hard parenting is. It was hard to see your child in pain.

He went home alone and told his wife what had happened. Both of them returned to the hospital the next day. They could see their daughter's pain and they vowed to stay with her by Locke's bedside for as long as it took. They now understood Anjali's love for this man. He saw her go to the temple, to the *Masjid* and to the church, feeding the poor and the homeless. She gathered the communities and told them to pray that a miracle would happen. It was the least they could do. Her father couldn't help but think John Locke truly was her *ardhangini*.

For the thousandth time, Anjali looked across the bed to where her parents sat dutifully. Her mother returned the gaze, compassion and sadness in her pained face. Her father similarly wished he could ease his daughter's suffering.

The door opened and a nurse walked in.

"He's in here," she said to a large man and a diminutive, beautiful woman. The woman gasped and rushed to Locke's side, stroking his badly bruised face. The man remained close to the door and took in the scene. He looked at Anjali, then at her parents and seemed to be thinking. Then he stretched out his hand and purposefully strode towards Anjali.

"Joseph Locke," he said, Anjali taking his hand and squeezing slightly. Anjali's father rose up and walked around the end of the bed. He too stretched out a hand.

"Vijay Sharma," he said, then motioned across the bed. "And this is my wife, Amita, and daughter Anjali. I am sorry to meet on such terms."

"Appreciate that, Mr Sharma. Allow me to introduce you to my wife, Daisy."

Daisy Locke turned away from her stricken son and nodded, before bursting into tears.

*

"We were to move away together," Anjali stated flatly. "But it was not in our faith or it wasn't God's will. Sometimes we plan things, but things don't always work out according to our plans. Life always intervenes."

Amita Sharma looked away when she heard the rebuke. Her husband bowed his head. Giving Anjali a hint that now was not the time to mention what had happened between them.

"I have to say, Anjali, John never told us you was—"

"Joe!" Daisy Locke said, sharply. Her husband looked a little pained. He had been trying to be diplomatic, but after a trip lasting more than sixteen hours over two flights, he realised even being careful might come across wrongly.

"Why would that matter?" Anjali said. "It's just a skin tone. You and I are humans first, not colours."

"I was just going to say that John told us he had a girlfriend and," he added, looking straight at Anjali, "it was clear he was very much in love with you, but that he never said you were Indian."

Anjali sighed and looked down the floor.

"You know, Mr Locke, your son could never understand why my parents would not allow me to be with him. My parents say they cannot allow it, that it will bring shame on my family, because our community affects our lives. Our life begins with marriage, not prior to marriage. The question we need to ask is does the character fit the description? I think if he were to hear you question my ethnicity, and he could do something about it, I think that might be the end of your relationship with him."

Joe Locke raised his hands in surrender. "I really meant no offence. I'm just... I just didn't know, is all. I'm sorry if I have offended you. Any of you," he added glancing at Anjali's parents.

"I do not think this is the time, Mr Locke, to be discussing such things," Vijay Sharma said. "While your son is still ill, I think we should not talk about race or religion." Joe Locke was about to say something but stopped himself.

"He was mugged," Anjali said, gazing at John's swollen features. "Two men – well, boys really – mugged him by the canal in the centre of Manchester. John, it seems, had been drinking heavily since I left him at the station and he had been in his favourite pub when he got thrown out. The police retraced his steps, which is how I know.

"Anyway, for some reason he decided to walk along the canal on his way home when he was attacked. Those boys stole his wallet but for some reason left his phone. They smashed his jaw, which is why his face is so swollen. The black eyes are from his broken nose. The doctors decided he had suffered a brain injury, which is why they put him in this coma. The police officer said it was likely his head had hit the cobbles and caused the injury. His skull is fractured, but it's all about how the brain hits the inside of the skull on impact, apparently.

"Anyway, it seems that despite all that, John somehow fought back and grabbed a scarf off one of the boys. He was still clutching it when he was pulled from the canal—"

"He was in the water?" Joe Locke asked.

"Yes. A passer-by heard the splash and saw just enough of John slowly going under the water that he had the time to rush down and pull him back out. That man saved John's life. Those boys tried to murder him, and they would have managed had it not been for that man."

The room became quiet save for the sound of the medical machinery. Then Anjali spoke again.

"His phone was in his pocket when he went into the water, but amazingly it still worked when the police dried it out. Because they had taken John's wallet, they didn't know who he was, but when they looked at the call log they saw I had tried calling him lots of times over the previous days, so they rang me. I nearly screamed when I thought John had finally called back but instead got a strange man's voice asking me to come to the hospital."

"That was the police officer?" Joe Locke asked. Anjali nodded.

"You said they are 'boys, really'," Daisy Locke said. "Does that mean the police have them?"

"Yes. They caught them almost immediately. Apparently, they ran straight into a policeman who knew them. One still had his scarf up, but the other didn't. They were searched on the spot as they were acting suspiciously and they had a load of money on them. Lots of twenty pound notes. It will have been John's money. They had already disposed of his wallet and the police are still searching for it, I think. It will be at the bottom of the canal somewhere.

"PC Harries came in with a detective yesterday. Those boys, they're sixteen. They've been charged with attempted murder. The clincher was the scarf in John's hand and the scratches he left on the boy's face when he grabbed it."

The door opened, surprising everyone. In strode a tall man in a long white coat. He looked about the room.

"I'm Mr Adefemi, I am Mr Locke's consultant." Joseph Locke immediately stood up and introduced himself and his wife.

"This might sound stupid," Joseph Locke said, "but we don't really know how he is."

"I will not lie," the consultant said. "John is in a very serious condition. We have stabilised him until the swelling goes down and we will find out the severity of his injuries, those to the brain specifically. We need to reduce the swelling in his brain, then see how he responds."

"Will that take long?" Daisy Locke whispered.

"I cannot say," the consultant admitted. "Injuries such as this are, as you can appreciate, potentially devastating."

"Do whatever you need to, Doctor. We've got medical insurance. And money."

Mr Adefemi smiled. "This is an NHS hospital, Mr Locke. The treatment is free to your son. We will do our best by him."

Joe Locke was bemused. Where he came from medical care was not free, nor was it cheap. Every American with any sense and enough money had medical insurance. He had assumed it would cover their son even if he was in England.

The consultant checked a few figures on the machines and looked closely at the notes on a clipboard before adding his own comments.

"There's no change," he said. "And it could be like that for a while. Talking to a patient in a coma can help, and sometimes they can hear you, but they can't answer you. It is good to see so many of you are here by his side, but it's best if you all get some rest and come back tomorrow. You cannot help here." Anjali was about to protest. "Especially you," Mr Adefemi said. "You are exhausted. You need rest."

"So who are you? And how do you relate to John Locke? You have no relationship," Anjali said steadily. "My identity is a woman and women are synonymous with sacrifice for everyone else."

"You are correct, Miss Sharma," the consultant said, raising his hands in surrender. "There's nobody more dignified than a woman. She associates herself with you in both sorrow and happiness. She becomes a lover and a guard. And our society calls her a maid. Your prayer cannot go unnoticed."

The room went quiet again and no-one quite knew where to look or what to say. The machines continued their monotonous actions and Locke's chest continued to rise and fall. His face looked terrible; blackened and swollen, flecks of blood still visible on his lips.

"You must stay with us," Vijay Sharma said, rising to his feet and motioning to the Lockes. "Amita and I would be honoured." Daisy Locke smiled and fresh tears rolled down her cheeks.

"Thank you," she said. "We didn't even bring a bag with us."

Amita Sharma also stood up and walked towards Daisy Locke with arms outstretched. The two women embraced and Anjali was proud. She just felt saddened that her John couldn't witness it. He was there. But then he wasn't.

*

It was the smell of spices that woke first Daisy and then Joe. It had become dark outside. Joe Locke sat up and rubbed his eyes, willing the jetlag away. His wife reached for and found the switch to the lamp on her side of the bed, the room suddenly bathed in a low, pinkish light.

When they arrived at the Sharmas' house, they were shown into a spare bedroom. Joe lay on the bed and, almost immediately, was asleep. Daisy sat on the end of the bed, staring but seeing nothing; only thinking about her son's survival. There was a quiet knock at the door and Amita Sharma walked in, carrying some beautifully coloured saris.

"It is all I have," she had said apologetically. "But I think they will fit you. Saris are very forgiving," she added, patting her stomach with a meek smile. "Or we can take you to the market if you prefer?"

"Thank you," Daisy said, and watched as her host placed the coloured clothes carefully over the back of a chair in the corner of the room. Amita Sharma left the room quietly. Daisy Locke yawned once and fell backwards into sleep.

When she woke up again, she saw the saris and went over to them.

"What's that, honey?" her husband asked.

"Indian clothes," Daisy said. "From Amita." Joe was confused. They just looked like sheets, but Daisy played with a swathe of blue material, trying to work out how it fitted. In a few moments, she felt she had figured it out and started to undress.

"You putting it on?" Joe said, surprised.

"Of course," his wife replied. "I've been in my own clothes for two days and our host gave me these to fit into. Amita will help me to get ready. I doubt Vijay has anything big enough for you, though. You'll have to stay like that 'til we get you some new clothes."

Joe and Daisy Locke felt a bit embarrassed as they entered the living room of the house. Joe was conscious that he needed a shower but had nothing clean to wear. Daisy had used the *en suite* bathroom and was now gloriously clad in a sea green sari that did, indeed, seem to fit her very well. When Amita saw her guest wearing the sari, she beamed and hurried across to her motioning for her to sit on the sofa. Vijay also smiled at Daisy.

"We will serve dinner in about half an hour," he said, then offered the Lockes some tea. Anjali quietly observed as her parents hosted. The situation the meeting of parents had taken place in was as horrific as she could imagine. But her parents were civilised people. She had caused it by leaving the love of her life sobbing on the floor of Piccadilly station. *No,* she thought. *My parents caused it.*

"Mother!" she called through to the kitchen. Amita Sharma reappeared, wiping her hands on a tea towel. "Please can you sit down?"

Vijay Sharma looked on, thinking he knew what was coming. The Lockes watched as Amita Sharma sat on the same sofa as Anjali, but at the opposite end nearest to Vijay.

Anjali had squashed into her corner of the sofa with her knees drawn up. She had wrapped herself up in a large blanket that covered all but her head.

"I need to say this because I think it is what John would want me to say. Mother, Father, you have stayed with me since we found out about John. You have been at his bedside almost the whole time I have. I have not been doing it for your benefit, but I think you must see my devotion for him."

Anjali raised her hand as she sensed her father was about to say something. Vijay Sharma remained silent. "I love our religion, culture and customs and I am faithful always in my prayers, but there are some things that I do not agree with and these are the things that John does not understand," she said.

"They have banned *sati* because it is outdated." Anjali looked across at Joe and Daisy Locke. "It's the act of the wife burning to death on her husband's funeral pyre." The Americans nodded as Anjali returned her gaze to her parents. "So I do not understand why we cling to other rituals. I do not understand why today, I cannot choose my husband and why I cannot marry outside of our system."

"Religion is given to us so we can follow the rules of Gods or God," Vijay Sharma said. "All may not suit us, but each has its values. There is a lesson to be learned. In no religion did God send scripture for just one religion or race. It was given to all mankind. And whoever understands it has the knowledge. We may not understand it now, but with time it becomes clear why science became advanced. And remember we are humans and we can make mistakes, but God is the creator. He can't do wrong for us. And why consider your parents your enemies even though we gave life to you and raised you for twenty years? We too have dreams and desires that one day we can give you away happily to your new home.

"As for your choice, you may be an adult, but it doesn't mean you understand the struggle of life or what's coming. There is a timeline between children and parents, which gives the parents an advantage in seeing how the world is changing. Whereas you Anjali can see the present life, not the future."

Anjali seemed to consider this. She turned to the Lockes. "Joe," she began, "I understand why you were shocked at my appearance when you first saw me. As I have said, John has never understood my parents' opinions on love and relationships, but I wonder if I know why he never told you that I was Indian. I wonder if he thought you might disapprove of your darling son marrying a different ethnicity."

"Anjali, I promise you," Joe Locke said, "I am no racist. My country has its problems and probably always will, but I don't see colour; I see a beautiful woman. I've known you five minutes and I am honoured my son has met such a strong, devoted girl. What I said in the hospital... I guess I was just tired."

"It's true, Anjali," Daisy Locke said. "I would not be married to this man if he had a racist bone in his body. The thing is, oftentimes he says the wrong thing for the right reasons."

Anjali thought for a moment and felt the comments were genuine. Amita Sharma wrung the tea towel in her hands tighter. She thought her daughter was being unfair but would leave it to her husband to speak.

"Anjali," Vijay Sharma began, slowly gathering his thoughts. "We have many things in our lives, but none is more important to us than our faith and our family. You are our only child and we have loved you and brought you up to be a good woman. I can see your faith is as strong as ours, but you have been brought up in a different world to us. When your grandparents grew up in India, *sati* was rare, but it still happened. When they came here they tried to cling on to their faith as a sense of identity. We, your mother and I, are forever grateful that the *jathakam* favoured us. The astrological chart brought our families together and we have never regretted it."

"But plenty do, Father," Anjali insisted. "You are the exception. Why can you not see that my love for John is real and there should be no boundary to that love? Love does not have faith, nor face, nor colour of skin. This is why love is elevated to the honour of God."

"Anjali—"

"I mean it, Father! Why have you done this to me? I'm not saying I'll be disrespectful or walk away, but don't I have the right to choose?"

"You will understand the day you become a mother, Anjali. Marriage is not a child's play."

Vijay Sharma tried to gather his thoughts. His wife was very close to tears. The silence in the room was uncomfortably long. Joe Locke looked from Vijay and Amita to Anjali and back again. Daisy Locke stared closely at Amita and wanted to go over and hug the woman.

"Anjali," Vijay Sharma began again. "Your mother and I have seen something truly beautiful in these terrible circumstances. We could never imagine such attachment as you have shown to John. We never realised until recently there was anyone in your life, because you hid him from us. We understand why you did that, and it has made us look at ourselves. Yes, we have our faith and our customs, but we also have our own minds and our own compassion. We have watched you pray for John and remain by his bedside in his time of need. We have done the same, for our daughter in her time of need.

"It has made us reconsider things. We are so very sorry for what we did and a thousand moons will not lessen our shame. You are our only child, our only daughter, and if it makes you sad that we have certain beliefs or boundaries towards you, then so be it. Becoming a parent doesn't happen overnight, it takes years of nurturing, of time and effort, but it takes only one second for that same child to rebel against their parents and walk away. Given what we have seen, we will throw away those beliefs."

Amita Sharma was openly crying. It was because she agreed with her husband. They had clung on to the old ways too long. Now they no longer cared what other families thought. If they were shunned, it wouldn't matter. Anjali jumped up, the blanket falling as she ran across the room and threw herself upon first her father, then her mother. Anjali and Amita sobbed. Daisy Locke joined them and the women laughed through the tears. Vijay Sharma stood up and headed towards Joe Locke.

"My wife and I wish to apologise to you," he said. "We behaved terribly towards your son, even though we had never met him. I am truly sorry for this situation, but you have my word and my honour in everything going forward. These last days I have prayed for John every minute. I want to get to know the man that has made my daughter so very happy. You and your family are welcome here for as long as you wish. I pray John will join us."

Joe Locke firmly shook Vijay Sharma's hand then pulled the smaller man into an embrace.

"I pray too."

eleven
or ended it

"And you're saying you believe this will cure him?"

"What I am saying, Mr Locke, is that this is a revolutionary treatment that, after extensive testing, appears to provide excellent prospects for individuals in a similar position to your son."

The emphasis was on the word 'appears'. The consultant, Mr Dixon, was a highly regarded British neurosurgeon. He had travelled up from London when he heard of the situation; having been waiting for some time for a patient displaying John's symptoms to present so that he could trial the treatment for which he had the highest hope for brain trauma victims.

"John's symptoms are extremely rare," the consultant continued, "in that we rarely have an individual in a coma who, we also discover, has a cancer such as John has. We have conducted the thyroidectomy and, as you know, he is now being drip-fed thyroxine while he remains in his current state. This new treatment, we believe, could satisfy two needs; it will fight any continued cancerous cells linked to your son's now removed thyroid gland, and it should impact on the damage to his brain we fear has happened and which is keeping him from regaining consciousness."

Joe Locke didn't know what to think. His wife Daisy held hands with Anjali. They were in a side room that had hastily become Mr Dixon's office on his arrival from London.

"You keep saying words like 'could' or 'should'..." Joe said.

"I know. And you are right to raise this issue. This treatment will be a world first. No-one has ever used a combination of Cobalt-60 with trace levels of Polonium-210 before. Cobalt-60 is a synthetic radioactive isotope with a half-life of exactly five years. Its use in cancer treatment is unusual, but not unheard of. What is unheard of is the inclusion of traces of Polonium-210, which is an intensely radioactive material, usually lethal to humans.

"Our research shows that the two interact in a very unusual manner, which alters the properties of each. The Cobalt-60 becomes more potent and therefore a better isotype for use in radiotherapy, whilst the Polonium-210 seems to lose its ability to cause radiation but appears to assist directly in the regeneration of stem cells. It means we can isolate and challenge the cancerous areas around John's thyroid, but also give his body every chance of regenerating the stem cells he requires to come out of his induced coma. I must advise, however, that saying yes to this treatment will make John something of a guinea-pig. It has been trialled extensively in mouse, rat and primate studies and has had a phenomenal effect. We think it can have the same benefits for humans as well."

Joe Locke sat back heavily into his chair. Daisy Locke exchanged glances with her husband. Anjali sat quietly to one side, trying to make sense of the science being explained to her. The Lockes had been staying with the Sharmas for a little over three weeks. It meant John was nearing a fourth week in a coma. His fractured skull and broken nose and jaw had all been operated on, and there had been work conducted to reduce the bleed on the brain diagnosed at the very beginning, which caused the original doctors to place John into an induced coma. But it was the surgeon tasked with inserting the plates that would fuse his jaw back together who first noticed the small lump evident in John's neck. It changed everything. It was the very specific set of circumstances that led to Mr Dixon's journey north to Manchester.

"How long before he comes round?" Anjali asked. Three pairs of eyes looked back at Mr Dixon, who sighed deeply and thought carefully.

"I cannot answer that. Animal models suggest very quickly, but results were not totally consistent, even though all specimens returned favourable outcomes. To extrapolate to the human level, it could be a few days, or a couple of weeks. But if he does not have this treatment no-one in the world can tell you when John will wake up or, and I am sorry to be so blunt, whether he will ever wake up. The longest waking coma survivor I have heard of is twenty-seven years. John's situation has so many what-ifs, there really are a lot of options open to you, but the reality is this revolutionary treatment, I believe, is the only one that will see John back with us in a short space of time."

Mr Dixon leaned forward and steepled his fingers, almost as if in prayer. "But I have to stress once again that while the studies are very positive, there are no guarantees. Absolutely none."

The consultant left the Lockes and Anjali alone in the room to discuss the issue. When he returned, all three had voted for the treatment. Daisy had made the one observation that clinched the issue; even if John was to wake up naturally, there was no guarantee he would be a fully functioning human again. The revolutionary treatment appeared to be the only option that improved the chances of a full recovery.

"I'll get the ball rolling," Mr Dixon said, nodding thoughtfully. Joe Locke wondered if he had just saved his son's life. Or ended it.

*

Five days later the unbelievable happened; John stirred and blinked. Then he opened his mouth. Joe Locke had been eating a steak and onion pie he had bought from the hospital shop when it happened. He leapt from his chair, startling Anjali, the only other person in the room, and stood over his son. John's head moved slightly from side to side.

Anjali also stood up. She had been resting her head on John's bed and had fallen asleep. She was instantly awake.

"John? John? Can you hear me?" Joe Locke said.

"I'm here, John," Anjali said. "Talk to us."

John's head continued to loll about on his pillow. He seemed to be trying to focus while he blinked and his mouth opened and closed. When he leant in, Joe thought he could hear sounds coming from his son, thought he heard him trying to talk. Anjali did the same and together they placed their ears as close to John as they dared.

"Three," John stammered.

"Three?" Anjali looked at Joe. "Is that what he said?"

"I think so," Joe replied. They both looked again at John. The head movements were more exaggerated. Anjali tried to settle him down.

"Three, point, one, four, one," Locke rasped, more clearly this time, but breathing deeply after every word. "Five, nine, two, six, five…"

Anjali's mouth hung open wondering why he was calling out numbers. Joe Locke did much the same, but he realised what he had just heard. He was an engineer, a very successful one, but his son was no mathematician.

"John," Anjali begged, "what are you saying?" She was scared. She didn't know what was happening. John slowly raised his left hand and pointed at what his father still held.

"Pi," he said. And fell asleep.

part ii
anjali

twelve

she would also die

Anjali rushed forward and pulled on the vivid red cord by the side of John's bed. A nurse arrived in seconds.

"He woke up!" Anjali said. "He just woke up and he said something. You need to get the consultants in." The nurse checked the equipment hooked up to John and quickly checked his pulse the old-fashioned way, just to make sure. She hurried back out of the room.

"He said 'Pi'," Joe Locke said. Anjali again looked confused. "The math formula. It's the ratio between the diameter and circumference of a circle. It's an irrational number in that it has an infinite number of decimal points. I think they've worked it out to a million or something. I know about it as I'm an engineer, but he sucks at math. I mean, really lousy. He'd never know what he just said."

The door to the room opened again and Mr Adefemi strode in. He cut a strong figure as he walked around the far side of John's bed, passed Joe Locke and looked at the readings on a computer on the bedside table. He looked back down at his notes, then turned to Joe and Anjali.

"Mr Dixon is on his way, but it's clear the new treatment has impacted on John. His readouts are normalising and as you have just seen, he has, albeit briefly, regained consciousness."

Tears rolled down Anjali's face and she started to sob. She had barely left John's side for four weeks and was exhausted. Just like the idol she worshipped at her home. She had increasingly thought she had in effect killed him by leaving at Piccadilly station in the way that she had, but Life was giving them a second chance and she knew there was now a new challenge.

She didn't approve but she understood why he got drunk to try to forget how she had hurt him. Now, finally, he was waking up from his nightmare and she was waking up from hers. She clasped John's hand tightly and sobbed some more when she felt his hand respond.

"The day I forgot about you or my love with my heart, this day will be the end of my life," she whispered. "Not a tear will be retained in my eyes. I'll never be somebody else's."

Joe Locke and Mr Adefemi looked at her.

"He's just squeezed my hand," she said, as more tears of joy flowed down her cheeks. Her hell was over.

Mr Dixon arrived half an hour later. Joe Locke had called his wife and Anjali had called her parents. Vijay Sharma was *en route* with his wife Amita and Daisy Locke in his car. They would be arriving shortly.

Joe Locke listened intently to the two consultants. Mr Dixon was clearly the more senior of the two in expertise and it was, after all, his research that had led to the treatment John had received. He was pointing to the large computer screen on John's bedside table.

"The ratio is key," Mr Dixon said. "I upped the grays in the Cobalt-60, but lowered them in the Polonium-210. Mouse models indicated that that maximised the potential for the treatment. The computer linked up to the photon emitter and provided the course over the proscribed period." He looked at the clipboard he was holding. "I have to say this has happened faster than I anticipated, but a brief moment of lucidity is exactly what I expected from the patient."

Anjali gazed at John's face, at the man she thought beautiful, and the man she loved with all her heart. At this point she felt she might die for the love she felt.

"*Ardhangini*," she whispered quietly, and knew her love was forever. "Don't take me out of your heart. I am your fragrance, don't let me fade away. I will always stand beside you."

Locke's eyes flickered. Then he opened them slightly. To his left two men, one white, one black, in white coats. Then another man, well-built and strong looking, with a full head of silver hair and a black beard. To his right an Asian woman; beautiful, smiling almost pleading in her eyes. Locke looked at her intensely, trying to place her.

"Ninety grays Cobalt-60 to ten grays Polonium-210. It's within the range, but not by much," Mr Dixon continued, unaware that Locke's eyes had opened.

"Too much," Locke said, barely audibly. But Mr Dixon heard something and looked down at his patient.

"John, my name is Mr Dixon. I am your consultant. How are you feeling?"

"Too much," Locke said again.

"Too much what?" Mr Dixon asked confused. Patients waking from a coma usually started with a "where am I?" or a "who are you?"

"You have given me the wrong dosage. It's too high." He closed his eyes.

Mr Dixon straightened; his face creased as if he was trying to work out the impossible. He looked at Mr Adefemi then turned to Anjali and Joe Locke; "Obviously with patients coming out of coma they are usually in a very confused state. You would be very confused if you had been asleep for four weeks and then woke up in a strange place—"

"He didn't sound confused," Anjali interrupted. "I heard what he said. How would he know that you have given the wrong dosage?"

Mr Dixon opened his mouth as if to say something, then closed it again.

Mr Adefemi stepped forward. "It's not too high," he said soothingly. "John can have no idea of his treatment. He has been in a medically induced coma for a month. He doesn't know where he is and he can't know what he has undergone."

"My son recited Pi to about a dozen decimal points before, doctor, and he can't do math. I don't know what you've done to him, but something's happened here and you need to be straight up." Joe Locke stared back at the two consultants who were, by now, exchanging confused and worried glances. Mr Dixon shook his head.

"No, impossible," he said. "John can have no idea of what treatment he has undergone. There are less than fifty people world-wide who have any knowledge of this branch of radiotherapy."

"Therac-25," Locke said. "1985 to 1987."

Mr Dixon paled significantly. His hand grasped the rail on John's hospital bed and Joe Locke moved to catch him should he fall. Mr Adefemi brought a chair for his colleague to sit on. Locke's eyes were wide open now; darting about the room and latching on to the four faces looking back at him. He kept returning to the Asian woman and her intense beauty. He tried to lift his hand to her face to wipe away the tracks of tears, but his hand felt heavy and he could barely lift it at all. The Asian woman smiled and held his hand a little tighter.

"What he just say, Doc?" Joe Locke asked. Mr Dixon simply stared ahead at Locke, at the scars still evident on the side of his now hairless head and at the tubes his patient was connected to.

"Did he say, 'Therac-25'?" Mr Adefemi asked.

Locke turned his head away from the Asian woman holding his hand. "Yes. It killed people."

Mr Dixon started to shake. Mr Adefemi had heard of the incident where a number of people in America had been given massively too high doses of radiation through computer error. He looked down upon his colleague and saw the agitation.

"Mr Dixon," he said, warily, "regardless of how he could, does John have a point?"

It seemed to have the right effect on Mr Dixon who regained his professional composure. He looked at his clipboard, then intently at the computer screen to the right. He made a few utterances, working out things mentally as well as double checking every part of the historical log of treatment. The other four people in the room looked on, waiting for a punchline.

"Can you show me the computer screen?" Locke asked. Mr Dixon raised a hand as if he was working out an extremely difficult mathematical formula and didn't want to be interrupted.

"If he wants to see, he can see it," Joe Locke said and walked around the two consultants.

"Be careful with that," Mr Dixon said. Joe Locke looked back at him and Anjali saw the disgust in the giant American's eyes. He looked at the apparatus and, satisfied that moving it would not pull anything out, he lifted the monitor and held it an angle so that his son could look directly at the figures. Locke glanced over the screen for a few moments.

"Wrong dose," he said. "You've given a dose far too high for this treatment." By now Mr Dixon knew his patient was right. Combining Cobalt-60 with Polonium-210 made the former typically stronger and the latter weaker. The consultant looked once more at his notes and made the calculation again.

"You're out by a factor of a hundred."

Mr Dixon had to agree.

*

Locke had fallen asleep and his father had returned the screen to its original place. The consultants left the room. It was clear there was an urgent conversation to be had. Joe Locke glowered after them, but smiled at a nurse who came in shortly afterwards to do some more routine checks on his now sleeping son. She had gone by the time the Sharmas arrived with Daisy Locke and Joe proceeded to tell them what had happened.

No one knew what to say. Daisy watched her husband closely. Incompetence was one thing he could not stand and it had regularly been the thing that had caused a rift with his artistic and not-at-all scientific son. For a change it was not her son's inability with numbers that was upsetting her husband; it was one of the world's foremost cancer and radiotherapy experts that was in his sights. Joe Locke had already used the word 'lawsuit' on several occasions.

Vijay and Amita Sharma crowded around their daughter, as if to try to protect her from whatever evil was in the room. It had been a lot to take in in the few minutes since their arrival and neither liked to hear Joe mention suing the NHS. Vijay Sharma decided he would talk to the large American when the time was right. The thing was it sounded like the patient knew more about the revolutionary treatment he had undergone than the revered consultant who had administered it. That made no sense.

Anjali was oblivious to it all. Yes, the conversation between her John and Mr Dixon had rattled her, but it was way beyond her comprehension. As an accountant she had a head for numbers, but not for science. She knew what Pi was, but never needed to use it.

As to the talk of radioactive elements, that was completely over her head and, she suspected, beyond Joe's knowledge as well. How her partner knew didn't matter. He was here. *Here* she thought, her heart almost bursting with relief. *My life is a safe keeping for you.*

She had cried again when her parents arrived, and they had cried with her. Her mother had embraced Daisy Locke for an age; mothers understood mothers much more than fathers understood other fathers, she thought, so she was surprised when her father had held Joe Locke in a similar fashion. She had turned away when the recriminations began; her only thought was her love was alive, not through machines, but breathing on his own. *The desire you have on your journey, that's where I'm going. You will find me.*

She looked at his chest; it was covered by a thin sheet, as if for modesty, but really it was because the room was quite warm and the nurse didn't want her John to overheat. The sheet rose and fell with his breaths, and Anjali noticed quickly that the breathing was different. When the ventilator did the breathing for him, his chest rose and fell steadily, in a constant rhythm. More than once the effect of listening to it had been so soporific, she had been asleep in seconds.

But now that John was breathing on his own, it was less rhythmic, as if the body regulated how much air was required for each breath and took accordingly. She noticed when he was breathing heavily, she felt a little alarmed, and when his breathing was lighter, he seemed more comfortable.

As ever she held his hand in hers and stroked his arm with her other. *Ardhangini* she thought over and over, realising that should John die, she would also die. Images of flames and funeral pyres had swirled inside her head a thousand times, but she had blinked them away. She knew she could not live her life without the person that made her whole and she had resolved to end hers should his be ended. *Until I live on, I shall live for you. Even after death I'll become the light upon your path*. She only thought after he had come round, that there hadn't been a consideration that he had, in effect, saved her life.

John's eyes opened and he let out a tiny groan. It was barely audible but Anjali heard it and so did Daisy Locke.

"John," Daisy said, "Oh my God, John! You're okay!" tears ran freely down the woman's face. By now aware of the situation Joe Locke put his arms around his wife as she leant over the bed to kiss her son on the forehead. "I've got my son back!" she sobbed and Joe Locke pulled her gently away so his wife didn't crush him in her elation.

Anjali beamed at her man, the man who made her whole, and felt the now common tears once again roll down her cheeks. *I'm that dream nobody saw,* she thought. *I am this story that, without you, is incomplete.* She had cried a lot over the last few weeks. Finally she could cry with joy. It was almost as if she had been holding her breath all that time and now the relief washed over her like the water from a Himalayan mountain stream.

John looked at faces staring back at him. The woman to his left was new, and she was crying. The man from before seemed to be holding her back. Or up; he couldn't tell which. The middle-aged Asian couple to his right were also new; they stood side by side and stared hard at him. The woman held her hand to her mouth and he could see she was crying as well. Closer to him, in fact holding his hand and stroking his arm, was the beautiful young Asian woman from earlier. She hadn't moved at all in the time he had been asleep, although he had no idea how long that had been.

There was an *impasse;* five looked down at the one in a hospital bed. John looked back and stared at each in turn. He raised his left hand and pointed in the direction of the white couple.

"I'm guessing you're Mom and Dad." He then turned his head slowly to the right, to look at the Asian couple and the beautiful woman stroking his right arm. "I'm sorry," he said, "but who are you?"

thirteen
she stayed in silent devotion

She dipped the cloth into the bowl of cold water and mopped his brow. She had been told to keep his room at a warm temperature, but not to overheat him. The soothing cloth left his forehead damp and she gently blew on the moisture.

Now I know what it takes to become a woman, she thought. *I was going to be a greedy wife, daughter and lover. Being a lover or a daughter is simple, but attempt to be a wife and you will see why a man considers a woman to be pious in his life.*

It was what he used to do to her when they made love; he would moisten her skin with a kiss and then blow. The effect was stunning. Her skin would tingle, perhaps even tickle a little and she would have to try so hard not to ruin the moment. He was so attentive for her, like an entity, but never more so than when he kissed her back and breathed gently.

The injury had left Locke bed bound, unable to move, change or go to the bathroom. To do the simplest job was difficult; even cleaning his teeth or drinking water. He moved slightly and Anjali held her breath. John had been back in his flat for three days. He had spent another week at the hospital while the consultants carried out tests and nurses nursed. Joe Locke had had the lawsuit conversation with Mr Dixon and had been surprised how quickly the NHS had started to try to smooth the situation. Vijay Sharma spoke quietly to Joe, who soon realised how Britain's health service was funded and seemed less inclined to carry out his threat. He held a caveat, though, and that was should anything happen to his son in the future, that he absolutely reserved the right to proceed down the legal route.

John looked at Anjali. At his guardian angel who never left his side. She changed his bedsheets and gave him a sponge bath each week, so he wouldn't develop bedsores. She gave him Indian herbs and spices, to help to strengthen his bones alongside his prescribed medicines.

He was getting stronger but he still slept most of the day, and simple tasks like talking and eating took a lot of his energy. Bedridden and unable to do the simplest tasks, his life seemed unbearable. When Anjali wasn't there, the room lingered in silence and he often called out, hoping that someone was there. He felt like a corpse, but did not realise it was the same feeling for a man without a woman, but with *ardhangini*. In every step he required help, and women become nurses without charge. He knew it was mentioned in the scriptures, that whoever has hurt or wronged a woman his life has been cursed forever. He had yet to walk, so Anjali massaged his legs just as the nurses had showed her, but she knew Indian massage, which helped the bloodstream run faster throughout his entire body. She first applied turmeric paste to his leg then all over the body and massaged it delicately. Then she wiped and washed his body. After that, she used lukewarm mustard seed oil and gave Locke another Indian massage. He still wasn't capable of movement, but the massage made him feel active and fresh. She did all the things she needed to get John back to where he was. The physical side wasn't a worry. But his memory was gone.

As she always did when he woke up, she made the shape of a gun with her right hand.

"Truth gun," she said.

"I'm sorry," he replied. "But thank you." He stared at her, confused.

Anjali lowered her hand and looked at her lover, *her husband,* for she felt *ardhangini* and although they were not married in this life, she knew they had been married down the ages and she knew they would marry again. Her parents saw it too, and preparations had already been made for when Locke would be able to walk unaided and marry his Indian princess.

Vijay Sharma made exceptional rules for his daughter to take care of Locke, but it was a difficult for him to do knowing that Locke was a stranger, had no blood ties and that his daughter was not married to him yet. The Sharmas' community had been supportive, but for the odd conventionalist who disapproved of marriage outside the religion. Those people gave him the looks that could kill. But aside from them, he had been a little stunned by the reaction. He was sure he would never have sanctioned such a development if it had happened to one of their friends' children, so he was amazed and delighted that others seemed to have little difficulty supporting him when it was his daughter taking the unusual path.

"Would like some food? A drink?"

"Just water, please. My mouth is a little dry."

Locke was propped up on cushions on his side of the bed to give him enough air to breathe. He sometimes woke up having a nightmare, brought on by the anxiety that he could no longer walk, or that he might be in a wheelchair for life, constantly asking for help. He sometimes woke up feverish and shouting, and Anjali soothed him by putting a moist tissue on his forehead, wiping his body to help cool him down. When the morning came, he had no idea he had been shouting in the dark. He often had trouble sleeping or would kick off his blankets without even realising it.

Anjali slept on the other side at night and spent the rest of her day sitting by Locke's side of the bed, attending to him. She thought often at how society viewed a woman's hand as a healing hand, and why most nurses in society were women. Men with women in their lives were lucky, but couples don't always recognise each other's potential or benefits. She had long since agreed indefinite leave with her work and Joe Locke had provided the money needed to live while John was so sick.

She always wore her sari, to make her work seem effortless. She knew a well-dressed woman who doesn't look tired has a positive effect on a man's heart, whereas an exhausted woman brings bad energy and bad mood. Not all women are suited to marriage or become 'wife material'. Few have that opportunity, but those with nursing hands can be a devoted wife. And so can those tested. In some cultures, the challenge is to gather pots and pans; the stronger they are assembled, the stronger the woman in that marital home.

Anjali smiled and got up to get some fresh water from the tap. His eyes were closed once more by the time she had returned; his anxiety and frustration of lying in bed felt more difficult than running a marathon. She left the glass on his bedside table and walked into the next room where she had a little shrine in front of which she would kneel down and pray.

Sometimes Locke would wake and try to reach for the water himself, but as often as not he would knock the glass over, the water spilling all over the floor.

All that she asked for was for John to recover. She thanked her Hindu Gods for his progress and begged for more. She never knew how long she stayed in silent devotion, and it was virtually the only time she was away from Locke. She knew a dedicated woman doesn't need a career, but that she has the consciousness, skills and knowledge to keep a home *alive*. It is an organism that lives just as the body does; if it's not cleaned or maintained, it can decay. Life is a balance between men and women and men earn the household wage for a better life.

But when the men are ill the women become the doctors, nurses and spiritual guides. Anjali prayed and begged, and in return she asked that her life be taken in Locke's place. She knelt in her buttercup yellow sari, the same one she wore when Locke had first found her in that little Hindu temple on that forgettable street in Delhi. Colours are the window for our souls, which is why she wore her brightest. She firmly believed it improved temper, luck, joy and love.

She was told to discuss things to spark his memory, play his favourite songs, or show him pictures of them together. She had played the video that had been shot of them dancing; David having edited it so that he never appeared and anyone watching would only think of the two people so in love as they glided around that dance studio.

But she rarely wore anything other than a yellow sari. She had asked her mother to buy her two more so that she would always have a fresh one to wear. She was desperate for John to remember his India and she had another canvas of her praying made, replacing the one destroyed in Piccadilly station. She hung it on the wall next to John's side of the bed so that he could see it all the time and hopefully remember it. He didn't, but he was lucid enough to recognise it was a picture of Anjali and agreed that she looked stunning in it. He was very impressed to learn he had taken it, but no. Nothing. No memory whatsoever came back to him.

Anjali prostrated herself on the floor in front of her shrine, her eyes closed, her arms lying flat, palms down. She stayed there for as long as she dared then rose up and raised her hands skyward, contorting and twisting her arms and fingers in her dance of devotion to the gods.

What is a woman without a man? What is a man with no wife? Nobody is as conscious as a woman. She stands by you when you're sad. She's in your life when you're happy. She became a dedicated wife, a mistress and a mother. Sacrifice and devotion are bywords for a woman. She attends to him day and night. She fasts and prays. She connects life with love. She shines like a moon and looks after him, bringing the darkness out of his life. She's the angel of mercy to him.

But she couldn't feel at one with herself because her husband was there in body only. She needed his mind to return and, until it did, until their past came back to him, she could not rest. She screwed her eyes tighter and once again embraced the floor in prayer, her buttercup yellow sari swishing quietly as she moved. Locke, as her future husband, was a result of prayer. But he who deceives his wife is not happy forever. Whoever said that was right. She heard the call and rose.

Locke was awake again. She sat down on the bed and gently raised the glass of water to his lips. His lips were dry and, to Anjali, he was drinking holy water helping and healing his life. He drank deeply, filling her with love once again. She didn't know where the love came from, but it felt stronger inside her every day. She knew it was without limit. He gasped, having drunk more than half of the water. Then she gave him juice and fed him vegetable curry like a mother.

Everything she did would be beneficial to his body, improving blood flow and joint pressure. She gave him walnuts, almonds, peanuts and cashews to help his brain. And she ended up with milk and turmeric, not that he liked all of this new food, but it helped him with his appetite.

"Thank you, Anjali."

"No," Anjali replied. "Thank you. You don't have to be sad or angry about what Life gives you. It's a life lesson for us. If you are in that place or in that state, there is a reason for that. It could be that you understand me or you need to think about your life, but today I desire to live again, today I intend to die again. No one can stop my soaring heart." Smiling, she moved her hands and wrists, twisting and making her jewellery jangle. "Today I desire to live again, today I intend to die again."

She was trying to lift his spirits as she always did. She could sense Locke was beginning to feel depressed again, restless, agitated, incapable of moving and stuck in one position. He had said he wanted to die, that he didn't want to live this life that he found so unbearable. Tears would often fall down his cheeks in spite of all her efforts.

"Life isn't going fast enough," he said.

*

The following morning Anjali awoke early. The sun was blazing, the heat intense and the birds were singing. It was a bright sky. She opened the curtains and the window to her room. The breeze flowed through the room. She took a deep breath. Locke screwed up his eyes and tried to turn away from daylight. She showered and dressed in another of her saris.

"It's a beautiful morning; we're going for a walk."

"How?" he said, incredulous. "I can't walk."

"I have a surprise for you," she smiled, then went into the bathroom, put toothpaste on his toothbrush, and brought him a bowl and a glass of water.

Later, she cooked breakfast for him, then changed his clothes and bedsheets and folded them neatly. She left the room once more and Locke stared at the door wondering what was about to happen.

"Surprise!" she said, returning triumphant and pushing a wheelchair. "You'll see the world with me today."

Locke looked on bemused, then felt the frustration return as Anjali struggled to get him in the wheelchair. He was a big man; over six feet tall, and even though he had lost a lot of weight since the attack, he was still much heavier than Anjali. But she persevered and got him comfortable. She pushed the wheelchair towards the window and Locke saw the sun for the first time in weeks.

"You need some vitamin D," she whispered in his ear before turning him around and taking out of their flat. Outside, the sun struck him like a razor, the wind alien on his skin.

"Where are we headed?"

"Anywhere you want. Around Castlefield? A stroll through the streets of Manchester? I could take you to Peel Park in Salford, by the River Irwell? It's not too far."

The wind was light, the rays were hot and sensuous. The wind blew and her sari flowed with the air as she wheeled Locke around the streets of Manchester. They stopped outside a Spanish restaurant on Deansgate where she squatted down in front of him, bringing herself to his level.

"I am not in control of my life; the heart is elsewhere and I'm elsewhere." She stared at Locke with a joyous smile. "I don't know anything about my life. My life is laughing at me and I'm smiling. Take a look, John. I'm neither wealthy nor a millionaire. I have no money, yet I feel as if I have everything. I have more to go on. Am I intoxicated or am I in a storm? Someone tell me where I am."

After hours and days with Locke, Anjali had found a new perspective on the world. There were old people, the middle-aged and the young. People had new lives, whereas some were disabled, others begging. But they all had something to say; everybody had problems or obstacles to overcome.

"The Earth thinks the moon is happy," she smiled. "The moon believes it's the stars. The waves of the ocean feel that the shore is happier than mine. Behind the happiness is the sorrow. Every view of the mountain is beautiful from a distance. When you come closer, you will see that it is made of rock and dust. The flower says the garden bed is happier than me. The bed in the garden tells me it's the wind. Behind the happiness is the sorrow. Night thinks daylight is enlightening. The warmth of the day tells me it's cold and black. Autumn believes that spring is blessed. The spring believes it's fire. Behind happiness lies unhappiness."

Locke's expression was blank, but Anjali was almost glowing she was so happy. He looked at her closely and she laughed.

"We just don't know what they're all worried about," she said. "Notice the trees, the birds, the people; observe them, see what this means. Look at those clouds, they all tell you a life story. I feel like I'm lost at sea. *I'm afraid I'll be lost on my voyage. This journey is new to me,* John. I can't take your place or your situation, all I can do is understand you. Come out of your darkness, John, embrace your new-found life. It's telling you something.

"*As I emerge from yesterday's darkness, I rub my eyes with new releases of life. Life is like spring with flowers everywhere, which is why I made the decision. I desire to live once again,* John. Life is beautiful, but when all you see is darkness, all you'll find is darkness. But when you see the light, you will find life."

She felt that John might hear his voice. And find hope for himself again. Locke smiled and stared into her dark brown eyes, willing himself to remember. There was a flash of a scene; darkness, but something yellow. Then it was gone. She saw the change in his face. He saw the yellow of her sari. He didn't know if he had remembered. It had been too fleeting.

*

John got slowly stronger and Anjali never left his side. Visitors came and went; Joe and Daisy Locke had had to go back to America, although Daisy stayed an extra week. Anjali never saw it, but Daisy had even gone to her parents' local Hindu temple in Oldham. She had only ever been mildly religious in America and figured that as she did believe in something of a higher power, it, therefore, didn't matter if it was a Hindu god or a Christian one. She had also taken to wearing saris almost the whole time, bemusing her husband who welcomed the generosity showed by the Sharmas, but remained very much the all-American man he was. Indian food became his new favourite cuisine though, as he told Amita Sharma every mealtime.

Hannah and David came a few times, despite the way Locke had spoken to them in his darkest hours. They told him about the night he was drunk and got attacked. David didn't want to, but Anjali insisted that they tell Locke everything just in case anything sparked a memory. Locke looked back at Hannah and David and apologised for something he couldn't remember. The frustration built from within.

His former work colleagues, Tony, Pete and Tom came. Another time Tony brought Tanya, even though they were no longer a couple and both seeing someone else. John could not understand how he could have ever been friends with the foul-mouthed man, and inwardly winced when Tony told the story of John being sick outside the curry house in Manchester. Anjali listened on; it was history she wasn't aware of and she didn't think it sounded like her John at all, but he had had a life outside of hers and the more people that came to see him the more chance he might remember something. That was all that mattered to her.

Tanya mentioned a Marie, but Tony shut her up quickly. Locke and Anjali both looked at the now awkward Tanya, and Anjali asked her to continue, even though she was pretty sure she would not like to hear whatever story was coming her way. Tony was very quick to add that John had not slept with Marie ("At least, not in the Biblical sense," he laughed out loud) and that it had made him question whether John was gay. As they left, Anjali asked Tanya to come back, bringing Marie with her. She knew she had to do everything for John, even if it meant welcoming potential ex-girlfriends.

Marie came alone the following day, which Anjali thought brave. Marie was certainly beautiful and easy to get on with. Locke listened to her talk about someone else's life.

"Why can't I remember?" he shouted, startling both women. He apologised. When Marie mentioned his refusal to physically sleep with her, Anjali felt a wave of love wash over her. He might not have known it then, or indeed now, but what she heard meant John was *ardhangini* to her before they had even met. She quietly thanked her Gods as she led Marie the door. The women embraced, surprising both.

When she returned to the bedroom, Anjali found Locke crying. She had no idea how he must feel, but she could see it was breaking him. It broke her heart too. She leant forward and cupped his face in her hands, wiping a tear streak away. He looked at her and she could see the frustration in his eyes. She caressed his cheek and felt the tears prick at her own eyes.

"We will get through this, John. I promise you."

Locke gave a weak smile.

"I hope so," he said. "It's killing me. I know who you are and what's happened in my life recently, but I can remember nothing. I am being told I am with the woman I adore, and yet I feel no love for you. I try, but nothing comes. How could I love you that much and now feel nothing?"

He was pleading with her and she couldn't do anything to help him beyond words.

"You will remember," she said. "I know you don't believe it but still I pray to my Gods. I know you will come out of this and I will know when because I will load the truth gun and you will fire the bullet to the brain. Life challenges us in many different ways. This is our challenge. You will remember the temple in Delhi, or the dance, or the wedding where we met. You will get those memories back, even the bad ones like the night you got mugged and hit your head, or the time I left you in Piccadilly. You will get better because you must. You and I are *ardhangini*. This illness will not kill you or me. We are together for life and have been for the many other lives we have had and will have. That is my religion and I believe it."

Locke had heard it all before. He simply couldn't believe it. He thought that if this was all about meeting someone again then at least he would feel something. But he couldn't feel anything towards his parents, even though he had accepted them. It upset him on a simple level that his mother was in tears so often as story after story of his life in America was retold and yet nothing came to him. Worst of all, the woman said she was his mother, but he felt no connection. Surely he would? He just had to accept that they probably were his parents and he would learn to love them again one day.

Just like he hoped to love the woman caring for him now. She was stunning and her kindness knew no bounds.

"Limitless or endless in space, extent, or size; impossible to measure or calculate," he said.

"What is?" Anjali asked.

"Infinity. I think your love is infinite to be caring for me like this."

Anjali smiled. Getting used to the newly-scientific genius that John Locke seemed to have become was perhaps the oddest thing in her new one-sided relationship. He would come out with phrases or numbers. She had given him pen and paper and later found it covered in mathematical formulae that she had no notion of. Later she managed to look some of them up online; Locke had been perfect in his recitation.

"I'll get you another drink," she said and stood up from the bed. Locke heard the swish of the yellow sari she was wearing and caught a glimpse of a woman in yellow. He screwed his eyes tight, but the image had gone. Was he seeing Anjali in the temple? Was he receiving the one thing he begged to get? Was it a memory?

fourteen
the last moments before death

He was getting stronger day by day, but could still only manage a few steps. His injuries were making him angry. He had been provided with a walking frame specifically designed for him to get him back on his feet as quickly as possible.

But it was a long and slow process. His head injury had affected his balance and he virtually had to start from scratch in learning how to walk again. He now had physiotherapy at the hospital three times a week; it had been one trip a week initially as the session left him exhausted for days. But his strength was returning and he could just about get himself to the bathroom and back unaided. It was the biggest victory yet; Anjali would do anything for him, but they were both keenly aware of how embarrassed he was when she had to assist with his bathroom functions. It was a step too far for Locke, but he had to accept it because his situation was so severe.

His injuries had been cruel, but he recited at length how common it was for someone to hit their head and lose any number of physical and mental functions. Victims often lost memory and the ability to walk as he had, but they could also forget how to speak, change character completely or end up in a permanent vegetative state and need round the clock attention. Some of the unluckiest might never wake from their coma, but those who had suffered worst would have locked-in syndrome; their only way of communicating was through eye movements or blinking. It was knowledge he had not had before.

"Imagine that," Locke said. "You are conscious, you are completely paralysed and you can only move your eyes. That is your only ability to communicate. It would be a living death."

Anjali didn't know where the knowledge came from. He might be on his laptop a lot, but he never seemed interested in anything scientific before his injury, except maybe when tinkering with the settings on his camera. But now he was voracious in his reading. Sometimes he said something clever to her that she had no idea about. He seemed to have reached a level of genius she could only explain as being the conscience of God. He was becoming a rare genius changing internally, but not externally.

She tried to stop him on occasion because it made him tired, but he always resisted. He often talked excessively. She did not like the idea of locked-in syndrome and shuddered at the thought of what those poor people had to endure.

"You said you've lost memory and the ability to walk," she said. "Do you think your personality might have changed as well?"

"I sense something, but I don't know what. But I do feel exhilarated." Locke threw his head back and laughed. Anjali was a little frightened by the maniacal shriek coming from her lover. "I wouldn't know, would I? I've got no fucking memory!" He laughed some more. A belly laugh, and false. He knew it was upsetting Anjali, but the frustration was never far away.

He knew all this stuff, equations, formulae, conditions, treatments. When he was moving around on his walking frame, he would talk incessantly about thrust, drag, friction, weight/ mass ratio and anything else that would explain the physical forces at play as he tried to make his way from one spot to another. He was speaking like he was on a par with Einstein and all Anjali could do was listen and make mental notes for when she next saw the consultants. She had a lot of questions for them.

She left the room to the sounds of his continued hysterical laughter and only came back in with a cup of tea once he had stopped. She thought about installing a camera to record his behaviour because she wasn't sure she'd be able to explain it all.

"Your accent has changed. You've gone back to being full-on American. You used to try to hide it and pretended to be British. That's gone." Locke had calmed down. It wasn't right that he upset Anjali the way he sometimes did. He noticed it was becoming more common and he put it down to his increasing irritation at being trapped in a body that couldn't do some of the most basic tasks with a mind that wouldn't allow him to live his life.

"I'm sorry," he said. She smiled and flicked at a stray hair.

"Why is it that Asian women have long hair?" he asked. Anjali sat down on the sofa and looked closely at Locke.

"We believe our hair contains knowledge of our wisdom and should therefore not be shortened," she said. "To cut it is to lose wisdom of a lifetime. That's why you see a lot of women in many cultures covering their hair. We also know the beauty lies in your hair; the longer it is the more men find it appealing."

John saw the action, heard the bangles tinkle and just for a moment thought he had a memory.

"Do that again," he said.

"Do what?"

"Touch your hair." She looked at him quizzically. "Something about your hair, your sari, the bangles. I thought I remembered something."

Anjali understood. It was a fact known to her that men's hearts beat faster when they see a woman in jewellery and hear the tiny tympanic rings. It was why so many Asian wore so many bangles. It helped in keeping their men focused; it helped stop them from looking at other women. She brushed her hair back again; she did it repeatedly.

There was something beautiful about the way she did it and he watched her intensely, concentrating his mind on the motion of the hand and the sound of the bangles as she exposed her face and eyes. Caring for her hair was an important element in her daily life. If her hair looked fresh, she would feel comfortable throughout the day. Ultimately, she figured, the first thing you see when you look in the mirror is your own face and hair.

Locke threw himself backwards into his pillow and cried out. Anjali placed her hand on his chest.

"*Kangana,*" she whispered, "listen intently, it is to call you and your name. The *bindi* about you, I see you day and night. I call out to you. You are getting there. Asian women have knowledge and wisdom when it comes to dressing. They don't dress for the occasion alone. They dress for themselves. So when it comes to speaking, she doesn't have to say a lot. Her femininity speaks for itself. Whereas in other cultures, women must double their efforts to attract men.

But the truth was he had many of these little episodes thinking he had a tiny flashback of memory. At first she was really excited and thought recovery was just moments away; it became apparent that wasn't going to happen. She did as she always did when he had what they now called 'a moment', and stood up.

"You know, John, if a temple collapses, you can build it again," she said. "If a *Masjid* is destroyed, you can reconstruct it again. But when a heart full of love is shattered, it takes years to repair. Therefore many are afraid to remarry. After years of praying for someone, your love begins to blossom. Trust begins to flourish. For this reason, lying is prohibited in a relationship."

In front of the picture of India wearing her yellow sari in the temple, Anjali started to slowly weave and flow as if being blown by a gentle breeze. Her body twisted and danced with her hands, she raised them skywards and then gently caressed her own cheek. She stroked her hair and swished it round, half-covering her face. Locke watched on and occasionally something would click; an image would flash before his eyes and then would be gone. He thought it might be a rush of blood he could hear, but each image, *each moment,* was accompanied by a whooshing sound as if a memory coming into focus had its own special noise.

Anjali continued, always a slow dance, always one in which she expressed her hands as much as she possibly could. Long before his injury, she remembered him telling her how captivated he had been when he watched her praying in the temple and she tried to replicate that dance for him now.

"I put henna on my hand. I draw complex motifs in my arm and the colour of my henna is named after us. The aroma that comes calls us your name. I put flowers in my hair, and flowers tease me. I wear jewellery on my ears, my neck and my body, without you it means nothing. Your eyes are the mirror to my soul. My entire body refers to you as 'John'. In your memory, I will vanquish my whole life. My life belongs to you, so come back and make me your bride. My bangles, *bindiya,* are all calling you.

"I had to do it, you know?" she continued. Immediately Locke did know. "I had to choose my parents over you."

"Please don't tell me again," he pleaded.

"I have to," Anjali said, still moving her hands making the shapes of ancient Hindu dances come to life in the room. "I'll never forget the moment my father pulled out a gun, and I will never forget the pain of my heart tearing in two when he tried to hand it to me and ordered me to shoot them both. How could I do that? How could I kill my own parents and live a happy life with you?"

Locke closed his eyes and listened to Anjali's voice. She told the story because it was a story she could repeat. It was a story that he had heard when he was well and he had heard it many times since he had lost his memory. It wasn't nice to listen to, but he managed to stop thinking about how the story ended with his injury and tried to remember the sights and sounds that would have happened when Anjali told him she could not leave with him.

"He pulled out a fucking gun," Anjali continued. She did not like swearing, but she had said it at the time when her world was collapsing in

Piccadilly station and she wanted everything to be as true to the reality as possible. "He held the barrel of the gun and he tried to hand it to me. I couldn't take it. You started to scream and there was a policeman nearby. You bent double, almost lying on the floor of the station, people all around looked at you, then you grabbed my ankle."

Whoosh... that was a moment. It was a new one. His eyes snapped open. Anjali was still dancing. Her sari slid gracefully over her body as she gently moved. Another whoosh. *The temple?* he thought.

"The policeman told me to go. He could see what had happened and he thought it best that he stay behind and look after you. I went and you screamed again and again. It was the worst sound I have ever heard. You were like a wounded animal in the last moments before death."

Locke had a brief image of a blurred scene, of Anjali running away towards some large windows. Then it was gone.

"I found out afterwards you had put your foot through your canvas picture; this canvas picture. The tear was visible." She looked at the photograph hanging on the wall, the one taken in the temple, the most beautiful image she had ever seen, not that she was being vain.

"This is the picture you destroyed, the one you couldn't bear to look at at that moment, and I don't blame you. I never did. I can't imagine how you felt at that moment, except that I felt something similar when my father stood in front of me holding a gun.

"Which is the greater sacrifice; the love of a parent or the love of a lover? Who gets first in your life, a parent or a lover?" Anjali stopped dancing. She looked sadly downwards, and turned slightly to look at Locke. "A fucking gun," she said quietly. She gave a slight smile and walked through to the living room. She sat down on the sofa and blinked away her own tears that were forming. She could not live without him; she knew that. The whole world knew it, she had said it so many times. Her parents had understood very quickly the devotion in their daughter. Knew too of *ardhangini* as they themselves viewed each other the same way, the way of centuries of Hindu belief and prayer. They could not allow their daughter to leave home to live with someone who to them was a complete stranger, one that had no faith in God. And Locke was an atheist who, to them, did not understand the basic underpinning of marriage. But they could let her follow her heart when they realised she was *ardhangini*. They had been so proud of their daughter as she spent vigil after vigil at Locke's side. They had brought her up the right way.

Anjali couldn't stop the tears from falling as she thought back to her parents and to that night with the gun. Not for the first time she questioned whether it had been loaded. She prayed not. She was thankful she had not so much as picked it up. To have done so would have shown at least a tiny amount of considering using it. But the more she thought the less she was certain. She thought she might have started to invent things that hadn't happened. Everything had become so difficult. She knew she loved Locke, but that in itself was beginning to worry her.

Locke wasn't there. He had been replaced by a different version; one that was scientific and no longer seemingly artistic. He was angry when he had always been so gentle. She understood why, but then she would think, why me? Or, better yet, why Locke? What did Life want to prove here?

He was ill but she was suffering too. She was questioning the journey of a lifetime with him. *Where are you taking me, John?* She tried to blank those thoughts out, but they wouldn't leave her.

She was *ardhangini* to *her* John, but to *this* John?

"No!" she said aloud. She believed in fate. She believed in Hindu *karma*. Maybe she had done something bad in her previous life and was given this situation as punishment. She could not pick and choose which areas of her religion she would believe. If she believed in *ardhangini,* she had to believe in *karma*. Truth is eternal, *Brahman,* the *Vedas* and *dharma*. She had to believe in all of them, and all of the other key beliefs of her religion. She was devoted to her religion but she was familiar with other religions and other texts, not just Hinduism. She was also devoted to her John and the two could not be separated. If they were, she would have been unfaithful to both. She was paying for the sins of her former lives and she had to accept that. Locke was part of that past. She put herself before the shrine in the living room and started to pray.

*

"Prosecco."

Anjali stopped praying and turned to see Locke leaning on his walking frame in the doorway.

"Pardon?" she said.

"Prosecco," he repeated. "At the wedding, when I was alone at the bar and thought you had disappeared, you asked for prosecco."

Anjali thought for a moment. She forgotten about that. She only drank at weddings and then only prosecco.

"I remembered," Locke said and the two of them looked at each other in stunned silence.

fifteen

the quiet chiming of bells

She was patient. She had been for months now. And she knew she would have to be patient for even longer. But she missed the physical life she had had with Locke. He had been such an attentive lover and she dreamed of his return. He showed no interest in her and hadn't since the mugging. She wondered if it was because he had gone off her or because the head injury meant he had undergone another character change. Maybe he just wasn't interested in making love anymore?

She castigated herself. Of course it wasn't that. They made love before because they were in love. But he couldn't anymore. He had put a huge amount of faith in Anjali to look after him because, after all, he still had no real idea of who she was. She tried to put herself in his shoes; would she believe everything she was told when she had no memory of it? She knew she couldn't. She could kiss him as tenderly as she could, be as gentle with him as his frail state required, but she could never get beyond the sense that he would be kissing a stranger.

The fact that he had remembered the prosecco brought about a change in him; the fact that now he could remember something from before the mugging meant that at least some of what Anjali was telling him was true. Until that point he had made certain not to touch Anjali or show any affection towards her beyond the purely polite. She would stroke his arm, or kiss his forehead, but he had used the excuse of his exhaustion not to have anything approaching a physical relationship. He knew he didn't love her as he had done and he was desperate for the situation to reverse, but until he remembered, then that wasn't going to happen. The prosecco memory changed all that and he stroked her arm, then the side of her face.

Anjali looked at Locke differently. Her deep brown eyes smiled and sparkled as she felt the first tender contact she had wanted for so long.

"What's brought this on?" she asked.

"Prosecco," he stated, simply.

"But you've not had any."

"No. It's because I have remembered something that you had forgotten. So you didn't tell me and now I know that at least some of what you have been telling me must be true."

Anjali smiled. "You've not touched me until now because you had to be certain first?"

Locke nodded. "It's still the only memory, but I'm willing to accept you're no longer a stranger."

She cried, held his hand against her face and leaned in to kiss him. He kissed her back. It went no further, but it was intimacy, and that was all she had wanted. It felt as though a corner had been turned. She was getting her John back.

*

"It will be £53.48," Locke said to the cashier at the supermarket as Anjali started to load the shopping onto the conveyor belt. He never missed an opportunity to count the cost of the shop before the cashier had run everything through the till. He seemed to enjoy showing off about his maths, but the more Anjali studied him, the more she thought it was just that he genuinely enjoyed working things out.

He could stand with the aid of a walking stick now and always insisted on coming with Anjali whenever she went food shopping at their local. They still drove, but he felt it wouldn't be long before he could walk the half mile or so.

The cashier gave a friendly smile. She had heard Locke rattle off the total before – it amazed her the first time, but not so much now. The last item went through and the till display flashed up. £58.26. Locke sighed.

"That side of salmon has twenty-five *per cent* off. Your till will say it is £19.12, whereas it should cost £14.34."

The cashier looked at the items on the till and there was a side of salmon at £19.12. Anjali held up the salmon in its white plastic wrapper. The twenty-five *per cent* offer was clearly on show, as was the revised cost of £14.34. The cashier called over her manager and explained the situation. Locke looked a little smug, something Anjali didn't like, as the manager rushed off to check the display. It turned out he had been right, just as Anjali knew he would have been, but to work out exactly what was wrong with the bill was more impressive still.

Anjali pushed the trolley and Locke struggled on alongside. He still had many difficulties and got tired far quicker than a young, healthy man of his age should, but his physical progress was almost taken for granted now that he had started to improve. He could do most things without assistance, as long as they weren't too energetic or took too long to complete. Walking around the supermarket would mean he would be lying down almost as soon as they returned to the flat.

But those at the hospital were delighted with his recovery. Mr Adefemi checked on him regularly and he underwent all sorts of tests Locke knew was to do with the excessive dose of radiotherapy he had been given.

Mr Dixon had returned to London, but kept in contact at least weekly. The dose he had administered in error became a trial in itself and although there was always that possibility of Locke, or rather his father Joe, going down the legal route should anything happen, he in effect provided that rarest of things; an experiment on a live human. Medical trials were usually exhaustive, but as Locke kept saying to his father, there was no substitute for a human model.

Once, when visiting the hospital for his latest check-up, he discussed at length a drug trial that went wrong a few months ago. Mr Dixon knew it well enough because all medical research had been put on hold before having to go through ever tighter regulations since then.

But what shocked the consultant, again, was the fact that Locke was able to explain the issues with the original drug trial and how the six healthy men infected managed to survive. Locke's knowledge was undeniable; how he got that knowledge seemed to defy medical explanation. Mr Dixon could not see how the treatment, and the excess dose given to his patient, could make him as scientific as it did.

There was simply no previous medical evidence to suggest what the case was clearly showing; that the treatment had somehow improved his intelligence massively. Locke had his own theories; the trouble was he spoke in a way beyond even Mr Dixon's or Mr Adefemi's medical knowledge.

The problem that remained was his memory. The flashbacks were still rare and images in his head elusive. Since the prosecco breakthrough and his finally remembering something even Anjali had forgotten, his mind stubbornly refused to offer more than the fleeting moments that seemed to tease him rather than help him get anywhere.

Always the whoosh as if a memory had its own sound and increasingly a sense that he was going to pass out as a moment approached.

*

The moon rose high over Manchester and it was a clear winter night. Locke had fallen asleep in front of the television; he was watching some programme about a bridge collapsing and kept saying things to himself as though he knew exactly what had happened. Anjali noticed the moon through a gap in the curtains and an idea formed in her mind. She got up and went to their bedroom, swapping the yellow sari for the crimson red one she wore in the dance studio. She then put on as many bangles as she felt necessary and spent an age over her make-up.

She continued to be Locke's carer, although she left his side more often now. He had a mobile should he need to call her and she knew he would able to manage simple tasks without her. She had no concerns about leaving him asleep in the living room while she nipped out. And what she was about to do was important.

Her breath frosted in the cold night air the moment she stepped out from the communal entrance to the apartments. It wasn't late, just past eight in the evening, but there would be people about. Anjali did not care for them. It was the moon she wanted. She had a question to ask of it. *Of her*. Of *Chandra*.

For the moon was important to her faith and to women everywhere. The menstrual cycle lasted one lunar month. It took nine lunar months for a full-term baby to arrive. The moon manifested sympathy and joy, enthusiasm and care. Most importantly she knew the moon was in its positive phase and that helped with memory.

Today was *Purnima* and *Chandra* was at her fullest.

Anjali stood in the middle of the small grassed area in front of the apartment building and hoped no one would see her. She began talking to *Chandra*. Or rather, she mouthed the words to her prayers as she asked the lunar goddess for help and guidance. She prayed for Locke's mind to return, for him to remember something, anything different to what she had told him. She felt he was getting better but the progress was so slow. She raised her right hand and stared straight at *Chandra's* white glare.

"*Witness the sun, moon and the stars are my witnesses,*" she whispered. "I know everybody knows you as a goddess, *Chandra*, but we are human beings and when we fall in love, we do not fully love the person we want. But one loves the Earth, the sun, the moon and the clouds. *Witness the sun, moon and the stars are my witnesses.*

"We find the Lord even in stone. Why? Because the land was the first place you passed us. Human beings are not. *Witness the sun, moon and the stars are my witnesses.*

"I came with one wish, *Chandra*, and it isn't about me. It's about somebody else. But I'm being selfish, because I fell in love with him as well. I hope you complete it. How do I explain him? How do I begin? There are times when I forget how sweet and innocent he is, sometimes when he is being mischievous. *Witness the sun, moon and the stars are my witnesses.*

"He is utterly unique. For differentiating yourself from the truth, *Chandra*, I've never known anyone like him. Sometimes I think he's kind of crazy. Sometimes he's just a genius. *Witness the sun, moon and the stars are my witnesses.*

"Sometimes he gets really upset. At times, he makes faces and makes me laugh. At other times, he's more stubborn than a child. And there are times when he feels like a devotee. *Witness the sun, moon and the stars are my witnesses.*

"What he is and what he can't be I could never convey it in words. But I'm not sure why I feel beautiful when he looks at me. When he expresses joy, I want to dance with joy. When he gets upset, I keep him quiet. I feel like holding him. Embracing him. *Witness the sun, moon and the stars are my witnesses.*

"And when he loves me, tears drip down my face. He makes me realise I was meant to be with him. And he was made for me. I love him so much, Chandra. Not for a moment, not even for a day or two, but for a lifetime.

"I'm coming to the door, *Chandra*, pleading with you, for John so you can bring back his memory. I acknowledge that you are far away; a million miles away from my touch. *Witness the sun, moon and the stars are my witnesses.*"

Anjali stretched her arms and set her hands to the moon. She made a promise; *I will marry John in every incarnation should you help him heal. I have asked this of no deity but you, Chandra, for you are the Goddess of women; you are my one true goddess among many. If you mend his broken mind I will marry him in every incarnation and I will devote my worship to you and you alone.*

Locke looked out of the window. He had woken and called out to Anjali, but she had not replied. So he used his stick and walked to the bedroom guessing she might have gone to bed early. The bed was empty, which puzzled him, so he walked to the window which looked out on the rest of Castlefield. He saw her instantly, and gasped.

There was a streetlamp nearby, but she wasn't bathed in a sodium orange glow; she seemed to shine in brilliant white light, her crimson red dress gleaming like liquid ruby. He could see her eyes were closed and her lips were moving. He dared to open the window a fraction to hear what she was saying.

The cold bit into him and he shut it again when he realised she was talking too quietly, or maybe not at all. Her breath sparkled on the gentle air and followed the same direction upwards as her raised right arm, twisting at the wrist, her fingers moving to some kind of rhythm. Light beams glanced off bangles like lasers as she moved her wrist in the moonlight.

Return his memory and I shall marry him in every incarnation. I shall worship you, Chandra, above all others. I will devote my life to you...

Return his memory and I shall marry him in every incarnation. I shall worship you, Chandra, above all others. I will devote my life to you...

The familiar feelings started to rush over Locke. He felt like he was going to black out. The whoosh didn't stop at the image; it didn't recede, but got louder and louder. He felt his head splitting apart. Outside, Anjali felt sensations pulse up and down her right arm. She kept chanting. He let go of the windowsill, the net curtain falling back across the glass. His hands went to his head and he screamed out at the searing pain. The image got closer and louder and he fell to the floor, clutching at his face, his skull. And then silence, briefly. The roar and the pain had gone.

Then he heard a sound. The quiet chiming of bells and an image of a woman, of Anjali, with her arms spread wide in the crimson red sari, its train catching on the breeze of a fan. He had seen the scene a hundred times, a thousand, as Anjali replayed the tape of their dance to try to get a memory, a moment of clarity. Only this time he wasn't seeing a scene from some recording; he was watching her dance from his perspective. From his own viewpoint; his own memory of the dance. He climbed to his feet and looked out of the window once more. But Anjali was no longer there. Instead he focused on the images in his head and of the wonder he felt for the woman in the crimson sari. The images were crystal clear and his hips began to sway as the voice of a man began.

Anjali returned to the apartment and walked purposefully into the bedroom. She didn't know Locke was in there, and gasped when she saw him. One hand had gone to his stomach, the other held across his chest. He was swaying and she recognised what he was doing instantly. His eyes opened and he saw Anjali open mouthed.

"I'm remembering the dance," he said. Anjali rushed to him and held him as still he moved. Outside, the moon, *Chandra,* shone ever brighter in the winter night sky.

sixteen

the entrance to a netherworld

With Locke no longer physically dependent on round-the-clock care, Anjali had gone back to work. His parents had come over a couple of times in the intervening months, but it was their money that had sustained the situation. With their son needing her, the Lockes made sure there was enough money in the pot for Anjali to do the caring. It was unwritten, but always known that as soon as he no longer needed care to that extent, Anjali would seek employment. And she had been glad of it; looking after him had not been a bind to her; it was what she had been put on Earth to do and it was what she would do, without question, if ever she needed to again.

No, it was the cabin fever; staring at the same four walls in Castlefield as she watched over Locke sleeping, or sat talking to him, telling him of old memories, or watching the TV shows they now liked. Before their viewing habits had been very different, but it was him that had changed. They both knew when that time had come. It was when Locke was walking unaided around the flat and when a trip to the supermarket no longer caused him to spend the afternoon lying down. He readily agreed.

He never said it, but his pride winced when he remembered once again that she was his carer. He didn't want to be a burden and, when he felt brave enough to say so, he suggested she go back to work, just to get her out of the flat during the week.

Her manager Joanne had been incredible; to have lost one of her best staff when Anjali had decided to run away to London with Locke had been a bitter blow, but days later Anjali had been back in touch and explained everything. Joanne's heart went out to Anjali; she was married, had two kids, a career. She was as happy as she needed to be and nothing felt better at the end of a good day's work than to go home to her husband and children and feel wrapped up in their love and warmth. Joanne didn't need anything else, but to imagine herself in Anjali's shoes turned her cold and she willingly offered to keep Anjali's job open, or at least make a place available for Anjali as soon as she was ready to come back. That had been the second week in April. By the third, she was back at work.

And apart from suddenly having to get up that bit earlier for the commute and do a full day's work, Anjali slipped straight back into the role she had previously left for love. It hadn't really been that long since she had last walked through the glass doors on Peter Street. The office reception remained the same and there were almost all the old faces still there. It was as if time had stood still for Anjali and she was inundated by work colleagues coming up to her throughout her first day offering hugs or handshakes from the more reserved. By lunch she was already shattered, but her close group of friends broke with tradition and they went out for a quick curry down a backstreet off Bridge Street, something they used to reserve for Friday lunchtimes.

She got home exhausted to find Locke on the sofa watching a programme about planetary observation. It was nothing out of the ordinary; he held a fascination for all sorts of subjects, usually way beyond her own comprehension. Happily, they were often way beyond her interest as well.

"How'd it go?" he asked, his eyes never leaving the screen.

"Good," she replied. "Really, really good. Joanne's been brilliant and all the old crew are still there, apart from Colin, but then I knew he was retiring, and that was from before you had your episode."

They had taken to calling it his 'episode'. It was how he liked to refer to it. He grunted and continued watching the television; planets orbiting stars providing clues to mass and density. Anjali shook her head at the subject matter and walked through to the kitchen. She needed refreshment.

"Cup of tea?" she shouted through.

"No thanks," came the reply. It struck Anjali just then that despite the fact Locke still couldn't remember the vast majority of their past, they were still very much living as an established couple.

*

Two days later she re-enacted the routine. The novelty of her return to work had already worn off for everyone in her office. For Anjali it was interesting to think that people could slip into the past with such ease. Reincarnation flashed through her mind; was everything a memory, in this life or any other? She would ask the question later when she prayed. *Chandra* was waning at the moment and Anjali's prayers to her goddess were reflected as such. It was the period of the month when she tended to pray to others, in her mind leaving *Chandra* in peace until her strength returned and she moved towards fullness once more.

"Hi," she called through as she shut the door to the flat behind her. No voice replied. She put the keys on the table by the front door and walked through to the living room. "John?" but the response was the same. Anjali checked all of the rooms, but the stillness was unmistakeable and she knew before she had finished her search that she was alone in the apartment. She removed her coat and her small-heeled shoes and rubbed an aching foot. *He's strong enough to be alone, he's strong enough to go out.*

Anjali busied herself with the kinds of mundane things that needed doing. That mainly consisted of taking washing out of the washing machine and into the dryer, getting changed into more comfortable clothes and making herself a cup of tea. She sat on the sofa in the living room and reached for the TV remote, stopping when she suddenly felt the silence in the room. There was no chuntering from the television about planets or mathematics or medical theory. John wasn't fidgeting, he wasn't even breathing and that was a sound she knew well.

A thought when through her mind; did *Chandra* wish to change Locke? Did a miracle really happen? Or was it a coincidence he seemed to be getting better, that his memory seemed to be returning? She looked towards the curtained window and imagined him out there in the early spring sunshine, perhaps taking a stroll along the canal. The image of her John being pushed in by the scum that had changed their lives forever floated behind her eyes. She blinked the thought away, took a sip of her tea and settled back into the sofa, into nothing but peace and quiet. Her mind went blank; it was bliss.

When she woke up, the late sun was no longer shining. A sodium glow radiated from the streetlamp outside and Anjali realised she had been asleep. She looked around in the half light and fancied nothing had changed.

"John?" she called, but knew there would be no answer. She'd been asleep for over three hours and he definitely should not have been out that long. He still wasn't strong enough for that. The panic started to rise in her. A sense of fear seemed to manifest in her stomach and her breathing shortened. Her head swayed as she struggled for oxygen. *Deep breaths, deep breaths.* Anjali focused on her breathing; exaggerated breaths in, exaggerated breaths out. Slowly she regained control and pushed the demons of panic and anxiety back. There were pins and needles in her hands and feet, but she wasn't worried. Somehow Locke had known that they were symptoms of her anxiety, said he had seen them mentioned in a programme he'd watched. She carried on with the breathing exercise; slowly her heart returned to a normal rhythm followed by the pins and needles receding to nothing. She clenched her fists almost to drive out the last of the sensations.

Anjali looked around the room again and sought to make sense of the situation. She felt no pain and that reassured her. It meant Locke wasn't in pain. She concentrated her thoughts and felt only happiness, no, *excitement,* come in. He wasn't hurt, or fearful, or tired or dead. Anjali was confident that whatever he was doing and wherever he was, he was enjoying himself.

She changed again, into a sari she wore rarely as she never felt sky blue was really her colour. She left the flat in darkness as she put on a warm coat and closed the front door behind her.

*

The route her thoughts took her was straight towards town. As she continued, she got the unnerving sense that she was heading straight back to her work. But there would be no reason he had gone there unless to surprise her. Maybe she had missed him and he couldn't get back? She dismissed the thought; all she could sense was that he was happy.

She passed a pub, several of them in fact, and with each one she wondered if he was in it. He didn't drink much at all in the flat; in fact together he drank much less than he ever had prior to his injury. She doubted he had been drunk at all in the intervening months. But then this week had been about his freedom, about his no longer needing his carer to care all the time. It had worked fine for the first two days, and now he was missing. *He's not missing; he's independent.* Anjali focused on the thought. If she couldn't let him go, then perhaps he would rebel and leave? She was convinced of her love; he still couldn't remember who she was.

She walked along Deansgate, dwarfed by the bulk of the old Great Northern warehouse to her right. She soon crossed Peter Street where her office stood and carried on. For some reason she felt the urge to cross over Deansgate and then, as she reached the Ramada Hotel, she turned left and headed downhill. Down here was deepest, darkest Salford, synonymous with the gangs that seemed to run Manchester. She reached the border between the two cities and stood still on the Victorian bridge that spanned the River Irwell below. It was dark now and a hundred yards off a wide junction where she could just make out the edge of a church with its sign no doubt highlighting services. To the right a curiously shaped building she felt could have been an old police station.

He's here.

She didn't so much hear the words as feel them. Her hand clutched to her breast and she closed her eyes. A plump older woman wrapped tight against the winter cold that wasn't there, eyed her suspiciously as she walked slowly down towards the crossroads. Anjali followed the route, but was slower now, conflicted by what she thought she could feel. She stopped. To her left two large men, one white and one black and wearing dinner jackets, seemed to be guarding a gaping, cavernous mouth that signified the entrance to a netherworld. They feigned ignorance of her presence, but Anjali was drawn into the building and stepped forward. The two men turned in towards each other, creating an immoveable barrier.

"Sorry, love, members only." Anjali wasn't sure which one had spoken; their expressions remained the same.

"My husband is in there and he is a member." She stared at them defiantly, despite the lie. They looked back at her, impassive. "John Locke," she added, effecting a steelier grit.

The black one turned and stepped back into the recesses of the doorway to look at a clipboard. The white one took a half step to his right to once again take up the centre ground. The black man tapped his colleague on the shoulder and the way parted immediately.

"Sorry, Madam," he said as Anjali stepped forward. Her heart was racing; *what the hell is going on?*

She slowly walked down the darkened flight of stairs then took a right turn. In front of her a young woman stood in the half-light wearing a skimpy black dress. The girl smiled as Anjali approached; she was acutely aware of her own attire not being in keeping with the clothing of the staff. The girl opened a door and light flooded out. Anjali stepped forward and waited for her eyes to adjust. She later thought it was like something out of Prohibition: chatter, tables, glamorous staff and less glamorous punters. Alcohol was flowing and there was chintzy music. She surveyed the scene, inwardly convinced Locke would never be interested in a place like this. But there he was, leaning forwards on a table, as if it was holding him up. She saw him the moment she walked in, and she headed straight in his direction.

He saw her and smiled, ignoring the look of concern on Anjali's face. "Grab a seat," he said, laughing and smiling as she reached him. She could see he was having the time of his life.

"What the hell are you doing here?" she whispered, the anger obvious. "Is this a fucking gambling den?"

Locke smiled again. "Sure is. Great, isn't it?" He hadn't moved from his hunched position.

"Great?" Anjali was stunned. "Great?" she said again. It wasn't a question. "We have to get out of here. Have you seen the security they've got? How much have you lost? We have got to get out." Her fury was matched only by her fear.

"Don't be silly," Locke insisted, gently laughing. "I've been here before."

"When?" Gambling was not an environment Anjali was familiar with. She had never stepped foot inside a casino, but she heard many stories of how they could ruin lives.

"Oh, way back." Anjali looked at Locke, at his beaming features and the unmistakeable twinkle. He looked away, then down at some cards he held.

"You remember this place?"

"Uh-huh."

Anjali tried to collect her thoughts. On the one hand enough memory had returned to him that he remembered how to get to this place he must have visited before he was attacked, but on the other, he was gambling and she couldn't abide by it. Like many things in her religion, it was frowned upon, if not fully blasphemous. She was angry and disappointed.

"We're in Salford, in an illegal gambling den—"

"Not illegal," Locke interrupted. He looked directly at her and she could see the mischief as the corners of his mouth lifted a little into a smile. He sat back on his stool, his arms no longer hiding the horde of chips beneath. Anjali's mouth gaped. She had no idea what she was looking at, but it was clear it was a lot.

"Ten grand plus."

Anjali closed her mouth. *Shit! Shit, shit, shit!* The reputation of the Salford gangs was terrifying, and she was looking at Locke take over ten thousand pounds from them. The croupier called out and a load more of the red coloured chips found their way to Locke's stockpile. He turned and raised a hand. A bald man, impeccably dressed in a dinner jacket and black bow tie, immediately made his way across to the table. Locke swivelled on his stool and slid off, his arm tracing its way around Anjali's thin waist.

"It's easy," he whispered, close enough for his breath to tickle her ear and her neck. She gasped. It was the most physical contact they had had in months. "We can go home now." Locke took her hand and they walked back towards the door that led to the stairs and to freedom. Anjali struggled to control her breathing. If there was more than ten thousand pounds coming their way, how could they possibly walk across Manchester without getting mugged? The bald man returned, carrying a small brown briefcase. Anjali turned away; that briefcase would be a calling card to anyone who knew what it signified. The owners of the club would have spotters outside, waiting to mug any punter stupid enough to walk the streets with the little brown briefcase. There might as well have been pound signs stamped on its exterior.

"Please come again, Mr Locke," the bald-headed man said, handing over the briefcase.

"Don't worry, I will," Locke replied, smiling. Anjali gripped his arm tighter and felt the relief wash over her as they exited into the dark Salford night to find a black cab waiting for them. Locke held open the door and followed Anjali in, sitting down opposite with a crash. The taxi moved off instantly, the driver not asking for an address. He turned left at the bottom of the street by the church. Anjali looked out of her window; there was a pub called the Black Lion curving around the edge of the old Victorian warehouse. She looked back at Locke. He leaned in conspiratorially.

"Counting cards," he said. "It's easy."

She looked hard at him. Did he know what he was saying? She didn't know what he meant, or whether he had cheated, but that club, which she was convinced *was* illegal knew him well enough to call him by name. He had clearly been a member before the attack and now he was back and taking thousands off them. They had got him a cab, but the cabbie clearly already knew his address as he didn't even ask.

"I can go to any casino in the country and take this off them."

Anjali looked away. An idea returned. She had been thinking about it for a while; Locke's case was unique. The treatment he received and the intelligence he now possessed had developed. He seemed to know everything.

She wanted him on TV, in the media, telling his story, making a comfortable life for them both by talking about what he had been through. Now he could defraud casinos.

He seemed to be able to read her thoughts.

"But I don't want to do that. I went to them with a proposition. I can take whatever I like off them as long as I train up their players. Their players go around the country, win big at other casinos and disappear. Then other trained players take their place. They can judge their own players against my success. I become the benchmark. Everyone else around that table was learning from me tonight. Soon they will be earning, and my fee is whatever I want it to be, I just need to pop in and count some cards."

Locke leaned back in the fold up chair as the black cab bounced along the streets of Salford, taking the back route to Castlefield. He looked out of the window, passing streetlamps lighting up his sharp features. In that moment Anjali thought he looked beautiful. But she remained quiet, deep in her own thoughts.

seventeen

i sensed you and felt you

Despite the brief moment of intimacy in the casino, once Locke's euphoria at winning had subsided, he and Anjali seemed to slip back to where they had been. She struggled to make sense of so many things: his continued memory loss against his memory of the casino, the fact that he had been there before and the fact that they obviously knew him very well. Was the card counting something prior to his attack or something his now formidable brain had worked out? Had he been to the casino more recently, without her knowledge? If so, how? Not so long ago he could barely walk unaided and a couple of weeks ago it had been an effort to even get out of the apartment block to a waiting cab. There was no way he could have walked the length of Deansgate to get to the casino despite his improvement since then.

And why didn't he tell her he remembered the casino? Why did she have to find him? It occurred to her then that he had not even asked how she had found him. She wasn't entirely sure herself, but was content to attribute it to *Chandra,* and she had prayed a lot to her goddess since the casino. She had confronted him, but he remembered nothing new.

The following weekend she walked slowly into the living room carrying two cups of tea. She handed one to Locke and sat down in her usual chair, placing her own cup on the table beside. For a few seconds she stared at the television programme he was watching.

"I don't give a damn about who Higgs Bosun is," she said.

"It's not a person—"

"I said I don't give a damn…"

He looked at Anjali and got the message. He turned the TV off. She took a deep breath.

"You're scaring me," she said, as calmly as she could. Locke looked on, waiting for more. "I don't like what happened at the casino. It's great you won and it's even better that your memory took you there, but it's a side of you I have never known and I don't like it."

The air seemed to thicken between them. This was meant to be about finding things out; it was almost as if a barrier had come up. And he hadn't said anything yet. She shook her head. *I am not going mad*, she thought. "When did you remember about the casino?"

"Weeks ago."

The statement was emphatic. It showed he had no remorse, but then was that what she was after?

"Why didn't you tell me? Every little thing that pops into your head you tell me about. I know you want to be the person you were again, so you tell me every memory you have." She was pleading with him. He stared back, blinking a little. "If you tell me everything, we can maybe move forward. If you don't, how can I help and how can we ever be what we once were?"

"You are a Hindu and your faith does not agree with gambling," he said. "When the memory returned I thought hard about telling you and decided against it. Instead, I decided to remain quiet and learn about betting patterns. I wanted to know if I could go out and win as the mathematics told me I should." He sat further back in his chair. "I knew you wouldn't agree with it so I didn't tell you. As soon as I was strong enough I decided to investigate. I didn't expect to do so well, although to be honest, I should never have had any doubt in the math."

"But you never gambled when you were with me," Anjali pushed. "Not once. The subject never come up and you only managed to come to me when you were free."

"I got burned in that place. I didn't owe them exactly, but I felt there was unfinished business. I didn't like how they had treated me previously." He stared at the switched off television. I got into a bit of debt with them. Not much, just enough for them to turn the heat up whilst I waited for a check from my dad. They had the money within a couple of days – the debt had already gone up, but I had asked for more than dad sent, so I could cover it. That didn't please them."

"So why did you go back? Why turn up at the very place you've had a run in with and who could probably make you disappear tomorrow."

"Oh, they could," Locke shot back. His stare made Anjali uncomfortable. "But do you know what? They only have two modes; with or without. In or out. I'm suddenly 'with' because of what I did yesterday. I'm in because they are interested in what I did. I put forward a proposition and I told them that if I took ten grand off them that it would prove I was someone they could do business with. They laughed, but said ok. Look what happened."

Anjali took a sip of her tea. It already felt a bit cold. "I don't want you doing it again," she said, trying to sound stern.

"I'm sorry, but I will. This is the only thing I have control over right now. I am trying; I am thinking all the time, looking over the pictures, the video, everything to do with our past. And when something comes back I grab it with both hands. I am not going against your wishes, Anjali, I am taking control of one of the very few things I know are me."

Anjali felt the tears fall and the sobs rise up from her stomach. She took a deep breath, looked at the ceiling and willed the tears to stop.

"I'm sorry," Locke said. "I am trying."

"Not hard enough!" she had not meant to say it, *to scream it,* but it came out all the same. He didn't react; his emotional attachment was still so low because he remembered so little. Anjali looked at him, and brushed a tear away. Her vision was blurred, but she could see no emotion in his face and cried again, louder this time. She leaped from her chair and ran into her bedroom slamming the door behind her. He listened to the sobs for a couple of minutes then turned back to the television. He felt bad for Anjali, but he just couldn't feel anything for her. His emotion was dead from inside. Now that he had enough strength back, he had wondered about leaving her and started to work out how he would do it, hurting her as little as possible.

*

Anjali's bedroom door swung open some minutes later and she stormed back into the living room. She had changed into the crimson red sari. Locke looked up in surprise and saw ever more tears falling. He turned the TV off once again.

"I wore this in the dance we filmed, the dance you have watched a thousand times. In India I wore yellow and you watched me thinking I didn't know you were there. I wore gold at the wedding when you found me again. I didn't know it immediately, but we are *ardhangini* and I sensed you and felt you in that temple. You saw me on the flight home and I gave you those words. They were Hindi and you could not have understood them. They got you even more interested, then my parents intervened."

She stopped, trying to control her breathing, the tears falling from her eyes.

"I wouldn't mind, John, but they are pretty fucking unusual memories. I am not some sweetheart from school, or that bitch that tried to bed you when all you could think about was me. I am deeper than all of that, so are you telling me none of that is in your head right now, despite everything? Are you telling me that you have a better memory of nearly getting beaten up by some wannabe gangsters in a casino than all that love you professed to me?"

Anjali was waving her arms around. Her face appeared blotchy, red around the eyes, her mouth peeled back not in a beautiful smile, but in the grimace of a wounded animal or the snarl of someone about to strike. She was not the calm Anjali Locke once knew. Women were supposed to be calm. That was their elegance.

"Are you?" she screamed.

Locke slowly nodded. "I'm sorry," he said. He had said a lot in last few months.

Anjali steeled herself. *This is it. Last chance,* she thought and pointed at the window. She hated how gambling could break ordinary people's lives. It was something she had seen in India culture as well as in the UK.

"Then go and stand there and look out of that window." He looked at her, uncertain. "Go!"

Locke did as he was told and went to the window. It was raining outside. He didn't see Anjali go, but he heard the swish of the sari and the bang of the apartment door. He pulled the net curtain back. Anjali walked into the centre of the small grassed area in front of the block, turned to look up at him standing in the window and straightened her right arm to point up at him. The first two fingers were outstretched, the thumb curled up, her hand looking like a revolver. It disturbed him. He didn't recall her looking as determined and aggressive as she did at this moment. Then the hand fell to her side and she started to dance. The sari was wet against her body, revealing the tight curves of her breasts and buttocks, the flatness of her stomach and the slimness of her waist. Her hair, usually so long dark and glossy was clumping in the wet and her make up began to stream down her face.

But she danced. Her arms flailed and made intricate shapes in the wet Manchester afternoon. Raindrops sprayed as she whipped her head around, sending her hair in arcs. A couple of young lads stood nearby laughing, but she didn't care.

Locke watched on from above. A whoosh, a memory, he closed his eyes. It was gone, then another whoosh and another. He stared at Anjali, watched her body gyrate and saw another shadow do the same in his brain. The two were separate, but seemed to converge. He let go of the net curtain and his hands clawed at his head. Could he get the two images to match? He was so close; his eyes snapped open. The lads had gone, but Anjali had not. She danced as if her life depended upon it. She could not stop as if to do so was to die. Other images swayed in and out of Locke's mind, the whooshing increasing then fading. His hands went back to his head and he let out a roar; a primeval cry of anguish, of pain and of anger. He seemed to howl.

His head spun; he felt seasick. He looked desperately about the room and focused on one thing – the picture of India that had remained hanging on his living room wall. His breathing quickened and he started to gulp down the air as if he was being starved of oxygen. He looked back out of the window and saw Anjali's prone body lying on the wet grass, the incessant Manchester rain not stopping. He lurched forward, bile rising in his throat as he fought the sensations coming forth from his body. He held on to the stair rail tight as he lowered himself slowly down the stairs, then crashed out of the block's front door and drunkenly rushed towards Anjali's prone form. He collapsed beside her, still gasping for air, and was soaked within seconds. His hands rested across her midriff. She opened her eyes, looked down to where he was touching her and looked back at him. His eyes had never closed.

"I remember," he said, simply. And began to laugh.

*

Anjali rose up to a kneeling position facing Locke, her knees sinking slightly in the soft ground. He did the same. Her right hand came up as it had done before she danced. Once again the first two fingers and thumb created the shape of a revolver. He frowned.

"Truth gun," she said.

"You left the temple by a side entrance and crossed that busy street to disappear." Anjali's breath caught in her throat. She swallowed hard, and pretended to shoot the revolver at his head.

"You were the last bridesmaid to enter the dance at the wedding." Tears rolled easily down Locke's face. She shot again.

"The day you left me you told me your father had put a revolver in your hand, but you couldn't pull the trigger." Anjali didn't shoot again, but lowered her right arm to her side. The rain poured into their eyes, down their backs, they could taste it on their lips, but neither moved. Then Anjali offered her hand and Locke took it. He held both her hands and blinked away the rain. It was over. He pulled her close and their mouths touched. They kissed for the first time in months. It was brief, but enough. They broke off and held each other tight, neither daring to let go.

"Truth gun," she whispered.

"I remember," he said. Then the sobs engulfed them both.

eighteen
crimson red petals

"There is no way I am getting dressed up like some fucking clown!"

"Joe!" Daisy Locke shouted, exasperated. "You will not talk like that to Mr and Mrs Sharma!"

"I mean it," Joe insisted, "he was born an Anglican and he'll die an Anglican. How the hell can he be anything else? Of course, you can dress it up however you want, but he doesn't look Hindu, any more than I look Chinese."

"No one is telling you to be Indian," said Vijay Sharma. "You are dressing for the occasion, a one-day occasion for couples. You're still Anglican. We make sacrifices for our children. Isn't that what parenting is about?"

Vijay and Amita Sharma were not pleased. And neither was Daisy Locke. They all thought the issues had been resolved weeks ago, not during the wedding itself. And now Joe Locke was acting like this.

"Our religion is peaceful, Joe," Vijay said, trying again. "It's been there for thousands of years without alteration. It does not claim to be better than any other religion. It is not Islam and yours is not Catholicism. They both say there is one true God. Hinduism is not like that. There might be many gods, but we conceive in one and we choose one god. Why would God grant humans miracles or wishes?"

Joe Locke looked at his wife and the anger writ large on her face. He then looked at Amita Sharma and saw the hurt in her eyes. Vijay Sharma's hands were held out, palms up.

"*Hamsa* – it literally means 'five'," he said. "The number of fingers on a loving hand extending blessings of faith, hope, strength, peace and prosperity."

"Enough, Joe," Daisy Locke interjected, imploring her husband to stop. "Please understand." Joe ran a hand through his thinning hair. He struggled to come to terms with the fact that his son was marrying an Indian woman. Or was she British? He could never work it out. He often wondered why his son couldn't just get hitched to a normal American girl? Or a proper Brit? Why did everything have to be so damn complicated?

His son had tried telling him once, but it made no sense. Something to do with empire. He was just glad America had broken away in 1776. Whenever he looked at Britain he saw a country far behind the USA. You only had to look at the health service. Back home if they had done what they had done to John, giving him the wrong dose, he would have sued the ass off the hospital. It was against his better judgement that he did not sue the NHS. He knew he was being sold a pup when he was told that suing the NHS was just the same as taking money away from the general public, rather than some rich shareholders sitting in an air-conditioned office somewhere. It had yet to occur to him that his Anglican faith stemmed from Britain. The irony was he was arguing for his son's adopted country on the matter of religion.

John Locke sat smiling at his father's obvious discomfort.

"Try to get with the idea, Dad. I am with her no matter what. You saw the state I was in; I could barely could walk and didn't know who I was. It's not easy to encounter someone who would stand by you in your time of need." He held hands with Anjali. "There is always somebody wanting something from you; who wants to benefit from you and take everything from you after marriage breaks down. It's not like that here."

Anjali looked on with an air of resignation. She had known her future father-in-law would react as he had done. This was exactly what her parents were worried about and they warned her often enough, but Anjali thought she had everything under control. If only her parents could agree with the wedding first. Joe Locke just could not get away from the all-American boy image he had tried to raise both his sons to be. Joe Jr. fulfilled that and worked as an attorney in a San Francisco law firm not far from the family home in San Jose. John had never and could never be what his father wanted. But Joe Locke sent the checks just the same. John may have been something of a disappointment, flunking college and falling for someone who wasn't blonde, white and, most importantly, American, but he was still his son.

"What is the problem here?" Anjali said. "Everyone is getting what they desire; two weddings, two different ceremonies according to each tradition and legal philosophy." She tried to stay calm and lowered her voice. She smiled. "I thought we had an agreement?"

"Darling, we did," Joe Locke said. "It's just this last little bit. I mean a divorce settlement? A dowry? Jeez, this tradition still pays out?

You're selling her like she's property. I ain't comfortable with that. Look, I'm sorry. Please forgive me. I just struggle with all this."

"With what, Joe?" Anjali asked. "What is there to struggle with?"

Joe Locke knew he was being teased, but he couldn't help himself. "Look," he said, uncertainly, "I'm an engineer. A simple engineer who made good. I don't have an opinion on much and I don't do politics, but my son is something different. Although he's not turned out how I expected, I will defend my son to death."

"But I have the same intentions," Anjali argued. "What makes you believe the same girl in your race will hold out with John forever? You can't guarantee me that. The statistic of marriage divorce is through the roof in your culture, but I'm not saying my culture is any better. Marriage is a fragile balance between husband and wife. Some last forever. Others learn from their errors. At least I can distinguish through percentages and marriage in our culture lasts longer. Being worried or concerned is normal and I don't blame you, Joe. Have faith, I will love your son for all time. Don't judge someone by their looks, religion or culture. Judge them by what's in their hearts.

"Our wedding is not about religion; it is about relationships. It is about the love I have for your son and the love he has for me. It is about my love for your family and John's love for mine. This is not about celebrating the differences between us, but about celebrating the ways in which we are the same. We are two people who have fallen in love, that is all. We didn't plan this. There is someone far greater who plans our life and we recognise him as the Creator. Although I believe in *ardhangini,* John, perhaps, does not. He may one day, I do not know, but for now I honour his beliefs as he honours mine. I believe honouring or respecting someone has more value than someone who believes only in his religion. Why? You may ask, because they discover human beings for what they are. We are just two people who want to spend the rest of our Earthly lives together. I do not see what is so difficult for you."

Her father, Vijay, shot her a disapproving look, but Anjali was determined to convert her future father-in-law from an ignorant bigot to someone informed of her language, religion and culture. Amita Sharma and Daisy Locke were both secretly amazed by the speech Anjali had just given. She was clearly a very powerful young woman.

Joe wasn't bad, Anjali had decided. He just didn't know. She turned to her own father. "Father, you should also know better. Our generation is becoming worse. More and more marriages are collapsing.

Many in our society have less faith in marriage. Why do you think that is? It's because people like you who value money over marriage. I know you require security for your daughter. This is not the only way. If you trust in your God, then why don't you have faith in him that he will protect our marriage? If you desire to give me anything, Father, give me your blessing so I can become successful. Let me remind you, my love is not for sale. I am not for sale. So don't scale our love in weights. You will always lose."

"I think what Joe is saying is that he doesn't realise the kind of wedding you are to have." All eyes turned to Amita Sharma. "I think what Joe would like to know is that after the Hindu ceremony, there will be the Anglican ceremony."

"No Mother, that is not it," Anjali said, but her mother ignored her.

"I think Joe would like to know that there is not one single ceremony but two ceremonies that make one wedding. John and Anjali are not being married as Hindus or as Christians; they are getting married as Hindu *and* Christian."

"No Mother," Anjali tried again. "This is about the divorce settlement, the settlement fee, if the marriage breaks down. I will obtain an amount, but that money wouldn't give me life. I will still be deformed as it takes us years to recover from the emotional past. No sum of money can compensate that. Religion is not God; it's a custom we apply. Culture is not a religious belief; it's a man-made thing. This is why we agreed on a two-wedding ceremony. To keep respect amongst our culture."

"Fine," Amita said. "If you don't require the settlement fee, then we'll honour your wish, but bear in mind you will be on your own, should it take place." Vijay Sharma nodded at this. "So you see, Joe," Amita continued, "this is not about John becoming a Hindu, this is simply about John becoming a husband to our daughter. We will gain a son, and he has accepted our way of life, and you will gain a daughter who has accepted your way of life."

"This is an opportunity to break down barriers, not put them up," Vijay Sharma said, "And we are sorry for the lump sum we requested. It is a custom that happens in our culture, but since Anjali doesn't want her insurance we are happy to revoke it."

"Okay, okay," Joe said, finally sitting down next to his wife. "I get it." John Locke smiled to himself. He knew that his father did not get it at all. But he knew the man felt foolish and he would have to put on a front for the rest of the ceremony.

*

John Locke performed his duties perfectly. He read up on the Hindu wedding ceremony and clarified which parts were to take place as he married Anjali. He had to explain several times to his father that they constituted the *vara yatra;* the groom's party, but Joe Locke never quite grasped what he was being told. They arrived at the *mandap* that had been erected in the car park of the Shree Kutch Satsang Swaminarayan temple in Oldham and there saw his bride for the first time that day. When they left the *mandap,* they would be husband and wife. Locke smiled at the thought; he chose to wear traditional Hindu clothing for his wedding and most of the *vara yatra* did the same. His *sherwani* of silver and gold shimmered as he walked and he wore a *sehra,* although he did not cover his face with garlands as others might.

His brother, Joe Jr. smiled constantly as the party moved further inside the *mandap.* He too was in a *sherwani,* as was David, whose wife Hannah was with the bridal party. He could barely contain his excitement at the thought of seeing her in traditional Indian clothing. Hannah's friendship with Anjali had instilled in both of them a deep love of all things Indian. David's expanding waistline paid tribute to his love of curry.

Joe Locke, once again, was the noticeable exception, preferring a standard westerner's suit of pale linen. John had been on the verge of saying something but Anjali had stopped him with a stern look. Still, John approved for different reasons; it took him back to his own trip to India. Everything took him back to that trip to India where his future was confirmed. And he did like the outfit worn by Hannibal Lecter in *Silence of the Lambs;* the archetypal Englishman abroad. His father cut a strong figure.

The assorted guests marvelled at John, some cheered, others whistled as he led the way into the *mandap.* Vijay and Amita Sharma greeted him and others, perhaps aunts, uncles and cousins danced and gave offerings of *akshat* rice and placed *tilak* dots on the foreheads of each of the groom's wedding party. Joe Locke even managed to smile as the red dot was placed between his eyes. *It'll rub off later,* he thought.

He scanned the room and saw his wife Daisy immersed in dancing with a group of Indian women. His heart melted a little as he saw her so happy. She'd not even noticed the groom's party had arrived, she was having so much fun. He thought about to Joe Jr.'s wedding back home; it was a glorious occasion, but compared to this? A little staid.

With John now in the *mandap,* all attention turned to the bride as the priest performed the *grahashanti.* Anjali was to be walked to the altar by her uncle *Navjot* and, once the priest had completed his invocation of the nine planets, she began her slow deliberate walk towards her future husband. The assorted guests gasped at her beauty and John looked on approvingly as she flowed forwards in her red and gold wedding sari. Locke knew why she had chosen those colours and, he thought, she had never looked more beautiful. He held out his hand and she took it as she arrived.

"You look stunning," he whispered to her when he thought she looked slightly nervous. But she wasn't nervous and he had got it wrong. This wasn't a traditional arranged marriage, but to effect shyness was considered graceful. It was a jewel in her culture.

The *kanyadan* passed and so did the *hastamilap,* their hands now tied together by many strands of cloth, indicating that they were to be bound forever. Seated in front of the holy fire, the priest recited mantras from the Hindu scriptures, and John and Anjali walked four times around the fire exchanging the vows of duty, love, fidelity and respect.

Anjali recited her own mantras, but not for anyone else to hear; just for her own heart and soul.

Help me with this journey, God, as I don't know where it might lead me. How far will I be tested before I break? My faith is in your hands. Touching the dust of your feet. I embellish my forehead. I worship you. My vermillion and my bindia say that only one woman stays married among millions. Only a lucky few have stayed married forever. You served your husband like he was some kind of god. As a woman, I don't see any distinction between a daughter-in-law and your daughter. I saw your face and I knew my own God. My job is to make the world happy. Let your sadness go to sleep. Out of a million, only one wife is married forever. When you look in that mirror, the mirror tells me you're every woman's mirror. Your smile resembles a river.

Locke smiled at his bride. This was the best day of his life. He had no idea of the internal prayer she was repeating, but he did repeat the Hindu scripture. He did not care for God's vows nor did he understand the meaning, but he played his part to maintain respect and honour between the two families. Considering he was an atheist, it was not something he would ordinarily do, but one thing he understood was his love for Anjali.

With that the Hindu service ended and there was a brief break where refreshments were served, before the congregation was recalled an hour later. Anjali now wore a traditional white bridal gown to look the part. She had smiled when she had looked in the mirror. To her she was already married to John. To him, it was only half done.

John stood smiling with the Anglican bishop, a cheerful-looking older man dressed in a white surplice with an emerald green sash. His brother Joe Jr. stood to John's right. Both the Locke brothers still wore their Indian *sherwanis* as neither felt the need to change. Locke's heart surged when he saw Anjali now transformed into a western bride in white. She walked towards him, slowly and gracefully, her father Vijay gently holding his daughter by the arm. After the usual gasps and clicking of cameras, the congregation settled down as the bishop began the Anglican part of the ceremony.

"Dearly beloved," he said as he made his way through the wedding vows undertaken by John and Anjali. Joe Locke had flown the Anglican bishop from San Jose to Manchester to make sure his own religion was properly represented at the ceremony. Bishop Arthur Hobbs-Browne seemed much more at ease with the wedding than Joe though, and his benevolent smile radiated warmth and love upon the young couple before him.

The ceremony had been agreed in advance. Once the couple had exchanged rings in the Anglican ceremony, the Hindu priest returned to oversee the *saptapadi*. After another short break John and Anjali recited the seven vows that would sanctify the marriage. A great cheer arose from the congregation as they were married. Rice was thrown and John Locke was finally allowed to kiss his bride.

*

"You've done all right there, little bro'," Joe Jr. said approvingly. The celebrations had moved on to a plush hotel on the outskirts of Manchester, the wedding breakfast taking place in the opulent ballroom. The dancing had followed a fabulous feast and continued long into the night. Only now was it beginning to wind down.

"You're not wrong," David added as the three men watched their women dance. The music had been a mixture of modern western tracks and Indian music. Towards the end of the night traditional Indian songs had been set to a western beat. Only the hardcore remained.

"She's amazing," Locke said. It was a statement, not an assertion. "And she is mine forever."

David looked across at Joe Jr. Both were surprised by John's comment. Possession sounded sinister. "I don't know about that, mate," David offered. "Hannah is my wife, but she's not *mine*."

Locke turned to look at his friend and smiled. "You're right," he said. "Absolutely right; a slip of the tongue. She is the most beautiful thing in the world, you will allow me. I have proof in that photograph on my wall you have both seen. But you see in Hinduism, in traditional Hindu marriages, the man owns the woman. Something like you're a god for her, and she may worship me, but I'm not a god. I do not believe that, of course, but it is written in the sacred texts. Go look it up." He downed the remnants of his beer and placed the empty bottle on the bar. Joe Jr. and David watched as Locke walked towards the remaining women on the dancefloor.

"Not sure I like what I just heard," David said as the two men watched on. "Doesn't sit right today."

Joe Jr. thought about his own wife, also dancing with the Anjali, Hannah and the rest of the women on the stage. "I'd have to agree," he said.

*

John and Anjali were to spend the first night of their married lives in the Lowry Hotel, just the wrong side of the River Irwell from Manchester. As the crow flew, they were barely a mile or more from the flat they shared in Castlefield, but they agreed, in fact Anjali positively pushed for it, to spend their first night as a married couple in the splendour of Greater Manchester's best hotel. Joe Locke had paid for it.

The limousine slowly approached the hotel entrance and a concierge hurried down the steps to open the vehicle's rear door. Locke stepped out first and turned back to his bride, holding out his hand for her to take as she exited the Lincoln Stretch. They were shown to their room and Locke tipped the porter as he closed the door behind him. The room was dimly lit; as per instructions that had been left with reception. Stark on the white linen of the bedding were crimson red petals placed in the shape of a Cupid's heart. Anjali smiled and turned towards Locke to show him. But he ignored her, instead rushing forward to kiss her forcibly on the lips. Since he had regained his memory and proved it via the truth gun, they had returned to their previous sex life and made love as often as they wanted to.

"You know how our wedding night would have been if we hadn't met or made love before we got married?" Anjali had pulled away and sat on the bed.

"Like what?"

"I would have sat down like a bride and you would have seen me for the first time. I would give you a glass of milk and we would speak all night long knowing each other until dawn. This is the dream every Indian girl has for her wedding."

The night suddenly felt hot, the atmosphere heavy and Locke was sweating. Anjali opened the windows of the hotel to bring in some air, then returned to the bed. He sat beside her.

"One day I will buy you the whole world," he said. "Someday I'll buy you a luxurious house with everything in it. I just need to figure out how. But I will."

"What am I going to do with all worldly things?" Anjali said.

"If you live on Earth, you require the things of the world." Locke touched her hand and stroked it gently. "Make a list of your desires and each year we will purchase something for our home."

"Listen, John, we don't appreciate Life's happiness through mundane things. We don't value things like love does. Value through your heart, like love does. The happiness of a man and a woman lies in the love of others, not with material things."

"But this is our life on Earth, Anjali. That is why we need things. But to get these things you need luck as well."

"With luck, you need money too," countered Anjali. "No matter what you have in life, if you think it's hell, it turns into hell. If you think it's paradise, it's paradise. The finest water we use each day. It's the same water people take out of the river. That is our mindset. The air emanating from the fan is the same tune that God gives naturally through our window. By the end of today it's a matter of sleeping or spending the night together."

"Will you pamper me?" Locke said. Anjali sighed.

"Let me show you the real world," she said and led Locke by the hand to the open window. "How do people live in this world? There. Look at that pair down there, asleep underneath the building. They are people, too. Whether the day is hot, cold, windy or rainy, that is their home. That is their bedroom and that building is a shelter for them. That woman the air for him. If you want to make yourself happy, John, don't look at someone above you; watch someone beneath you and you will see the beauty of life."

Locke continued to look at the two homeless people holding each other tight in the car park under the building across the river. It was a life he did not appreciate and he did not want to have to consider their plight on his wedding night.

"Let me kiss those lips," he said instead, turning to look at his bride. "This is not my desire, but my heart talking."

"Behave yourself!" Anjali half joked. Locke had always been an attentive lover before the attack and his subsequent episode; now he had changed a little. She noticed it each time and sometimes he got a bit close to the edge. The kindness and attentiveness had gone. He was more mysterious and dominant. She believed his passion had been unleashed by his treatment and, if she was honest, it was exciting.

She fought for breath as Locke continued to kiss her. It was rougher than normal, but then he had had a beer or three at the wedding, not that he was drunk. Emboldened, maybe, but not drunk.

"Wow," she said, panting as they parted. "Someone's eager."

Locke stared at Anjali. She was incredibly beautiful, but that was not what he was thinking at that moment. He meant to have her. He pushed her backwards hard; her legs hitting the frame of the bed causing her to fall. The Cupid's heart was no more as the petals were crushed and dispersed. Locke straddled Anjali, who felt fear as he stared down at her. It was like he was a different person, one with dark thoughts on his mind, rather than love. He bent forward and kissed her forcefully again.

How beautiful you were, she thought. *Give me a chance to come to you. That is all I'm asking. The colour of you has changed. The circumstances and the situation have changed. I can see the beauty inside you. There was something innocent in you. You were the only thing I desired. I could feel the rhythm of music when you touched my body. I thought of you as an idol. There was love for you in my heart. You felt like the perfume in my hair. There was love in your eyes. How beautiful you were...*

She didn't resist. The champagne remained on ice. Long after Locke had fallen asleep, Anjali remained wide awake. They had not made love like that before. He had been much more forceful than normal. The more she thought about it, the more the night had turned into a nightmare. She lay still. She wondered what had just happened. She felt like a dead corpse.

part iii

zoë

nineteen
the pressure on his brain
2009

"It was the best day of our lives. At least it was until Sachin arrived and topped it. You were so thrilled that day and everyone said so. I was so proud to have you as my husband, but the thing that many seemed not to notice was how much *I* was also thrilled. It was the happiest day of my life to finally marry you."

Anjali turned the page and more radiant images spoke of a time long since gone. Bright outfits and brighter smiles paid testimony to a day that looked so wonderful. To Locke, none of it meant anything at all, but Anjali was a woman who believed that marriage was meant to be hard sometimes and that everything should be done before that life was abandoned.

"You looked incredible in your *sherwani*. You all did. Even your father, although he refused to wear one. It makes me laugh to think of the *tilak* on his forehead. He was uncomfortable at first, but your mother and brother had a wonderful time and eventually your father settled."

She flicked slowly through the pages of gaiety and happy people, of two religions and two peoples coming together to celebrate the lives of two lovers married. She lingered on the last image in the photo album. Anjali and Locke shared a kiss, the photographer expertly capturing the moment and blurring slightly all those who bore witness to it into the background. The assorted shades of saris and *sherwanis* became a riotous kaleidoscope of colourful joy.

She looked at her husband, searching his features for any semblance of recognition. All he could see was the woman telling him stories, but his mind couldn't connect with her memories. Locke closed his eyes and slowly shook his head. Anjali gently placed the book down on the coffee table and reached for another album. He caught her arm and she pulled away. *Life shouldn't be this complicated,* Anjali thought bitterly.

"I was going to show you the pictures you took at Hannah and David's wedding…"

"I know you were. It's just not working. I'm sorry, but my head hurts. I'm trying, I really am, but..." Locke looked back at the beautiful woman sat beside him, "there's nothing."

Her family had told her to let Locke go, that he would find his own way one day. But the idea of not knowing where he was or what he was doing was what haunted her the most. What if he was hurt, or someone took advantage of his vulnerability? It wasn't in her nature to walk away. She looked into the furthest corner of the room and he knew tears were forming in her eyes. They had done this so many times before and it never got easier. He tried to feel compassion for her and he genuinely felt sorrow, but she was a stranger to him, despite all the evidence she put in front of him.

"I'm sorry."

Anjali rose from the chair and looked down at her husband. She saw the concern etched on his face; it was always there when she tried to jog his memory. She did everything she could to trigger a response, but nothing worked; not old television programmes or the music he once liked, nor places or events he had been to or witnessed. Not even his own wedding album. And as the worry manifested in his furrowed brow, she felt the tightness in her throat as she tried to keep her composure. It wasn't his fault any more than it was hers. She saw the love of her life as though he was hidden behind tinted glass. It was John, but it wasn't. As long as he couldn't remember, she knew she couldn't see him clearly. To her, suddenly, he was just a man in a body and he had neither personality nor identity. She continued with the mundane daily charade and went to boil the kettle.

Locke watched after Anjali as she went into the kitchen. *If all this is true, why can't I identify my love for her? Is there more to it?* He looked back at the large photograph he had apparently taken of her in a Hindu temple. She told him that he had taken the picture while he was travelling in India and she was visiting relatives. It had been a chance encounter, but they had met again on the flight back to England and once more in Manchester. It was why Anjali insisted on saying they were meant to be; that they were something called *ardhangini*. She had explained it many times, not that she needed to. He understood what she meant; it was just remembering his past he couldn't do. *Why can't I rediscover myself?* Locke felt the bitter thrust of anger rise in his throat, the frustration shaking within his whole.

She had told him how he had had the photo blown up and framed on his wall for months before fate once again brought them together and she first went back to his flat with him. He had forgotten about the picture hanging; apparently his face was its own picture when he found her looking up at it that first time. Luckily she hadn't run away, but at the time she couldn't decide whether she should have felt flattered or scared.

Luckily? Was that a recognition? Or just his own mind rehashing what Anjali had told him? It didn't matter. His headache was worsening and he was tired. He admired this woman as she continually insisted that, as his wife, she would remain beside him for the rest of her life. But it was suffocating. He wanted to break out of the apartment and get away from the woman who claimed to be his wife. She barely let him out of her sight and he struggled with that. He felt constrained, like a prisoner, with her constant watching over him. Worse, he sometimes felt like a toddler, with an over-fussing mother watching for some inevitable fall. He understood why, but it didn't sit well with him. He stared again at the picture. It was beautiful and the woman in it certainly was. But he felt nothing for it. It was just a picture. Life seemed to be taking a different turn.

"You nearly broke your foot over that," Anjali said trying for an air of normality, of humour even. "I split up with you at Piccadilly station in town. We were due to run away, but my parents found out and stopped me. You put your foot through that picture and kicked the wall behind it. You can still see the tear where I fixed it with tape. You were lucky you weren't arrested, or so I was told."

Anjali smiled at Locke and placed the cups of coffee on the table.

"It wasn't my finest hour," she said, "but we got through it and this is where we are."

The silence lasted longer than was comfortable. Anjali shuffled slightly, her red chiffon sari, the one she wore constantly in a bid to jog his memory, rustled as she did so. Locke didn't move. Life was a distant memory to him.

"Do you want to watch a Sharpe?" she asked finally. "Or a Men Behaving Badly? You loved watching both of them. You were so excited when they brought Sharpe back for a couple of episodes and found out it was filmed in India. I don't know how many times you watched it once you managed to record it. Then you relapsed and I nursed you the first time. I bought the DVD and played it to you as often as I could. You didn't seem to mind. Your memory had returned by the time they brought out the second of the India Sharpe stories. You watched that constantly as well. Do you want to watch—"

"Stop!"

The air left Anjali. Locke raised his hand in apology.

"I'm sorry," he said. "I didn't mean to shout. It's just..."

"I know," Anjali muttered, looking down at the floor.

"But that's it," Locke said. "You don't. You have no idea. There is nothing. I am trying and trying to remember but there is nothing."

He turned to look at Anjali and took her hand in his. She didn't reciprocate; her hand remaining limp as he squeezed it. She knew this moment too well. It was the only physical contact they ever had since his second amnesic episode.

"I know why you are doing this and I thank you for it. But I cannot remember any of it. That is all there is to it. I am not being obnoxious, or awkward. I just cannot remember. It's getting so I know what you are going to say and it's getting harder to take. You talk about photos and how wonderful it all was. I can see it's a fucking photo and I can see that I am in it! But an image is just an image; it's not a human feeling. Until I regain my feeling, my appreciation, my identity, you're just an outsider to me. There's something beyond my body that my spirit wants. I have to find myself or find someone. Without loss, we never appreciate what we have."

Anjali pulled her hand away. Locke breathed deeply.

"Look, I know you are trying, but it isn't working. You're no doctor or psychiatrist and I'm not some dumb child, so please stop trying. I can see you are my wife from the pictures. I can see the people who say they are my parents and I know how I got into this state. I see that little boy you call our son."

"He is our son!"

Locke raised his hands in surrender. "I know. You have said it so many times. And he is wonderful. I just—"

"Don't say it..."

"I just don't feel anything. For any of you. I want to but I can't. You cannot force love. With money you can buy houses, cars or land. You can buy any amount of luxury goods, but you can't buy emotions. That is why love is free will."

Anjali's hands were clasped in her lap, her knuckles white. She felt she had failed as a wife, that she had failed in God's eye. She looked up at the ceiling to stop tears from once more forming. *Why me?* The voice echoed through her mind as she fought to keep control. *What have I done, God, that you make me cry? Don't leave my life in tears, the life you gave me is dying.*

"Marriage is a struggle, circumstances change," she whispered. Locke looked hard at her and she stared back. "What's the truth and what's false? Tell me God. Let the world know. Don't let your worshipper perish. This is my test to see how much I can take. Whether I can resist the struggle or fight it. If I've done anything wrong, tell me or test me, or take away the stain of this pain. What is your decision, my creator? For once, come to Earth and share it with the world. We are told it is you who does justice to everyone. Share your knowledge with us."

Locke watched on, blank. This was new. Anjali's new god seemed much bigger than his depression, worries, anxiety and anger. And it was much bigger than their pain. He realised once again that every step was a test for her as well.

For an instant, one tiny pinprick in time, she began to believe the moment had come to let him go. She shook the thought away and picked up the remote, pointing it at the television. The opening titles rolled and she wondered again why the DVD still worked. She had put it on what seemed like hundreds of times.

Locke shrunk back into his seat and sighed. The familiar music played and Sean Bean's haggard face appeared. She may have been right; he may have loved Sharpe once. But not anymore. Putting it on now was a form of torture. He stared at the screen, but didn't watch. Instead he thought and tried to make sense of what was happening. What was the connection between the brain, memory and soul that she was desperately trying to regain? What was it that identified the individual? If it was personality, Locke's made him feel dead inside.

They sat in silence for an interminable length of time. The sounds of gunfire and deceit echoing from the television. Anjali had remained alert in her seat, Locke now slouched. Outside a wet Manchester afternoon in mid-January blanketed. The sky darkened noticeably, shadowing the room. Christmas had been and gone. The gloom pervaded the atmosphere and Locke began to feel cold. And distant. He noticed goose pimples on Anjali's arms and his heart ached to be able to take her out of her suffering.

"You once said she reminded you of me." A beautiful Indian princess had appeared on screen. Locke grunted.

"I've never said you are not beautiful."

"She is beautiful," Anjali persisted. "You always said she had such grace and you loved the clothes she wore in this."

"I know. You tell me every time you put this shit on." Irritation, frustration, anger all grew the more she reminded him of his past, and he was starting to resent her.

"Please John. Don't get angry." Locke leant forward and picked up his cup of coffee. He'd not touched it yet and it was going cold. But he needed something to do, anything to break out from the constantly repeated scene the two of them were playing out. He took a mouthful, and felt colder still.

"You said—"

Locke hurled the mug of coffee across the room towards the image of Anjali in the temple. He narrowly missed but cold coffee had gone everywhere: the floor, the sofa, on his forearm. The mug shattered on impact with the wall and fell in a dozen or more pieces to the floor. He had wanted to throw the coffee in her face but resisted the temptation.

"I'm not a fucking lap dog!" he yelled.

Anjali screamed and leapt up, running towards the door to the spare bedroom where she now slept, and closed it behind her. She leant against it, feeling its protection, but she couldn't stop the sobs and they always came. The doctors, *the fucking doctors,* had told her to keep trying to jog John's memory and always she tried. And always it ended like this. Should she give up? Did she even like her husband now, let alone love him? She slammed the palm of her hand against the door and prayed. It was the darkest moment of her life but she knew she had more to come. She was being tested and it was the hardest thing she had ever had to do.

"*Raatein dhalati nahi,*

"*Din bhi niklta nahi,*

"*Usaki marzi bina patta hilta nahi,*

"*Rab jo chaahe wahi toh hona hai.*

"The day doesn't become the night,

"The day has not passed,

"Without God's promise no leaves turn,

"Only that which God desires shall come to pass."

Her eyes had been screwed tight as she prayed, her forehead pressed hard against the door.

"Every one of us is a puppet to God," she said aloud, trying to convince herself she was right. "Life is a play and we're the characters in it from the moment the curtain opens to the moment it closes again. We salute ourselves with greetings. We are the players in that life. The audience sometimes cheers, sometimes boos because in the play we are the good or the bad and we put our names at risk. Life is a stage play for us. But what is true? Don't ask me. Humans are fake. Nobody knows. No one recognises us. We create situations like this. We are the protagonists in this life."

Anjali opened her eyes and they slowly adjusted to the white paint of the door an inch away. "He gave me a place to live. At that house, he gave me love. As a blessing he gave me a happy family. Live your life with each smile. Because tomorrow, no one knows what will happen in the future. Let each dream count."

Locke had not tried to come in. He had once and his face had crumpled when he saw what he had reduced her to. He had not come in since.

She knew his life was a living hell, but so was hers. It was like living with a stranger from the street, rather than her own husband.

Locke sat forward on the sofa and put his face in his hands. He felt so weak and so utterly impotent about everything. It wasn't fair. All he knew was what Anjali had told him. Repeatedly. He wanted to end it all, to get away and to not have the constant reminders of what he was meant to have done once upon time. He wanted a new beginning and to forget his past, to be a person he could define as his own; he wanted a new identity. He dug his fingers into his eyes, as hard as he dare, and screamed. It was loud, almost psychotic, and he screamed again. Anjali heard him from the other room. This time it was quieter. He banged his fist down onto his own leg and felt the pain rise. His voice cracked and at that moment, he felt totally alone as he tried to release the anger inside and the pressure on his brain. His head pulsed with the stress, causing him to rock back and forth on the sofa.

The life that apparently once teamed with joy felt dead. Slowly his breathing calmed and he took his hands away from his face. In the other room Anjali wept quietly, but he could still hear her. He looked across at the picture of her in the temple and at the splatter of coffee where the mug had hit home. Either side of the temple picture was another; to the left a black and white photograph of Locke holding a baby Sachin whilst Anjali had an arm around them both. All three were smiling at the camera and it was a stunning photograph. But it wasn't so much as a distant memory to him. To the right of India was a newer monochrome picture of Sachin. He looked every inch a happy three-year-old as he held on to a favourite cuddly toy tiger, beaming up at the photographer. *Life wants you elsewhere, John. It wants you away from here.*

"I want to be there too," Locke replied to his own thoughts.

There was barely light enough in the room for him to distinguish the features in the photographs, but he knew them by heart. And it crushed him every time he looked into that little boy's deep brown eyes. He clenched his jaw and fought back the tears that tried to come. He was dead inside and knew he could no longer be that guy. He decided he wasn't going to wait to find out.

Locke stood up and felt for his wallet in one jeans pocket and his phone in the other. He took out his phone and dropped it gently on the sofa, giving the room one last glance. *If what they say about love is true, perhaps I'll find my way back one day?* By the front door he picked up his keys to the flat and looked at them for a moment. He didn't need them where he was going, so he put them back on the rack. Wrapped up in his heavy-duty coat, he took a last look back along the corridor to the living room. He could no longer hear Anjali, but he felt for her and hoped she could feel his remorse as well as his pain. Quietly he closed the door behind him and walked out into the Manchester rain. He looked back at the building as if someone was calling his name. He had heard someone say, perhaps in a film, that if you looked back as you walked away, then you were sure to return. He knew he wasn't going far, but he wasn't going to be found either.

He sensed the weight lift the moment the first cold, fat raindrop hit his face. *This is a new destination; an unknown destination.* The thought shook him slightly, or was it the cold air that made him shiver?

"I'm free," Locke said to himself.

twenty

a single muffled word

John Locke turned back to the canvas and applied a little yellow. Then he added some paint mixed with glitter and placed it on canvas. He felt satisfaction and allowed himself a little grin. He loved how something was transformed by a lighter shade, how layer upon layer turned a two-dimensional entity into a living, almost breathing, thing as height and gradient and carefully placed shadow turned the image into something that seemingly moved when looked at from different angles, as though it was trying to escape from the picture and become *real*. Only painting gave him memories now. He lost himself in the composition and the pangs in his heart lessened as the memory of the day he walked away faded to almost nothing. Now the subconscious mind brought him a new release in Life.

He no longer thought of his previous life. He had somehow managed to shut it off. The human spirit is a powerful thing that enables us to see only what we want to see. It helps us find out what we expect from life and our hearts are primarily responsible for these actions. It had not been easy, but for a while he had dwelt on what had happened that last day in his old apartment, not that he had been a full participant in his old life. Walking out had been the best thing he could have done. The people calling themselves his parents, and he had no reason to disbelieve them, paid for his new flat. He felt nothing for them, but thanked them and viewed them as if they were kind Samaritans.

The flat was in one of the non-descript new apartment blocks on the Salford side of the River Irwell. His view across the river gave the impression of a canyon between neighbours as he felt that he could almost touch those living in the older, red-brick edifice that stood in Manchester on the opposing south bank. Whilst his building was all glass-fronted balconies and light-swathed rooms, the red-brick building harked back to an industrial age where the river gently lapped at its skirts. Locke could imagine the swarm of small boats crowding a polluted Irwell in days gone by, bringing or removing goods for distribution across the country and perhaps beyond. A hundred years ago? Two? The images in his head were fascinating to him; of Empire and England being the centre of the known world. He had no idea why the subject interested him so much, but it did.

He had been told he was American, and he knew he spoke with a West Coast accent, but again, no memories of a formative life over there, just an interest in all things English. Someone had tried to explain, but it hadn't helped.

When he first entered the apartment he found a book on the kitchen table about Michelangelo's artistic canon. It had been left by the previous tenant and it felt like a sign. Almost immediately images started to form in his mind and he realised he had found something to keep him busy. It turned out the former tenant had been an artist and with a knowing nod he appreciated the quiet resonance in the room. With the estate agent trying to look interested, Locke had walked towards the balcony and opened the doors. The wind rushed in, warming his face and blowing his hair. He breathed deeply letting the moment wash over him. "I'll take it," he had said.

The picture was coming along, and he was actually rather proud of himself. It depicted the inside of a temple, Hindu, he thought, and showed a woman deep in worship to a shrine set against a wall. The way he had painted light streaming in from a hidden window drew the viewer to the deep and stunning yellow of the woman's sari. He called the shade 'buttercup' for it fairly shimmered with gold and silver as he passed his paintbrush over the canvas, accentuating curves and ripples in what was unmistakeably silk.

The woman radiated beauty. Her arms were slightly raised and her wrists he had captured in the moment of prayer, as if she was dancing before her God. Or Gods. He had not bothered to look up the Hindu religion; he just remembered checking once early on in his painting career. He laughed when the word 'career' entered his head. He hadn't gone to night school, or tried to get enlisted in an art college; for Locke, painting was a way of escaping the outside world. For a long time it didn't occur to him that what he was producing was actually any good. It didn't matter; what he was painting he was sure came from some kind of memory.

When he closed his eyes to breathe the air of Salford, images of ethnic beauty flashed through his mind. He was captivated by the beauty of his muse, by her hair, her face and her jewellery, as if she was calling him. But he didn't know who she was or what she meant to him. But she remained. She was like a supernova or a blossoming flower, or a dream turned into a poem. She was like the early morning sun or the night of the full moon. She had a graceful smile and a shyness. She was like a lamp in the temple. But why did he think that?

He didn't know why, but only when the brush scraped, leaving an expertly delivered new shade of paint, did he feel truly alive. The woman in the painting seemed to speak to him on occasion and he wondered whether there was someone like this, a woman worthy of his worship as she worshipped her Gods. He knew he was engaging in fantasy, and continued to paint.

He stood at his easel for hours as it was the only thing he liked doing. He didn't enjoy going out and tended to pull up the collar of his coat when he left his flat, wearing sunglasses the moment he left the main entrance and walked out into the Salford throng. Within a short walk there were all the mini supermarkets he ever needed. And there was an arts and crafts shop nearby where he got most of his materials. The rest he ordered in with his computer. Nothing else held an interest for him and he had the luxury, for which he was truly grateful, that his apparent parents turned out to be very wealthy and kept his current account well stocked with all the money he needed. He didn't take advantage. Beyond his art materials, his diet was simple and he wasn't a big eater. He made sure the ingredients were fresh, and cooked the food himself, if only to give a little necessary respite from the incessant painting. An hour was all he needed to make and eat a lonely meal, then it was back to his brushes, where he no longer felt alone.

Initially he was afraid of introducing himself to society because of his amnesia, and he often questioned what people might say or do. He had been afraid that people would take advantage of him or worse, pity him. The outside world was so cruel and indecisive. But as time passed, those thoughts lessened. He began to think less of society and more about himself, often questioning who he was or what was his life purpose would be.

Silence came back at him.

He was no longer interested in the television or what happened around the world. He kept his radio on low, just to take the edge off the silence, but he never listened to it. He just didn't want his apartment to feel empty. Sometimes he heard the echoes as he moved through the rooms. That made him feel alone. Occasionally scared.

*

He sat on the sofa in the flat's open plan kitchen/ living room area and gazed deeply at his painting. It wasn't small, three foot by six, and it dominated the corner between one wall and the glass doors that led out onto his balcony. Every day felt new, he saw the seasons unfold in front of his eyes. The wind came and knocked on his door. And he welcomed the wind as if it brought news or letters. The light was fading; his room descending into a dim, warm quality whilst the setting sun emblazoned the building opposite into the most incredible oranges and reds. Later still that building would glow almost purple as the final rays disappeared beneath the horizon. He marvelled at the phenomena; mixing paints creating myriad colours was a passion for him, which he felt amplified his mind.

Locke loved his latest painting. It wasn't quite finished, but it was almost there. It was the best one yet; he felt as though he could sense the feelings the woman had in her own mind as she silently recanted her prayers to the shrine. He was forever just on the edge of the words coming, as if he removed some headphones and the sound of outside world would pour in. But it never quite came.

He looked at the other paintings he had done, most of the same scene, all of the same woman praying to her God. He had named the series of pictures inside the temple *'Wisdom of God'*, and always thought he sounded fucking pretentious when he uttered the title out loud. The other paintings he was not so fond of, but he recognised them for what they were; his development as an artist.

Initially he had painted scenes of outside the temple, others where the emphasis, or at least some of it, was on the jewellery worn by some Asian women. Another depicted a woman with her sari flowing in the wind and, when he studied it, he marvelled at the details he had captured; her face beautiful, eyes the colour of onyx and her mouth deep red. Her nose, ears and neckline glistened with jewellery. All of his paintings he felt were striking and, with the earlier ones, the more he paid attention to them, the more details he had added.

But it was the *Wisdom of God* series that he liked most of all. They were all of much the same scene, but to him they were markedly different. He could see where each had an altered tone in the dress, his muse's skin, or her hair, even the dust motes spiralling in the ray of light from the hidden window. It was all there and Locke didn't give it a thought. Or, rather, he gave only as much thought as each painting demanded until he moved onto the next. There was no one professional to appreciate his work, but he knew that with each incarnation of the same image, he was getting closer to hearing for the first time. What he was to hear he didn't know, but he was sure that one day he would get so good that his paintings would talk back to him. Each version had improved him as an artist and each had built on the last. One day, he was certain, a painting would speak to him. And he knew it was the only way that he would ever regain his memory and with that came his former life.

He looked back at the current version and was instinctively stunned at how he had got so much more depth in this version than even the canvas he had finished last month.

Did something flicker? He peered more closely, slowly got to his feet and walked purposely towards the easel. His heart rate increased and his breath became shallow as he strode forward, never taking his eyes off the woman in the picture, seemingly swaying in her buttercup sari and with her twisting hands. *Twisting.* Locke's eyes widened. Did the painting move?

A voice seemed to emanate from the painting. *Who are you looking for? What do your eyes want? I'm standing right here. Your search for me above and below. But you didn't search for me where I really was. You didn't look into your heart yet. You're going through all the wrong places. I'm right here with you. I dance in accordance with your orders. I break all traditions and come to you alone. You're the story of my life and I'm the story of yours. More than beauty, personality is a deeper skin than genuine beauty. Break that tradition up in front of me. I'm standing right here. And you don't even know who I am. Memory triggered by scent are much stronger than memories triggered by any other sense.*

His brain felt slack and tired and he looked at his watch, convinced it must be late. The light in northern English latitudes could last until almost midnight in summertime. But it was now early September and the sun had gone down. It was just past eight and it was dusk outside. He looked back at the painting and gasped as a sound formed in his head. Had he imagined it or had he actually heard a word as if spoken by someone? *As if the woman in the painting had spoken to him.* He scrunched his eyes tight closed and heard the blood rushing through his ears. He opened his eyelids once more and heard it again, not that he believed it. A single muffled word, but becoming clearer. It *was* coming from the painting, and he was as sure of it as much as he was sure no-one else would ever hear it. There it was again, becoming more frequent, more intense, more *insistent*.

Locke closed his eyes against the dim light, covering his ears with his hands to block out all excess noise. The sound intensified. An infectious laughter amongst the white noise as the word became clearer. His eyes snapped open.

"India," he gasped, and felt a tear prick at the corner of an eye as he realised he had finally remembered something.

twenty-one

am I getting close?

Locke liked this pub. It wasn't the nearest to his flat, nor was it the most salubrious, but he had found it soon after he had left home and the woman claiming to be his wife. Two things had caught his attention when he had first walked in: the paintings on the walls that showed images of old battles and regiments, which was probably why the pub was called the Briton's Protection, and the second thing had been the landlady seemed to recognise him. He couldn't cope with the same thing happening day after day after day with the woman who said she was his wife, but he liked the idea that he might have been inside this pub before and that it might jog the odd memory without anyone pestering him all the time.

He ordered a lager and a whisky; the pub had seemingly hundreds of different bottles of the latter and all were listed in a menu he liked to peruse, and went into the room at the back with its depictions of the British soldiers of yore. He liked the mounted sabre-rattler in one of the paintings and studied it closely as he did every time he came into the pub. He put the whisky on a table next to him and took a large gulp of the ale as he admired the look of fury on the horse rider's face.

"You know what that represents, don't you?"

Locke turned to his right and found a pretty brunette woman standing beside him. He had not noticed her arrive. Now he couldn't help but notice her with her bright blue eyes and perfect smile.

"No, I don't believe I do," he replied.

"It's some artist's impression of a scene from the Peterloo Massacre. It happened near here a couple of hundred years ago." The words meant nothing to him. "It's a very important part of Mancunian history. I can tell you about it, if you like?"

There was something about the suggestion that appealed to Locke. And it had been a long time since he had spoken to anyone. He hadn't been looking for company and he rarely found it when he went to the Briton's Protection, but on this occasion the idea of someone to talk to suited his mood. He saw the empty glass the woman was none-too-subtly waving in front of him and understood. She smiled and sat down at the table where his whisky waited, while he went to the bar. His evening had just improved.

*

He soon found out her name was Zoë Lawrence and she worked as a receptionist in a private dental practice in Manchester. *That explains the perfect teeth,* he thought idly as she talked enough for both of them. At first she explained about the Peterloo Massacre and why it was important in the history of the city he lived in, then she moved on to her own interests. Art was very high up the list and a good friend of hers apparently ran a gallery in the city centre, which she said, Locke just had to go and visit. He agreed that he would, saying he liked a bit of art himself.

But he didn't mention his own pictures and whilst Zoë continued he wondered why he hadn't. He wasn't sure how he may sound in front of this stunning blue-eyed woman. It occurred to him that he was attracted to her and that wasn't a sensation he had had for as long as he could remember. She just seemed... *right*. He raised his eyebrows a little as he gave Zoë a second, deeper look.

"I've never seen you in here before," Locke said as he returned to the table carrying another Sauvignon Blanc and a Highland Park double measure for himself.

"Oh, I've been in before, but usually with a group of my mates," Zoë replied, effecting indifference. "If I'm being totally honest, I find it a bit drab, but the boys like to start their pub crawls here, so I just tag along."

"Are they here tonight?"

"On a Monday? God, no! We've all grown out of that," she said, taking a sip of her wine. "No, my confession is that I saw you walk in and decided I should talk to you. There is something interesting about you. I'm getting a vibe and my curiosity got the better of me." She saw the surprise in his face and smiled. "You might not have seen me in here before, John Locke, but I have seen you. Twice in fact. You've been alone both times, ordered a lager and a whisky each time and spent however long looking at that painting each time. Are you lost?"

"It's complicated," John smiled. "I don't want to bore you."

"It's the last bit that made me follow you in when I saw you arrive earlier," Zoë continued, ignoring Locke's remark. "I'd never normally come in here on my own."

"So you followed me?"

"No, but I saw you cross the road just ahead of me and decided this was the time."

"Time for what?" he asked as he took a sip of the fiery whisky. How he loved that sensation.

"To introduce myself. You seem nice, so I thought I'd say hello. I also thought you may not notice me; you always look so lost."

"I would have noticed you, if I had been looking for someone. But you've never spoken to me before, so why do you think I'm nice?"

"Maybe not nice," Zoë mused. "Maybe I meant to say interesting, as if you have the weight of the world on your shoulders. Are you saying you're not nice?" her eyes widened and Locke saw the mischievous smile appearing at the corners of her mouth. "I can read people sometimes. I don't get it right all the time, but there are few where I am wrong."

"People can be judgemental," Locke said quietly. "I didn't want to give wrong impression. I'm all right, I think. Maybe a bit complicated."

"Complicated? I can live with that. So I think it's time we had dinner, don't you? If I have another large wine on an empty stomach, I'll be anybody's."

Locke laughed. Her personality shined. It might have been the whisky dulling the edges of his own senses, but this beautiful little woman now had his full attention. He felt a sensation in his groin and decided he would play along. It was a sensation he hadn't felt for a long time. It didn't matter if she turned out to be a disappointment; right now he liked the idea of her company and if it led anywhere, he was fine with that too.

*

Zoë suggested a Japanese restaurant down a side street off Deansgate. Locke had never been before and they marvelled as a chef played with an egg, spinning it with a spatula then flinging it skywards and catching it in the chef's hat he was wearing. They laughed when he missed and one of the diners took offence at raw egg splattering her ankle.

"Bit of a bitch," Zoë said as they watched on. The woman's protestations were excessive, but she calmed down a bit when the head waiter waived the bill. The chef wasn't happy. "So, what's your story, then, John Locke? You've not told me anything yet and all I have so far is your accent. American? Canadian?"

"You would run a mile if you heard my life story."

"Try me," she said. "I've heard it all."

Locke took a bite of his prawn tempura and used the time it took to chew to decide how much to tell her. He didn't know where the night might take them, he wanted to come across mysterious, but not scare her off, but he had decided that if he was going to invite her back for coffee her answer would probably depend on what he said next. He decided to tell everything he could remember; and that was just the eight months since he had started living on his own. It wasn't the conversation she had been expecting. For some reason he felt he could trust her even though he had met her barely an hour ago. Or maybe it was the whisky talking. He didn't know.

"Jesus," she whistled. A couple at a neighbouring table looked up. "So you literally remember nothing? Oh my God! That's... well, that's... you're right, you are complicated. I never expected that. It's like a story from a romantic novel."

"It's not," Locke said. "I don't know my past and I know that when I tried to remember it, it was the worst feeling of all. So I decided to break with a past I couldn't remember and start working on a present that I can."

"And the future?"

Locke shrugged. He knew the future would sort itself out. He had no control over that. "I've no idea if the past will come back, so I am working towards my future. I'm happy right now. My life's pretty good. I don't want to go back. The more I look forward, the less I'm bothered with what I have left behind."

"So you are a blank canvas. I wish I had that feeling," said Zoë. "I wish I could forgot my past and start anew." She was no longer interested in her own meal. What she had just been told begged a million other questions and she didn't know where to start. It suddenly felt like the beginning of something, but she had always been unlucky with finding love. There had been men and she was surrounded by them most of the time, but none had stayed around long enough to truly discover her. Locke pushed his own plate away.

"Love is truly hard to find," Locke said. "If only people could understand the importance of our hearts."

She considered this. "And what have you left behind?"

"I don't actually know. I do know that what happened to me happened in August last year when I woke up in a strange place with strange people looking at me. They all said things about who I had been and what I had done but I couldn't remember any of them or any of the things they said I'd done. I had two months of that and left. No one knows where I am and I like it that way."

"But aren't you curious? I mean, is there a wife? Kids?"

"I don't know," he lied. He realised he had lied very easily. But in his defence he had not thought about the woman who said she was his wife for a long time. He briefly tried to remember her name, what she looked like, but quickly banished the thought. He knew then he didn't want to know and that Zoë, if she was still interested in him, would have to accept that. He looked deep into her face, trying to read what was there. Zoë held the gaze briefly then looked down at the floor. *It's been a long time since anyone's looked at me like that,* she thought.

"This is a lot to take in," she said at last. "I won't lie, I know it was only a first date, but I thought there was a spark between us. It was brave of you to tell me about yourself."

"I'm not sure about 'brave', but I felt the spark."

"I like the mystery you hold in yourself. I like the honesty of your story. I can tell you there's not a lot of men like that around." Zoë laughed aloud and grabbed her glass of wine. "Fucking hell!" she said, before downing the last of the drink. She looked back at Locke, a strange kind of smirk on her face. "Fucking hell!" she said again more loudly. She didn't notice the disapproving looks of other diners. "Why the hell couldn't you have been straightforward? Yeah, got married early, got divorced, couple of kids, they're my world, blah, blah, blah. Fuck's sake!"

"Shall I get the bill?" Locke said, his hand already raised to catch the attention of a waiter. He surprised her.

"Oh, that's ended quickly." Zoë said suddenly feeling deflated. In that moment she realised she really liked him. "Sorry, I've lost my manners. We'll go halves."

"No need," Locke replied as she fumbled about in her handbag. "You can get the next round in."

She stopped rummaging for her purse and looked back at Locke for a moment. Her heart beat a little faster. *Damaged goods, Zoë, you need to walk away,* she thought. "All right," she said, "but I'm choosing the pub."

*

What pleased Locke the most was that Zoë seemed to move on quickly from the shock of his amnesia and whatever life he had had before it. He couldn't tell whether she gave a shit or she understood the seriousness of the condition. He realised the reason why he had not even considered dating over the past few months was that he didn't want to spend endless evenings with women who walked away the moment they heard his story. If Zoë was anything to go by, he needn't have worried.

She had chosen a more exclusive bar in the centre of the city. By happy coincidence it was closer to his flat than they had been all evening. She nodded rather than spoke when he invited her back for the coffee and they walked arm in arm down Blackfriars before turning left onto Chapel Street.

"Careful" he said, half catching her as she stumbled into the lift.

"Don't worry," she laughed. "It's the heels, not me. I'm not so drunk as to not know what I am doing."

"And what are you doing?"

"Making a fucking big mistake, probably!" Locke smiled and pressed the button for the eighth floor. The lift doors opened out into a pleasant lobby area with several doors off it. He walked diagonally across holding her hand as he did so.

"Make yourself comfortable," he called through as he switched on the lights and went into the kitchen. "Do you actually want coffee, or something else? I've not got wine." Locke turned around. Zoë stood in the middle of his living room, her mouth gaping. *The paintings...* he could have kicked himself. He was so used to seeing them he almost forgot they were there. He decided to brazen it out.

"I call her 'India'. I don't know why I keep painting her." The silence held. Zoë didn't quite catch what he had said. She was captivated by the art.

"You never told me you were an artist."

"I'm not, well not professionally. It's just a hobby." Locke went over to the double doors to his balcony and pulled the curtains to. With the lights on at night, anyone from across the Irwell would be able to see into his flat. It was the one thing wrong with where he lived.

"She's beautiful," Zoë whispered. "Who is she?"

Locke shrugged and held his palms out.

"She must be someone. Otherwise why would you keep painting her?"

"I genuinely don't know."

"I love the colour, the texture and the jewellery she's wearing; it really brings you in to focus on her eyes." Zoë pulled herself away from studying the latest incarnation of the woman on the easel and looked at the others that had already been hung on the walls. There were five in total and all very similar but in slightly different poses.

She stared hard at Locke, trying to read him. She was small and stunning and, in that moment, a bit frightening. He feared the evening was about to end. He gave what he thought was a shy, coy look, trying to tempt her away from his paintings.

"I think you do know," she said eventually. "I think this is someone important to you. This isn't a muse; this is someone real. You said people had been telling you who you had been. I bet one of them was this woman. I think she is your girlfriend or your wife. Am I getting close?"

"I really don't know," he said.

"Which? Girlfriend or wife?" Zoë persisted.

"Honestly, she's just some fantasy woman. But I wish I knew her, and sometimes I feel she is calling me from some distance in time or space, but our dreams don't often come true."

"Why do you keep painting her? What do you think it means?"

Locke sighed. "It's a mystery I am willing to discover, but I can't make the connections. It could be my past or a reincarnation of my past."

"You believe in reincarnation?" said Zoë, teasing.

"No, but I'm open to the possibility. I keep an open mind. Any possibility is better than no possibility, don't you think?"

Inside Zoë's mind warning sirens were pinging left, right and centre. She knew there was a story here, just waiting for her to discover it. But she also knew she wanted him so much it was beginning to hurt. If she let him in, she was afraid of what she might be getting herself in to.

"That I really don't know. There's this image in my head and each time I paint it I do it better. More details emerge each time, but I don't know why I do it." He sat down on his sofa, then looked up at Zoë.

"Can a relationship really have this much effect on us? That even after she has left us, we still remember her, hear her? Our eyes search for her as if she will come back any minute now."

"Not that I know of," said Zoë. "But the thing is, I smell bullshit."

"It's true. I don't know who she is and I don't know where the setting is. It looks like a temple, and I seem to be capturing her devotion, like she is almost speaking to her Gods."

Asking God to protect me wherever I may be?

"But I don't remember ever going to a temple. It might even be in India, but I don't know. You only see half of her face, for God's sake; it could be anyone." He sounded weak and he knew it. "I'm sorry. It didn't even cross my mind all these pictures were in here. Or that it would spoil our night. I'd forgotten about them. You had helped me forget. Until now. I've never spoken to anyone about my paintings. You are the first. But I haven't got the time to examine all this properly. I don't want to be psychoanalysed."

Zoë said nothing but Locke watched on as she slowly looked at each painting in turn. She stopped at the unfinished version and leant in closer, studying the face of India and reaching up to touch it. But she thought better of it and pulled back.

"This is too fucked up," she said at last and pushed past Locke on her way to the flat's door.

"Zoë wait!" Locke said as she fumbled with the latch. "We can talk about this," but she was already out of the door and he decided not to follow her. He had fucked up when it came to being intimate and he knew the night would have gone differently if his paintings hadn't been on show. He walked back towards the unfinished painting.

"What do you fucking want from me? Why are you in my mind, my thoughts, even when you aren't with me?"

He felt the tears of frustration splatter on the wooden floor. But then again he hadn't gone out looking for anyone or anything and he certainly hadn't planned on bringing anyone to his flat. He looked at the unfinished painting of India, then at the curtains blocking the world out. His watch said it was getting close to midnight and he felt guilt that he had not seen Zoë safely home or at least into a cab.

But when he walked out of the lobby of his block of flats, she was nowhere to be seen.

twenty-two
if only he would let her

"But he admitted he was married, Babe. You can't go there."

Zoë looked upwards at the dark ceiling of the coffee shop.

"Not in so many words. He never explicitly said so. But yeah, I know."

"So that's that, then. Time to move on to your next victim."

"What do you mean by that?"

Liam Anderson leaned across the table and took Zoë's hands in his. He flashed his cheeky grin, the eyeshadow making his deep blue eyes look huge. "You have form, you gorgeous little slut, as you well know. Hardly a shrinking violet in the bedroom, or so you tell me."

"Piss off!" Zoë hit back, pulling her hands away. "If you weren't so bloody gay, I'd show you exactly what I can do in the bedroom!"

Liam pulled his face, as if the thought of sex with a woman was the worst thing in the world. It wasn't strictly the case and he had slept with women before, even since he had come out all those years ago. But there was something about Zoë that made him doubt himself. Was he actually bi-sexual? Only Zoë made him question his sexuality like this and yet she was his closest friend. He had harboured thoughts about her but nothing came of it. And then they had grown too close. Still, he had those thoughts and when they chatted like this, over a coffee, he struggled to keep his mind where it should be. He was sure she had no idea about what really went on in his head.

He sat back. "But you still know you can't go there. A married man? Big no-no." The silence hung between them. "Kids?"

"He said he didn't know. But I don't know if he is lying. I genuinely think he's been alone for some time. I think I was about to be his first in a long while."

"Excuses, Babe. You're trying to justify what cannot be. You just need to forget and move on."

"Yes, but there's sincerity in his words and glances. I really don't know if he's lying. I think there is a passion in him that I've not found in any other man. I think I've been searching for a John Locke for a very long time."

Liam winced inwardly. Those strange feelings rising to the top of his thoughts as he listened to her outpouring of love for some bloke who reckoned on having amnesia. It was a neat trick; women far less intelligent than his beautiful Zoë would fall for it. And all the while, he sat in front of her and couldn't bring himself to tell her what he really felt.

"But that's just it," he said instead. "There is justification. How much do we know about this guy? His past, his history? For all we know, he could be a serial killer."

"He doesn't remember his past, Liam. He has no idea. Doesn't he deserve a second chance? John said he was leaving his past because not being able to remember it was the worst aspect of it all. Imagine if day in day out someone keeps telling you something you don't agree with.

"How long would our friendship last if I told you every day that you weren't really gay, that you were putting it on? You'd show me the door within a week. Now imagine if I said you used to be straight. You have no memory of it. You can't believe it. You'd get offended and angry not with me, but with yourself. Do you see? How awful must that be?"

Liam was about to reply; Zoë had no idea how close she really was.

"He's a genuinely nice guy," she continued. "Gorgeous looking and a cute American accent. He is not some scumbag running away from his responsibilities; he's ill."

"You're developing a sympathy for him," Liam said. "That's not love. If you go there, it will end badly. You'll be broken a few months from now and I'll have to pick up the pieces. I've watched you break up a couple of times now, and it breaks my heart."

"I know. But the more I think about it the more I see the positives. I'm not about helping him remember, I'm going to be there to help him to forget. I know that sounds weird, but I think it's what he wants and I think I can help him to do it."

"The past still haunts you, you know? Remember that. You helping him to forget, helping him to not remember? I think it's selfish. I think you're playing on his vulnerability." His voice had risen slightly and they both noticed it. *Why the fuck are you talking like this, Liam?* The identical thought in both their heads.

Zoë sighed. "I know I'm probably being stupid and setting myself up for a fall, but I just can't get this idea out of my head. I know I'm going to go back to his flat and if he doesn't want to know, then so be it, but—"

"But nothing, Babe. I don't need to tell you why this is so wrong. You already know it is and I don't want to see you hurt. There's a woman out there and she'll be back. Hell, she's probably looking for him right now. Think about her, the kids he might have. Think about how Daddy is ruining Mummy's life."

"Stop it, Liam! That's not fair! He said there were no kids. I have to believe him."

"And when you find out there are little ones..."

"I said stop! I mean it, Liam. I can't deal with that right now. I need your support not your judgement. I need you not to be like this."

"I'm trying to give you clarity, but you seem hell-bent on diving to the bottom. Why is it you never see it as I see it? You know I love you and it kills me to watch this happening all over again. Why are you always picking up men who are lost?" Liam saw the look on Zoë's face and realised he had gone too far. He had almost let his true feelings out at a time when her head was somewhere very different. He raised his hands in mock surrender. "Okay, okay. I get it. But you need to be so fucking careful, Babe. I'll be here for you, for always, but you've got to be careful. When this blows up, you've got to be prepared for your world to end. Because it will. This will be worse than either of Damian or Steve, because this guy has admitted lying to you even before you've started a relationship."

"But that's the point. He's nothing like Damian or Steve. And I don't think he's lied. He's been upfront from the beginning and his situation is very different to anything else I've ever experienced."

"Maybe that's true, but yet again you gone for a fucked-up guy. When will you realise these guys aren't for you?" The silence lingered between them. Liam knew he had lost the moment. "Will he get his memory back?" he asked.

Zoë nodded. "Probably, or so he says. But it can take years and years."

"But it can also happen in the next day or so?"

"Please! Just stop it! I know what you're saying, but just stop, will you? Yes it could happen tomorrow, although not suddenly, I don't think. He might get a flashback that leads to another and so on. But it's not a quick process from what he told me. He didn't know himself, just what doctors had said. Life must have been unbearable for him."

"And for her…"

"If there is a her."

"You know there is. And are you up to it when he does remember? Are you strong enough? Nothing is permanent and this is just a health condition. Circumstances will change. You have to open your eyes and come out of the fantasy."

"Yes," Zoë whispered. "I am strong enough. For him." She took a sip of her coffee, but it was cold. It seemed as though they had spent hours poring over John Locke's life. Or, rather, his past life.

"Another?" Liam asked.

"Please," Zoë said feeling as conflicted as she had ever been.

*

It was dusk in the mid-October night as they stepped out from the coffee shop into Manchester's bustling Northern Quarter. Once run down, the area had seen a transformation in recent years and was the nearest thing the city had to a Bohemian district. Independent brewers and bars rubbed shoulders with independent restaurants and cafés, the chains deliberately spurned to make the area different.

"Food?" Liam offered.

"As long as it's not Japanese," Zoë said with a laugh. "I've had it with flying eggs."

"Takeaway," Liam said with determination. "And we'll have it back in the gallery. I do my best thinking there."

They crossed a road and made their way to the small Chinese restaurant that had become Liam's go to takeaway. Service never really came with a smile as the little woman behind the counter always looked completely overwrought. She never showed any recognition and Liam had long given up any pretence of small talk while he waited for his order.

"This is a sweet and sour pork kind of night. A bit of brain food for stimulation. And some prawn crackers, wontons, salt and pepper wings and a Tom Yam soup."

"Bloody hell, Liam! Are you ordering for both of us? You won't stay in that shape for long."

"I eat a lot when I'm upset. I've listened to your nonsense for hours."

Zoë ignored the jibe. Then the food came suspiciously quickly, which annoyed her as she was still trying to process the jumbled thoughts in her head. She knew what Liam said was right; she was heading for trouble, but there had been something about Locke that had caught her and reeled her in. Yes, he was beautiful and friendly and had been the perfect date until the paintings and the spectre of a possible wife turned up, but for all his confidence, he was damaged. He had been living alone for months, only seeing people when he ventured to the shops or the pub and never really talking to anyone. That was assuming that everything else he had said had been true.

She tried to ignore Liam as they walked the short distance to G1NQ, the art gallery he owned thanks to a highly lucrative few years as a city trader in London. He was weighed down by the food, the plastic bags straining to the point of bursting whilst she walked alongside weighed down by the thoughts in her head.

The main lights in G1NQ were off as they made it to the glass front door, and they remained off as they walked through the dimly lit gallery to the office at the back and settled down to their meal. She loved the place.

When it was closed the only lights lit had been carefully placed so that it was clear there was a painting, but not what it was. Zoë thought it very effective, but then Liam was artistic; maybe not to the point of being an artist in the conventional sense, but being able to create something so beautiful and, at night, rather haunting. There was no doubt he was very clever. He had a very keen sense for art.

"It's a shame you're gay. I think we'd make a great couple."

The comment surprised him. *If only you knew…* He looked across at her. Little make up, no frills and yet a stunning beauty. He gazed at her skin, like glistening gold in the half light, and at her pearlescent smile and lips of the deepest rose red. She was amazing. *When you have nothing to lose, nothing matters.*

"My mother always wanted grandchildren," Liam said, effecting indifference. He saw Zoë startle. "Don't be so ridiculous, Babe. You'd never be able to put up with my moods, gay or otherwise."

"True," Zoë said, before taking a mouthful of her own Tom Yam soup. "Nor you mine. Then again, maybe we would have been so blissfully happy that neither of us would have any need for moods."

"Distasteful, Babe. You're my best friend, but you're putting me off my pork." Zoë almost spat her latest mouthful out as Liam found himself funny. "Seriously, though, I've seen this before. When you go all melancholy about your love life, you start talking about me. You've got it bad for this guy, haven't you?"

Zoë put her spoon down and dabbed the corners of her mouth with a piece of tissue. "I think so, yes. That night was perfect until it wasn't. It was just so... natural. Even when we were talking about his condition, he remained calm and gracious—"

"You're making him sound like a vicar."

"—and funny," Zoë continued, ignoring Liam. "And I want to help him. Why can't all men be like him?"

"Because then we'd all have the same personality and personality is what we fall in love with. Sure, our looks count, but when they fade with time we are left with just our personality." Liam looked deeply at Zoë. "Anyhow, help him do what? Remember the wife? Or the kids, assuming there are some?"

"No, Liam! Please stop it. I want to help him move on. I want him to be natural and happy in himself. I want to be there for him because I'm sure he gets lonely and the thought of that hurts me. I've spent so long thinking about it and that's why I turned to you."

"You always turn to me. It's what I love about you, Babe. Your heart is pure. You are looking for true love not like some gold digger. You are lost just like him."

She gazed into Liam's eyes and felt a little tearful. And, for the first time she felt something. For a split-second she saw something in him. "I love you too, you amazing human. Whatever happens with John, I know I've always got that love to protect me. You're such a beautiful man!"

"I told you, stop trying to turn me!" Liam said. Inside he was breaking *Take your chance, you idiot...* But he couldn't.

"I'm not, you tit! I'm just... very grateful to have you in my life."

Liam leaned back in his swivel chair and twisted on it slightly. "Without the sun there is no moon. Without day there is no night. Without clouds there is no rain. Without you there is no me."

"What chick-lit did you read that in? Cosmo?"

"I didn't" Liam stated, a little annoyed. "Anyway, you said he paints," he added, breaking whatever moment had gone between them.

"Amazingly in my opinion, although I know I'm no expert."

"Do you think he'd welcome visitors? Those of an artistic bent who can maybe exhibit some of his work?"

"I need to see him again first," Zoë said. "I need to go on my own, and see where that takes me. I have a horrible feeling it's all over before it's begun, so you can pick me up again when I fall. But I'm going to visit him again soon."

"Sure you wouldn't want me to come along? I doubt he'll see me as a threat, especially when I call him 'Daahling'."

"Not yet. And you don't have to camp it up for him or anyone. I think he'd take one look at the size of you and know he could snap you in half."

"Harsh." Liam looked at his arm and flexed a bicep. "I suppose I am a bit on the puny side. Still, it's not the size of the dog in the fight—"

"—it's the size of the fight in the dog," Zoë finished the cliché for him. "But you're not a fighter. It's another reason why I love you."

*

Zoë refused Liam's offer to walk her home. She needed time to think and the cool air hit the back of her throat as she made her way across the city centre in the direction of Locke's apartment building. She walked part way down Blackfriars Street to the bridge over the River Irwell and looked up at where she was sure his flat was. It was to the left-hand side from where she looked, but there were no lights on where she thought his flat was. She tried counting the floors, but wasn't certain she was looking at the right one. Temptation flooded her mind. It didn't matter.

The idea of John Locke sitting there in the dark upset her. She needed to hold him and nurture him. A strange sensation took hold in the depths of her stomach, as if it had been years since she had seen him. It was not as though the thought of Locke never entered her mind, it was as if she was yearning for something. *Are you lying to yourself, Zoë?* That or she was nervous. Surely she didn't have butterflies? She realised she felt like lovelorn teenager, not a confident woman in her late twenties. The moment she had woken up that morning and started mulling over what had gone before, she knew she was going back to his apartment to try again. There was no bigger red flag to her than a man being married, that's if he was, and Liam was right to be suspicious, but Locke was very, very different. He was an enigma to himself and it excited her. She had a project; a damaged man she found incredibly attractive. Damaged was what she fell for. It had happened before and had happened again. He was broken; she would give him new life.

    As she leant on the stonework of the bridge, gazing up into darkness, she knew her mind was made up. She turned back up the slope towards Deansgate looking out for a taxi to take her to her own flat in Higher Broughton. It wasn't late, but she was ready for bed. All that stood between now and her next life was a night's sleep and a shift at the dental practice. This time tomorrow night she intended to be making love.

    If only he would let her.

twenty-three
it was disturbing, but *he* wasn't

By four o'clock Zoë was sweating. By five she was almost shaking. Patients looked at her oddly and her co-receptionist was starting to think she was ill.

"Why don't you take an early dart?" Siobhan said. "I can cover the last hour. Jo'll be fine about it."

Zoë paused briefly from inputting further figures into the program she was using. It was a new system and made little sense to her why she was doing it.

"I can finish those off," Siobhan said almost soothingly. She was a big woman, late forties, with more than a hint of tough Oldhamer about her. Right now she was doing her best impression of caring.

"If you're sure..." Zoë said, annoyed at herself for sounding so feeble.

"Of course, I'll square it with Jo."

*

It was cold outside and Manchester was serving up one of its many grey days. A light drizzle had started falling during the night and it was still going monotonously onwards as it often did in England's wettest city.

Zoë pulled the collar of her coat around her neck with one hand and held a pathetic little umbrella with the other as she stepped out from the sanctuary of the practice. She turned left and immediately felt the force of the wind blowing up John Dalton Street and almost inverting her umbrella. It was as though the wind was inviting her subconscious to meet with Locke. She pushed on, trying not to think about the carefully brushed hair that would be lank and wet in minutes.

By the time she reached Deansgate, her mood had lifted. It was a skill she had; no matter how bad things got, quite often her thoughts could change completely in a very short space of time. Instead of being a beautiful but nervous wreck in front of the current man of her dreams, she could be a rain-lashed stunner, breezing into his flat bringing more than a hint of the weather with her. Much more disarming, she felt. Had she kicked herself every time she dropped a clanger in the practice that day, her legs would have been black. Her mind was so far elsewhere and she had started to panic on a few occasions, as if she knew she was leaving sterile but easy pastures and chasing rainbows that would only take her to desolate moorland despair. Or worse.

Why the hell was she being like this? In her more lucid moments, she knew she could have such an impact on his story. But was she was losing her mind? Locke was a catch; a handsome man she found funny, a blank canvas of a guy and talented. And she was drawn to him like a magnet. But that was all. At other times, she made herself sick at the thought of talking to him, as if she held him on a pedestal like some modern-day Messiah. She did it every time; this was how she felt when she had fallen in love. But this *was* different. It was as if she was going for a job interview with a million-pound wage tag attached. She had heard it being said that the longer it takes to fall in love the more effect it has on the mind. Her life might change from this moment on or, and she knew this the more likely, she'd been stupid, her heart had won and she refused to listen to the warning signs. She was infatuated with someone she should have walked away from at the very beginning.

Zoë stopped on the bridge that always reminded her of Concorde with its soaring central white support looking like the great aircraft's nose on take-off. A little upstream was Blackfriars Bridge where she had been standing the night before, hoping to catch a glimpse of Locke in his apartment. A voice inside kept telling her to go to him, that he was waiting for her. But then the devil on the other shoulder; *will he let you touch him? Will he ask if you love him?*

"Breathe, you idiot," she said aloud. She was closer than last night, and again sought any sign of movement within the apartment. She desperately wanted to see him. Just one fleeting movement would be enough; a single brief impression of him to steady her heart. Or make it beat a hundred times faster. "Love just happens once," she tried to convince herself.

Again she saw nothing and again she couldn't be sure she was looking at the right apartment when she tried counting the floors; she thought the bottom two might actually comprise the building's entrance hall, so wasn't certain where the eighth floor actually was. Maybe he would come out onto his balcony, coffee in hand? Or a whisky? He was introvert, but she had seen the table with its solitary chair just before Locke had closed the curtains. She was sure he was the sort who felt Nature, and the changing of seasons, just as clearly as he could work with changing colours. But what if he changed? She had a sudden strange vision of him pouring her a glass of wine, of everything being perfect. Except he didn't stop pouring and the wine overflowed. She cried out, but there was a look on his face, as if he was full. Still he poured. She wanted to drink from Locke's glass, but he had to stop first. The more she wanted it, the more he poured. Wine spilled onto the table, the wooden floor, seeped into the rug. John Locke was this intoxicating wine and she was an empty cup. People would say that she's still feeling for him.

The image disappeared. Below the silt-brown waters of the River Irwell gurgled and rolled on its inevitable way. The Manchester drizzle gave the surface a slightly rough texture and for one brief, ridiculous moment Zoë thought about jumping off the bridge into the river. Love was so hard to find. Even if we're staring at someone day in day out, we can't tell if he or she is there for us. She drew a deep breath and shook that thought away.

Was that a suicidal thought? The idea shocked her; she had never been suicidal in her life. She put it down to the daft nerves that had afflicted her all day and took a purposeful stride towards Locke's apartment building instead. The image of India came to her. If love was to be defined, she knew it would have to be in the form of this idol woman. The whole world wants to be in love, but not many of us find it. By midsummer, if the heart is lost, what will you do? What *can* you do?

She reached the apartment block when reality struck; she hadn't considered the difficulty of getting in without a pass card, but then slipped in through the open door as someone else left the building. The reception desk being empty was another bonus and she hurried along to the lifts. She was outside Locke's apartment within a minute and suddenly didn't know what to do.

"I didn't expect to see you again." Zoë spun around as the soft American tones sounded loud in the confined space. "It's a bit wild out there."

Locke's hair was plastered flat to his head and water streamed down his face. He held a carrier bag in each hand and Zoë realised why he hadn't been carrying an umbrella. She also realised that her cunning ploy of rain-lashed stunner had gone out the window; Locke was pulling that one off with much more aplomb. He held out one of the carrier bags.

"Mind holding this for me?" Zoë took it without speaking as Locke fished in his jeans pocket for the door key. She remained where she was as he headed into his apartment. "You coming in, then?" he asked as he held the door for her.

What's wrong with you? The thought wouldn't leave her head as she demurely walked through. She gave her legs another metaphorical kicking.

*

Locke walked through to the kitchen leaving Zoë in the short hallway leading to the main room. He returned and asked to take her coat, then proffered a seat on the sofa.

"Coffee or something stronger? I've even got wine this time. Sauvignon Blanc. You see I can remember some things." He gave one his smiles that he thought hooked the ladies in. Zoë saw it and melted a little inside. *Those eyes...*

He knew he hadn't lost her. He knew there was always going to be a second chance. The thought appealed and he seemed to grow an inch or two taller as he stood up straighter.

"Wine would be lovely," she said, and instantly regretted it. She didn't really have a plan, but was determined to tackle him on the possible wife and kids before anything else. She knew she shouldn't compare herself against the painting, but she couldn't help herself. India was like a flowing river or a dancing deer. Sometimes like a hare, sometimes a butterfly and other times she shone like the moon.

But how do I compare? she thought. *Am I a poet, sometimes a secret personality, sometimes a teardrop, sometimes a lit candle? Everyone wants her to become the ideal woman and no one likes me. Why shouldn't I envy the lady in the painting?*

Soon she'd have alcohol in her hand and, if she spent any time in the apartment at all, her judgement would be shot. She knew what she hoped would happen, but she resolved to clear up the domestic situation first. She was not going to have a relationship with a straight-up married man.

This was different, though, and she needed to convince herself of that. As the wine arrived with another smile, she realised she was already lost, whatever he said.

"So," Locke sighed as he handed her a glass and sat opposite her in the single armchair. He suddenly looked like a king on his throne, sipping his own wine, she noted. His other hand stroked the arm of the chair as if he was stroking her back. *He's fucking flirting!* she thought, then fought to keep her emotions in check. She took a sip of her own wine and tried not to look at the paintings of India adorning the walls. Soft music came through from somewhere and she wondered when he had managed to put it on.

"So," she replied. "I think I need help."

Locke raised his eyebrows. "Not what I was expecting. Help with what? Moral or financial?"

"Moral!" she stated and took another large draught of her wine. *Get a grip, Zoë, you've met men before.*

Not this man, a voice inside replied.

"That's a good start," Locke said. "I don't think we know each other well enough to discuss money."

She took another mouthful of wine then put her glass down on the table beside the sofa. She was not going to get pissed before she'd had the conversation.

"It's about last week," she started. Locke took a sip of his own drink and waited for her to continue. "You told me things that I can't really comprehend. I mean, I get that you're ill with your amnesia and I think I understand how you found it so frustrating that your only option was to leave that life behind, but there are other things you need to address and I need to address before I can truly give myself to this relationship." Her eyes widened as she realised what she had just said.

"But we don't have a relationship," Locke replied, softly. The smile had gone. He knew what was going on the moment he saw Zoë standing on the bridge looking up at his flat. It gave him a bit of time to prepare himself as he followed her to his building. But to tease wasn't right anymore. He liked this woman and, being honest to himself, he really liked the vulnerability that came across in between the bouts of strength she sometimes displayed. This was someone he could be proud of yet knowing she would need the odd bit of reassurance. She was living real life and doing a bloody good job of it. He was hiding in plain sight, living alone with his paintings and talking to few. It excited him that despite his position of weakness, he could support her just as he was sure she would help him.

"I know it was a lot to take in on a first date, if that's what we can call it, and I understand completely why you ran. You were right to challenge me about being married and it was wrong that I lied to you about that. But you realise that my situation is different and that I am not some shit that's baled on his wife and family."

Zoë's lips pursed open as she heard the word. *Family.* Locke's fingers drummed on the arm of his chair. He saw the recognition in her eyes.

"There's a boy, Sachin, and he's five, maybe six. It's the second time I have had amnesia. The first time was in 2003, and then again last year, five years to the day, or so I am told, to the attack that left me with amnesia first time around. I'm not sure of the significance of that. These are things I have been told but do not remember. To have that happen to you daily is a living hell and I had to go. I have tried to block that time from my mind and start afresh. It may sound cynical, but it's the truth; I know I am married and with a family, but it's better not to be there because the man they thought I was simply wasn't there either. These are the things I have been told. They are the things I am trying to forget, because I can't remember them.

"Anyway, this woman, Anjali's her name, tells me she brought me round eventually last time. She helped me to remember and apparently we had this idyllic relationship strong enough to get married, have a child and live happily. I'm not sure how long it took for me to regain my memory that time, but I know it wasn't quick or easy. But, you see, none of that matters."

Zoë made to say something but Locke raised his hand and stopped her.

"None of that matters because all of it is *told,* but none of it is *remembered*. I have tried so hard to believe her and everything she has told me. And I have tried so hard to love that little boy because I figured the one area amnesia could not get me was with the love of my own child. But it has. I looked at a cute little boy, big brown eyes and a lovely smile and I think, *he's bonny, he's cute, he's funny.* And then I think, *but who is he?* I can't get past that. It's so hard and yet so easy to be in a situation where you know you should be feeling something and yet, because you feel nothing, you are not in that situation. There is evidence, lots of it, but when nothing comes, all that becomes nothing."

He looked closely at Zoë as she tried to follow what he was saying to her.

"Let me put it another way. Have you seen that photo in the kitchen? The one of you and me on top of Ben Nevis when we climbed it last year? Your head right now is telling you there is no photograph, because in your mind it didn't happen. Okay, but what if I go into that kitchen and come back out with that photograph and show it to you? What if you stared at it thinking *what the fuck?* What if I started telling how the views had been amazing on the way up, but then the clouds rolled in and we couldn't see a thing on the summit, how we got a bit scared trying to find the path and then descended, seeing or hearing nothing save the crunching of our boots and the occasional sheep bleat? Do you remember how cold we were when we finally got back to the car? It was dark and I nearly shit myself when that sheep baaa'ed right next to me."

The story seemed to hit her right in the chest and slowly descend to the pit of her stomach. Locke laughed, loudly, as if he was playing to an audience of many.

"I had no idea the fucking thing was there! Do you remember? Do you Zoë? It was one of the best days we ever had. We never laughed so much. You fell asleep on the way home. Seven bloody hours of you passed out in the seat next to me and me driving us all that way home."

He leant forward, "You do remember that, don't you Zoë? Do you remember your son, Sachin? Or the day we got married? I was wearing a red and gold sari. You said I looked more beautiful that day than any other. Do you remember? Do you remember how cold it was at the top of Ben Nevis? Do you?"

He sat back in the armchair. His eyes dark as the rain outside worsened and the light failed. Zoë reached for her wine and gulped the remains down.

"I think I need another drink," she said, holding the glass up. Locke understood and smiled.

"It's not easy to understand," he said, "but maybe you get an idea now? It is cold on Ben Nevis, and there are sheep there, but I've never been there either. At least I don't think I have. But say it with enough conviction and you can mess with your own head. This is why I am trying to forget what I can't remember. Just think; *trying* to forget what you can't remember. I can tell you, it's fucked up."

*

Locke returned with the wine. Zoë took another large mouthful, still trying to process what had just happened. For a moment she had actually tried to remember being on the mountain before it came back to her that this guy was performing some kind of mind trick. *It* was disturbing, but *he* wasn't. As she began to make her way back to the actual reality of right now, she glimpsed a moment of what he must have been through and why he seemed so happy to have got past it today.

"Do you think we could order some food in before you knock me over completely?"

"Sure, what would you like?"

Zoë thought for a moment, wondered if her little joke was in poor taste, then said it anyway: "Maybe not Indian."

Locke laughed and she smiled back. *From now on no one will love you like me,* Zoë thought. They both knew it was going to be a long night.

twenty-four
melancholy, perhaps

Things had moved fast. They'd been together just over a week and, although she hadn't officially moved into Locke's apartment, Zoë was already spending pretty much every night with him. They hadn't even gone to her apartment yet and his was much more convenient for work. Liam had warned her to be careful, but she was flying high with her new lover. They fed off each and conversations about amnesia were thankfully very few. It was how he liked it and for her, she decided ignorance was bliss. And life with him was; he was caring, funny, handsome and the sex was fantastic. If she was to describe *Love,* Locke would be a symbol of it. She was making love and she thought, if not already, that he also would be making love to her. She didn't mind. For now she was happy to hold him close afterwards and not think about his unusual situation. She tried not to think about it as her issue as well.

She had her own pass card now and hummed a little tune as the lift took her up to the eighth floor. She found Locke painting as he did every day. He had started a new painting and, so far, it seemed identical to the others. It was in its very early stages, but it was clearly a woman in a sari. Jealousy stabbed at her.

"Do you think you'll ever paint anything different?" she asked, trying to keep her irritation in check.

"I don't know. I never thought about it. I tried other things before, they didn't work for me. I don't think of myself as an artist or painter. I always thought it was therapeutic. And as soon as I picked up the paint brush this image came from nowhere. I didn't think about it; I just did it, if that makes any sense to you. The image in my vision was so precise that my edits have been many. For now this is all I have in my head; it seems to be the only thing I want to paint." He took a step back, to better see the full painting. "It almost feels real. It almost feels like destiny, as if I stole upon her by chance. If I was to describe love, this would be it. Love is soul to your heart. Love and desire together is to worship. Devotion is a reason to live."

"You can be an insensitive shit at times!"

Locke stopped the brush work and turned to look at Zoë, a quizzical expression on his face.

"I'm sorry," she said quickly. "I didn't mean it. She isn't real; you are. There isn't anything to feel jealous over."

"But you did. And I do get why. We've talked about this; it seems to be the only way for me to move on. I need you to move on with me."

"But you're constantly painting pictures of *her*. Do you not know that? Do I know that? It's just a woman in a painting, you keep saying. That's the one thing you do or say that reminds me every time of your situation. No, that's not right. It's *our* situation! There are three of us in this relationship. I just want there to be two. Just us."

"With you there's no darkness, no cloud," Locke said. "You do realise that?"

He put the brush down on the easel and crossed towards Zoë. He checked his hands for wet paint then carefully stroked her cheek. "It's still early days for us, but I like what's happening. You are the woman I desired. Your loyalty and dedication have kept me alive. I think we are good together and I think we work for each other. I will get there and I want you by my side. You are my hope."

She looked up at him, the irritation subsiding. He said the right things at the right time. "Have you given any more thought to my idea?" she asked. Locke pulled his hand away.

"This is where I find it hard," he said, walking back to his painting. "You hate the idea of my paintings, yet you want me to exhibit them?"

"Because when I get my head out of my arse, when I stop resenting, I look at them and I know they're really good. I am sure Liam—"

"Bugger Liam! I don't know who he is and I don't want him looking at my paintings. I certainly don't want anyone else to be looking at them. Only you. I keep telling you, I am not an artist. Don't try to make me into one."

"It would be a life altering opportunity," Zoë said, quietly. "And why only me? Can't you see how weird that is and how it's a situation entirely of your making? You want me in your life but I'm the only one who can still see your ex? That's a bit fucked up, don't you think? Why don't you start painting me? Don't you find me attractive?"

John didn't answer. Of course she was attractive, but this image has a deeper meaning, which he still needed to discover.

"And if you do exhibit them, maybe that will offer some kind of release? Maybe something that will help you take the next step to your recovery or redemption or whatever the hell it is?"

Locke sighed and turned to look out of his window at the old red brick mill opposite. It was a clear Spring day and the Irwell sparkled below. "I've told you this; I don't need to recover and I certainly don't need redemption. I just like things the way they are. I do my paintings and they give me a purpose. Then you come home and we're wonderful together. But each time you mention my paintings, I know you're trying for something I cannot give you. You need to accept that. These paintings are why I exist. I've no idea what would happen to me if I stopped painting or, perhaps worse, tried painting anything else.

"If the sky's in love with the land, then he should show his loyalty first. Only then will love prevail. If love lives in the mountain spring, pray or worship him and only then will these waters come upon you."

Zoë came and stood next to Locke, looking at the same view. She ignored what he had just said. She failed to understand that trust was the foundation of any relationship. Increasingly he came up with these little phrases. They sounded sort of mystical to her, and she wasn't entirely comfortable with his saying them. She felt as though they put him on a higher level of intelligence and that she couldn't keep up with him.

"Why don't you stop for tonight? Maybe we can talk if it doesn't annoy you or tire you out? What if Liam comes and has a quick look? He'll know in seconds whether he's looking at something. I think they're brilliant and I think he will too." She turned to face him. "He's not far and, if you're uncomfortable, then you don't need to be here. Liam could take a look and we could all meet up for a drink somewhere, neutral ground, that sort of thing. I'm putting a lot at risk, here."

"How?" Locke asked, searching Zoë's face for answers.

"Because I think exhibiting these, if they are good enough, will help you move onto the next stage, whatever that is. I don't want to scare you off, John, but I think I love you. I think I have since the moment we met in the pub that time, looking at that picture of the soldier on his horse. When I think about it, I am stunned to have received such a precious person into my life. Finding someone is never easy, but I see things in you I have never seen in anyone else."

"Not even that Steve, or Dan, or whatever he was called?"

"Damian and yes, Steve as well. I was much younger then and they were both bastards. I went through hell because of them, but I am much stronger now and you are very, very different. I'm not sure there's a man on the planet like you."

Locke snorted. "Probably just as well. We only live once, we only die once, and we fail in love just once."

"Look, I'm not some silly little girl expecting a Prince Charming. But I think I might have found him and I'm willing to risk everything to be with you. I think exhibiting will at least move us on. If it doesn't kill us, it will make us stronger. I know it will."

Locke turned away again; he stared at the painting and he could see the potential Zoë was trying to make. But was he ready to let go? His gaze moved on and he stared at the old mill's windows gazing blankly back.

"I've been in touch with Liam today," Zoë pushed. "He wants to look at them because I've gone about them so much. I think it's time."

Locke nodded and headed for the bedroom, taking his painting shirt off as he did so. "I'll be in the Briton's from seven. He can come then or not at all."

*

"You weren't fucking wrong, Babe; these are amazing." Zoë felt an odd pride as Liam scanned Locke's paintings. "These are utterly incredible. I'm not a university-educated art expert, but I know when I like something and these are so detailed. I don't know how he's done it; they are all identical yet every one has something different about it that I can't pin down. It's like he's painting the same thing but with a different emotion and you can see it."

"That's what I've been telling you. I thought they were great, but I could never quite work out why. I still can't, but it's got you behaving the same way."

"I want to see him. These need to be in my gallery. A big fuck off display; we'll get the local rags in. Fuck that, we'll get the national rags in. Everybody needs to see just how amazing this guy is." Liam looked at Zoë who thought he looked a bit mad. "Where is he?" he asked.

"The Briton's Protection."

"The where?"

"Not your normal hang out. Old man's pub. But it's not far."

"It will have to do. Lead on, Babe!"

Zoë laughed. "Hold on a minute, Speedy! I need to text him first, tell him we're on our way. I don't want to suddenly appear in the room with you slavering next to me. Besides, I need to get some slap on if I'm going out."

"Bugger your slap, Babe, I'll be slapping him about if he doesn't say yes."

"You'd lose, Liam," Zoë said leaving the gallery owner to fawn over the paintings by himself.

*

Locke steadily nursed his second whisky. He was nervous and had gone for a Talisker, just about the hardest hitting Scotch there was. On the table two white wines and a pint of lager. He had no idea what Liam might drink, so he played it safe. He knew what Zoë would have, though; it never changed.

The picture of the sabre-rattling horseman remained and he had spent his allotted length of time looking intently at it. When he sat down he wondered why he studied it so much. Compared to his India creations, it was a simple, fairly amateurish pencil and watercolour, washy, lacking precision. He just liked it.

Zoë walked into the room smiling, although she looked a little on edge.

"Liam's getting them in, but I see you've done so already."

"I didn't know what he'd like, so I got him a choice." Zoë leant down and kissed Locke on the cheek.

"That's you being very sweet; I'd like other people to see how gorgeous you can be."

"Maybe one at a time."

Zoë had placed her coat on the back of a chair she had arranged for Liam to sit on and took her place next to Locke. The gallery owner entered the room a short while later. She smiled at the thought of his face when he first walked into the pub. This kind of establishment did not register with the urbanite.

"Ah, I see we're double, no, triple parked," Liam said as he placed a white wine, a whisky and a gin and bitter lemon on the now crowded table. Locke rose to his feet to accept the proffered handshake.

"My," he added, keeping the handshake slightly longer than was necessary whilst winking at Zoë, "you told me he was gorgeous, but you didn't tell me just how manly. Do you mind if I call you 'Darling'?"

Locke felt the colour rise in his cheeks. "Not really, if that's what you want." Zoë patted Locke's leg in encouragement. She recognised when her boyfriend was out of his comfort zone just as much as she could tell when Liam was trying too hard.

"The paintings are amazing, John. I can't tell you how good and I'm not bullshitting you. I want you to exhibit at my gallery. It's small fry, but I am certain that you will go on to great things with your art." Locke began to say something, but Liam was in full flow. "It's not just the beauty of the subject, apologies for the insensitives, Babe, but she's a fine muse. No, it's the way you have drawn five identical paintings that are all completely different."

"Completely different?" Locke moved forward slightly. "I don't see them as different, just better each time."

"Better...?" Liam thought on the phrase. "Better? Not different? How interesting. I think we are both right, John. I see completely different paintings that are identical. You see improvements each time. Zoë has told me a little of your past, I hope that's okay, but perhaps what you and what I see are the same thing? I thought it was your personality shining through; one is sad, another thoughtful, another dare I say it, happy. Maybe each painting is actually representative of the way in which you are moving on with your amnesia? Perhaps in the first you are still conflicted about having left the wife," Liam raised his hand once more, giving himself the chance to draw breath. "Apologies again, Babe, but she exists and she might be in these paintings. So, the first one is conflict and you're confused, no, wait, you're angry at your situation and, by default, at the subject of your painting."

"No, you're wrong," Locke countered. "I'm not confused or conflicted. The painting represents how one person can see a woman in many ways. Every man loves a woman, but there is a certain pose a man can see in a woman which grips his heart. Images are moments; the shape of her face, how she stands by her side, the shape of the stance, all of the hair to one side of her face. Poses create images in our minds which can last forever. We capture them with our eyes, but we store them in our heart. That's why our eyes are called the window to our soul. Those are the images I like in a woman when I'm taking a photograph. Obviously I didn't do these paintings with the help of a camera, but I did do them with my heart."

Liam thought for a moment, then carried on regardless. "The second one? I saw a softening. Melancholy, perhaps. Like you can't stay angry forever, but that doesn't mean you're now happy. No. Melancholia is correct." Liam looked from Locke to Zoë. "Babe, your man is a genius. Keep hold of him if you can."

"Give it a rest, Liam, and let John get a word in." Liam saw the daggers coming from Zoë.

"Sorry, Babe."

"I'm not sure about exhibiting," Locke stated flatly.

"Oh, I know!" Liam countered. "Worried the ex might see and come and find you? I'd seen it coming. Very brave of Zoë, but then she's an absolutely rock of a woman, aren't you, Babe?"

Zoë's mouth was wide open. Locke looked at her, worried. Liam realised he'd gone too far and held up his hands.

"I'm so sorry to both of you. Really. I'm very excited about your paintings and the world needs to see them. I'll waive my fee for gallery space, I'll even pay you to have them hung, I know that this is the start of something special, and I'm just desperate for you to take this opportunity." The air flowed out of Liam. "I apologise with everything I have. I've gone too far. I'm truly sorry. Do you forgive me? Both of you?"

*

The room was dark, save for the outside glow. They'd stayed in the pub until closing and Locke and Zoë had got in one cab leaving Liam to hail another. Liam's infectious enthusiasm had disarmed Locke completely. He was no fool, but he believed the gallery owner to be completely genuine.

They fell into his apartment and alcohol played its part as they hammered into each other the moment the front door was closed. They had never made love like that before; for Locke some beast inside had been released. Zoë had hit back, her own animalistic instincts brought out by the euphoria of the moment and they lay back panting, the curtains not drawn, not that anyone was likely to be able to see them. He turned towards her, her head resting on his left arm, the fingers of his right hand caressing her flat stomach. They stayed like that for minutes, their breathing returning slowly to normal, Locke's eyes closing as passion subsided into love.

"It's going to happen, isn't it?" Zoë stated.

"What is?"

"She's going to come. To the exhibition."

Locke's eyes opened. He pulled away slightly and Zoë raised her head to free his arm so that he could lie on his back. They both stared ceilingwards.

"I don't know," he offered, annoyed the subject had come up again. And at such an exquisite time. She really knew how to turn situations sour. Her jealousy and insecurity always conflicting in her mind.

"I think you do know, and I think you will. It will be the final test of us."

Locke breathed deeply. "You might be right," he said, somehow aware of the tears rolling down her cheeks.

"Why doesn't love last forever, John? Why are we always lingering in the middle of the road alone and feeling depressed?"

"If we don't respect what we have in front of us, it will eventually became corrosive," Locke replied.

Zoë rolled further onto her side of the bed. She could feel it in her heart. And her heart was breaking.

twenty-five
it's not there in nature

'Seven for seven-thirty for the Seven Faces of India', the invites stated. No one was to come until after eight, though, to raise the anticipation levels outside. A nosey crowd had started to mill once the music blared and the doormen took their places. Liam had pulled out all the stops; passers-by wondered whether there were going to be celebrities to gawp at. The venue simply *looked* exclusive. Apart from the deep house tones of a specially recorded mix, nothing escaped the blackout curtains erected across the glass frontage of G1NQ. A red carpet had been laid out in front of the glass window, ushering people in whilst giving the assembled photographers something to snap. Some of them had been there long enough for the little viewing pen on the other side of the bouncer-flanked doorway to fill up. Many wondered what was so exclusive tonight, but Liam knew how to put on a show for Manchester's rich and famous.

    The early mood music was nineties dance. A local DJ, specially chosen for the Bhangra set he was to play once guests started arriving, was discreetly placed near the front of the venue. His light set could not interfere with the main gallery but it was an excellent backdrop to the dark and winding route approach Liam had decided upon. Guests would be treated to a tunnel-effect; black curtains and exhibits hanging in such a way as to focus purely on the images presented as they meandered towards another set of doors. They were of pictures of India; as raucous and bright as the DJ's flashing lights, women in saris matching the reds, blues and purples of the lasers, leaving the guests to study the images of interpretation. The effect was both confusion and exhilaration, but it was to be lost on most.

    The same slightly claustrophobic effect was designed the other side of the doors where guests would be offered their champagne and the canapés made to order by a nearby Michelin-starred Indian restaurant. Here hung something entirely different: images of Locke, bleak, black and white compositions of his face, his eyes, working at his easel. Liam was pushing for a drab existence in the painter, as Locke insisted he be referred to. Zoë's agreement made the vote unanimous that there was to be no mention of amnesia. The art had to speak for itself and if Locke mentioned his medical condition during the speech he was dreading he had to make, then so be it. But no-one would know until he spoke the words. Instead, they would see perceptions of a new 'artistic genius', so said the invites. In a surprising perhaps even disappointing way; Locke was to be the dull meat of the three exhibitions. He was the grey that followed the light show and the drab before the guest finally set eyes on his amazing paintings.

Liam had been relentless. In the intervening three months, he had got Locke to paint two further paintings and all seven were to hang on an intricate pulley system. Initially guests would see the paintings hanging side by side against one wall, draped in beautiful almost transparent coloured chiffon. The silhouette of India was just visible through the thin material, enough to get guests wondering at what was really beneath. When the time was right, a button would be pressed and the furthest left would silently move forward, it's chiffon mask falling to the floor, followed by the next, then the third.

From the viewing area each painting would briefly appear close up before the next became dominant. Liam had designed a 'catwalk' for Locke's paintings which would all return to their original position on the far wall before moving once again in the same rhythmic fashion. Only at the end of the staged viewing session, when the seven paintings returned and remained in the original positions, would Liam announce the guests could move in for a closer look.

They would all take that opportunity, not only because they had been wowed, but because displays of personal wealth were necessary. Each painting had a price tag of at least one hundred thousand pounds and Liam had estimated that everyone in the room, bar Locke, Zoë and the hired help, could afford to buy one. His only doubt was whether he should have gone for an auction instead. Regardless, the plan was simple; to put Locke on the artistic map for people to acknowledge and appreciate his art.

"I'm not sure about this," Locke said, fretting whilst nursing a second whisky. He had a decent alcohol threshold and promised Liam he'd be careful.

"It's going to be the making of you," Zoë whispered back. She'd walked the floor show three times now and felt immense pride in what her friend had achieved. In contrast Locke had become shy and feared a washout with no guests or sales.

"I'm not sure I want to be made. I'm quite happy with what I've got. You have come into my life like a goddess, or a messiah, when I had no one to trust or to be with." He smiled down at Zoë, then bent forward to kiss her.

"Ewww! Get a room!" Locke laughed as Liam passed by, the picture of efficiency. Zoë could taste the whisky on her lips. "Remember, John, this is your night. Just do as I say and you'll be heading for superstardom with a half of a million in your back pocket."

"But that's not what you want, is it?" Zoë asked.

"Not really, no. I want to know why those bangles, those earrings call to me. Why do those eyes have a thousand things to say to me? If the painting tells me night is day, I'll believe it. It's as if it tells me to die for it, I will. I just don't get why I'm so mesmerised by her long hair blowing in the breeze. When the breeze blew on her sari, I felt I was closer to her than ever." Locke's expression barely changed as he looked back at Zoë. "Other than that I'm just happy as I am."

"Let's hope you still are in about three hours' time," she said, reaching out for a passing canapé, feverishly trying to push down her thoughts of what Locke had just said. The fire of the spicing hit the back of her throat to disappear into a creamy after taste. She had no idea what she had just eaten.

*

Sixty had been invited. Liam had orchestrated things in such a way that demand for the tickets at the invite-only event had soared so he could he handpick his audience guaranteeing a mixture of wealthy local business leaders, footballers and predominantly actresses from Coronation Street, specifically the more beautiful and red carpet friendly ones.

He also made sure there was a good smattering of wealthy Asians and the region's most Bollywood-esque celebrities. Photographers would go home happy with shots they could sell to the papers. Liam would go home happy as the seven paintings made their way at the end of the night to the vast mansions of Cheshire. He didn't care who bought them, but he suspected the business leaders he had chosen would buy one if only to show they could.

A couple of footballers were the first to arrive, one from City, one from United and Liam knew them to be old mates. The blondes on their arms looked identikit and the four happily posed for the paparazzi before going through the glass doors to be hidden from sight. The DJ's music had changed to Bhangra; the sense of expectation in the main gallery rose accordingly. Zoë was a bag of nerves and Locke was virtually mute, but Liam was in his element and he effortlessly met the first guests with the kind of decorum they expected.

More guests arrived and the room began to fill. It wasn't the largest, because G1NQ had been split into three, but it was warmly lit, compared to the first two rooms. Liam's plan had been to keep the main gallery a little in shadow until everyone had arrived. The big reveal was to take place at nine. By then everyone was to have been on their second or third glass of champagne and the switching of the lights would have gained everyone's interest.

Locke lost count of the hands he shook, or the cheeks he pecked. He smiled dutifully but said little. Zoë was never far away; she was his rock for the night. He wasn't worried about being surrounded by beautiful women, and neither was she, but if he needed her to step in, Zoë was there with a ready smile.

A few guests asked for a preview of what was going on, particularly the reporter for one of the local papers who had been invited on the proviso of total discretion. Zoë stepped in and gave a suitably banal response. The reporter was there to observe; interviews were to take place later.

Locke's focus changed. A breeze brushed at his face and ruffled his clothing. He looked for the source of the draught, but could see none. Nor did anyone else seem to have noticed it. *I am coming, John...* His head whipped round; the speaker must have been right next to him. A woman, seductive. But there was no one close enough to him to have said it. He wasn't suspicious, or spiritual, but the words seemed to him a warning.

*

"John, it's time." A focused Liam grabbed the artist's hand and took him to a chair that had been brought into the room. Locke sat on it, feeling ridiculously like a fake king on his plastic throne. Zoë stood to one side. They held hands. Liam had hurried to a spot just below and left of the first painting where a pulpit had been erected. As he reached the top step a spotlight fell on him. The main lights also changed, bathing the room in new brightness. The murmuring guests quietened and turned to see what was going on. The DJ's music dropped so as to be barely audible.

"Ladies and Gentlemen," Liam began, his delivery surprising both Zoë and Locke, "welcome to the Seven Faces of India, a unique exhibition by a quite incredible artist. This man has a level of skill that I have never before seen in my career running a gallery. I do not pretend to speak as an art expert, rather as one whose appreciative eye I like to think is better than most and as one who can see something of the artist in a painting.

"What you are about to see is truly astounding. This artist has managed to capture his differing moods in otherwise identical paintings. I do not wish to preach when I say those of you with the eye will be staggered by what you see. For others without the same level of brilliant judgement, you will nonetheless see an incredible depiction of such natural beauty and peace as to be rendered, I suspect, mute, even if for just a little bit."

A murmur swept through the assembled guests, some offering a wry smile or a gentle laugh as Liam continued. Locke tightened his grip on Zoë's hand. His hand started to sweat.

"I'm not feeling so good," he said, using his pocket handkerchief to dab at the sweat running freely down his brow. "Something's coming, I can feel it. It's like a ghost."

Zoë shushed him. "We will talk later," she whispered, staring at the audience with barely contained excitement.

"Without further ado, I give you the mesmerising art of John Locke who," Liam said raising a dramatic finger, "I dare say will become the most celebrated living artist on this planet. He is right here amongst us and this is his art. This is his Seven Faces of India."

Out of view of the audience a few feet in front of him, Liam pressed a button. The light in the room grew brighter still. The first of the paintings, initially held upright on the pulley system, tilted forward slightly as the wires began to whirr quietly and the blue chiffon cover sheet fell to the ground. The painting moved smoothly forwards towards the audience, levitating wraithlike on the near-invisible wires.

It was Locke's least favourite effort and he had to stop himself from covering his mouth. Zoë squeezed his hand as the painting stopped a few feet in front of him then started to move to the right. The second painting started to move, its lilac chiffon sheet similarly falling as the painting pitched forward. No one spoke until the last painting had followed the same sequence and all seven hung back in their original positions.

They then moved forward as one, seven ghostlike apparitions advancing as if to bow to a theatre audience. They stayed there for some moments giving all the opportunity for a better close up of paintings that were no longer moving. Locke's eye was inevitably drawn to the right where his most recent creation hung proud. Liam had been right; his mood was captured in these paintings and the latest one was joy. They had decided to not call them by moods – better to leave that to the audience, but with the last brush stroke of that painting, he remembered feeling complete. He looked up at Zoë and they exchanged a glance. He felt his heart might give out.

"The Seven Faces of India!" Liam called out over the audience left in awe by the mesmeric display. "I now give you their creator, the quite indescribably brilliant John Locke!"

The crowd broke into polite applause. Locke stood up from his chair and embraced Zoë with a kiss on her cheek. She was beaming. He climbed the stairs of the 'pulpit' and embraced Liam who also kissed him on the cheek making him both smile and blush. The audience laughed politely at his slight discomfort.

With Liam's encouragement, Locke breathed deeply. The ambient lighting in the room darkened once more leaving the two men lit up by the single spotlight.

"I'd like to thank you all for coming," Locke began, his speech shaking wildly in his hands as he read it slowly and deliberately. "If I am completely honest, I don't know why you are all here."

He waited for the sympathetic laughter and gentle applause to die down. "No, really. I'm just a regular guy who can paint a bit. Liam is the first person who has seen anything in these paintings, and I include me in that. He sees in my art something more than me and his positivity surrounding these seven depictions has given my life something of a direction.

"How much do we truly love someone? No one knows, yet many of us still say "I love you," to another, daily. And for millions that makes our hearts miss a beat. I don't know why I painted these pictures, only that I painted what my heart saw and my eyes obeyed. The seventh face is the final finished image and it stands in front of you now. She is a woman worthy of worship. She has consciousness like no other. A woman who is a gift to our society and whichever home she lives in, she brings us light and happiness."

Towards the back of the audience a woman gasped, causing others to turn around.

"You see, I am a damaged human being," Locke continued. "I have amnesia and I do not really know who I am. I have been told of my former life, but I remember none of it. It's like having dementia, yet my passport says I'm twenty-nine years old. And I know it's not dementia."

Under the lights, the audience seemed to be one dark mass of people. Locke became aware of some movement at the back of the audience, like it was splitting in two. Those at the front remained unaware. And that included Zoë.

"If I had dementia, do any of you think I could create each painting essentially the same but for me, and hopefully you, intensely different? Would you believe me when I say the paintings speak to me? Because they do. The more I create, the better I get, the closer to perfection I think my paintings are. And with the final seventh painting, it was like my heart was speaking to me, or as though someone's prayer had been answered. Do we make decisions based on our hearts or our minds? Or do we use both? The heart does not have its own brain, but I would say the decisions I have made have been based on my heart. We are forgetful. I don't mean in the sense of amnesia, I mean that we forget what made us fall in love in the first place. Our heart reminds us of that.

"This series of paintings is called the Seven Faces of India, because each time I look intently at them, a tiny piece of my puzzle falls into place. When I look at these paintings, I hear the word 'India'. And it's a real voice. It's not in my head; it's called 'clairaudience'. Just like clairvoyance where people see things that aren't there, so clairaudience is where people hear something when it's not there in Nature."

The murmurs and gasps in the crowd became louder; they were realising something, but none of them could quite believe it. The audience had now split completely in two, forming a kind of guard of honour for someone to walk through. At the front stood Zoë and she had turned to one side. Locke could see her looking down the corridor of guests but still couldn't make out what was happening.

He found his place on his speech and began again, aware sweat was rolling down his spine. "I don't know why I hear the word 'India', because I'm not spiritual, so it can't be real, can it? I don't know why I paint, but it gives me a kind of solace, and I don't know who I paint because I can't remember."

"But I remember, John. I remember everything."

Locke stopped at the softly spoken words emanating from the crowd. The spotlight blinded him just enough that he couldn't make out the features on any face. The woman's voice continued, seemingly floating towards him out of the light.

"I am who you believe in, whom you love. It is me your heart calls because my eyes never stopped searching for you, because you were in my prayers. The sun faded. The ambiance started to burn. I remained motionless and the ground began to move. My heart started to pound. My breath stopped.

"Could that be my first love? It was such a beautiful moment. My dreams started to become a reality. This is how my love will always stay. Meet me at that birth after birth. Because of you my life is full of colour and I'm losing myself."

There was electricity in the air. No one moved. Locke's mouth had gone dry. In front of him he could make out the silhouette of a woman. *India*. Her hair seemed to blow in breeze that wasn't there. Her yellow sari floated on the air. She took a single pace forward. Now she was at the front of the spellbound audience. Anjali spoke.

"I became the shoreline. The sea becomes thirsty. Hide me in your stargaze. In these eyes, we have created a house in which we can live together. How can I explain what you represent for me? I swear to the Lord. You look like a god to me. You live in my heart as my god. Place me in your world as my god. People speak of living multiple lives. They speak of dying in love for one another. Regardless of what you want to do or accomplish, do it in this lifetime.

"Without you, John, my life is only half. Together we have one heart, one life. You are not just my night and day; you are my better half. My beauty and my body belongs to you. This fair skin belongs to you. If you are earth, I will be your sky. If you are the waterfall, I will be your ocean. I am hidden in you John. Still I desire you more."

Locke raised his hand to shield the spotlight. In front of the crowd stood a woman in a bright yellow sari. Her black hair fell in cascades down her back. Her eyes, he could see, were fixed on him.

"If you say it's day I will agree. If you say, it's night, I will agree." Locke felt his skin draw taught. Cold washed over him. Hairs stood on end. "Give me the permission to live and I will live. Tell me to die and I will die."

Zoë stood to the right of the woman in the yellow sari, and Locke never forgot the look on her face. Liam appeared next to her and oddly, Locke wondered how he had got down from the pulpit.

"It's me, John," the woman said softly. "It's Anjali; I am your India. You sang songs, read poetry and played games with me. It had no effect on my youth or beauty, but when your voice reached my heart. I felt like a sweet voice of *koyal* was speaking to me."

The noise from the audience grew; there was not a guest in the gallery who couldn't immediately see this mystery woman was the woman in the picture. Anjali continued forwards as Zoë watched her go, the taste of saltwater on her lips, Liam whispering quiet support in her ear.

Anjali reached the bottom of the pulpit and Locke descended its stairs. The spotlight went off and the room returned to its pre-speech cosy dimness. The DJ started back up, though it seemed out of place.

Anjali held out her hand and Locke took it, as if he was seeing her for the very first time. She was mesmeric. He looked over at Zoë and Liam; they weren't where they had been.

"I think it's time you came home," Anjali said. "You have dreams in your eyes. You have words on your lips. I will dedicate my life under your name. Because of you my night shines. A man only paints the woman he truly loves. Whether you become happy or sad, I will take all of your pain, if you give me permission to live.

"Seeing you is all I need, John. Desiring you is all I ever wanted. Finding you was my destiny. If only I get your love, I will forget the rest of the world. Give me the permission to live, I will live. Give the permission to die. I will die.

"Every inch of my body is calling you, my eyes search for new paths. I live in your breath. If you search your heart you will find me. *You* are calling *me*. Even after death I will belong to you. I will worship you, I will want you, that's my promise."

"Sir? Madam? Could you follow me?"

The woman was dressed smartly in a black suit with white blouse. Locke hadn't seen her before, but she was clearly one of the staff for the night. Anjali nodded and he found himself following the woman with his wife at his side. His memory had started to come back.

The door to Liam's office was open, light shining out into the corridor. Zoë's face was puffed up and red and she looked away when she saw Locke standing in the doorway. Anjali was just behind him, not wishing to look at the woman she knew to be the woman her husband had been with.

"John, I'm sorry," Liam said, his hands resting protectively on Zoë's shoulders. "But it had to be this way."

"What do you mean?" Locke was trying to process the sudden flood of images in his head but couldn't. "Why are you sorry?"

"Because, much as I like you, I couldn't have you hurting this one anymore." Liam squeezed Zoë's shoulders. She looked bleary eyed at the doorway, at Locke and his wife half hidden beside him. "I feared that, with all the publicity I've laid on, your wife would have to find us. I gave security an instruction to let her in if she showed up. I didn't know she'd wear the sari, but I guess she did that to trigger your memory."

Anjali nodded at the implied question. It had been exactly her plan.

"You engineered this?" Liam looked down at an incredulous Zoë.

"I'm sorry, Babe. I didn't think John was lying, which meant this day had to come. If she hadn't turned up, then maybe it was all in his head. But she has and we move on. You need to move on, Babe."

Zoë sniffed and dabbed at her eyes. She would be more honest with herself in the coming days, when she accepted what had happened, but just then she knew Liam was right and she wanted to punch him in the face. She had been a conduit through which John, *her John*, had learned to love again. She knew it was his life, that Anjali was his destiny. And it was tearing her apart.

"Look after Zoë," Locke said. "I know you love her. I can see it in the way you look at her. I know you can't say it, so I'll say it for you. Life is short and you never know when it will end. To find the perfect woman is rare; don't let your love hide in the shadows. Don't miss your chance."

"John, do you want to go out the back way, away from prying eyes?" Liam asked, tears welling in his own eyes. "I think perhaps you and your wife need a bit of privacy."

"Thanks," Locke said weakly allowing himself to be guided. At the backdoor to the gallery he stopped. Anjali turned to face him and he suddenly realised she was holding his hand. "What just happened?" he said, looking back down the corridor where a scream sounded from Liam's office.

"We happened, John," Anjali said. "*Ardhangini* happened." She saw Locke's puzzled look. "I will always find you, that's my destiny. We're together again. I'll tell you why when we get home."

part iv
john

twenty-six
and then, bang...
2018

The applause began as soon as the host said his name. A pretty assistant motioned the direction Locke and Anjali should take then pulled back the curtain for them to walk onto the stage. With ready smiles they passed through the doorway side by side. Anjali waved her hands into the breeze and gave *Namaste* to the audience, feeling the heat from the studio lights as she did so.

VC Gadkari moved towards the pair, arms outstretched ready for an embrace that suggested long-term friendship. He looked out into the audience and struggled to see beyond the stage lights, but waved anyway as if he recognised some in the audience.

The applause died down. Locke and Anjali took their cues from Gadkari and sat down on leather armchairs. The host did the same, then leant forward and touched Locke's knee, smiling, before greeting Anjali with a *Namaste*.

"I am honoured to be in the presence of the world's second most intelligent man," Gadkari said still smiling. "After myself!" The audience laughed. Locke took the joke for what it was and gave his own mock applause. "But seriously," the host continued, "you must actually be the world's most intelligent man. We know the why, but we do not perhaps know the how, or indeed the *who* of John Locke. What is each day like, for you?"

"First of all, I am not an intelligent man. I still have a long way to go before I can claim that title," Locke replied. "And I wasn't always like this; I was just an ordinary guy, like everyone here."

Anjali smiled at the answer. He was being modest and she liked that. Locke moved slightly in his armchair, feigned concentration and steepled his fingertips, as if the realisation of his fame had just sunk into his psyche. Somewhere in the audience a cough.

"It is like every day for everyone," he began. "I wake up, I look at my son and my beautiful wife and I feel happy. I am no different to anyone else lucky enough to have that nuclear family. But I suppose I am lucky in other ways. It's not every day you get attacked and wake up with some kind of 'super brain'."

The audience laughed as Locke made light of his injury. He laughed with them then winked at a camera pointing straight at him. He knew now how to play to the crowd.

"But there must be something more," Gadkari persisted. "Your story is so amazing, so incredible."

"All I can say is I was in the right place at the right time." Locke stated. "Not that it felt like it then. I had had my heart broken by the woman I loved, I think I was heavily drunk, which was not a good way to be, and then I was badly hurt. I was in a coma for weeks and I had to learn the simplest tasks again. It took me an age to walk again and all the while I had no memory of who I was."

Photographs of Locke's injuries flashed up on the big screen behind the trio. An occasional gasp emanating from the audience. He leaned across and took Anjali's hand in his. "It was Anjali who give me life. At that time we weren't married and she had just left me as my girlfriend, which is why I was drunk that night and why I was defenceless when I was attacked. But she came back into my life when I needed her the most."

Gadkari turned his attention to Anjali. "So, you have broken up, you are no longer together and yet you go back when you hear of his injuries. What made you do that?"

"Humanity," Anjali said without hesitation. "If you can't help another human being, then you aren't leaving a good example in life to other human beings. You don't need to be in a relationship to aid others." The audience broke in to spontaneous applause. "You need a heart," she continued, once the clapping had subsided. "We should forget race and religion and put it to the back of our minds. We are human first, race and religion comes later."

More applause, then Locke took up the narrative. "Of course, the story is not incredible because it has happened. To find it incredible, is to not believe it. I had my incident, Anjali nursed me back to health, and now I am changed with a greater mind than I had before." Locke pretended to study India's most foremost chat show host. "I think you believe all that, don't you VC?"

Gadkari threw up his hands. "Of course, I do. The whole world believes." The audience loved it; laughter and applause combined. Locke waited for it to end. It was a polished performance that he had honed in many television studios across the globe. His newly developed intelligence had him on the screens of the US and the UK and, because of Anjali, India as well. His books had sold millions, and his other activities had brought him adoration from billions.

"You know," Locke said. "It's easy and difficult at the same time. Easy because I have used my knowledge in a way that helps people. I have upset many corrupt organisations by exposing how they abuse the ordinary man in the street. I have broken up cartels by looking at the evidence properly. I am proud of these achievements, and yet pride is not necessarily a good thing. And then it is difficult. But I have my family; my wife and my child. I have incredible support. When you possess the right *ardhangini* in life, life is suddenly much easier."

The TV host placed his hand on his chin, as if he was thinking deeply. He paused for effect then looked straight at Locke. "There was an affair in the middle of all this, wasn't there? How do you feel about that looking back?"

Locke's face darkened. He had not expected the question and his publicist usually insisted it did not come up. Perhaps Gadkari had forgotten. Perhaps deliberately.

"It's the most shameful thing I have ever done," Locke said.

"No, it is not," Anjali said, abruptly. Both Locke and Gadkari turned to face her, surprised.

"John was having one of his episodes. He had lost his memory and the pain of having me try to bring him back was killing him. I was telling him what had happened and he could remember nothing. I didn't know what to do and so I kept doing the same thing, saying the same thing over and over.

"Then John left and I lost him for almost a year. I understand why he left and I understand why he tried to create a new life for himself. But an affair? No. John was *told* he had a wife, but he didn't *know* he had a wife. That is why he did not have an affair."

Gadkari nodded, still seemingly deep in thought. "I think I understand. It is a special woman who can forgive like that. Tell me, Anjali, what do you serve him with? He still has medical conditions. Do you still not know why it occurs? Is there a cure?"

"I serve him with love and support," she said. "It is all I think any wife should seek to do, and it is the same for men; their first job is to love and support their wives. But as to his condition, the science hasn't evolved enough yet. We don't know if there will be a cure, but the interesting thing is the world's foremost expert on John's condition is John himself. Five years to the day he was treated for cancer during the recovery from his initial attack, he relapsed and lost all memory and identity. Five years to the day and it happened a second time."

"It's something to do with the radioactive isotopes used in the cancer treatment," Locke interjected. "I anticipate another episode in a few months, but I won't bore you with the science."

Anjali ignored her husband. "That is a conflict for me. I have to find him first, bring his memory back and remind him I am his wife. It takes a while and last time it was months until his memory came back. And it is so hard for him. During his first relapse he left me because he couldn't take it anymore. I was telling him all the stories of his past life and he could remember none of it. I showed him photographs, videos, played TV shows he used to like, everything and anything that might help him remember. But he couldn't, and it nearly killed him. He left and I lost him for almost a year, before I finally found him again. That's when he started to remember. And when he is back to normal, he develops a fresh identity, new talent or a new skill. It is a challenge in our spousal relationship, but we have made it."

"You are a brave woman," Gadkari said. "You are a good role model and inspiration for our new generations." The audience signalled its support with polite applause. Anjali radiated strength and beauty and modesty. The chat show host turned his attention back to Locke. "You say you won't bore us with the details, but you are certain you are due another episode?"

"I know I will have another episode in a few months' time and although I know why, it still scares me," Locke admitted. "I have had three episodes of amnesia. The first when I was mugged and the second and third because of the radiation treatment I had during my recovery from the head injury I suffered in the mugging."

"And that is the radiation half-life…" Gadkari suggested knowingly.

"It is. My doctors and I agree that is why I have these blackouts every five years."

"Are you worried or scared, Anjali?"

"Yes, of course," she replied. "But we know when it's coming so we can take precautions."

"Most days I don't care," Locke added, "but some I am truly scared. My intelligence is natural, but the treatment somehow made me able to remember everything having seen it just once. That doesn't happen to normal people. It didn't happen to me before I was treated. I was never good at mathematics, I mean I knew the basics, just not the detailed equations. I always envied others' intelligence, really, as I wasn't a bright guy. I used to wish I was more intelligent, but now that I am, Anjali reminds me all the time that having a heart is much more significant. It's how people judge after your appearance."

"And what do you mean by that, Anjali?"

"The heart in our body gives us personality," she stated. "But with intelligence you become lost and proud. And we forget our God, our creator. We sense we are self-sufficient. We feel as if we are God. But we forget who give us the intelligence in the first place. And we forget to thank him or remember him."

"So you believe in God?" Gadkari asked.

"Yes. That's my whole existence."

Gadkari turned his attention back to Locke. "What about you, John? Do you believe in a God?"

"No," Locke said. "And I can't believe in the concept of God, either. I believe in the seen not the unseen."

"If you know everything," Gadkari paused for effect; the audience suitably silent, "do you not know if you will retain this... this superpower or intelligence?"

"Well, of course, I don't know everything, but with regards to that question, I haven't figured it out yet. There is no reason why I should lose it, and I don't think I will, but strange things happen. I guess they could 'unhappen' as well."

Gadkari returned to Anjali. "What do you think about this question?"

"It is an interesting question, and one we don't hold an answer for in our Hindu culture," she replied. "But there is a belief in Islam that intelligence belongs to God. He presents it to whom he wishes. It can occur at any age. This is why some people are regarded as having developed greater intelligence or knowledge at early stages of their lives, so maybe as young as six, and others much later, perhaps in their forties, fifties, sixties or even later. That is why Muslims don't worship idols. The Muslim consciousness is higher; it's because they're allowed to worship without idols. And few individuals or cultures can do it. Even now, humans still cannot worship God without idols, including me. Although our Scripture says *'na tasya pratima asti'*, which means that God did not have pictures, paintings or carvings. They ask Allah for intelligence and he might bestow it upon them. If you look at the table of *chakras,* you will see that the highest consciousness is called Allah. It's above our heads and not everyone can achieve this consciousness or use it. That makes us ordinary human beings working with our labours or our minds. Only by achieving this do you have the intellect."

Gadkari considered this. It was definitely a more highbrow conversation than he had expected to come from Anjali Locke; he expected all of the intellectual comments to come from her husband. He was about to say something, but Anjali wasn't finished.

"If you look at the story of an individual named Srinivasan Ramanujan, he was an Indian mathematician who studied at Cambridge University in 1913. He did not resemble any other genius in the history of the world and yet his work now forms the basis for superstring theory and multidimensional physics. Ramanujan used to say that his genius came from God.

"If you examine Muslim history, there is a belief in Muslim civilisation that Muhammad was given his revelation from God. The man was illiterate. He never claimed that he was a genius or wrote the Scriptures. Even today, it is a sign that there is something greater than human consciousness. Either intelligence belongs to God or knowledge belongs to God. And God is called all knowing. Their mind is already in a superior consciousness. They call upon God or Allah to give me intelligence and knowledge. Not everyone uses it well or receives knowledge. And if you look at the anatomy of our brain, you will notice a deep slope in our frontal lobe, which indicates that our brain is configured to worship or to incline down."

The audience broke into spontaneous applause. Gadkari followed with his own applause.

"How do you know this?" he asked.

"I seek knowledge about other religions," Anjali replied, easily. "Scripture is not sent to any single religion; it was sent to all mankind, and whoever reads it has the knowledge of the universe. But as human beings, we love to separate or divide; even one God in hundreds of thousands of 'gods'. Our history shows people who told the truth from their consciousness were ridiculed by society. To name a few: Christopher Columbus, Giordano Bruno, the Wright brothers, Andreas Vesalius, William Harvey, and Galileo.

"Mathematicians are the language of God. History has proven that name over and over again. This is why I think John's knowledge was given to him by God and that, someday, his belief will be restored."

Locke smiled, looked out at a faceless audience he could not quite see, and heard the applause. This audience liked what they were hearing, and he was gratified that they were listening so intently to his wife.

"Going back to the question of knowing everything," Locke said. "I don't know everything, because I have to learn it all in the first place. I don't choose the subject I desire to earn; it just happens, as though it is choosing itself, or as if someone is pulling the strings and leading me in a certain direction. You could call it fate, a miracle or destiny. It just happens. And so the fear of losing that ability isn't there either, it's just that my brain gets reprogrammed every five years.

"But my condition is unknown. The question we should be asking ourselves is, is it God's gift? Is it a miracle? Is it supernatural? I don't mean in the sense of ghosts and phantoms, but that avenue still needs to be analysed. We know why this happened to me to the best of Man's knowledge, but we don't know whether this *superpower...*" it was a word he hated, but again some in the audience tittered, "... is infinite for example."

"The answer lies in religion *and* science," Anjali stated. "The problem is, we're splitting religion from science. If you look at the history of Mesopotamia and all the scientists, you will see that they all succeeded in reading the scripture which leads to new scientific discoveries. Religion gives us signs, science gives us the how. It means we need to find out what religion is real."

VC Gadkari held out his hands in supplication, as if Anjali had said something profound and the audience dutifully applauded. Locke thought it ludicrous, but then he found many people ludicrous nowadays. He didn't let it affect him. He looked over the audience and basked in their glory a bit more, then looked back at Anjali. Their son, Sachin, was at home with the nanny. She had chosen to come to the show. It was her role, especially in India, to show her support and devotion to her husband.

Gadkari leaped up from his chair and clapped loudly. "Much more from John and Anjali Locke after the break." And the audience applauded once more.

*

"So, you're in India for an extended period, I believe?"

"I am," Locke said, after the latest applause had died down and Gadkari had asked the question. "That is to say we are here for three or four months whilst our house gets built in England. We will return when it is finished and I will prepare for my next episode."

"You designed your house?" Gadkari asked, apparently shocked.

"I did. As is my good fortune, I studied architecture for a short time, then used my newly acquired architectural skills to design the house."

"So it is not just knowledge you can learn easily, but how to use that knowledge practically?"

"Yes, that's right," Locke said. Gadkari leant forward conspiratorially again.

"We have a video we would like to show people," the chat show host said, taking on a more serious tone. "It's of you performing an operation."

"Oh no!" Locke laughed out loud. "This is terrible! I did this quite early on, in about 2007. But to give it some background, I first time got interested in medical science was when Anjali was pregnant with our son. Very soon I knew more about childbirth than the consultant and I decided on a home birth where I would deliver the child. Fortunately my wife didn't agree. She said it was her body and of course she was right. I may have this exceptional intelligence, but that does not make me omnipotent or immortal. As it was, it was a normal birth and our beautiful son arrived, but I could have delivered him easily.

"The second incident was when I was walking in Manchester one day and this man keeled over right in front of me. I ran to his aid along with others. I checked his vital signs and I'm thinking, *why are you doing this? Phone an ambulance.* But it was like it wasn't me; it was as though I had medical training and I was using it.

"I was aware he was slipping away, so I started to bark orders at people – it's a blur but that's what I did. I knew his breathing was failing, as if he was choking, so I decided to do a tracheotomy. I shouted for a pen, or any kind of narrow tube, and someone handed a biro to me. I took the lid off and removed the pen and ink cartridge, then I pushed the narrow end of the tube down on the man's throat, trying to gain entry to his windpipe. There was a crunch and the tube went in. Suddenly this man is gurgling as the air flows back into his lungs. He tried to sit up, but we made him comfortable until the ambulance arrived. I told them what I had done then walked away.

"I couldn't believe I had done that. It was my first ever open surgery without any medical training and I was lucky it worked. But then I always knew it would. Why? That I can't explain, but after that I realised I wanted to save lives. I took to studying and researching and in a matter of a few months, was good enough to become a surgeon."

"Those two incidents led to this third one."

"Let's roll the tape, shall we?" Gadkari said. An image appeared on a big screen behind the host and Locke watched between his fingers, feigning embarrassment. "What is happening here?"

The image was of a man, lying on his back with just his lower face visible. A much younger Locke came into view wearing a surgeon's scrubs. His face was covered but the eyes were unmistakable. He looked at the camera.

"A friend of mine plays a sport known as rugby. It is a very rough game in which you physically need to overpower your opponent. Sometimes this organised violence can descend into actual and illegal violence. My friend was punched and he has broken his jaw in two places. In this video I will show you how to set it back in place."

The video blacked out briefly before showing an incision being made in the tissue of the patient's lower jaw. Locke talked as he performed the cut.

"One of the breaks is immediately below the front teeth of the lower mandible, and I am making the incision at that point. You can already see were the gum has ruptured along the line of the break. I will realign the mandible and secure it using titanium plates and screws." Locke looked up at the camera as an assistant sucked up some loose blood made by the incision. "But don't get too excited – he won't set off the airport alarms!"

Back in the studio some laughed at the joke. Locke had lowered his hand and pretended to watch. To his right, Anjali beamed even though she had seen this video many times. The footage jumped again, Locke still talking to camera as he secured one of the tiny screws in the plate below the patient's front teeth.

"And that is the front plate in place. The other break point in this instance is below a wisdom tooth on the left side of the face. I am now going to remove the tooth and put two plates across the second fracture; it's longer than the first so I need to make sure it is properly stable."

The footage jumped again, to show Locke closing up the incision in the patient's mouth. He finished and cut the last of the stitching thread, then looked back at the camera. "And there we have it. In total there are now fifteen pieces of titanium in my friend's mouth. His jaw will take up to three months to heal, so he is on soup for a while, but he will make a complete recovery."

The footage darkened a final time and Gadkari turned in his seat to be facing Locke. "So am I right in thinking that was your second surgical procedure?"

"Procedure, yes, you are right," Locke said. "It would have been my third had Anjali not been completely correct about giving birth in the hospital. I just wanted to prove I could do it. In fact, what you don't see is that I actually invented a new method of stitching wounds such as those; instead of just using a thread which I noticed caused gaps in the mucosa, that's the area where the incision takes place below the front teeth, I added a non-toxic glue that held either side of the incision together while it healed naturally."

"That's amazing!" Gadkari said. The audience applauded as one, spurred on by the prompter who chose when there should be clapping. "And you didn't operate again?"

Locke took a sip of the water on the table next to him and shook his head. "No, I didn't. Some things I learn I like to continue with them, whereas others I have done it and don't need to prove myself capable anymore. A surgeon watched that video back with me and he pointed out where he thought I had gone wrong. I corrected him on those points; he's retired now, but for the last years of his career he used my methods."

More clapping. Locke's smile was genuine. But at this last comment Anjali did not smile. Her face was set hard. She didn't like it when he showed off. He sometimes struggled to stay humble.

"I have knowledge, more than anyone can learn in their lifetime. Some people achieve one skill in their lives. I have three. Just call me God!" Locke laughed, more deeply this time, and to some he crossed the line from sanity.

"John, stop!" Anjali said quietly, realising he was making a fool of himself in front of millions. She waited until she was sure the camera was on the host, or her husband, then quietly rose and walked off stage. Gadkari hadn't noticed; he and Locke was still laughing at Locke's excitable manner.

"You mentioned you were designing and building your own house?" Gadkari asked.

"Yes," Locke said, "and being an architect and being a surgeon are not that dissimilar. The human body has a design; the upper and lower jaw move in a vertical plane so that your teeth chomp up and down pulverising your food, for instance, or where your fingers have multiple bones and joints making it possible for you to grasp things. So when I decided to build my own house, I did a bit of research and started thinking about a design."

Locke shuffled in his seat, took another sip of his water. "But where this is different to surgery is that with architecture, I have a blank canvas and I can put my own ideas into the building. The body is already designed; I could only repair it. But with the house I can do what I like.

"One of the things I always had was a passion for art. But I couldn't draw, so that's why I took to photography. I used to take photographs. In fact, it was on a trip to India where I first saw my future wife and photographed her in a temple. Isn't that right, Anjali?" he said, turning in his chair only to find her seat was now empty. He didn't break stride. "Before I had all this intelligence, I simply had an eye for beauty and my photographs were good. That's what cannot be taught; art. I can study the great painters and copy their creations, but I cannot *create* as they would have. Art and beauty are indefinable. They are the kinds of qualities you have, or you don't have.

"So I can rebuild the Taj Mahal or Buckingham Palace, but I relied on my own art to create Locke Towers to the correct building specifications that anyone can learn. My home will be an extension of me and unique. Another architect may create a design and others will think it more beautiful than mine. That's fine – but I am trying to understand the secrets of art, to see whether, just like knowledge, I can learn to do perfect art. I am not sure. But it's exciting to study."

VC Gadkari sat back in his chair. The audience remained quiet, waiting to see what the TV personality would say. He sighed. "The episodes," he said. "Tell me about them."

Locke seemed to think for a moment; "It's simple, really. I was given an incorrect dose of radiation which somehow opened up my brain's abilities to retain information. I have my theories about that, but I am the only person in the world that this has happened to. It must not happen again, although I believe there are some scientists in countries such as Russia that are trying to replicate my condition. It's terrifying to think that there might be an army of super intelligent people being created.

"But anyway, we had reconciled my intelligence by the time of my first episode. I had already started writing books about improving brain power, annoyed the casinos by explaining how to count cards and win, performed that operation you have just watched. All those things happened before my first episode. As did the birth of my son. And then, bang..."

Locke clapped once. The noise resonated throughout the studio. Gadkari startled a little.

"It took me around six months to get my memory back again. History had repeated itself; I lost my memory after I was mugged and I lost it again. Amnesia is a terrible thing and it is one thing I am desperate to cure. It tears your life apart for you and for your loved ones. Think about it; it's bringing about new personalities in me. I didn't trust my wife, my beautiful wife, for six months. I didn't know who she was. I didn't recognise our son or the rest of my family or hers. She had to go through the whole process again.

"But it was easier the second time. There were videos of me doing things with my wife, with my son. There was the video of the surgery we have just seen. All of these things existed and so I could see myself on screen. Slowly the memories returned. With the third episode I was ready; exactly ten years after the wrong dose was applied and exactly five years after my first collapse, I collapsed again. But this time I had footage of my wife and my son and my wedding and other things, I was sure I'd get through it."

Locke sipped his water. "It happened right on cue. This time I was lying down on a comfortable bed so that I didn't collapse and hurt myself somehow. My wife knew it was coming and we tried to explain to my son, but that was hard with him being just eight at the time. I know why it happens; the radioactive isotope has a half-life of exactly five years. But I don't know why that causes the seizures and the amnesia. I'm working on it."

"You're due another episode shortly?" Gadkari asked sensitively. "Is that correct?"

"It is. I've prepared for it differently this time; I've recorded videos where I talk to my future self. But I am also designing parts of my life into the building of my house in England. I will have it built by then and it will be our home while I convalesce. In the meantime, we are in India. We have our charities over here: my wife's school and the funds we have to help the country's street children. We are taking the opportunity to further them ahead of the inevitable."

"What is the motive behind the charity?" Gadkari had, by now, also realised Anjali had left her seat.

"It was Anjali's idea. At one point my condition wasn't getting any better so she started up a charity organisation. She believes in helping the poor and receiving blessing from millions. She felt it would bring spiritual harmony into my life. She's not been proved wrong so far."

The audience broke out in spontaneous applause once more. It was what Locke had hoped for. He knew there wasn't long left in the interview and he wanted to make it about his stay in India and not just his fame, fortune and life history. VC Gadkari smiled wanly.

"Are you nervous?" he asked, forcing Locke back to his condition.

"Yes," Locke replied, curtly. "The collapse is horrific; blinding headaches and nausea. It's not pleasant for me or my wife or anyone who witnesses it. It will only be my wife and doctors this time. Same as last time. So until that happens, and it will happen on the fourteenth of August, I am here in India trying to do some good for the world."

"You say you are trying to work out why it happens. Why don't you know?"

"My circumstances change," Locke said simply. "And I am not smart enough. People may think I'm a genius, but I haven't find the answer to my life."

"Why not?" Gadkari countered.

Locke gritted his teeth. "I can learn things with ease. I retain information. But if the information is not there, then I cannot learn it. What's happened to me is unique and there are no papers explaining it. When there is, I will be able to understand it instantly. But it is not so easy to create theories as to actually learn the latest science. There aren't many things I don't understand, but my episodes are one of them."

Gadkari leant forward and again placed his hand upon Locke's knee. He tried for a look of cheekiness, as if he and Locke were best friends.

"What else don't you understand?"

Locke knew what the chat show host wanted. He didn't like the question, but he knew how to play the media. He took a deep breath as if weighing up whether he should make his statement.

"Women," he said. "I don't understand a woman's sacrifice for a man. I don't think anyone does. Why else do we have so many divorces in our culture?" Locked laughed again and the audience laughed with him.

Gadkari had his comment. A light-hearted ending to the interview. Fake whoops of shock and surprise mingled with the laughter in the studio. Locke smiled and looked out into the throng. Laughter turned to applause and the studio lights moved, brightening the area where Gadkari and Locke remained. The host leant across and shook Locke by the hand, then turned to face a camera and gave his closing remarks.

"Isn't it refreshing that the world's most intelligent man admits that not even he understands women? Finally, I have something in common with the unbelievable Mr John Locke." Gadkari pretended to wipe a tear from his eye, as if he had been crying with laughter. It was how he ended every programme. It was what the audience came for.

From where she now stood, Anjali watched on. She could see her husband was a little uncomfortable, as he looked around. *Why say it?* she thought. She saw him smile and wave to the audience. Anjali didn't smile; she didn't take her eyes off him. She could feel a change developing in John Locke.

twenty-seven

a rabid obsession for revenge

"You didn't have to say it." Anjali stared out of the window of the limousine as it snaked its way west from the television studio and through the busy Mumbai streets towards the mansion they were renting.

"I haven't said anything I didn't want to say. It's my life. This is my story. I can present it how I like. I don't need permission from you." The anger simmered away just under the surface. Locke was livid. "Why the hell did you walk off the stage? Do you know how humiliated I felt?"

Anjali had walked out during the interview, surprising both Locke and Gadkari. She had done it just after Locke had mentioned he didn't understand women. That comment hurt, but then he went further and she left. Gadkari made a joke about her departure and Locke laughed with him. She had remained in the studio, though, standing in the shadows just beside a camera, observing her husband and his body language. He was proud of his achievements.

"Where is the John I fell in love with?" she had whispered, eliciting an angry glare from the cameraman. She ignored him. "Where's the John that wanted to change the world? He was humble, and loving."

She returned to the present, gripping the car seat a little tighter as the chauffeur took a corner a bit fast.

"I didn't want to leave, but you were getting out of control," she stated. "'Just call me God'"? Are you dumb or stupid? Why would you say such a thing? I'm in utter turmoil about that right now. I start talking about humanity and you make a joke about being God. Where were you when you didn't have this knowledge? We are human first, not God. It's a gift, John. A gift you didn't have before. Look around you; everyone has a brain but not everyone is intelligent like you. It's so rare."

Anjali looked out from the darkened windows, barely making out the lights still on in late night shops or Mumbai's mansions.

"I couldn't help myself," Locke said finally. "The audience was cheering me on and I got a bit excited."

"You do know there are millions around the world observing us? We're under the spotlight and you go and say that. If I knew you were going to behave like that, I would never have suggested we went in front of the cameras. My family, my friends, everyone I know will have seen that, and you are saying this in a country where God and intellect is considered as God's knowledge. If they didn't see it live, they will when word gets out."

"When did you start to care about what people thought?" Locke felt his fists tighten. He might be the world's cleverest man, but he wasn't infallible and he knew how stupid it sounded to compare himself to God.

"I don't care," Anjali insisted. "But I still need to answer to people and wider society. You may be famous, John, but our lives are forever interlinked."

Locke said nothing. He stared out of the other window, feeling Anjali's sense of anger and defeat. He turned to look at her and saw a face he didn't recognise; gone was her serenity and patience. In its place a woman he saw with wisdom and knowledge when it came to worshipping her husband. But right now she was as angry as he had ever seen her.

"What has gone into you?" Locke said. "You've never been like that before. You have never talked to me like this before."

"I realise that and that is why it's hurting me. You are my husband, my *ardhangini*. It's my occupation, duty and responsibility to show you the right path and tell you when you're getting it wrong? People see us as just a woman, or just a housewife but we are much more than that. We bring luck and change your lives. We bring fulfilment in your lives. Without it you are alone. Your life has no purpose. Why do you think men are constantly searching for a woman? They may have sex in mind but it's company they are searching for. That's what *ardhangini* means. You aren't the person I fell in love with fifteen years ago. You are changing, and I can see it happening."

"Calm down," John hissed. "The driver can hear what you're saying. This isn't the time."

"I fought for you with my family, with my society and my wider community. Why? Because synchronising thought between a man and woman is important. Doesn't that mean anything to you?"

Locke didn't answer; he was too deep in thought. But the thing was, he didn't know *what* he thought. He felt the interview had been a success. Gadkari had been happy and so had the audience. He just couldn't wait to get home, but the Mumbai traffic was getting worse, not better. He had to get out of the car, couldn't handle being in the same space as Anjali when he had done this to her.

It had been a throwaway remark, but he knew the damage was done and he could never go back and rectify it. The anger simmered below the surface once again when he thought about how hard he had worked to provide for his wife and son.

Money doesn't grow on trees; has she got any idea where ours came from? The publicity alone will bring in more. He thought hard, his head pounding. The moment the interview was over his mind was on other things. But Anjali kept poking him, trying to get a reaction.

"And why did you think it was okay to mention women like that? That we're *strange*. You didn't have to say that either, John." The car slowed and waited for the gates to their temporary home to open. "You know how irresponsible it was. Women in India are not treated well. Every day a woman is treated badly just because she is a widow. Men discover that women are the source of their failure in their marriage. She is miserable. A man demands a higher dowry just because she is a woman or in a caste system. Women have to get an abortion as soon as they find out they're expecting a girl.

"People may worship the Goddess in our temple, but in the outside world, we are processed like dirt and prostitutes. Men sell women in the markets but they forget she is the same as they bring into their home and call her their wife. We give birth and the first thing a child sees is its mother. Yet still we are ranked the lowest of the order. When women can't afford to work or don't have an elder brother, we are traded for a higher dowry in marriage so the husband can provide for her family.

"After finding it's all over the news the number of rapes that are happening. Suggesting women are *strange* dehumanises them."

"I didn't say it like that. You're making too much of it."

"Whatever you thought you should have clarified it."

"My comment was positive," Locke insisted. "How can anyone know what's in a woman's heart or mind? We still don't know women after millions of years. There is a deeper root to a woman. That kind of thing. That's what I really meant. You are looking at this the wrong way."

"And young men will hear what you have just said and think women are beneath them. They can do what they want with them. That's the way I am looking at it and you know it."

"That's bullshit," Locke said as the car came to a halt by the grand staircase that led to the huge entrance of the house. Two male servants, both in full red and gold regalia, hurried down the stairs to open the doors to the car. Locke stepped out, not looking at his servant, and marched towards the house. Anjali quietly thanked the man opening her door and watched as her husband strode up the stairs two at a time. Another servant held open the door to the house and Locke breezed in. Anjali watched him turn left. She would check on their son alone.

*

"How is Sachin?" she asked the nanny standing outside the closed door of her son's bedroom. The nanny bowed.

"He had a full dinner, played some video games and was asleep by the eight-thirty, madam."

"Thank you, Meena," Anjali replied and quietly entered her son's bedroom. She controlled her breathing and let the anger leave here. She was now being a mother, not an angry wife and she never forgot to check in on her son. She looked down dotingly at the young boy, his eyelids flickering slightly as if he was in the middle of a dream. She stroked his soft forehead and bent down to kiss him on the cheek. Such innocence never ceased to her with deep love.

"You look just like your father," she whispered. "I just hope you don't turn out like him. Be innocent, be kind, be loved, even if you do have a low IQ."

Sachin had struggled with the temporary move to India. He was initially very excited as he had travelled to the country several times previously and met with much of his extended family, but this time they, or rather his father, chose Mumbai instead of Delhi. He said he wanted to be surrounded by Bollywood money and spend time with the rich and famous. Which is what they did for a bit, but Sachin didn't bond too well with any of the sons and daughters of Bollywood's great and good. He didn't seem so keen on all the glitz and glamour, and he had not been born into it like the other children. He seemed to be developing something of a photographic memory. He could recognise objects in much more detail. Reading and collecting knowledge was becoming apparent. It looked like he might be following in his father's footsteps and becoming a genius in his own right.

Not that his parents noticed, but his mind was developing fast and he became more isolated and soon stopped wanting to leave the mansion grounds. At the same time he heard his parents arguing and took to hiding around the house. Neither his mother nor his father realised.

Locke was the same. After a couple of weeks eating out in Juha's most exclusive restaurants, living off his fame as being the world's most intelligent man, he seemed to get bored. Now he rarely left the substantial room he had turned into his office. Anjali didn't venture in there often, but the first time she did she had been shocked. At least a dozen computers, a huge TV screen, fridge, freezer and a bed. *Even a bed.* It was a self-contained flat where Locke could work away at whatever grand plan he had, without ever leaving the room. To her it felt like he had walked out on her and Sachin again, only without actually leaving the marital home. Soon he didn't come out much at all and she wondered whether to contact his consultant, not that Locke would take any notice.

*

The phone buzzed on the bedside table. Slowly Anjali turned her head to look at it. She had been awake for hours, trying to process last night's argument with Locke.

"Hello mother. *Namaste.* How are you?"

"I'm fine, Anjali."

"Then why have you called? It's usually me calling you." Anjali looked at the alarm clock shining bright red LED lights next to her and sat up in bed. "It must be half four in the morning. Has something happened?"

"Can I only ring my daughter when there is a problem? I just got a sense that you might not be feeling well, mentally. I'm sorry for calling, but I just had to. I need to know for certain and I need to hear your voice. Are you doing okay? Are you happy right now?"

Anjali said nothing. She was tired and she felt she would cry if she spoke.

"What's gone wrong, my darling?"

"Nothing, Mother," Anjali lied. "Nothing. Nothing!" She could barely control her emotions, desperate not to burst out crying.

"Oh, Anjali, I can hear the upset in your voice. Please tell me what I can do."

"I don't know what to do anymore, Mother. He is not the same person I fell in love with. We are constantly arguing, quarrelling. Right now he is sleeping in a different room."

"You need to have patience, my darling. He will come around eventually. He really loves you. Perhaps you should just quieten down for a bit and listen to what he has to say? Marriage is about understanding your husband, about understanding his feelings and his needs. It's likely been a difficult time for him, being in a different country. I always thought it was a risky decision to go to India. It is so different to here. Why don't you try mediation? Do some prayers? Ask God to give him light and discernment. Being a wife is about being patient. That's why we are called the consciousness of men. Maybe you can help him to find his way?"

"I will try that, mother," Anjali said. "Thank you for calling, I really am all right and I will talk to him later."

Quieten down for a bit? Wasn't that exactly what she railed against with his comment about finding women strange, and yet her own mother was suggesting her husband needed her help, not her criticism. That didn't sit well. The TV appearance had come at the end of a day of interviews with newspapers and radio stations that would be broadcast across India. Anjali had followed, just to be with her husband. She wondered now whether she should have done.

Locke had not checked on Sachin as he had gone straight to his 'lair' as she sometimes called his huge office. He was neglecting his son and he was neglecting his wife as well. The image of Sachin sleeping gave her the impetus she required and she put her dressing gown on as she crossed the landing to her son's bedroom. He was still asleep and still looked angelic as his chest rose with each of intake of breath.

And that innocence. It made her think about herself. Was she being too trusting? Was she just happy with Locke because he earned the millions that kept them in splendid wealth? Did she need more from her *ardhangini?* Or was it another challenge? She was being tested like never before.

She returned to her bed and fell asleep thinking about her life and was soon confronted by an image of Locke running away from the police. Patrol cars blocked the exits to a large, clearly English, field. There were seemingly hundreds of policemen, some on foot and some with police dogs, and the dogs were barking as one. Loudhailers were shouting instructions for people to stay inside while a helicopter hovered noisily overhead.

She could no longer see Locke but for some reason she thought she remembered him running through the streets of Manchester. Then she was walking along a quiet street having visited her local temple. Locke burst out of a side alley and crashed into her. There was a look of sheer terror on his face.

"What are you doing here, John? What are you running from?"

And then the shot rang out, piercing the dream. Locke's eyes glazed over as the life left his body then he slumped, straight down. Sightless eyes now looked upwards and Anjali saw the sky reflected in them. She screamed, aware of heavy boots running somewhere nearby.

"Help him! Someone please save him!"

The sounds of boots got nearer. There was shouting, but she couldn't tell what was being said. She knelt beside the body and touched his face. It was already turning grey. Tears stung as she stared down at the broken body of her husband. His eyes moved to look directly into hers.

"I'm sorry," he said. "Why did I do it? Was it greed? Or pride. I don't know. I couldn't keep your word." Then his eyes closed forever.

Anjali sat bolt upright in her bed, instantly feeling the wetness on her face and the drenched nightgown sticking to her skin. "John!" she called out. "You can't leave me, John!"

She took the hem of her nightgown and rubbed the sweat from her face, then grabbed the glass of water by her side and drank it all, gasping for air once she finished. Pieces were beginning to fall into place and she hurried to the shrine in the hallway, several of the staff trying hard not to stare.

"Hey Krishna! Radha! What am I doing wrong? Why are you showing me this? Please help me. Was this a coming sign? If I have done anything improper, please forgive me. But don't take John away from me. If he has done anything wrong. Please forgive him, but in return, you get hold of my life."

Anjali lay flat on the floor in front of the shrine for hours, touching the foot of the idol and asking for her husband's forgiveness. Slowly her breathing eased and she began to get back to her feet. She gave *Namaste* and walked away, aware of people looking at her. She pretended she couldn't see them, but one thing was clear; whoever was watching her walk with lank hair and soaked clothes, John Locke wasn't amongst them.

His next episode was just a few months away and it worried her more than ever. Was the bond between husband and wife weakening? Or was her love faltering? Was it even there anymore? She determined not to cry at the thought of her life. Elsewhere in the building, she fancied she could hear her husband tapping away at the keyboard of a laptop. It was nonsense, of course; he was too far away. But in her head at least, the tapping wouldn't stop.

*

Locke looked at the clock in the bottom right-hand corner of the computer screen. Just after eleven in the evening local time, so about half six in England. Not for the first time he felt irritated at the usage of half hours on the world clock. He thought it stupid, but then he found a lot of things stupid, many that didn't matter. He wondered about Anjali; was she stupid in clinging on to the smallest point of spirit? Not ordinarily, but he seemed to be getting more annoyed at the things she said. *Why does she always have to be right all the time and why can't I think right?* That nonsense about understanding women – how could she possibly extrapolate that to mean the demeaning of women? Why not focus on the fact women were enigmatic? Or that their beauty often didn't reside in their physical features, but in the intricacies of their minds? Was it not enough to adore her for bringing their child into the world? And what if he had said he did understand women? The opposite would have happened; millions of women worldwide would have scoffed and so would Anjali.

Can I ever be right? The argument wouldn't go away and he went over it time and again, fuming in his thoughts. But he hadn't been talking to Anjali; he had been talking to VC Gadkari and the chat show host was more than happy with the levity at the end. It had ended the show succinctly and neatly and everybody was happy. Everybody except Anjali. The situation was bothering him. He didn't have control and he thought there was something deeper within his wife that he couldn't fathom with pure logic. Was it because he was a man, or an atheist? He couldn't decide whether he believed and his non-belief mattered.

But we still managed to fall in love. What is the connection here? What is the lesson? Will I ever find an answer here? What can she see in me, that I can't see in myself? Is she a psychic? Can she tell the future?

He shook the thought away, sighed and started tapping at his keyboard. He struggled hard to concentrate as the thoughts kept creeping up on him. He strained to obliterate the thoughts that kept forming in his mind. *Concentrate, you fool!* He wanted to catch his contacts in England before turning to the Indian issues he faced. Something was brewing back home. He could feel it. The emails coming through from trusted sources were changing. He had long since removed the sycophants from his networks so that when an email came through now, he knew he could take that individual at face value, which meant he could take their comments at face value. The syntax was changing. He noticed it increasingly of late. Whereas before everything was definite and on track, 'woulds' had become 'coulds' and 'I will' became 'I'll try'.

Then there were the gangs he had contacts with. Now they *were* stupid, and he liked to play with them, but as he always knew, they would get greedy. It was the only truth about any criminal; until they were stopped, they would demand more and more. The Salford lot had long since ceased to be important. He had outgrown them quite quickly, and the lucrative business of ripping off casinos the length and breadth of the UK was no longer interesting. When the casinos retaliated, their own muscle stepping into the lawless void of modern England, Locke quietly got out. His books were starting to take off and it was clear the gambling industry changed as a result. Governments around the world started to legislate and gambling dens either became fairer to the gambler or ceased to trade. Locke had taken precautions; the stupidity of greedy criminals often morphed into a rabid obsession for revenge.

But the Salford gang knew him. They were the only criminals that knew his identity. Once he had earned a decent profit from the gambling scams, and he was started to get noticed in media circles, he knew he had to protect his identity. No one involved in any of the little scams he created knew his name, his face, even his voice. He was meticulous. But he had to cut the Salford gang another deal which gave them something else to do illegally and he quietly stepped away. True to their word, they never divulged his name – at least it had never appeared in the press – but periodically they would come back to him. He supposed when they ran out of money. They had become an insidious memory that occasionally raised its head. They had been in touch again. Locke decided it was the last time.

But outside of them, things were different. There were different people doing different things, all just the wrong side of the law. Even now Locke felt a frisson of excitement each time he was involved with them, and they were all there when he opened his encrypted emails. It was so simple; he had an email address that literally anyone in the world could find and all emails came through on that address. But each email was sorted automatically, and before it landed in his inbox. Should anyone look, his emails were in the tens of thousands daily and, hidden within, emails from his not so upstanding contacts would be there. His programme automatically changed those emails into something benign while he looked at the message. If anyone looked at the sender's email, they would see the 'translated' email and a stock answer from Locke Enterprises politely replying to that individual. Each time someone emailed, the code for them reinvented itself based on what was in the email. It was untraceable, and yet it was sitting there, plain as day, in his inbox.

But the real beauty? The dodgy emailers had no idea who they were emailing; they just thought they were using the cover of Locke Enterprises' address. They didn't know they were dealing with John Locke himself. If any succumbed to a police investigation, they would have no idea who they were emailing, and neither would the police. Any enquiry from a police officer was met with the correct shock and denial from the unsuspecting staff, who routinely said they thought the emails were spam. Only Locke himself knew, and he liked that. It was the secret of his success; he knew more than anyone else on literally any subject. He was unstoppable; he was in the public domain and he now had a much darker side no one knew about.

He smiled like the devil himself and fired off an email to a stockbroker in London and another to a horse trainer in Ireland before turning his attention to the one from a small-time shipping contractor from the Isle of Man. It seemed the skipper was getting cold feet. Trade had been good while it lasted, but it seemed he no longer wanted to be involved in the smuggling operation Locke had set up. And that was both a pity and a problem.

The diamonds, sapphires and emeralds making their way into the UK were helping Locke Enterprises massively. Trade in precious stones were nothing new, but the authorities, at least those governing the UK, had clamped down hard in recent years. That was what made the trade lucrative and the guy on the Isle of Man helped Locke facilitate it. But now he was 'trying to get over to Ireland in the next week or so', and it wasn't good enough. The shipment was ready as the horse trainer had told him so. The stockbroker in London was primed to put the gemstones on the market using the lapidary Locke himself had sourced. The plot had not been that long in the planning, but any change at this stage would infuriate him.

The guy in the Isle of Man said there had been an increase in patrols on both sides of the Irish Sea. Locke clenched his jaw. And typed a little more angrily than he might normally. The shipment would go ahead as arranged. He had no remorse for anyone involved.

*

Locke looked again at the clock in the bottom right-hand corner of his screen. It was nearing four in the morning. Anjali would have been asleep for hours, so he convinced himself it would be fine to sleep in the bed in his sprawling office. He was tired, but he had trained himself to get by on just a few hours' sleep. Four was usually sufficient, although he would know if he needed more and would routinely use the weekends to catch up. He'd go to bed now and get up at eight. He needed to get up for breakfast anyway, as he knew his wife would want to see some interaction with Sachin.

  He had gone to his office in a little show of petulance that he was still unhappy with Anjali's comments. But he had to maintain the façade of family life, especially where Sachin was concerned. He fired off an email to the school Locke Enterprises had set up in Anjali's name, helping transform a once grindingly poor Delhi neighbourhood, before a final email to the separate street kids initiative he had going on in the same city.

  The school was legitimate, but the street children plan was not. Should it come to the attention of the authorities, the only people to go down would be the managers. He smiled; how easy it was to mess people up? His managers had no idea he was behind the protection racket that turned street kids into forced labour. The racketeers had no idea they had been employed by the guy who owned the initiative. It was self-perpetuating. Locke knew kids disappeared, but no one would tell him and no one could trace it back to him. He pressed 'send'.

  "Bed," he said to himself and rose from his chair. He usually felt satisfied after making his plans. It humoured him to show the world one face, the generous genius side that they all seemed to love, when in another world he was a criminal, dangerous to society. It was as if he had developed a split personality. Oddly, he didn't feel satisfied at all.

*

In her own bedroom some distance away, Anjali Locke could hear nothing but the gentle lapping of Indian Ocean waves on Juhu beach. Sometimes the moon would beam through the French windows, basking the room in a silvery glow. Occasionally a car would go past on Military Road. It was a quiet area out of the hustle and bustle of noisy neighbourhoods. She rolled onto her back and saw no John. Her bed had felt empty for days. She missed the warmth of his body against her skin. It was a feeling as if she had lost her *ardhangini*. She stared upwards at the ceiling. Her pillow was still damp. Her thoughts had been clouded for weeks now. She was living with a different John, and he was no longer carefree and loving. He spent less time with his own son and more time locked away in his office. It was a room she knew nothing about except that it was a workplace. It was a room of knowledge and mystery. And she was becoming a stranger in her own home. He spent virtually no time with her at all.

The comments on the TV show had been indicative of his behaviour; "Just call me God" was all over the TV. It wasn't normal John. Fair enough that he had also mentioned the school in Delhi and the street kids initiative, but that also worried her. She started to question herself and the millions that had been donated to help orphaned children. She couldn't remember seeing much improvement in the school, so what had happened to the money? Was it being laundered and how could it be? It was raised legitimately through the business and she got to choose where to put it. If someone was laundering it, how were they getting it back?

On their latest India trip Anjali and Locke had done nothing for her school apart from a flying visit one day. Outwardly the school and its children appeared to be doing very well, but Anjali cast a mother's eye and saw the little things; a child looking undernourished, a uniform a bit too dirty. She saw discrimination, the caste system, skin colour and religious difference when it was meant to be about education and equal rights. And the children were quiet apart from the couple of super confident kids chosen to walk around with them. *It just didn't feel right.*

She wanted to discuss it with her husband, but never found the right time as the flesh of managers, teachers and the local MP were pressed, smiles were forced and flashbulbs went off. Locke had decided to fly them there and back himself so even then she couldn't really talk to him. Of the street kids initiative, she knew nothing at all. All that she knew was the donations were happening and the school and the lives of its children should have been improving. That should have meant lots of blessings should come their way which she was sure would benefit Locke ahead of his next episode.

But she realised something was wrong. The school seemed to be much more Locke's little secret, so she had done some research. On the face of it, it was doing really good for the children in that neighbourhood of Delhi. But then there was a local newspaper and it was asking questions. It was there, online, in plain sight. She didn't know from the coverage whether the police were involved, but a journalist was writing articles and what they suggested worried Anjali. She blinked away a tear.

"What are you up to, John?"

twenty-eight
be glad of what you have

Locke sat by the pool in the mansion's sprawling grounds. It wasn't yet hot enough for him to head back inside to escape the midday sun. Instead, a gentle breeze wafted over from the Indian Ocean and a sprinkler system swashed the verdant gardens. Traffic hummed the other side of the compound's high walls.

Sachin raced out from the house and bounded down the staircase to where his father sat on a sun lounger, a vast book across his lap. The boy was carrying a cricket bat and ball and was padded up like a batsman.

"Dad! Throw some down for me?"

Locke looked up from his book and gazed at his son, but the boy could not see his father's pride through the mirrored aviators.

"I've a bit of work, son," Locke said smiling. "But I can throw some down later? Why don't you get Singh to play with you? If his own bowling is too slow, you could use the machine?"

Sachin was beginning to notice changes in his father, that he had no concern for himself or his family. He felt that something was very different. He was about to say something then thought better of it. He turned and walked slowly back up the steps. There was a teardrop at the corner of his eye, but Locke couldn't see it from the distance between them. The boy gave a final glance in the direction of his father but saw no change in him.

He looked upwards, to where his mother stared down, and she witnessed his tears. Locke sighed as he watched his son disappear into the house. The trouble was, he did have work to do and everything he was doing was full of risk. He knew he was overlooking his family, and it was having a significant impact on his life, but for now it was a situation that could not be helped.

He took a sip of the chilled orange juice and returned to the book in his lap.

Anjali had seen it all from the balcony of her bedroom. She crossed to her own bedroom door and opened it just in time to see Sachin close his. She hurried down the staircase and towards her husband.

"What are you playing at, John? He just wanted some time with you. Can't you give two minutes to your son?"

Locke lowered the book once again. He wasn't getting the peace he needed.

"I have work to do. You know that. It's not as if I'm not doing anything. I'm not some dumb husband. And it's not like it's the end of the world yet." Locke looked up at Anjali. "I'll give him a little time later."

"A child can't understand that. John. They only see disappointment. And you have a son that wants nothing more than to play a bit of cricket with his dad. This time, this age is precious for a boy.

"You can spare five bloody minutes! This affects a child psychologically. This will be remembered for the rest of his life if you don't fix it." Anjali's face was thunder; hands were on hips. "Well?"

Locke said nothing. Anjali threw her hands up in disgust. What could she do to make him see sense? She tried again.

"Listen, John, imagine being a couple that have no kids. They feel infertile; a tree with no fruits. They try to have a child. They visit mosques, churches and temples. They pray. Why? Because they mourn over a child. And you've got this chance. You're lucky. But you wants to give it all away!" Locke slowly closed the tome in his hands, took off his sunglasses and folded them away into the pocket of his shirt. He got up from the sun lounger and faced his wife.

"You are his mother, where is your responsibility? A child needs his mother more than his father. And I have work to do. Play comes second." He walked away from Anjali whose mouth was open. He rarely dismissed her like that. She regained her composure and ran back into the house. She found Sachin in his bedroom looking quietly down at a book about cricket. She saw his upset and ran to him, hugging him tightly.

"Father no longer loves us."

"Of course he does, Sachin. He loves you and me. He's just occupied at the moment. There are lots of things you can play with; it doesn't have to be cricket. Listen, I want you to remember one thing; parenting is not easy, but parents always love their child. I know that as a child it is difficult to see and understand this because all you do is observe your circumstances, not the whole circumstances."

But Sachin did understand. His brain was developing rapidly and he was beginning to look mature for his age.

*

Anjali knew where her husband had gone, but chose not to follow. Instead she went back to her bedroom to find her laptop and turned it on. The history brought up the stories she had found out about the street children in Delhi that were going missing, a lot from the area around the street kids initiative Locke had set up. She rushed back down the stairs and burst into his office. Locke had his back to her, but she saw him stiffen as she dared enter his domain. A little too hard she put the laptop down on the desk in front of her husband and stepped back. Locke looked at the screen and read a little of the story. He knew what he was looking at instantly and quietly marvelled at how little time it had taken her to start to work it out.

"What are you suggesting?" he asked, feigning surprise.

"Is that us? Is that you?" Anjali stammered, struggling to control her anger. "Help me understand. Why are the press after you?"

"Is that me, what? Do you mean is that our initiative? Are you asking if the kids we are helping are somehow disappearing? What would I know about that? Our task was to give the funding and we did. What goes on afterwards isn't really anything to do with us."

"Are you seriously asking me if we are involved in this?" His eyes bore into Anjali's. "We *help* kids, in case you had forgotten. There is a school in your name that is the best in its area, by far, because I can do what the Indian government chooses not to do. There is a street kids initiative that I set up helping India's millions of street kids providing them with a bed, with food, with security and with a roof over their heads so that they don't need to sleep in the gutter. You find one bloody story suggesting something bad's going on and assume it's true." Locke rubbed at his forehead. "The press is waiting for an opportunity to blame me. I think you're waiting for an opportunity to blame me too."

"There's more than one story—"

"I don't give a shit how many fucking stories there are! That initiative helps kids. We help kids. What the fuck are you suggesting?"

Anjali stepped backwards. She had not seen her husband like this before. She paused, weighing up how to fight back. She had been sure there was something in the articles she had read. But there wasn't enough. She couldn't dismiss the fact the children weren't being treated well; she'd seen it with her own eyes, but could her eyes have deceived her? She had always considered the possibility that the journalist was after something that wasn't there, and was happy not to let the lack of facts get in the way of her story. The idea of contacting the woman flitted through her mind. *What was that journalist looking for? And was it there?* She shook it away. But she was also damned if she was going to be cowed in her own home. She took a deep breath and rose to her full height.

"Consciousness is a gift, John. Knowledge and intelligence are gifts. Your own is a rare example. Your mind is your consciousness and it has a connection with God. I don't care if you believe it or not. Don't take advantage of that knowledge. Use it to benefit everyone. Your consciousness is closer than you think."

Anjali raised her hand as Locke started to protest. She was well aware that he didn't believe as she did. "I was never going to try to convert you, because that has to come from you. He shall show you a sign, but by the time you recognise it, you may lose something valuable. Consciousness relates with God and it applies to the whole of humanity. The only thing is that not everybody understands religion or the concept of God. It has been around for thousands of years yet we still get its concept wrong.

"Don't lie with your consciousness. You may fool the world, but you will not fool God. Be glad of what you have; your knowledge, your wealth and most importantly, your family. But look back to when you had none of those things. You are not self-sufficient; there is somebody above you. And be careful what you wish for as you might not like the consequences. Your accident, your episodes may be the cause of why you became this genius, but have you ever thought it might just be a coincidence for you to get here?"

Locke suppressed the urge to clap mockingly. His eyes never left Anjali's, and he saw the fire there, the inward rage that sometimes appeared and always thrilled him. He used to mistake it for passion, that he had somehow managed to channel her fury into sex, but this was different and he pulled back from clapping or saying or doing anything at all. He had done nothing wrong and he kept up the denial. He thought about those convinced that what they were doing was the right thing, but they didn't face reality. He had not committed the physical acts. Anjali walked away, her head held high, then stopped by the door and turned once more to face her husband. Her chest heaved.

"If you want to earn money John, make your earnings legitimate because I don't want blood money. Lie to me, John, and you lose me. I am your *ardhangini;* it is my right to know when you are doing something wrong, to help put you in your right place, to show you or to tell you that you are on the wrong path in life. That is also *ardhangini.*"

She paused, then, more quietly, "lie to me and you lose Sachin."

*

John Locke was thinking hard. He might know how to do just about anything, but *what* to do still required thought. He reopened the book he had been reading that morning and found his place. He didn't know why he was bothering as he knew everything it said already. But for some reason, he felt a little different seeing the words on the page rather than in his head. It was a study relating to frontal lobe damage in the brain and a victim's apparently increased risk-taking as a result. The mugging fifteen years earlier had left him with damage to his frontal lobe and ever since he had read every bit of research he could find on the subject. The one constant was the increased risk-taking.

If anything, as a young man he had been more cautious than most of his friends. But not so much that he stood out or was called names. No-one made jokes about his intelligence when he couldn't answer the questions. Now was different; he got a thrill out of being able to do things no one else understood. And it sometimes worried him. He often thought back to the time he had been in that casino in Salford and Anjali had found him. He had been shocked that she was so scared. He had made a deal with the casino, did what he said he was going to do and got rich off the back of it. At least rich enough to keep him in funds while he started to work out what else he could do to make money for no effort. Where was the danger?

But he was more impulsive and didn't necessarily weigh up the consequences. And that he knew. He fought hard against himself to make sure when he was plotting that he thought of every eventuality. It wasn't something he found easy. He started small with the gambling books. Those didn't seem to hold much danger unless he fancied plying his wares in Las Vegas, which he had no intention of doing. As his fame grew, he started appearing on television. He knew then that anything dodgy he did must not be traceable back to him. He was not happy with Anjali's role in it all. It had been her idea to go public and tell the story. Only if he had hesitated, but then he figured she might suspect him; it may raise more questions. So he played it smart. He followed her lead.

His varied interests continued to grow; he read medical journals to understand his own situation, but then Anjali became pregnant with Sachin and so he started reading everything he could about medicine and not just head injuries or amnesia. He read everything there was to know about birth and by the end of it the delivery, he was telling the consultant what was going on with Anjali. He stopped when Anjali shouted at him during another powerful and painful contraction. Afterwards, the consultant took Locke to one side and asked, somewhat angrily, whether he was a qualified obstetrician. She was shocked when he said that he had just read up on the subject. His knowledge seemed better than hers.

That led to his fascination with all areas of medicine and culminating in his conducting that operation on the broken jaw. He looked for a subject and found one quickly. He discovered a rugby club that was crowd sourcing the necessary funds to build a new clubhouse. Locke promised to pay for it all if he was considered first when it came to healing a fracture on camera, should it happen. He also offered a considerable financial payment to the unfortunate player. It wasn't long before someone had a suitable injury and Locke got his video. It added to the mystique, to the image of the man who knew everything. He had got into a little trouble for that because he didn't hold the correct qualifications. The fact was he held no qualifications, yet the operation was conducted better than it would have been done on the NHS.

He considered enrolling in medical school to become legitimate, and he knew he would get to the right level in half, no, a third of the time of normal students. Maybe even less. It was just so simple. He read up on surgery procedures and had already been rich enough to get the equipment, facility and assistants together to do an experiment. But the player got his jaw fixed and the club got its new clubhouse. Locke paid for it as he had promised then, at the official unveiling, realised he could have built a better one. That was when he started to think about designing his own house.

The risk-taking was still there and, if anything, the urge was getting stronger. Bored one day, he wondered if he could scam his own bank and not get caught. Within a week he was a million pounds richer, a sum he felt small enough for the bank not to notice, especially as it had been made up of thousands of much smaller amounts. He didn't think it would even show up in an audit. He, of course, told no one. And the increased risk-taking remained.

Locke closed the book when he finished the conclusion to the paper on frontal lobe injury and placed his fingertips together. Anjali's words had bitten deep. He went over them in his head and thought about his son, dressed as a cricketer and wanting a knockabout with his dad. He thought about the street kids initiative and what Anjali thought she had worked out. He had been aware of the claims but hadn't yet figured out how to get rid of the journalist. There was time yet. It might just take a little word in the correct official's ear. It might take a little more; veiled threats or direct action, but that might raise more questions in Anjali's eyes. He had ideas; he just wanted to work out which method was best, and he was back to realising, painfully, that he might know every fact, but he didn't necessarily know how to make the right decisions. The decision was made, however. The journalist would cease to be a problem.

Anjali. *Anjali.*

Locke was concerned and he didn't like the sensation. All that religious crap she spouted at him, but she was right about one thing; she could read him like no one else. Could she tell when he was lying? Did she have a power over him? She seemed to be able to see the unseen, to see what he had kept hidden, and he didn't know how she did it. He was never so confident about his own poker face that he would gamble with cards, so was there something in his mannerisms that meant she knew he was up to something? *Ardhangini?* More times than he cared to remember he had considered that phrase. And he knew Anjali was absolutely certain it was true. No amount of reading about all of the world's organised religions could get Locke to believe, but his wife did and he saw its effect. That was the key difference between them. And they still fell in love. Silent thoughts would differ when it is a question of God or no god. And she would never persuade or convert him. All she said was the truth. But for her, there was something in it. Could the power of belief overcome the reality of Life? He knew there was no higher power, but did belief in a god make an individual stronger? It wasn't just that Anjali felt protected through her Gods, but she believed in the unseen when the rest of the world thinks only of the visible, needing proof. She felt empowered too. Could the power of religion in one conquer the certainty of right in another?

"No," Locke said aloud and moved the mouse on his laptop. The screen came to life and his emails appeared. One struck him immediately. "No, religion cannot beat me. But I can beat others."

Keys were tapped and messages sent, all in sure and certain knowledge that he was back doing what he knew he could do. Anjali faded to the back of his mind to join Sachin, who had been there for some time. He would confront his familial issues later; for right now something was happening just as he predicted it would. He replied to one email and sent another. Then he booked a flight back to the UK. The hairs on the back of his neck rose up. Yes, Anjali could wait one more day. This could not. He realised he was taking the biggest risk of his life. He realised he was getting excited. He realised the thrill of deceit made him feel smarter and cunning.

 He chuckled.

twenty-nine
sat there like fucking rats

Locke shivered. After the overnight flight, the temperature was considerably cooler in Manchester than it had been in Mumbai. The cab took him to his current home on the outskirts of the city. It was early, but the sun was very much up and the city was very much alive with people getting ready for the day ahead. Locke sent two texts, then went into his garage to make his final arrangements. He was at the building site of his new home by nine, taken there by an exclusive chauffeur service. The driver was to wait for him.

In front of him the clatter and dust of the new palatial home he had designed. It was taking shape, and was going to be painted white eventually, a turret to one side because he liked spiral staircases. Eight bedrooms was excessive in his own mind, but then Anjali had a lot of family so he wanted to be able to put up as many as possible.

The Lodge was an existing four-bedroomed house in the grounds which he had kept so others could have extended stays if necessary. He was thinking specifically about both Anjali's parents and his own. He had only mentioned her mum and dad when talking her through the plans, and he had let Anjali design the décor to help make her think she had something to contribute. A woman's touch was needed. A feminine twist was what made a home a home. Without that, it would be little more than bricks and mortar.

Rob Thomas, the site foreman, walked across the building site yard that would become Locke's extensive driveway. The huge man's hand was outstretched, his hard hat almost hanging off the back of his head. Locke switched his briefcase to his left hand and the two men shook.

"Good to see you, Mr Locke," the builder said. "How's it looking since you were last here?"

"Good, Rob, good," Locke answered surveying the scaffolding surrounding the shell. It had only been a few weeks since he had seen it when there was little more than the foundations in place. But the walls of the shell had gone up and Locke knew the roof joists would be on there soon. "On schedule?"

"Ahead, Mr Locke," came the reply. "We've had good weather and the lads have been working hard. That incentive really does work. The Lodge is finished as well."

"And so it should be," Locke said walking with a smile slowly towards where the front door would be. His incentive had been fifty percent more if the house was built on time. He looked at his foreman, "Okay if I walk around?"

"As long as you wear a hard hat, Mr Locke," Thomas said, holding a spare red one he had brought with him. "The law's the law."

Locke smiled; Rob Thomas was a kind man he decided. Someone who worked hard so his team would work hard. He trusted him. But the law? That was an ass. Only one other person in the world knew what Locke was about to do. And the law would never know.

"I've got a bit of work to do," he said as he started to wander off. "Make sure I can get in the Lodge."

*

Locke sat in the back of the cab and pretended to read his newspaper. It was his best chance of avoiding conversation with the driver and that was crucial for him. He did not want to be memorable. He scratched at the fake beard he was wearing and determined not to touch the prosthetic nose that was making him itch. So were the fake eyebrows. He had also grown his hair in the last few weeks, long enough that he could create a parting and tuck the sides behind his ears. He would go back to his normal crop soon enough.

The taxi turned off the motorway and carried on a short distance into Worsley. It had not taken long, and neither would the next part of his plan. He got out in a pub car park not far from his destination and walked calmly away from the taxi, turning left up the road he needed. He was glad of the Manchester cool as he could feel his skin pricking under fake beard and nose. He removed them as he walked and felt the fresh air soothe.

He was dressed in a dark blue suit with a white shirt open at the neck. He thought he looked inconspicuous. The tie he had been wearing earlier was neatly folded and in his jacket pocket. The only things he carried were his wallet, a pay as you go mobile phone and a pair of mirrored aviators he put on as he approached the house. He liked his sunglasses and particularly the anonymity the mirror effect gave him. The door opened before he reached it and a large, shaven-headed man greeted him effusively.

"Sam," Locke said perfunctorily and smiled as he walked into the small house. He waited patiently as Sam closed the door behind them and showed the way into the living room. To one side a long sofa where two gruff-looking young men sat. In another room Locke could hear someone busy making tea, or coffee. Locke didn't want either. Sam offered Locke an armchair.

"I'm ok, thank you," placing the briefcase on the floor beside him. "This won't take long."

Sam Roper eyed Locke warily as he sat down. He had been rehearsing this moment for a few days now. He knew he had to play it carefully as he had sensed Locke was tiring of him. He wasn't aware his guest had flown in from India specially, though.

"Mr Locke, we've known each a long time now, and I like to think of it as a good relationship we've got." Locke nodded, giving Roper confidence. "Thing is, we've come into a bit of bother, like. Our Pete's inside. Went on a job I hadn't sanctioned. Got himself and a couple of others caught. Thing is the others were Sean Merrick's lads, and you know what he's like. He blames our Pete. Which is why he's after my blood."

"What did they do?" Locke knew; he just wanted to be certain he was being told the truth.

"Went on the rob down in Cheshire. Only it was some footballer with top notch security. They was sat there like fucking rats while the police turned up. Been Pete's idea, Merrick says, so he wants us to stump up. If he can't have his lads, he wants our business. Look around you Mr Locke. We're not rich."

Locke looked around. The story checked out from what he knew and his surroundings were, indeed, humble. A three-bed semi-detached in leafy Worsley wasn't much, but then Locke knew it was one of the sons' homes; Jonno Roper. He was on the couch with his brother Ricky. For all the warm words and pleading from their dad, the Roper twins looked ready to attack at a moment's notice. But Locke also knew about the five-bed Sam Roper had across the village. It was one of the most salubrious properties in the area. Sam Roper was not of few means.

"We need to pay him off, Mr Locke. We're going to double our efforts at the casino. Goes quiet in the day, so thinking we'll open one of those caffs in it. All that poncey crap people want nowadays. Hoomus and advacado. Charge them a fortune for it. Got the chef lined up already. We just need to pay Merrick off now, then we'll be free to make it up to you through the caff we got planned." Roper leaned forward. "We've had such a good relationship for years now, Mr Locke. I'd hate for that to end when it wasn't even our fault."

Sam Roper sat back in his armchair, trying to look relaxed.

"How much are we talking?" Locke said.

"Hundred grand pays 'im off. Hundred and fifty gets us set up so we can start paying you back straightaway."

Locke smiled despite efforts not to. This was the sixth time the Ropers had asked for money from him. He set them off with the card counting and they made plenty before it became less lucrative. They got that for an initial ten thousand pounds and even that Locke had won legitimately. There had been no deal in place, really, other than to let him walk out with the cash if they accepted his offer of help. But since then there had been a number of begging emails, all with the same underlying threat. It was never the Ropers' fault; and they would hate to alter their arrangement with him. It had taken Locke until now to finally decide what to do. The Ropers were the only people who knew who he really was. He had no doubt that tongues wagged with the ale, but it was only their word for it. If anyone ever came knocking, he would admit his very earliest involvement with them. None of the money he had paid out to them was traceable; they would have to explain it; all one point something million of it.

"I'll give you two hundred," Locke said. "But that's your lot. Pay off the Merricks, set up this café, save some for retirement. But don't ever come looking to me for help again. Do you understand that?"

Sam Roper got up from his armchair, eager to shake Locke by the hand. Locke stepped back and Roper's hand dropped to his side.

"I mean it. It ends here."

"Yes, Mr Locke. I, we, fully understand," Roper said. Locke had all the information he needed. Ropers' boys could be trusted just as much as their brother rotting away in prison. Pete Roper was his one concern. But Locke knew he'd been given twenty years and wouldn't get out inside of ten. It may only have been a robbery, but it was certainly not his first. Merrick's lads had got much shorter sentences.

Locke reached into his pocket; Jonno Roper started forward but stopped when Locke pulled out a phone. Sam Roper had gone back to his armchair and breathed satisfaction as he watched on. It had gone as the meetings always did. He had John Locke by the bollocks and this would not be the last time he took money from him. It did solve the Merrick issue, though.

Locke pounded away at his smartphone. "As always, the money will be with you tomorrow." He held the phone up as if it was proof the transaction had been made. If he had wanted to pay it immediately, he easily could have. But the money was never going to leave his account. He looked at the message on the screen. *'All four. Including the woman.'* And pressed 'send'.

A smiling Sam Roper showed Locke the way to the front door and closed it after a reasonable number of seconds. Locke walked back down the Ropers' street and turned right into a narrow footpath. He waited then heard the reassuringly loud roar of a powerful motorbike coming up the road. He had chosen it specially. From his vantage point he saw it speed past the entrance to the footpath. Locke turned and continued on his way, briefcase swinging in his right hand. He heard the engine cut out just as he turned left onto a different street and made his way to Worsley village green. He felt his pulse rise as he faced the one gamble in his plan; that there would be a black taxi at the rank. There was. Inside of five minutes, he was back on the motorway heading towards Sale and his shell of a mansion.

*

"How do you like The Lodge, Mr Locke?" Rob Thomas asked as Locke walked up the pathway towards the back of his new mansion. It was just after ten thirty; he had been gone less than two hours.

"Beautiful. My wife has an excellent eye."

"She has, Mr Locke," Thomas agreed. "Your guests will love it."

The two men walked slowly together around one side of the building.

"Are you staying long?" Thomas asked as Locke stopped to look more closely at the frame of the turret. It was to be double walled, so there was room for people to hide in the gap should the need arise. The builder had been surprised by the idea, but Locke assured him it was just a bit of fun borne out of his delight at priest holes and secret rooms.

"No," Locke said eventually. "I've a little work to do in Manchester then I am going back to India tomorrow morning. It literally is a flying visit. I intend to be back here in a couple of months, though, so this place should be finished."

Thomas did the calculation; "If it's eight weeks exactly, we should be finished building and well underway with the furnishings. Ten weeks total."

"And the bonus is yours if you stick to that. Right down to the cleaner having gone over the marble with her duster."

Locke laughed with the builder and handed back the hard hat and the key to The Lodge he had provided him with. His chauffeur remained a hundred yards away, clear of the dust of the building site. Locke got in and placed the briefcase on his lap, tapping at the thought of the fake beard, nose and eyebrows he had in there. He would incinerate them shortly.

*

Massacre in Manchester read the headline. Locke thought it excessive; hardly a massacre. *Four slain in peaceful village setting.* He read the report with interest picking up anything that might be of use. There wasn't of course; only a mention of the motorbike heard going up and down the Ropers' street. The article in the paper didn't even go as far as saying it was the Ropers that had been killed, just the approximate age and gender of the victims. He was shocked when the age of the female was given as *'mid twenties'*. He had assumed it was Sam Ropers' wife in the kitchen, but it must have been one of his sons' girlfriends. He didn't think either was married.

"Bad that, isn't it?" Locke looked towards the sound of the voice. Behind his left shoulder stood a small man with a bald head and round glasses. "It'll be gangs."

"Yes," said Locke, "I suppose it will be."

The announcement went up calling on Mumbai passengers to go to their gate. Locke rose up from his seat, folded the newspaper and placed it under his arm. He didn't make eye contact with the bald-headed man who watched him walk away dragging a small suitcase behind him.

Rude, he thought, and ordered a coffee.

thirty
her lips lingering

Anjali looked out from the living room window and stopped. She saw Sachin standing at one end of the cricket net looking back at his father. She realised it had taken them a long time for them to bond, given the recent changes in Locke's behaviour. When she changed her position slightly she could see Locke standing still, hands-on-hips, looking down at the ground. Her son looked anxious. He was making an effort, but she thought the mind and heart just weren't there.

By the time she reached the cricket net, Locke was using the bowling machine to send balls down. He liked this activity with his son and Sachin was getting good at it. They had toyed with the idea of getting a coach in full time, but Singh the gardener had played a decent level back in the day and was more than capable of teaching the boy for now.

Another ball fizzed down the track, bouncing off a length. Sachin spun around on his feet and smashed the ball into the side netting. He was showing rare talent.

"Four, that, dad!" the boy shouted. Locke didn't even hear him.

"What is it, John?" Anjali asked quietly, walking up to her husband. Locke startled. He hadn't realised she was there.

"Nothing. I'm fine." He put another ball in the machine and Sachin despatched it to a different place on the imaginary boundary. Anjali rested a hand on her husband's arm. It was an indication of concern that only a wife would acknowledge. A woman who could see that something was not right and that her husband needed help.

He looked into her eyes and saw the fear and concern there.

"You look tired," she said at last.

And it was true. He'd been back from Manchester for a week, but he had barely slept. He kept telling himself the four hours a night were enough, but he wasn't even getting that. Not that she knew it, but he had crossed a line as surely as if he had pulled the trigger himself. He couldn't get the thought of the Ropers out of his head.

To start with he had watched the UK news online for any mention of the murders, but it didn't seem to be important enough to make it to the national channels. And it had only appeared a few times on News North West. The Ropers were well-known in Salford, but they were not popular outside their own circles. Watching closely, Locke thought the journalists were doing the minimum on the story despite all the earnest comments from the police officer in charge of the investigation. That cheered him; fewer people likely to talk, not that there was anything anyone could say. He had been meticulous in his planning and the contract killer thought he was dealing with someone from Scotland.

That had been a nice touch; getting the hitman to go to a lonely bit of hillside in the Scottish borders to find the weapon on the new motorbike that had been bought for him. The man who had left the pistol there had no idea it was destined for Manchester. He would have a better idea now that the news had broken, but if the killer had followed Locke's instructions to the full, the gun was gone and the Glasgow gang were happy with the money they had been paid for it.

"I'm not tired," he said at last. He pulled at the dial on the bowling machine, making it fire the balls five miles an hour faster. One zinged down the track, too quick for Sachin. The next one clattered into the stumps. As his son rearranged the stumps, Locke turned and walked away. Anjali stayed and played with her son.

*

Locke had been different ever since he had come back from England, both mentally and physically. And he had only been there a weekend. Anjali had tried to engage him at mealtimes which they still made every effort to spend together. More often than not, since his return, Locke would push the food around his plate eating very little. He had lost some weight, which he claimed to be a bit of Delhi belly, but she knew that he was lying, making excuses for some reason. The chefs they employed were meticulous in their hygiene, but, more than that, they knew to make food for western palates and western sensitivities. Besides, neither she nor Sachin had been ill and they had all eaten the same food.

They usually ate at six in the evening to give Sachin time to wind down and be ready for bed at a reasonable hour. That night Locke didn't appear. Anjali knew she had to speak to him again, but about what? She seemed to have lost the means to connect with him and start a conversation.

The romantic bond seemed to have vanished. It had been the longest few weeks of her life and these chats were becoming commonplace. She couldn't put her finger on it; one day he was fine and the next he spent staring into space or throwing himself into his work. She had no idea what was on his mind, and this connection was a significant part of its *ardhangini*.

"And you're not a mind reader, Anjali," she had said out loud, half hoping he would hear. He didn't, or pretended not to. She had tried to find out and she had failed.

She cast her mind back; Locke seemed fine when they first came to India. It had actually been his idea. Anjali had been content to stay in their old house while the new one was built, but Locke had insisted. Sachin's school weren't happy, but the complaints predictably disappeared when school fees were mentioned. The trip had been sold to her when Locke said it would be good for both Anjali and Sachin to get to know a bit more of their Indian family and to see a bit of the school and street kids initiative they were responsible for. All of which seemed totally reasonable. Sachin was only missing the last term of school. Locke was going to home school him over the holidays so their son missed nothing. It all seemed like a great idea.

But then they arrived in Mumbai, which was nowhere near her family or the school and street kids initiative they bankrolled. It was Bollywood stars instead and Anjali had been unimpressed. Things had gone well for a couple of weeks before Locke started acting a little strangely. It had happened before the TV interview and Anjali had noticed the change. She tried to dismiss it, but she felt she saw it during the interview and in the days following. He was worse since his return from the trip to England. She didn't know what was wrong and he dismissed her when she asked. He was unable to look at her; something was consuming him. Was it guilt or conscience? Or both. With Sachin in bed, Anjali slowly made her way across the vast hallway to Locke's office, holding a photograph of their wedding day. Increasingly she felt uneasy about going in there and, for the first time, she knocked before doing so. She heard nothing from inside so opened the door and walked through.

"Can I get you a drink or something?" she asked. Locke looked up from the monitor in front of him and shook his head. He held Anjali's gaze for a brief second then looked back down at the screen. Anjali walked towards him and pulled up a chair to sit down next to him. She remained quiet as he worked. She couldn't read what was on the computers; it looked like lots of columns and figures, but then there were various images and bits of text on other screens, none of it making sense to her. She was about to ask what he was doing but changed her mind. She was right to.

"Can I help you?" Locke stated.

"I think it's more if I can help you, John. I'm worried about you." Locke said nothing.

"Remember this photograph of our marriage?"

"Yeah. What about it?"

"You know why Indian women wear jewellery?"

"To look beautiful?"

"Yes, to be beautiful, John, that's true too, but do you have any idea what that means or represents?"

Locke said nothing. Anjali put her finger on the photo.

"It's called a *tikka*. It goes between the left and right of your hemispheric brain. And beyond the *bindi, which is* the third eye. Our wisdom and judgement originate there. It shows the eyes and the strong connection to the temporal lobe." Anjali's moved her finger to another part of the photograph. "These are called *Sahara* or *Kaan* earrings. This part of the brain helps us analyse our life circumstances, understand speech and raise awareness. It points to the frontal lobe. The left and right of its cerebellum hemisphere. The finger moved again. "This is called the *maang tikka* and these two chain snares around our brain. That depicts the cerebellum and parietal lobe. All together jewellery is the crown of women's consciousness. We dress our head like a bride, because the knowledge is hidden behind it. It complements all of our brains. These jewels represent and remind all women that we are the awareness and guidance of our man. But not every woman uses it well. When we are the one who should be calm, so we can better handle our men. Men lose their way and that is why He gave you a woman to support you."

Locke sighed and Anjali braced herself in case he was going to shout at her. But he sighed as if the air had rushed out of him. He leaned back in his chair.

"I'm tired, that's all." He held out his hand and Anjali took it. She pulled it closer and used it to stroke her own face, kissing his fingers, her lips lingering over his wedding ring. Locke pulled his hand away, but not sharply, and looked adoringly back at his wife as he cupped her cheek. His conscience bothered him still and he wondered if she could work it out just by looking at him. He had tried and failed to find a flaw in his plan. Doubting himself was new. And he didn't like it.

He looked at his wife in a way he hadn't in weeks. He smiled, pressed a few keys on the keyboard and Anjali watched the computer go into lockdown.

"It's true, I am tired," he said. "I've not been like this for years and I'm not sure what's wrong with me." Anjali held his hand again.

"Is there a problem? Do you want to speak to a consultant? You can have privacy if you like."

No answer.

"Is it something to do with the new house, or Sachin's school, or our things in Delhi? You've not been the same since you returned from Manchester."

Nothing. She took a deep breath.

"Is this about another woman? Am I getting close?"

"No!" Locke shot a glance at her, then looked away. She saw it. There *was* something.

"Is it a crime, have you done something illegal? I'm getting closer, aren't I?"

"Please don't push, Anjali. I don't think I could take it. I've got a lot on at the moment, but I promise you, it's all legitimate. There's nothing dodgy going on."

Anjali blinked. Initially, she had wilfully looked away from the possibility of there being something illegal going on. But what he just said; he must be up to something. The concerns over the street kids initiative hadn't been mentioned again, and despite all her searching, she could find no new news stories from the Delhi journalist about it. The woman seemed to be focusing her attention on the climate these days, making Anjali wonder if she had been moved *or silenced*. But why say there was nothing dodgy? That sounded more than a little odd. "*It's all legitimate...*" sounded odd too. He saw the look.

"I'm telling you, it's nothing I can't handle. I am a genius, you know!" Locke laughed, but it was hollow. "And it's nothing to do with money or schools or houses, okay? Please don't ask me again."

Anjali let slip of Locke's hand, her mind racing.

"Do you want to go for a walk?" he said suddenly. "Along the ocean?" Locke was already on his feet and striding across the room towards a large wardrobe. He selected a linen jacket, dark blue to go with his chinos, and walked back towards his wife smiling. Anjali looked down at her own outfit and decided it was fine once she got a shawl to counter the evening cold. She smiled and nodded.

*

It would have been lovely, except a million thoughts rushed around Anjali's head. Locke had been distant for a while and now he seemed preoccupied on something big. Why couldn't she read him? All she could tell was that something was wrong and she thought she knew her husband well. Yet again she doubted herself, her intuition. Was his intelligence changing him? Was he up to something criminal? Or had he simply gone off her? She felt confused. *Am I blind to him?* The question in her mind scared her.

His hand held hers a little more tightly as they walked barefoot along Juhu beach, the waves quietly crashing on the soft sand. Anjali felt the fear from his clammy grip and wondered if she was about to lose him, though no words had been said. The sun was setting on another day, but the street vendors still called and the decadent smell of spices floated on the cooling air. Anjali brought a savoury snack from a street vendor and they shared it as they walked. The beach was busy, but not too much. Some stared as the white man and Indian woman walked hand in hand, each lost in their own thoughts. Some startled because they recognised them from the television interview with Gadkari. Some came towards him, wanting to shake his hand. His smile started to return a little.

Regardless of the reason, neither of them took any notice; they were used to it.

"Do you still love me?" she asked suddenly, causing Locke to stop. He turned to her and their eyes met in the dusk.

"Of course I do," he said without hesitation. "You and Sachin. Everything is for you and Sachin." It sounded defensive; an automatic response rather than the whole truth.

"Am I asking a lot of you? Too much need for luxury?"

"No, but I'm responsible for giving you that lifestyle. Women leave us. Nobody wants to know the failure; everyone wants to know the successful one. Isn't that the game here?"

"Then why are you so cold all the time? Why do I feel that I don't know you anymore?"

Locke kicked at the sand, then looked at the shoes he held. He dropped them and took Anjali's left hand in both of his.

"I don't mean to be. I don't want to. But things are driving me towards it. I don't feel I have any control over it. I just have a lot on. I have a reputation to maintain and it's a huge responsibility. I feel like I'm living two lives, two personalities, which nobody can understand. I keep telling you this."

Anjali searched for her husband's face for clues. He smiled softly and gave her hand a reassuring squeeze. "I promise you this Anjali, I promise you that it will end soon and we can get back to being normal. It will set us up for life even more than we already are."

"But are we in need of more? Isn't what we have sufficient? Look around you, John, people are in a much worse place. We have this and we have Sachin. We ought to be happy now, so why aren't we? If it is doing this to you, is it even worth it?"

Locke bent down to pick up his shoes and turned away. They walked further along the beach, just above the tideline.

"I need to finish it," he said.

"But finish what? We have enough. I would live with you in a tin house."

"Once I have then it will all be over," Locke said, ignoring her plea. "We know I've got another episode coming up, so I just need to get this done before that happens."

Anjali could hear the strain in his voice. He wasn't cold; he was breaking up. Whatever was going on was hurting him and she couldn't help because he wouldn't let her. He wouldn't involve her.

"I love you," she said, barely above a whisper.

"I know," he replied and let go of her hand. Trust persisted in their relationship; the foundation of a marriage.

*

They made love that night. Locke snored quietly beside Anjali, her eyes were tightly closed, her face wet with tears. She changed her mind; it wasn't making love, it was sex. He seemed to try harder than normal and it felt rougher. She didn't like it, but she didn't complain. He was in a bad place and she didn't want to make it any worse. He was always so tender with her. Tonight she experienced a different lover, one she still couldn't read.

Does he really love me still? Do I believe him? Thoughts tumbled through her conscious. *Is this the new normal? As long as I live, no one respects me or values me. I'm worthless to you. Maybe by the time I'm dead, I could be worth something. I only wish I could die in your arms.* Her eyes snapped open and stared into the black. A new thought had swum into focus and terrified her. But it wouldn't go away. She gasped.

Do I still love him?

thirty-one
i know about you

"There's someone here to see you," Anjali said as she popped her head around the door to Locke's office. He looked up, surprised.

"Who?"

"I don't know, but he turned up with two police officers. I've put him in the living room with Vijay."

John Locke rose up from his desk, thoughts flitting through his mind. He took a deep breath to compose himself and shrugged his shoulders, more for Anjali's benefit than his own.

Vijay stood to attention outside the door to the living room. He gave a slight bow as Locke walked past him and into the splendour of the largest room in the house. It was ridiculously ostentatious, but then this was Mumbai, home of Bollywood, and many a Bollywood legend had stayed here. He closed the door quietly and walked towards the figure standing next to the fireplace.

"It's a Landseer of Isaac Van Amburgh," Locke said motioning towards the giant painting the visitor was looking at. "Van Amburgh was an American animal trainer. I think the owners like it because there's a tiger in it."

The visitor looked back up at the picture, then back at Locke.

"You're much more conversational than when we last met, Mr Locke."

Locke was taken aback and regarded the small bald man with his round, wire-rimmed glasses. He felt the flicker of recognition an instant before he spoke.

"You'll have to enlighten me," he lied.

"Manchester Airport," the man said. "About three weeks ago. You were reading the paper about those murders in Salford. You said nothing to me when I engaged you in conversation. You just walked away. Very rude, I thought."

Locke stared at the visitor.

"Look," said the small bald man, "how about we start again? My name is Gregson and I have some very interesting information about you, Mr Locke, that I think you should hear. Once you know how much I know about you, perhaps we can get down to business. Perhaps we could take a couple of seats and get something to drink? Bottled water? Perhaps your butler could bring some?"

"Vijay!" Locke shouted and the door to the room opened immediately. "Iced mineral water," he said, without bothering to turn to look at the butler. The door closed again quietly.

"Oh come, come, Mr Locke. There's no need to be like that. We have ascertained that you can be very chatty when it suits. I've seen you on the television many times." Gregson had chosen a large yellow armchair as his seat. He motioned to another opposite, suggesting Locke take that one, as if he was a guest in his own home. Locke did as he was asked and sat down, wondering why he was allowing the interloper to instruct him in his own house, but then he was furiously trying to work out who precisely it was that was seated in his living room. It felt back to front and he didn't like it. He wanted control and Gregson didn't seem to want to give it up. The door to the room opened and Vijay walked in carrying a silver salver with two glasses, a jug of ice and a large bottle of mineral water upon it. He placed the tray on a table nearby and stood to attention. Locke waved the man away.

Gregson got up, poured two drinks, handed one to Locke and retook his armchair. "I want you to cast your mind back to 2011 where you did a little audit of some accounts. You'll recall it wasn't strictly legal what you did. In fact, you'll recall that it was theft, pure and simple, of a million pounds from my client."

Locke took a sip of his water, his mouth had gone a little dry, as he sought to stay calm in front of this new, confident guest. He placed his glass down on a table next to his chair.

"Mr Gregson, I've no idea what you are talking about, but I can assure you that I do not take kindly to being threatened or accused in my own home."

"But I have not threatened you, Mr Locke. I've not threatened you at all. I have merely stated facts which I can happily prove to you in an instant."

Locke felt trapped. He still couldn't work out how Gregson could know. But he clearly did know.

"I just felt we could avoid all the humdrum and get straight to the point," Gregson continued. "*I know about you.* I know what you have done and I know you will be very interested to hear what I have to say. So, can we proceed in an orderly manner?"

Locke stared hard at Gregson who, after a brief wait, sighed. "I can mention that initiative you have going on in Delhi if you wish? That journalist was getting close, wasn't she? It was me that put the call in to her editor. Or rather, it was me that spoke to the Delhi chief of police, who put the call in. As you will find out shortly, the initiative will be closing very soon. There will be a raid tonight by the Delhi police and, as you have so meticulously planned, the correct people will be charged and found guilty.

"You, given your standing in society and the fact that your charitable work has been so undermined by a ruthless gang exploiting child labour, will go on television talking of your sadness and revulsion. You will also make a sizeable donation to the Indian government to aid their own charitable endeavours."

Locke remained impassive, but mentally his brain felt like it was on fire. He kept coming back to the same conclusion; the man was bluffing; there was no way anybody could know what Gregson suggested he knew because the measures that Locke himself had put in place could not be overridden by anyone. But somehow he did know.

How? He folded his arms and feigned mild intrigue.

"For heaven's sake, Mr Locke, this is beneath you. I'll not talk to you about those murders in Manchester as you have ignored me on that topic once already. I guess it's not something you would like to discuss, given your role in it."

Locke was about to protest, but Gregson silenced him with a raised hand. "You stole from my employer, Mr Locke. Seven years ago, you decided to take what was not yours and you did so despite having seemingly more money than you will ever need. Given my work in tracking you down, I have been tasked by several other organisations keen to use my services. I am here on behalf of four of them, to see which if any you are interested in working for."

Gregson reached down to pick up his briefcase. He placed it flat on his lap and pressed the buttons to unlock it. He took out a white A4 envelope, then closed the briefcase and put it on the floor again. He held the envelope, as if weighing up whether to hand it over, then held it out as he leaned towards Locke.

"Take this and have a good read. I return to London tonight, but my contact details are in there. You have seventy-two hours to decide what to do, Mr Locke." Gregson looked at his watch. "Actually, let's be generous; you have seventy-four hours and thirty-six minutes. I will hear from you by five pm British Summer Time on Thursday. If not, then you are more stupid than anyone in the world gives you credit for."

Gregson rose from his chair and picked up the briefcase. "I'll show myself out."

*

The envelope remained unopened on a desk in Locke's office. He stared at it, wondering about its contents. Earlier Anjali had come in asking about Gregson, who he was and what he wanted. They rowed. Locke played ignorant, busy trying hard to process the information, to work out where he must have gone wrong. But even as he tried to bluff it out, he knew he was no actor. He could tell lies when there was no pressure, but Gregson was something different.

She didn't say it, she didn't have to, but he heard the words she had spoken a few weeks earlier; "Lie to me, John and you lose me. Lie to me and you lose Sachin."

But he couldn't admit that Gregson was right or, and it was this that he tried to convince himself was not possible, that for all his genius, his actions could be tracked. Anjali ran out of his office crying, right after he had screamed at her to get the fuck out.

He heard footsteps in the hallway, Sachin pleading with his mother and then the front door to the mansion slammed shut. Locke breathed heavily as he heard the engine of the Porsche start up. He gave little thought to where Anjali was going as they didn't have any friends in Mumbai – certainly not anybody that would take her in like this. The wealthy they had met and made friends with were not reliable. Scandal trumped friendship when money was at stake.

She hadn't had time to pack; so she wouldn't be going to the airport. Just a drive around until she calmed down was most likely. Which gave him time to consider the envelope and its contents. Gregson definitely knew things about him that no individual could. And it went back seven years to the week he decided to take thousands of small payments to make up the million he stole.

Seven years. Had Gregson been after him all that time? Or, more likely, someone noticed the missing amounts and Gregson was their go to man to work out what had happened. Computer security had changed massively since then, but if Gregson had worked him out early enough, he would have been able to follow him near enough constantly. He could conceivably know about every time Locke had siphoned money from one bank or another. And he wasn't pissing in the wind when he mentioned the street kids initiative or the Manchester shootings. He couldn't be, could he?

Locke decided against doing anything with the envelope. Instead he wrote a press release. If the police in Delhi were to raid the initiative tonight, he would have to provide a denial very quickly to appease those wanting to try to link him with the child labour scam he had set up.

"This is a test of the world's most intelligent man," he said aloud. "Nothing more!"

He sat down in front of his computer screen and began to type. "They certainly cannot link me to the murders..." he whispered, then stopped typing. *Which murders?* Locke pinched the bridge of his nose; if Gregson knew about the shootings in Salford, and he had made a point of talking to Locke about the murders when they were in Manchester Airport, then he could easily know about the children missing from the initiative. He was aware of fourteen and he had presumed most if not all of them were dead. The journalist had not even got close to discovering the truth; it was far worse than even she had worked out. But Gregson? What did he know?

Locke banged away at the keys again, the words forming on the computer screen. He didn't hold back in his denials and used every cute phrase he could to paint the shock and outrage that he must surely feel that his good name had been dragged through such an horrendous episode as that that befell the street kids at Locke Enterprises' flagship charitable work.

He printed the denial out then went through it with a pen. He was on version six when he heard the engine of the Porsche as someone, presumably Anjali, brought it back to the house. He put his pen down then rushed out. Anjali got out of the car alone.

"Where's Sachin?" Locke asked.

"I've taken him to a friend's house. He's staying over."

Anjali breezed past Locke who saw the redness of her eyes. She must have been crying the whole time she had been out. "Which friend?" but she kept on walking, slamming the front door behind her as she went into the house. Locke looked at the Porsche, then at some of the garden staff. They quickly got back to whatever they had been doing. He ran into the house and hurried up the vast staircase to their bedroom. Anjali sat on their bed with her back to him. He decided to keep his distance.

"It's the street kids initiative," he said. "You were right; there was something going on. When you said about that journalist I got an investigator involved. I still don't quite know what has happened, but Gregson came here to tell me what he thought he had found. I've instructed the Delhi police to raid it tonight. The point is I didn't know until you mentioned it. I got Gregson to look into it and it doesn't look good. It seems some gang was using it as a front. Anjali, I…"

He knew he was laying it on thick, but he prayed it wasn't too much. He walked around to her side of the bed and sat down next to her.

"Gregson thinks it has been used as a sweatshop, that the kids have been used as child labour." Her hands were together in her lap. He decided against holding them and instead gently touched her chin, trying to get her to look at him. She shrugged him away.

"So that journalist was onto something," Anjali whispered.

"Yes, and that is why she was moved from within the paper. I got the editor to pull back on articles about the initiative while Gregson looked into matters."

All lies. But he had rehearsed these ones while Anjali had run off somewhere. It would be easier to handle Anjali first then Gregson, and he needed his wife on side. He was confident in his argument and knew she would believe him. He thought again about touching her, holding her hands or face, then decided against it.

"It gets worse," he said quietly. "Children have gone missing."

He looked at his wife who slowly turned towards him. Fresh tears rolled down her cheeks and he felt an overwhelming urge to kiss her deeply.

"Why didn't you tell me?"

"Because I didn't want it to be true."

"The school?"

Locke shook his head. "Gregson found nothing. The school's fine."

Anjali allowed herself to fall towards her husband and he caught her in an embrace as she sobbed into his chest. He stroked her hair and gently kissed the top of her head. He tried to regulate his breathing and thought once again about the white envelope.

Whatever was in it, John Locke wasn't finished yet.

thirty-two
you know I can walk away

Locke left Anjali on the bed saying he had some things to do. He went back to his office and, finally happy with the drafting of his document, he picked up his mobile and made a call. Within the hour VC Gadkari was seated in the same armchair that Gregson had been in earlier that day. Technicians fiddled with lights, cameramen looked for the perfect frame and two women frantically scribbled on a notepad, editing the script that the TV anchor would use to question, gently, for it had been a stipulation, John Locke about the revelations surrounding Locke Enterprises' street kids initiative in Delhi. A make-up artist busied around Gadkari's face, making sure there wasn't the least sign of sweat, but the truth was Gadkari was nervous. He wasn't used to being summoned, and he wondered whether he should have agreed to Locke's request. Guilt by association and all of that.

The door opened and Gadkari turned to see Locke breeze into the room. He rose from his seat and the men shook hands.

"Are we ready to go, VC?" Locke asked as he sat down in the opposing armchair.

*

"What's going on, John?" Anjali asked from the top of the grand staircase as soon as the TV crew left the house and Locke closed the front door. "I mean it, what is really going on?"

Locke stared back at his wife. When was she going to give up? She had not listened in on the interview, but the moment the crew had gone and he was alone to collect his thoughts, she was back at him. It was like she was his shadow, always there, never giving him a moment's peace.

"You know what, Anjali? I'm tired. Is it okay to be tired? Is it okay to get a little time to myself?"

It was a tone she was becoming accustomed to. Marriage was an extended relationship and the longer it lasts, the better it becomes. Her 'reality' was far from that 'truth'.

"You're always having time to yourself," Anjali spat the words at her husband. "You always seem to be up to something and I never know what it is. John, I am your wife and as such I have rights. My job isn't just to look after Sachin and run the household. Who will you get help from in your time of need? I need to know if you are doing things you shouldn't be, because one wrong step doesn't just affect you; it affects me and Sachin as well. It affects all of our lives. Getting married is easy; staying married isn't."

"You don't need to fucking know!" Locke started to walk towards the vast staircase, stopping in the middle of the grand hallway.

"There shouldn't be any secrets," Anjali stated firmly as she looked down on Locke. "We are husband and wife, *ardhangini,* and we have met through the ages to be married time and again. You cannot exist without me and I cannot exist without you. But when you are in your office, I am alone. There is only me and Sachin and you hide from him as well."

"Don't bring the boy into it."

"Why not?" Anjali gripped the marble bannister, her eyes never leaving Locke's. "You only have us here. No one else. And you have spent so little time with us."

Locke threw open his arms and spun. "Look around you. Look at all this fucking splendour. Do you think it pays for itself?" He stopped twirling. "I am working. I am working for all of us and the minute things get difficult, and you have no idea just how difficult, you don't help me. Sometimes I need to be alone. You don't understand my pain, my hard work. You don't earn it. No wife ever does it. You're a housewife, that's all. A domestic bee. You hinder me. And when the time comes, women leave with half of the fortune. A man has to protect his identity, his *honour,* by himself. Is a woman prepared to do this for a man? You are getting in the way, you are interrupting my days, my hours, trying to do something good in the world. There is no appreciation for a man's hard work in society, let alone at home or in the eyes of a court. The more this goes on the more I am thinking about this bloody *ardhangini* crap and the more I am thinking about how I might be better off existing without you. You know I can. You know I can walk away."

Anjali remained calm at the top of the stairs. Inside her body was raging, but she didn't want to show any weakness. The silence lingered for a few moments.

"Tell me, then," she said

"Tell you what?"

"Tell me why things have become difficult. Am I the trouble here?"

Locke raised his arms in frustration and stormed off towards his office. Anjali watched the door slam shut. Now she could feel sadness. She couldn't understand his sense of frustration.

*

Sachin returned to the mansion early the next morning, but already a large gathering of press photographers and journalists had started milling around, trying to get a photograph or a word with Locke. The Umrigars, with whom he had stayed, decided on sending him back as soon as they realised something serious was about to explode around John and Anjali Locke. They wanted nothing to do with it. Ramnath Umrigar watched with horror the interview with VC Gadkari, which had been broadcast to coincide with the arrests that were taking place at the Lockes' street kids initiative.

Anjali hurried to her boy and held him close. Singh, the gardener and sometime cricket coach, closed the main door behind him, awaiting instruction. The press scrum outside the front gates had frightened Sachin, who had no idea why they were there or why he had been woken up so early and taken back to his own house. He hadn't even had time to say goodbye to his friend, Junaid. He knew nothing of the interview or the news.

His confidence began to return as his mother hugged him. He wondered about his father and he looked across the grand hallway to the door to his father's office. Its door was resolutely closed. Again, he wasn't to know, but his father had spent the night in there. His mother, having watched the interview and news reports, had retired to bed alone after she had managed to placate Sunita Umrigar enough so that Sachin wasn't dragged from his bed that night.

The door to the office opened and Anjali, Sachin and Singh watched on as Locke strode across the grand hallway and into the reception room that just twelve hours earlier had resembled a television studio. He was carrying the white A4 envelope that Gregson had given to him. Anjali didn't know its significance, but Locke had opened it and what it contained turned him cold. Seconds later he came back out of the reception room and crossed the grand hallway again.

"Dad?"

But Locke didn't hear his son, or ignored him, and closed the door to his office once again.

"That will be all, Singh," Anjali said, getting to her feet and taking Sachin by the hand to lead him towards the kitchen. Her boy would be hungry.

*

Locke checked the time, smiled to himself, and pressed 'Enter'. It was done. It was Thursday and in six hours' time, Gregson would have the reply to his ultimatum. Now all Locke had to do was wait until nine-thirty in Mumbai and turn on the global news outlets. He chuckled; he would not be watching the British ones, though.

"Time to make another statement," he said to himself as he headed out into the garden at the back of the house. The sound of leather on willow had started to permeate as his brain began to wind down with the job finished. Sachin crouched and got his body behind the ball as Singh sent another one down. The ageing gardener was still good enough to bowl a ball, although he had confided in Locke that he ached for hours afterwards. It was why Locke had bought the bowling machine.

"Sachin!" Locke called out. "Four runs!"

Sachin and Singh both turned to see Locke striding across the lawns to the cricket net. The boy dropped his bat and broke into a run, hugging his father seconds later. Locke looked over to Singh, who understood.

"He is getting very good, sir," the gardener said happily. "He gets better every day," he added, before making his way back to his day job. Sachin's grin grew wider.

"Fancy sending some down, Dad?"

"Absolutely," Locke replied, smiling as his son almost waddled back into the net with the oversized cricket pads hampering his progress.

From her bedroom window, Anjali watched on with shock and delight. It was the first time either she or Sachin had seen Locke in two days. The rugby scrum at the front gates had made them virtual prisoners, but Locke insisted it was business as usual as long as no one left the house. When the police came, it was to see him alone. They had not wanted to speak to Anjali or anyone else in the house. They had stayed for over four hours before leaving. The arriving and departing shots of them at the mansion gates would make the front cover of the Indian nationals the next day.

And now this; for two days she had wondered about her very existence, about her life, her son, her wider family. And she had wondered about her marriage. She had been so sure of Locke, almost from the first moment they had 'met' in the temple.

I'm a dry desert riverbed. He was a vibrant ocean full of life. In the dry bed of the desert river the water of the ocean does not penetrate. How did I get cheated on? How did I become a crazy lover? Now I'm a life-long love story.

He had found her and that meant everything to her. He had found her twice more; it was fate, it was *ardhangini*.

Whose steps do I hear? Why do I hear my heart beating faster? Is it my memory giving me a flashback, or is it someone else? It's hard to put my memories behind me. The memories flood back. Am I now just a love affair? If I can't grieve, what else can I do? I was a shy girl running from a mirror.

But Locke's behaviour had frightened her. It was erratic. She now knew better than to try to talk to him when he was in one of his moods. They could last for days and he could explode at the slightest thing. She watched as father and son played their cricket. It was the first proper contact they had had for many days now. She would give them a bit more time.

"Enjoying yourself?" she asked thirty minutes later as Locke sent down another ball that Sachin defended with ease.

Locke laughed. "He's getting really good, Singh says. He's been doing a great job."

Anjali picked up a cricket ball and waited for Sachin to get in position. She dropped it into the chute and watched it fizz down the pitch towards her son. He defended this one as well.

"It's good to see you," she said, quietly. "I was beginning to wonder if we were to see you again."

"I know," Locke replied, looking at the ground. "I have had a lot on my plate, and you've seen it on the TV. But we're coming out the other end. It's going to be fine."

The anger had gone and before her stood the old John Locke. His plan was a success. The act he created in the stairway had worked perfectly and left Anjali confused.

"Is this about the street kids initiative? I know they've arrested those men, but surely they can't think you had anything to do with it?"

"No," Locke said, not entirely truthfully. "I don't think the police believe I had anything to do with it. The court of public opinion might have something to say on social media, but then everyone becomes a keyboard warrior, don't they? I'm sure there's plenty of vile things being said about me. Not that I care."

Anjali caressed Locke's face, staring intently into his eyes, believing, or wanting to believe. He smiled back and stroked her face. Somewhere behind them Sachin made gagging noises, as if he was going to be sick. Anjali and Locke embraced, then burst out laughing as their son stood impatiently, with his hands on his hips waiting for the next ball to be bowled.

Later they ate together, again for the first time in many days. Sachin had been desperate for a burger and the chef had gone to town creating something amazing that Locke said rivalled anything he could remember from his childhood in the US. Then they watched TV and Locke read to his son at bedtime. It was another of the cricket biographies that Sachin couldn't get enough of. Locke was beginning to think that whatever he did in life, his son would be wearing whites a lot in the coming years. He wasn't wrong, but for Sachin, something else was happening outside of his cricket.

Anjali raised her glass to her lips as Locke came back downstairs, his father-son bonding done for the day. "What would you like to watch?" she asked as he flopped down on the sofa beside her.

"Something light," he said. "A comedy, maybe."

Anjali flicked through the channels, then decided to look for a film. Locke took the TV remote from her and headed for the comedy section. She looked at him quizzically.

"I can use a remote, you know," she said in mock outrage.

"I know," he replied scrolling down the programmes. "I've just got something on later, so I don't want something too long."

He settled on an episode of *30 Rock* and noticed that Anjali had changed her seating position to make it harder for him to touch her.

*

By the time Anjali woke up, *30 Rock* was no longer on the TV. They had watched a couple of episodes before her eyes had closed. The TV was still on, but it wasn't comedy any more. Locke was watching a news channel from the US and his face was full of horror. She looked at the screen and did the maths in her head. New York, where the news broadcast came from, was nine and a half hours behind Mumbai. It was a little after one in the morning local time.

The television pictures showed smoke rising from what looked like a bad car crash, then the scene changed to show a number of ambulances parked up as bodies lay in a street. Anjali's eyes widened. The scene changed again, this time to the view from a helicopter; ambulances and police cars were hurtling through the streets, a view of Tower Bridge made it clear the pictures were from London in the UK. In fact all of the scenes were from the UK. She looked at the strapline: 'UK hit by multiple incidents'... 'situation is ongoing'... 'reports entire UK internet failed' ... 'death toll stands at fourteen'.

"That's not right," Locke said quietly. "That can't be..."

"Oh my," Anjali said. "What's happened?" She looked back across at Locke, his expression the same as before. "John? What's going on? What are they saying?" Locke began to shake his head. His mouth was open, his eyes never leaving the TV screen. "John?"

"Get out, please." The statement came out in a whisper.

"Why? What's going on in Lon—" Anjali didn't get to finish her sentence. Locke turned his gaze to her and what she saw terrified her. His eyes bore into her, his mouth a snarling fury as he spat the words that had her running for the door.

"Get the fuck out now!" he screamed.

thirty-three
missing for a long time

John Locke hammered away at the keys and stared at the four different screens positioned so that he could see across all four at once. On one the news reports continued. He had set it up so that he could see the pictures being broadcast on the now restored BBC channel in the UK, as well as Russian, US and German news outlets. He wanted to know when reporting turned to speculation and there had been plenty already.

The US outlet had repeatedly blamed unnamed terrorists or possibly a state operator, with Russia mentioned often. Russian TV settled for terrorists and argued the UK had been technologically weak and therefore not ready for cyberwarfare.

It was what Locke had wanted. He had planned the UK's internet shutdown, for one whole hour, at the moment Gregson had insisted he was to provide his response. This was his response, and it was untraceable. What Gregson would also discover was that the entire money reserves of the bank he represented had been wired to its five top competitors in billions of tiny transactions during the five minutes before the internet stopped in the UK.

No news reporters had mentioned the run on the bank yet. Which would have disappointed Locke, but for the fact there had been deaths. The toll now over a hundred amongst the thousands of accidents that had happened across the UK.

Deaths.

They should not have happened. Locke banged away at the keys again, taking his eye off the news reports to another screen. Computer code, white against a black background swirled and scrolled at a rate impossible for any human to read. But Locke continued to type, looking for the one thing that would make sense to him.

The door to his office opened slowly. Locke raised a hand without looking up.

"Do not come in."

The door closed as slowly. He didn't see the tears well in Sachin's eyes or hear his son sob. He heard the clatter of a cricket bat thrown onto the stone floor, though.

Locke pressed a button and watched a screen as a transparent luminous green depiction of the world appeared. He pressed another key and looked on as a trace enveloped the Earth, nodes in every country and on every continent. Anyone deciphering his code would eventually follow the trace to any one of a number of Russian Cold War military sites which they would assume was the source of the hack that had closed down the UK's internet. If they deciphered it again, they would find themselves taken to a different Russian Cold War military site. The code would keep jumping; it would never actually appear to have a source because every source the decipherer found would be different, but with one constant; it was located in Russia. That work would take intelligence agencies weeks. In the meantime, Locke knew, without answers the press would speculate and Russia would already have many fingers pointed at it.

But the deaths.

No one was meant to die. Locke steepled his fingers and glanced again at the news streams running simultaneously. He felt the pain behind his eyes, but was determined not to give in to the sobs he could feel in his chest. How had it happened? The sensation was new and very real and it frightened him. He was the most intelligent man on the planet and he had got something wrong, somehow. Initial claims of terrorism being responsible were being scaled back, except for Russian TV news who pushed the point further and further, seemingly blaming any Islamist terror organisation at will. What the BBC was broadcasting now, however, was how the incidents happened. The worst occurred in London when a lorry driver ploughed through a crowd crossing at a set of lights. The driver was in custody, but before he was arrested someone had filmed him running back from his lorry to where sixteen people lay dead. He was heard saying his SatNav had gone off, before an angry mob leapt on him and restrained him. Police arrived in minutes and took the man away. He turned out to be a Romanian national, and that seemed to further the Russian angle for American TV. Locke shook that thought away; Romania hadn't been part of the Eastern Bloc for thirty years.

"The SatNav go off! The SatNav go off!"

Locke buried his head in his hands and wept. He had considered navigation a risk, but did not expect people to be so obsessed by it that it caused accidents. There had been thousands. He knew aircraft would be safe, apart from the one that crashed on take-off in Wales, but then he reckoned that was an isolated example of pilot error. He was not going to take the blame for the three killed when that light aircraft dropped fifty feet and burst into flames. He had also knew ships and trains would be fine, but he had underestimated the general public's love of their phones and satellite navigation systems. It had left more than a hundred of them dead. At least the emergency services had been able to use radio rather than internet. It was small consolation, but that one point had undoubtedly saved some lives.

"Why are people so fucking stupid!" he shouted to the room. "Why? Why?" Locke grabbed at the screen showing the news outlets and pulled with all his strength. It smashed face down on the ground beneath his feet, its power cable swinging wildly after it had been wrenched out. He pushed at a second screen that shattered on the floor behind his desk, then he picked up the remote keyboard and threw it as hard as he could. It struck the wall to the right of the office door, just as the door opened. Anjali screamed. Locke looked on in horror as she touched her forehead; there was a thin trickle of blood where a piece of keyboard had caught her. He became aware of a brief sharp pain and reached up to his own forehead. When he looked back down at his hand there was no blood, only his shaking palm.

He looked back at Anjali and saw the terror in her eyes. She tried to comprehend the scene before her, then slowly stepped into the room, closed the door and turned the key. She eased towards the panting, distressed-looking man that was her husband. He seemed confused and unhinged and she wanted to calm him down before anything else. She realised he was upset by the news, but had no idea he was responsible. She became aware of a strange sense of dread in her stomach and her forehead stung a little, but nothing compared to the fear in her heart. She realised that Locke looked cornered and wild and he needed her right at that moment. The explanation could wait.

Remove the mask; let me see the real John.

"John," she whispered, and he looked at her, dazed. There was sweat on his top lip and his hair was unruly. "John," she said again and held out her hand. He stared at its graceful beauty and at the ring on her wedding finger. He saw the smudge of blood where she had felt for the nick on her forehead. He looked up at her face and saw the tiny sliver of crimson close to her hairline. He looked into her eyes and could not hold the tears back.

She hugged him, walked him to a sofa and sat him down. She held him there as he wailed into her breast. She kissed the top of his head, made soft little utterances to soothe and calm him. She did not feel like his wife; she felt like a mother reassuring a child that had fallen and scraped a knee. She didn't know the man in her arms. She wanted to know where her John was and she was going to do everything to find him. She felt all of her love flow through her, enveloping her with an aura so deep she believed it tangible.

She had not felt like this for some time and, as the old feelings returned, she felt lighter as if she was floating on an astral plane, as if her prayers had finally been answered. But she needed to catch a glimpse of her old John. The man she loved.

She pulled away aware that her top was soaked with her husband's tears and that he had gone quiet, no longer sobbing. He looked back at her, appeared ashamed and looked away at the computer screen in pieces on the floor and at the two remaining screens, one still flashing up images of code and the other live updates of the markets.

Suddenly a flash of red appeared on the second. He peered closely from the sofa, trying to make out whatever was happening. He realised then that his forced run on Gregson's bank had gone the way he wanted it to. That made him smile and he finally looked back at Anjali, blinking away the tears.

She frowned; she had not expected him to suddenly smile. *Years have gone by,* she thought. *So many events have taken place. The man I fell in love with; he never made it back. I can neither see nor smell it.*

"Are you okay, John? Do you want to tell me about it?" Distraught one minute, happy the next? She wondered if this was what was meant by being bi-polar. "I need you to come to me."

This was also new for Locke; he had broken down and now he needed to explain it away quickly. He averted his gaze and stayed silent, buying time, fearing he was about to lose her. He could not let her in on what had happened, on what he had done. To do so would have been to signal the death knell of his marriage, of his being with his son, of his own freedom.

To do so would also have been to admit his own failings and he could not comprehend that.

No, she would never understand what he had caused and why he had done it. Anjali was spiritual and he accepted that as people needed a crutch; they needed a higher being to help divest their own sins when they felt they had done wrong. But there was no such higher power in his head. Only guilt and coming to terms with what he himself had done. He saw it all the time whenever people who had nothing to do with a certain incident, suddenly took it upon themselves to wallow in some shared grief. They were trying to identify and connect with an occasion when they had played no part. They called it compassion and Locke understood that. But he saw it for the weakness that he considered it to be.

"It's the street kids initiative," he said, adding a sharp breath for emphasis. "I just can't get over what has happened. Those poor, poor kids." Locke pushed his face close to Anjali's chest again, hoping she would react to the gesture. She did and he felt her arms tighten around him. But this time she understood it was related to the news and that Locke was lying. She remained silent, not letting on. She was desperate to see the John she knew, but her eyes felt bruised and a fire burned in her core. She wanted him to find his own destination, but in her direction. She couldn't see it and her heart bled for him.

It had taken him till now to mention the missing children and, since the story had broken three days ago, he had spent his time as he always did; planning and plotting, staring at his beloved computers, locking himself in his room. He had made himself distant. That was something Anjali could not understand. She had been sickened by what had gone on as she had watched the television as much as she could bear.

She had searched for answers, but amongst thousands of possibles, she stared at the one probable. She stared at John and understood. She had seen the unsmiling faces of the men who had managed the initiative on behalf of Locke Enterprises. She had even met some of them on walk rounds she had done in the past. The initiative had been wound up immediately; the doors closed and the remaining children, all two hundred and eighty-six of them, had been rehoused straight away. She could not believe it had happened at all. And yet this was the first time Locke had mentioned it since it had happened and he had done the Gadkari interview. Something wasn't right; he was even watching American comedies the night before. There had been no sign of guilt or responsibility then.

I'll find the true John here. That's what I have to find out. That's all I need to know. Remove this false world, unveil the real John. Take that stranger off his face.

"John," she breathed, "you weren't to know. We put our faith in those men and they abused it for their own ends. I can't believe it, and certainly not of Amar Rajmi."

Locke nodded his head at the mention of Rajmi; he was the general manager at the initiative and a man he actually liked. He winced a little as he considered, for the first time, that it wasn't just the children that were victims. He shrugged the thought away.

"Me neither," he said. "He was ideal for the kids. A schoolteacher and a local councillor? He should have been perfect for the job." Locke looked back up at Anjali. "How could I have got him, and the others, so wrong?"

"Because you know facts and figures," Anjali said. "Because you can create things and because you can put in place the structures that normal people can manage. But you cannot possibly understand what every person is thinking. I'd swear on my life that Mr Rajmi was a decent man and not guilty of what he is accused, but you cannot tell what anyone is thinking at any one time."

Locke smiled inwardly. Anjali didn't know how right she was. He pulled away from her embrace and considered her. The scratch on her forehead had stopped bleeding, and the pain on his own forehead had receded. That was strange. He forced the thought away. He still hadn't got himself out of the woods. He leant forward and kissed her, just gently, on the side of the mouth. Anjali kissed him back before Locke stared down at the smashed computer screen by the desk.

"I'll need to get those replaced," he said, rising from the sofa and walking carefully through the debris. Anjali watched her husband as he went to the door and called for Dhaljit, their housekeeper. Locke smiled once more at Anjali and left the room.

She waited, her forehead creased in confusion, trying to understand what had happened in the last ten minutes. She touched the sodden patch on her blouse, as if to reassure herself that at least Locke had actually been crying. But the rest? Was it really about the missing street kids? He had gone from crying like some crazed wounded animal to normal in a matter of minutes. Every time she felt she had got close, Locke had made himself more distant. It wasn't meant to be like this. She was meant to understand her husband before he himself understood. She was supposed to be everything to him and he was meant to be everything to her. That had been missing for a long time. Just when she thought she had made a breakthrough, that he had confided in her, he snapped back into the new Locke she could not read.

Dhaljit hovered in the doorway uncertain whether to come in. She stayed there until Anjali rose and walked out of the room. The housekeeper had been made to wait for over an hour.

thirty-four
one final, withering look

Locke barked into his phone. Everywhere men walked carrying stuff to and fro, loading up the trucks with all their belongings or going back into the house to get some more. It was a huge process that was accompanied by a lot of shouting, and not just from Locke as he got increasingly animated in conversation with the person on the other end of the line.

Anjali descended the staircase wearing a stunning sky blue and gold sari. A few of the removal men stopped to gawk before their foreman shouted at them again. Sachin was outside having a last net session with Singh. The boy and the gardener had grown very close during the Lockes' stay in Mumbai and Locke rewarded that friendship by donating the bowling machine to a local cricket club Singh was still involved with. He could have easily had it transported along with everything else, but instead he promised to build his son a state-of-the-art cricket net at their new mansion in Cheshire. He had already drawn up the plans and told his representatives in Manchester to lodge the application. He reckoned on it being a formality. Locke killed the call.

"John," Anjali said, "can we talk for a minute?"

Locke regarded his wife, still seething at the conversation he had just had. Then he smiled. "Sure," he said, and led the way into the main reception room with its Landseer depiction of Van Amburgh and his tiger. They sat on a plush leather sofa together.

"What is it, Anjali?"

"Gregson," she said flatly. "Who is he, what is he and why does he keep coming to our house or calling you on the phone?"

Locke's smile vanished. It had been Gregson on the phone, and it had not been pleasant. But Gregson was showing his hand too quickly; it meant he had no proof. He was beaten. And it was the last criminal thing Locke wanted to do. The run on the bank was genius; the collapse of the internet had terrible consequences, but he had brushed them aside as the fault of others. Things had gone too far and he had done too much. He knew he had to stop. He wanted peace from now on; a new beginning. Was it time to trust his wife? To tell her the truth? Or just some of it? He increasingly found lying was something that came easily and he liked it. But a moment later he would realise how he no longer seemed to have control over it. He wondered whether the lies were killing him, turning him into something he wasn't.

"He's from a bank in the UK," Locke said after a few moments. "He is accusing me of a number of things that are not true. He is threatening me with arrest when we return to England and he is being what I think the British like to call 'an interfering cunt'."

Anjali was shocked at the use of the word. It was not something she could ever remember Locke saying before. He saw the shock and raised his hand in surrender.

"Sorry. I meant to say 'an interfering busybody'."

She nodded an acceptance of the apology, but Gregson was clearly getting to her husband.

"Which bank?" Locke shook his head. "Okay, why is he after you? What is he accusing you of?"

Locke sighed. *How far do I go?* "Theft," he said. "He is accusing me of stealing a sum of money from his bank seven years ago. He is threatening my arrest and the seizing of my assets. He is threatening me with the Proceeds of Crime Act and he says he has the evidence to prove it." Locke looked at Anjali, her face creased in concern.

"And does he have the evidence?"

"No. But I did do the crime." It was the first truth he had said in years. Was he wrong to have done that? Was telling the truth true payback? He felt as though he was about to find out.

"What?" Anjali stood up quickly and stared down at her husband, and then at the opulent room they were in. Her breath shallowed slowly and she started to panic. Locke reached for her, to bring her back down to the sofa. Her mind screamed, *don't touch me,* and she resisted to start with but eventually acquiesced. Her breathing stayed the same and she fought to get it back under control.

"I did it to prove that I could. I was challenging my new found knowledge and intelligence, you know, giving it a bit of a test drive. I took a total of one million pounds in thousands of tiny withdrawals. It was after the gambling, the books, the surgeon work that I did for a bit. I was bored doing what I was doing. It was never challenging enough for me. I became a risk-taker and I was intrigued to know if I could do it. Everything I have done since my change has been about expanding my knowledge to see if I can outwit every organisation's experts. Gregson is the only one that believes he can trace anything back to me."

"And can he?"

"No, because I have hacked his computer and erased all the evidence he says he had on me. The thing is, he's started to get desperate, which to me means he has not got it backed up properly, or on a separate disc or something. He tried to play me; I have played him."

"So you think you're smarter than everybody else?" Anjali stated, her eyes blazing. Locke didn't answer.

"The let me tell you a story about a lion, a king of the jungle," she said, never taking her gaze off him. "He believed himself to be stronger and more intelligent than everyone else. And every day he ate another animal. One animal every day. The other animals were afraid of being his next meal. A courageous mouse thought he would be next in line to eat, but when he walked in the lion laughed and said he wasn't even enough for an aperitif!"

"I apologise, my king," the mouse said, bowing, "but I hear there's a larger, stronger, smarter lion than you in the jungle."

"Who dares to come into my kingdom?" the lion roared.

"He wishes to challenge you," the courageous mouse replied.

"Take me to him!"

So the mouse took the lion to an isolated place in the jungle where there was a well. "He's in there," he said.

The lion looked inside the well and roared. His reflection also roared and the lion could not differentiate between himself and his own reflection in the water. In anger and wrath he jumped in the pit and died." Anjali paused. "Being intelligent is fine, but being proud to be intelligent is not."

Locke smiled, then laughed. "I get what you are saying, Anjali. Gregson was persistent and irritating, but now he is beaten."

Anjali's breathing had slowly normalised. She felt the control come flooding into her. Locke showed no remorse for what he had just said.

No remorse. Psychopaths show no remorse. Keep a straight face, and lie in front of it. He thinks he's smarter than anyone. Including me.

She formed her right hand into the shape of a pistol. "Truth gun," she said. "Lie to me, John and you lose me. Lie to me and you lose Sachin."

Locke's laughter faded and his jaw clenched. Anjali was a far more difficult proposition than Gregson. He realised she was thinking about their marriage, how she must think it hung in the balance. Her grit and determination were why he loved her, and that love was now at risk.

"Is that the only crime, John?" He hesitated. Anjali placed the 'gun' to her temple, but he gently pulled her hand back down.

"That won't work anymore. I am going to tell you what happened. It wasn't the only crime."

"Tell me," she stated. Locke sighed, weighing up his options. All sorts of images flashed through his mind of the scams he had pulled, of the gangsters he had played, the companies he had ripped off, the TV appearances, the medical procedures, designing his mansion with its many false rooms. All of them came to him as he thought back over his litany of crimes that no-one knew about. And then came the final two; the ones he could not rationalise in his own head, the ones that kept him awake at night, the ones that haunted him: the footage of Amar Rajmi being led away from the street kids initiative and the unsteady video of the Romanian lorry driver running back to the bodies in the street, screaming.

"The SatNav go off! The SatNav go off!"

"Everything I have done, I have done for us and for Sachin—"

"Careful, John..." Anjali interrupted. "I didn't ask for your fortune like a lot of women in society might. I just asked for a husband." Locke saw that determination, that bloody determination that smashed him down. He knew that she knew. She knew he was still lying.

Locke had remained seated and Anjali began to walk around him, just as she did at the wedding *mandap*. He knew she was sizing him up and working him out. It made him nervous.

"I have done everything to prove to myself that I could do things and benefit my family and give us the lives I think the world's most intelligent person should have," he said.

"But money cannot purchase love or emotion," Anjali countered. "It can only buy you luxury. Therefore it is said in all cultures that love is eternal. You're nothing but a human being. Why should you understand that?"

"We are not the richest people in the world, but I don't need us to be," Locke insisted. "I just want what is befitting of my ability."

"And you thought turning to crime was the answer for you? Tell me about the crimes, John." Anjali formed her hand into the shape of a gun and pointed it him.

"Okay, the truth. Every last bit of it." Locke cleared his throat. "It started with the gambling. I went into that casino and showed them I would be able to take ten thousand pounds off them and that they would let me walk away with it if I promised to show them how I did it. I know you were scared when you found me, but we were safe. I took the money and went back to show them how. They went into casinos all over the country and cleared each of thousands of pounds. All legal. But as the casinos saw they were losing, they changed the rules.

"I wrote the books off the back of that, sold all those copies and made us wealthy. But there was a problem. The gang I worked with at the start got greedy. They kept coming back for more money. The last time was about a month ago. They were the only people who knew I was not completely legitimate."

Locke closed his eyes and took an exaggerated, deep breath. It was the biggest step he was about to take and he felt as though he was falling.

"They're dead now."

Anjali's mouth opened and the hand pointing at Locke lowered.

"You killed them?"

He shook his head. "Had them killed. They were gangsters. They were career criminals that had never worked a day in their life. I may have won ten thousand pounds that night, and made them rich into the bargain, but they have since taken over a million from me, *from us*. That trip back to Manchester was to get rid of them. I set up the hit and only one of them that has seen me in the flesh remains. He is currently in prison for a very long time."

Locke stood up and slowly walked around the room. Anjali's eyes never left him. *He's a murderer...* the only thing going through her mind. *He's messed with God's consciousness, he gave you this knowledge, this life as a gift. And you used it to become a criminal, to lie, to murder...*

"I can justify it because they were bad people. I know it is wrong, but there are now fewer bad people in the world as a result."

"What about you John? Aren't you a bad person?"

Locke kept walking all around the room. "I could pay them the million because I had made legitimate money through the books and TV appearances. The money from the bank was just curiosity. They missed it so much they only realised seven years later. In the meantime, I've done a number of other scams where no one has noticed."

"*Karma* has a habit of coming back to haunt you," Anjali whispered. "So you think you've committed the perfect crime?" Locke was secretly impressed with his plan, and his wife.

He smiled. "Yes, if you like—"

"I don't bloody like, John!" Anjali screamed, Locke's smile disappeared. "There is no crime or sin that is perfect. No one but you thinks so. I can't believe you're saying all this! You're a criminal! A fucking murderer! Murdering a human is a sin. If you killed one person, it is as if you have killed the whole of humanity. Life is not for us to take. Only a creator can do that."

Locke raised his hands in an attempt to pacify. Anjali reacted by pointing her hand straight at him, almost making him flinch as if she were holding a real gun.

"Every genius has a weak spot. Yours is losing me." Anjali's eyes burned with hatred at that moment, as the words hung in the air between them. To her left, on a table, she saw a fruit knife next to a bowl of oranges. She picked the knife up, Locke's eyes widening, and placed the blade against her wrist making it clear she was ready to slice her own flesh if Locke lied again. "Gregson's bank. What is its name?" she demanded.

"The bank? That's not important," he said, his eyes darting between the knife and Anjali's face, trying to read her, trying to beg her not to slit her own wrists.

"I'll decide what's important, John! What's the name of his fucking bank?" Anjali's face screwed up in fury, tears fell freely from her eyes. Her breathing was irregular as she took great lungful's of air. Then realisation. "Oh. My. God. It's the one that's collapsed, isn't it? The one that had a run on it and all its money disappeared. You caused its collapse."

John nodded weakly. "Yes," his voice barely audible.

"And the UK internet crash happened immediately after the run. They are linking the two. The moment the run ended, the internet went down. People died because of that. And you did it! You!" Anjali slashed at her wrist. A single downward motion and the blood flowed. She dropped the knife and ran at Locke, screaming. He didn't know what to do, but at the back of his mind was the stinging pain coming from his own wrist. He looked down and saw blood. *What the fuck was going on?* He had never seen hate in her eyes before, but he did this time. She launched herself at him, crashing into him with enough weight to knock him staggering backwards, sending a small table careering across the room. Decanters of rare whiskies, rums and brandies crashed to the floor and smashed as Locke tripped, landing heavily on his back. He winced from the pain and looked up to see Anjali holding the small of her back just as he now held the small of his. He blinked. She was in the same pain as he was. Just like when she got that small cut on her temple and he felt pain in his. *Ardhangini. It's real.*

Anjali saw the recognition in Locke's face. *Finally he's got it,* she thought. *And it happens when he's told me all this!* She looked down at her husband, lying amidst the broken glass and spilled alcohol. She pointed again at Locke, only this time it was a single, quivering finger. She had gone beyond the truth gun. "You killed people." Locke shook his head.

"No! They were accidents! I didn't think people would be so affected they would crash their cars!" It was a lie. He had considered it a possibility, but he had gone ahead anyway. The stupid bastards that were so obsessed with their SatNavs that they had crashed into people, parked cars, each other. Those senseless, selfish little pricks had ruined his meticulous hacking programme. Anjali stopped. Her hands went to her stomach and she wretched. She wretched again, but nothing would come out.

"Anjali?" Locke said, never taking his eyes off her as he carefully got up. He placed a hand on a shard of glass and gasped in pain. Anjali immediately grabbed the wrist of her right hand with her left. There was a cut in the centre of her palm. She looked down at it as Locke pulled at the shard in his own palm and saw the blood collect there.

They looked at each other, the realisation hanging between them like a curtain. Locke dared not move. For the first time since he could remember he didn't know what to do. They stared at each other, each nursing a cut palm, each wondering what stood before them.

"The street kids initiative." It was a statement, not a question. Locke tried to read the thoughts going through Anjali's mind. This would be the final straw. If he told the truth now, it would be over. It probably already was. But he could not tell her the truth. Children were missing, almost certainly dead, and what the men had done to them before murdering them was a cross too far for Locke to bear. He shook his head slowly. Anjali let go of her right wrist and raised it up into the shape of the truth gun once more. She walked towards Locke, her hand pointing straight at him. She stopped when the nails of her extended fingers touched his forehead. She pushed, digging them in and feeling the same sensation in her own forehead. A droplet of blood fell from her cut palm.

"Lie to me now," she hissed, "and you lose everything you have ever cared about. I'll see to it, John. A wife can forgive and forget the wrongful acts of a husband because she has a relationship with him. But when any company, society or authority finds out, they will hunt you down."

Locke dared not move with the truth gun pointed at his head. He could feel the sweat on his forehead trickling down, and of the wetness in his trousers where he had lain in the spilled alcohol. The cut on his wrist stung most, though, and he still couldn't work out how that had happened. The knife had been nowhere near him. He looked deep into Anjali's eyes and saw the rage within. In that moment she terrified him. She had the power. She was the strong one. *She was the good one.*

"I had nothing to do with that," he said, "any more than you did. I had no idea any of them were like that." Each word came out slowly and deliberately. "I have had nothing to do with those poor children's disappearances."

Anjali lowered the truth gun and allowed her hand to fall to her side. They stood looking at each other.

"There's no need for me to kill you, John. You're killing yourself."

Locke still could not read what she was thinking. For the first time he saw that the marriage had taken place in the sky. Two souls meet and find their way on Earth. He put out a hand, a small gesture to try to connect, to take her hand in his and hope to God she would let him.

Her right hand went quickly to her own temple, her fingers once again making the shape of the truth gun. "Now I know you have lied. You lose, John." Her hand flinched, mimicking the recoil when a pistol is fired. She made to look like she had blown her own brains out. Anjali gave Locke one final, withering look and walked away. "You didn't only lie to me, John, but to your consciousness as well. He will give you your judgement, your outcome, because he was the one who gave you this genius knowledge as a gift."

Locke didn't move. The door to the room closed firmly behind her as Anjali walked out. Locke fell to his knees and sobbed amongst the broken glass and spilled whisky.

part v
anjali

thirty-five
let me be the first to die

Anjali looked down at the journal in her lap and wiped away another tear. It was a futile gesture; her handkerchief was drenched. She knew her make up would be smeared all across her face, but she didn't care. She looked around the room; at the door to the walk-in wardrobe, the huge mirror dominating one wall and the writing bureau sandwiched between two tall windows. Streetlight filtered through either side of the thick maroon curtains. Her heart had ached so much over the previous week she felt it might tear in two. She missed her husband. The touch. The feel. The smell. And the way he thought she was beautiful. It was the definition of beautiful.

She missed her John. At times she had thought she might be having a heart attack. Each time she saw Sachin's image and the pain subsided. She had to keep it together for her son. So far he had not asked questions. He knew something was wrong; the silence lingered over his mother's face. He was happy to be back in Manchester and having his father away from home was nothing new to him, but his friends were starting to notice his smart responses.

They were at home in their old house in Didsbury, and it felt so much better than India. They both thought it, but for different reasons; Sachin loved being back with his friends. He'd gone for a net at Lancashire Cricket Club and they had put him on their books there and then. They said they had never seen so much talent in a twelve-year-old. He could capture any moment in seconds. But he had only played with Singh the gardener for a matter of weeks. He had never picked up a bat before then.

For Anjali, being thousands of miles from her husband was the only way she knew she could be true to herself and no longer accept his criminal path. But she couldn't reconcile those thoughts, her actions to what she truly believed in; *ardhangini*. She often believed separation was a curse on a wedding when it was really a blessing because it helped people think about their lives, their experience, to look at what had gone wrong and how they could have done better. How could she separate from the man that made her whole? She started to consider why God placed this test upon her life. And did she learn something about life? *He said I do. I said I do. And God was our witness.*

She held the diary in her lap. It was nothing remarkable; just a small book with a light pink cover, but she had the secret of his heart. It harked back to a younger Anjali, where the wind breaks away slowly and gently blew at her hair like the beating of tree leaves. It was an Anjali she now remembered well after finding the journal amongst the possessions they had left in the UK. She shuffled slightly on the silk-sheeted bed and looked at the first words again. *I love John Lock, that's my secret.* She smiled inwardly at the misspelling of his name then took a deep breath and lay back down, her hair soaking up the saltwater on the wet pillow. She thought about what brought them together. What was the secret and the sign? Why John when there were millions of Indians in her society?

*

Dear diary, it is not in our culture to fall in love with a stranger, but this doesn't mean it doesn't happen. Many must have gone before me in finding their own love story. How come humans seek love? What significance does it have in our lives? What did the ancients leave behind and who invented it? Who made up this love affair in the first place? The question is always whether my parents will accept it. That is where I am right now. Why is it not respectable to my family? Why does my society shun it, my home?

I understand how tenuous my life is. If I fall pregnant it will be my name and not John's that will suffer the stain of shame, but the scriptures say a single person is good for you. However, today's society says that several partners are what they want. And they gave it a name; dating. I will suffer the burden of my child and raise it with all my heart. Alone if necessary. Will my parents, or society, let that happen? Or will I be slain in the name of an illegitimate child? I know it's my parents' greatest fear. I will only marry once. I believe that with all of my heart. Is it John? Can it be John? As my mother still says to me, "you only get to live once, not many times, you only die one time, not several, so you get married once, not many times."

I never thought I would be one of those who falls in love with a stranger. I am Hindi. Romance is everywhere in our scriptures, but does that mean that society is going to allow me to live happily ever after? Love has such an evil reputation when men turn away from their words. I live in England, but my heart is in India. The life I live at home is a different one to what I experience outside. There I am modern, I am educated, I am working and supporting myself and my parents. I am an independent woman with all of those qualities, but it still doesn't give me the right to make independent choices. For I am yet young in the eyes of Life's experience. And knowing something isn't the same as experiencing Life.

This is my problem. It doesn't mean that doesn't happen in my culture, in my civilisation, only that I choose not to take those decisions because I believe our life is a circle of Life. That what happens today carries on into our future.

I think my life is about to change. Whatever I believed in is about to change. I feel shy and ashamed when meeting a man like John, but am I wrong to think about him or to feel about him? Is Life telling me something, encouraging me to fall in love? Is one look enough to fall in love, to think, he could be the one? My judgements are all over the place. I saw him in the temple, taking my picture. I saw him on the plane and I whispered to him, not that he understood. A silly little game that left him confused. That was cruel, but I have to know if he is serious about me. Will he seek me? Will he find me?

But then I saw him at Hannah's wedding yesterday. This time we spoke. This time we kissed. Was kissing a stranger a good thing, knowing that I might be somebody else's? Why do we lose ourselves when you come to Earth? And why do we split up after marriage only to be together again? Do I still have regrets about meeting John? I don't know.

Anjali sniffed and dried her eyes. Her mind went back to that day on the moors with its excitement and dancing and love. She remembered it vividly. The colours had not faded at all. Being the fourth bridesmaid down the aisle and the dance on the stage she had choreographed with Hannah and the other bridesmaids. She had spotted Locke as he gaped at her, his camera held listlessly in his hands. She thought she had maintained her dignity.

People say we are showing more energy, love and expression of our feelings when we dance. Why do we say that? Why is dance viewed as our true sentiment?

He had not seen her recognise him even though her heart skipped a beat that she was looking at the man she had seen in the temple and on the plane home. She wondered why she had left the room as soon as she did; did she not want to know the real John Locke? Why even then had she been so shy? In hindsight, she needed encouragement. Perhaps she was too nervous. Or just too Hindu and shocked by the thought she might have fallen for an Englishman? It was out of her culture to fall in love. Her belief was sealed; it would be an arranged marriage. Whatever she felt, Anjali remembered the courage it took her to follow him to the bar and to whisper in his ear.

"And I'll have a prosecco."

He had nearly leaped out of his skin and she smiled at the memory. And she remembered how he called her "India", providing a reaction she had not expected. *Am I a woman or a country?* she had wondered. They had talked, quietly, at a table by the window, then danced and found out what each other was really called. Goosebumps rose on Anjali's skin as she thought back to how he captivated her from the very beginning, how he was shy, but confident and how he was American and not English. She realised very quickly just how much he was infatuated by her. It was the kind of love that every Asian woman seeks.

She wanted a man that would worship the ground she walked on. And then the cab ride back to his apartment and the first time she saw the picture on his wall. She was an idol for him. The huge image of her deep in prayer in the temple in Delhi. She remembered her initial shock and how she batted away the brief concern that Locke was a stalker. She felt she already knew him, perhaps better than she knew herself. She was embarking down a road that would lead to confrontation with her parents. But she knew from the beginning that John Locke was the one. That he was her *ardhangini*. Relations are not like the grain of sand one can throw away. It's not like a letter you can read and then tear up. Even after separation, it's not actually broken up. This is the connection in a relationship. And now she was still looking for a solution to help John's life.

She suppressed a sob as she thought back to John's youthful purity and how he had changed. There are seven heavenly places, seven oceans and seven lives in our midst. There are seven different vocal tones. But the most incredible tonality is the one she liked the most. It had been a long time since she had cursed his attackers who had tried kill him by throwing him in the canal. That assault was the catalyst. How might his life have been different if that hadn't happened? Would he have still been treated for his cancer in the way that he was? It was discovered sooner because he was in hospital and in a coma. But perhaps if the tumour had not been discovered then, could it have killed him? That came later and there were already too many ifs.

Anjali turned the page, and again delighted in the memories. She read her own neat handwriting as it took her back to the conversation she had with one of her girlfriends. She had written it just a few days after Hannah and David's wedding. She had not told the dairy of her innermost memories, certainly not of that first night she had spent at John's flat. She knew why – in case her mother had found her diary and read it. She had ended at the dance, that was far enough if prying eyes ever saw it.

Instead the diary moved on to the *Mela* in Manchester. It had been her friend Lexi's idea; she wanted to avoid another of her mother's ferociously hot curries.

"Be cool," I said. "Tell my mum and dad to keep it mild. You know how they love to feast."

Then Lexi asked me about my mystery man, about John, and teased me about my thoughts about the Universe. She told me it wasn't how the world works, but her beliefs are quite different from mine. How I wish I had given him my number. I just couldn't bring myself to do it.

We went to the Mela and it was amazing. I wasn't sure what caused me to go there, but my heart said I could find something valuable.

We had a ball on the rides and I felt so proud that my culture was taking centre stage in the heart of my city. I wore a white sari with a veil, my nod to the Mela, my show of being Indian British that day, rather than British Indian. It felt right, somehow. It was significant. It didn't rain, but it was windy and my veil caught the breeze and flew away, high into the air. I let out a little scream and Lexi and I laughed as we chased after it. It now feels like a sign but at the time we just thought it was funny or weird. I saw it land amongst a group of people, or at least I thought I did, but it actually landed beyond them and I saw someone bend down to pick it up. I recognised him immediately. I can't believe I am writing these words, but it was John! I stopped and we looked at each other. Lexi joined me by my side and seemed to understand immediately. I was still trying to make sense of the situation. All I could hear was a little voice saying "ardhangini" over and over again. And the sound of my own beating heart.

He looked at me and smiled, my veil hanging limp in his hand. "Hi," he said. "Anjali, isn't it?" He was acting cool and nonchalant. I didn't like it, much, but I don't think I really heard him. I was still stunned by the sight of him. Romantic music seemed to be playing in my head. "I'm sorry, you look familiar, you remind me of someone I used to know."

He was being funny and, I realised, flirting as well. He smiled at me and my heart raced some more, only not from running, but from the fact I was once again talking to him. I smiled back, and took the veil, wrapping it around my head and breast with timidity before a stranger.

I decided to play his game. "I see you remember me."

"Why wouldn't I?" John asked. "You gave quite a performance and left me with something to remember you by."

*

Anjali put the diary down on the bed. She knew the words by heart she had read them so many times. She closed her eyes and imagined herself back in time and space when John Locke had walked towards her.

"What brings you here?" he said.

"It's the *Mela*. Who doesn't like a funfair? I've had an amazing day."

"Oh, really? Nothing else?"

"I wasn't expecting anything else," Anjali said. "What about you? What brings you here?"

"You have to ask? I think you know I love all things Indian." Locke stepped forward. *"All things Indian"*.

The meaning was obvious. Anjali blushed. Lexi tapped Anjali's arm and melted away into the crowd. Neither saw her go; they only saw each other.

"You want to go for a ride?" she asked, breaking the silence. He raised an eyebrow. "On the Ferris wheel," she said more firmly, ignoring the twinkle in his eye.

They had queued but not for long and took their seats. The wheel started with a jolt, Anjali gripping Locke's arm for security. She didn't know why she had chosen the big wheel; she wasn't that fond of heights. But as they reached the top they could see out over the houses of Manchester away towards the dark moors and towards Rochdale where Hannah and David had got married. Each took it as a sign.

They walked around the fair, arms linked or side by side, saying little. They didn't have to. The moment was sufficient. The way the wind blew her sari gave the occasion a magical twist and blew at her hair, all the while trying to catch his gaze.

The sky began to darken and Anjali looked at her watch.

"It's getting late," she said. "I need to head home."

But he wasn't ready. He turned to look deep into her dark brown eyes. She felt weak as she looked back at him. "Have one lunch with me. One date," he said.

"What do you think this is?" It was clumsy, she knew, but she also realised it was how she felt. Some go on dates to get to know the other. But for her, one look was enough to know this was for life.

"It's been a decent day, but not a date."

Anjali smiled and looked away. "It's been a date for me," she said, then turned and walked away.

Locke stared at the ground. Not sure what to say. She had wrong-footed him. "You can ask me anything you like, then you can decide, whether I am worthy of you or not."

Anjali stopped then slowly turned and walked back towards Locke. She started to sing.

"Agar zindagi ho tere sang ho.

"Agar zindagi ho tere sang ho.

"Agar maut ho toh woh ho tujhse pehle.

"Agar maut ho toh woh ho tujhse pehle."

"Balmaa, balmaa," she whispered. Her head rested on Locke's chest as she put her arms around his waist, pulling him closer. She felt his embrace tighten.

"That's beautiful," he said. "What does it mean?"

She reached up and kissed him on the cheek. Then placed something in his hand and walked away. Locke watched her go, maintaining his gaze long after she had disappeared from view. He looked at what she had placed in his hand; a business card. He was surprised, until he realised it had her phone number on it.

*

Anjali quietly sung the song to herself once more, only this time in English. She had not told Locke what it meant. She wondered if he had ever translated it once he started getting his incredible powers of memory and intelligence.

"If there is a life, I wish it to be with you.

"If there was death between us, let me be the first to die.

"My love... my love."

Sachin Locke stood outside the bedroom door and listened without a sound to his mother's heartfelt singing. She had switched back to singing in Hindi and he sensed the tone of the music. Then he heard her gentle sobs.

He walked across the corridor and down the stairs into the hallway. He knelt before the shrine to Radha and Krishna and prayed for his mother to bring her happiness back.

At the top of the stairs Anjali looked down on her only son and felt more alone than ever before.

thirty-six
maybe he's addicted?

"It's the Russians. I bet you a pound to a penny, it's the Russians." Hannah placed the cup of tea on the table beside Anjali and sat down in her favourite chair. On the television a news report was still speculating on what caused the collapse in the UK's internet that led to all the deaths and injuries.

"There'll be a poisoning next, just you watch. Whenever the government keeps quiet about something, it means it's going on at the diplomatic level. They'll be pointing the finger of blame at Moscow anytime soon."

And it was true; the rumour mill was in full swing and anybody who was anybody had appeared on television stating Russia was behind the cyber-attack. Government ministers had recently started talking about the involvement of a state power and even the prime minister had made noises to that effect.

"It can't be anyone else," Hannah continued. "The North Koreans haven't got the technical nous, and I don't think the Chinese are that belligerent. It's got to be—"

She stopped. Anjali held her hand to her mouth and tried hard not to break down. Hannah saw it and rushed across to the sofa where her friend sat. The women embraced, and one of them convulsed into sobs. Hannah stroked Anjali's hair.

"Let it all out," she said.

*

Anjali paced up and down the large living room, a bay window looking out onto the scene of suburbia beyond. Hannah watched on desperate to help, but she could see her friend was toying with something huge and she didn't want to push her. Anjali kept wrestling with the key problem she had; should she give Locke up? Or was it enough to distance herself from him? Would they understand or would they judge their relationship? Regardless of the options, she was either separating from her husband or betraying him. Should she blame the medical condition or John for what he had done? Did he have a choice? Was she being naïve because John was her husband? Silence lingered in the room while the thoughts tumbled. She couldn't even begin to think of the horror when she had to face society, her parents or explain his father's deeds to Sachin.

She thought of the legal consequences, for each and every one of them. Could John survive this? Could his condition and subsequent treatment justify the lives lost due to him? Surely a good lawyer could prove this. But then what would happen next? Would he ever be allowed out again or would he grow old in prison? Even if the Salford murders could be kept out of it, people had died because he had shut down the country's internet. May my God forgive him when the scriptures say that if you have killed someone it's as if you killed all humanity. He wouldn't get a short sentence.

And by the time he came out surely they would have changed the law? They would have to have done something because, as Anjali knew, the court of public opinion would not let him be seen to get away with anything. And that meant her son was at risk as well, in fact her whole family, and John's family in America. The press would be all around them. On one side, John Locke. On the other, the rest of the world.

In between, deeper than the seven oceans, the fiery heart. If she didn't swim, she would be burned. She was stuck, both with him and because of him. She was a devoted wife; that was all she had ever wanted to be. That and be a mother for her son to be proud of. What she did next would certainly determine what happened; it would either speed things up or let them run their course.

Hannah took another sip of the freshly brewed coffee. She had sat down and the television was switched off. She waited some more.

The consciousness of God. The phrase tumbled through Anjali's mind like clouds of superheated steam escaping an erupting volcano; dangerous, malevolent. *The consciousness of God*. So rarely understood, she thought. Even though that knowledge had been given not everyone uses it well. Humans were good at exploitation, at corruption, and profiting from it when it was given for the benefit of society and humanity. She didn't need society with her on this one; she just needed one person to believe and that was John. Who was missing. Could she ever make him understand? Or get him to repent and confess? *Now there's a well-known story about Ranjha and Heer, where she's always calling for his name*. The stress had got to her. She looked down at Hannah, and saw the concern etched all over her friend's face.

"It's John," Anjali said at last. "I don't know how to get through this. I don't know what to do."

"Start from the beginning, Anj. Tell me everything that happened."

So Anjali did. She told Hannah everything apart from the Salford gang Locke had had killed, and the fact that it was Locke and not the Russians, or anyone else, that had caused the blackout on the UK internet system that had led to the incidents that had resulted in further deaths. She mentioned the street kids initiative, but didn't connect Locke with the missing children. She couldn't go there. The room remained silent for minutes as Hannah tried to process the information.

"Oh my God!" was all she could utter, finally.

Anjali looked hard at Hannah. They were best friends and they had kept closely in touch despite Locke's stratospheric rise to superstardom and global fame and wealth. Anjali saw no reason why they couldn't stay friends even though they moved in very different circles now. In fact she saw her friend as the brake on her runaway lifestyle, and it was a brake she desperately wanted. Whether Hannah ever knew how Anjali viewed her friendship, she couldn't guess, but she was about to discover it. The truth is not something that every person can swallow. It was why people try to conceal it, but it was only when the two of them were together that Anjali ever felt anything of her old self. Without exception prosecco was poured and also without exception, they went halves on the food bill, even though wherever they ate out, Anjali had the means to buy the entire restaurant, let alone settle their bill.

"It wasn't meant to be like this, Hannah. He wasn't meant to be like this. The man I met and fell in love with is different to the John you see today."

"Where is he now?" Hannah asked. Anjali shook her head.

"I don't know that either. I just packed up and left India. This is our home, not Mumbai and the Bollywood lot. Sachin is happier as well. Over there he spent more time with an old man who played cricket with him than he did his own father. Now he's got his friends back.

"So no, I don't know where John is or what he's doing. He's not tried to contact me and I haven't tried to find him. It's just such a mess and I hate it."

"Are you telling me your marriage is over?"

"I don't know. It can't be, not in my culture. This is unique." Anjali looked hard at Hannah. "Not in my heart. Do you understand that? Because I can't understand it fully. He's done terrible things and he will pay for them, but in my culture we are two halves of the same whole and neither can live without the other. Have I failed him as a wife? A woman's role is to lead him in the right direction. How could I not see that? I was his conscience. His *ardhangini*. Is it my fault—"

"Don't ever blame yourself, Anj, not ever!" Hannah stared hard at her friend and decided against going back to give Anjali another hug. "From what you have told me you have done everything expected of a wife in any culture. You have loved him and you have made a life together. You care for your son as much as any mother and you care for your husband as much as any woman I know. I always thought that because your marriage was difficult for both sets of parents, so you and John had to work that bit harder. Now I think it's down to the fact that you love him just as much as he ever loved you. I think you are the strongest couple I have ever known. But don't let him off the hook by blaming yourself. Too many women do that and it's not their fault."

"Then why didn't I see all this?" Anjali hadn't meant to shout. Hannah jolted, shocked by the anger. "I'm sorry, Hannah, forgive me. This is what I mean. I don't know what to do. If we were so perfect together, why are we now in this mess?"

"No marriage is perfect," Hannah said. "You can't ever know what's in someone's thoughts. Being perfect isn't what marriage is about. Marriage means testing your strength. It is to know if you can keep the promise you made before God."

Anjali stood up again, wringing her hands and looking frantically about as if she was missing something that was in full view in the room.

"Do you know what this sounds like?" Hannah offered. "It sounds like a band splitting up because the lead singer got a better offer to go solo. I don't mean like the Beatles and John Lennon finding his Yoko, I mean George Michael being better than the other one. John's just got the bug for fame and wealth and it's taken him over. Maybe he's got bored because of that mind of his?"

"Maybe he's a psychopath?" Anjali shot back. It wasn't the first time the idea had entered her head, and it was the one that caused her the most distress. If Locke was a psychopath, what more was he capable of?

"He's not that, Anj—"

"What if he is? What if his head injury made him this way? He explained something about risk once, about how his injury meant he was more likely to take risks. But this? There's taking risks and there's turning criminal. Why do people always come up with new ways of hurting each other? Why can't they see what they have got is to help other people? Why didn't I see it? That house was a temple for me. And after the Lord, I worship that man. That's why people tell you never to worship a man as a god. They're always going to disappoint you." Anjali stared down at Hannah still sat in her seat. Hannah shuffled uncomfortably and took a sip of her coffee to buy a little time.

"Anj, I think you should sit down and have some of your tea. I didn't put sugar in it – I can see you're hyper enough as it is." Anjali's stare softened.

"That's better. We're not going to sort this in the next ten minutes, but we might if we take our time." Anjali sat back down, the constant whirring in her mind seemed to slow a little as the tea touched her lips and the hot liquid gave her throat a pleasant scold. At that moment it felt like she'd taken some sort of drug turning her instantly calmer. Not that she had ever touched drugs.

"I'll never be able to sleep again," Anjali said.

"It sounds like it's all to do with the head injury," Hannah suggested. "I get that he wouldn't be who he was without ever have gone through his ordeal, but if one side effect is that he is suddenly super intelligent and another is that he is more of a risk taker, then perhaps it makes sense that he was always going to try to outwit other people using his brain and his risk-taking took him to ever higher levels of danger. It starts with the head injury, but maybe now he's hooked on danger? Maybe he's addicted?"

"But there's still a choice to do what is right. We are people, we have free will. It could be that he just wants to keep proving himself, but why go so far as to put all of it at risk if what you are doing is illegal?"

"Is that not the point?" said Hannah. "Isn't this all about going further and further? Do you think he thinks he's above the law?"

"No. Maybe. I don't know." Anjali stared at the carpet in Hannah's front room. "Now he's become alien to me and then I became a stranger to him. Maybe it is just like a drug, like it gives him a shot of testosterone when he pulls something off? All that money he took from gambling dens and 'greedy banks', as he calls them, maybe that was all about redressing the balance?"

"You think he sees himself as Robin Hood?" Hannah said, incredulous.

"No! He could never be Robin Hood; he does nothing for the poor!" Anjali replied, emphatic. "Well maybe that's where it started. Remember, he still didn't remember who I was when he got involved in that gambling den in Salford—"

Hannah gasped. "Is it the same lot that got murdered the other week? You know when four of them got shot dead in their house." Anjali couldn't reply. "Oh my God!" Hannah gasped again as the knowledge that Locke was behind the murders burst through her brain like a locomotive. "Oh my God! Oh my God! Oh my God!"

"Hannah—"

"Jesus Christ, Anjali! You said you had told me everything. Oh my fucking God!" Hannah was on her feet. "That's a different fucking level! He's killed four of them!"

"He didn't kill them, it was the—"

"It doesn't fucking matter, Anjali! That's murder! Plain and simple. He has had people killed and it's no different than he'd pulled the trigger himself." Hannah looked at her best friend, shaking her head from side to side, her mouth open, her eyes wild. "You've got to get out. You have got to get out right now and go to the police."

"I can't! Don't you think I've considered that and nothing else? He's my husband."

"No," Hannah said slowly, trying not to let her emotions spill out. "He's a murderer and he will take you down with him." She turned away. "Jesus! I can't believe we're having this fucking conversation. You've left him. Now you've got to make it permanent and you've got to make it right."

"But he's my husband. Sachin will lose his father. I'll be mocked by society. People always blame the wife. I can't face the disgrace." Anjali screamed at Hannah's turned back. "He makes me complete. How can I send my husband to the authorities?"

"He makes you complicit," Hannah responded quietly, still looking anywhere but at Anjali.

"I have failed him. I need to atone for my sins."

Hannah's shoulders sagged. She turned slowly and sat down next to Anjali, looking closely at her eyes, at the fear and the distress within.

"Don't give me any of that moral crap, Anjali," Hannah said slowly and deliberately, her hand resting on her friend's knee. "You did none of this. You were a perfect wife for him. You cannot be a perfect wife for a murderer.

"You have got to get out completely. You've got money, you can go and hide, taking Sachin with you. Move out before he turns up here like he's bound to. Block his numbers and his emails. No amount of your *ardhangini* justifies you staying with him after what he has done. And when you leave him, you will still be whole. You were whole before, you will be again. Time will heal your pain."

"That's just it," Anjali said. "I wasn't whole until I was united with John. I can't go back. It's forbidden. The henna I have on my hand is eternal. The name stands forever. Once you put that on, it can never get out."

"No, it is not forbidden." Hannah spat the words out. She wasn't religious; Anjali's faith was her own, but this was something else entirely. "If you don't go to the police by the end of the week, I will."

"No! No! Please don't!"

"I am your friend Anjali, but I have limits. If you don't tell the police by Friday, I will and our friendship will be over. I understand your beliefs, but where does it say that you must remain with someone outside the law, that you as a modern British woman has to stay with a murderous husband? What if he turns on you? Or Sachin? Whatever happens, he will take you down with him. I guarantee it. And you have made me complicit by telling me this."

*

Anjali stumbled slightly as she made her way down the steps of Hannah's town house in south Manchester. The gravel crunched underfoot as she walked towards her car. She had stayed as strong as she could, but now that Hannah couldn't see her face, her expression broke. She was a friend who did not understand *ardhangini* and the importance of a woman's obligation. Instead, she had become a friend who had made a threat to her. Who could she talk to when she had a criminal for a husband? Who can comprehend these circumstances, is it God or justice?

Tears fell like rain as her mouth opened in an horrific rictus grin. She prayed she would make it to the Audi before breaking down completely. She got in and gunned the engine, driving as carefully as she could out onto the residential road before she turned the volume on the radio up loud and howled. A tsunami of animalistic feelings of loss and self-loathing smashed over her, turning her cold, then red hot, and she pulled over barely a hundred yards from Hannah's house. The car stuck out an angle, but she didn't care. She howled again; the primeval cry of a dying animal, or of a mother losing her child. Or a wife failing her husband. And she *had* failed him. She had told Hannah about the Salford murders. Another now knew and there was no coming back from that. A million thoughts rushed through her brain as the music blared and the engine ticked over. She didn't notice the beeping behind her; that she had blocked the road. Then the knocking at the window. The angry motorist stepped back as soon as he saw Anjali's face; the red raw eyes, the tears, the cruel, dreadful bared teeth.

She was wedged between the truth and the lies and the protection of her husband. Was this another challenge she faced in her marriage? Life continually defies its strength.

At the end of her gravel driveway, Hannah stood with arms folded. She looked down the tree-lined avenue she called home and at the three cars now blocked by Anjali's Audi. She thought she could still hear the loud music her best friend must have switched on to hide her true feelings. She suppressed her own feeling to run to her friend and help her once more. She stayed where she was and felt totally empty. Their friendship was probably over, she realised. Certainly it would never be the same again. Another car's horn blared. Hannah looked at the phone in her hand and pressed a few buttons. She held the mobile to her ear as she walked back up her driveway knowing she was leaving Anjali utterly alone in the world.

thirty-seven
never watched her leave

She looked out across the desolate scene in front of her. Wind whistled through her hair as clouds scudded across a marauding sky. The hills looked foreboding; they looked threatening. She pulled her coat tighter round her shoulders and shuddered.

A few feet away Sachin knelt down amongst the grass tussocks, playing with something. Anjali couldn't quite see what it was, but it was occupying her son while her mind was on everything and nothing at the same time.

There had been no contact with Locke, no further news from India about the street kids thing, but then again that was no surprise as Indian justice could be very slow, or corrupt, or both. As soon as a news programme began discussing the internet outage, she changed the channel. She didn't know why; she didn't really watch the news and right now she even found those terrible reality TV shows preferable, not that she watched any for long.

She turned her face away from the teeth of the wind and looked once again across the moors. Grey skies and grey hills. Grey gullies and grey tarns. The ancient drystone walls were grey. Even Sachin's blue jeans and tee-shirt looked grey in this light. The only colour she saw was the white of her own coat and the black of her hair as the wind tossed it around, every gust blowing it in a different direction.

She steeled herself, took a deep breath and stood up. Her mind thought back to the last time she had seen this view; Hannah and David's wedding when she finally got to know John Locke.

Behind her stood the beautiful hall where the marriage had taken place. The mansion did not look beautiful today, but ominous, and Anjali looked at it just briefly as she turned and made her way back over the break in the drystone wall.

She called out to Sachin, who obediently left what he had been doing and followed his mother back to the car. They got in, Anjali unaware that her son had just balanced nine stones on top of each other, leaving an amazing little tower for someone else to discover. That was if the wind didn't blow it down first. Sachin was confident it would remain upright for a while yet.

*

Anjali stopped the car at the top of the familiar street and wondered what the next couple of hours would bring. Despite Locke's wealth, her father and mother had chosen to stay in the house they had bought when they first came to the UK nearly thirty years earlier. They no longer had any need to work, but they had wanted to remain in the close-knit community that had welcomed them all those years ago and which they now saw as their extended family.

"Are Nanny and Grandad going to be there?" Sachin asked. He knew something of what was going on, and never pushed his mother about where his father was, but sometimes his mother needed a nudge; he was increasingly noticing those times and would say something to deflect her attention and bring her out of whatever trance she was in at that moment. He had tried to act as normally as possible as he felt it was the only way he could help. He understood the situation to a certain degree, but he realised he was too emotionally immature to be able to discuss marriage with his mother. It still hadn't been that long since he had last seen his father and he expected he would see him again soon.

"I hope so, darling," Anjali replied, putting her foot down slightly and causing the automatic start-stop to ignite the engine. The Audi rolled slowly down the road; a curtain or two twitched, she noticed. Even when it was barely moving the car's engine was powerful and that made it noisy. Not many powerful cars made their way down this little street.

Halfway down Anjali pulled over to the right and they both got out. A final deep breath and then the knock. Amita Sharma opened her front door a few seconds later. She knew it was Anjali from the sound of the car, but she always waited for the knock.

"Anjali," she said, smiling happily. Then she looked at the boy. "Sachin!" the older woman squealed and rushed past her daughter to give her grandson a huge cuddle. Sachin was almost as tall as his grandmother, even though he was only twelve. Anjali smiled at her mother and son and turned to enter the house. Vijay Sharma stood in the doorway, a very happy smile on his face. He opened his arms and Anjali readily stepped forward to feel the embrace. She was surprised; she had expected to burst into tears the moment either of her parents showed any sign of affection towards her.

Maybe she was becoming immune to the mental anguish that clouded her every waking thought? Or perhaps there were no more tears to shed?

"We didn't know you were in England," Vijay said as he walked ahead of Anjali towards the kitchen at the back of the house.

"We've been back a few days, that's all," Anjali replied. Already she knew her father had worked out that something was up.

"Oh? And what about John? Did he not want to visit us?"

Anjali followed her father into the kitchen. Tea had been freshly brewed, but then the kettle never really stopped in this house. Tea was a close second behind religion for the Sharmas. Sachin bounded into the room and hugged his grandfather, Vijay Sharma beaming down at the boy.

"John is still in India," Anjali stated coolly. She would wait until Sachin was elsewhere before telling her parents everything. It wasn't long; Amita Sharma gave Sachin a can of fizzy pop, which was all he needed to head back through to the living room staring at the screen on his iPhone.

Vijay Sharma sat down at his kitchen table with a heavy sigh. Anjali was quieter taking her seat whilst Amita Sharma busied herself. "*Malpua?*" she said.

"Yes, thank you," Anjali replied, strangely comforted by the thought of the pancakes she would dip in her mother's amazing sugar syrup. It had been a favourite since childhood and just the thought of the sweet snack almost made a mockery of her thinking that she could no longer cry.

"So tell us, what is going on, Anjali?" Vijay Sharma said. "I can see there is something wrong." Amita Sharma placed a plate of pancakes on the table and brought her husband and daughter a cup of tea each. She returned to her stove to gently warm through the syrup. Anjali looked at the pancakes and then at her father. She found it remarkably easy to tell her parents about her separation from John. The rest, the thefts, the murders, the internet outage, she would hold that in reserve. Her parents didn't need to know about that. At least, not yet.

When she had finished, a silence filled the room. Amita Sharma was nervous and looked from her husband to her daughter and back again. She desperately wanted to say something, but Vijay would get the first word. Anjali waited for the inevitable backlash but was almost past caring. She was simply doing her daughterly duty; she needed nothing from her parents but their blessing that she had done all she could. She didn't think she would get it.

"I knew it was a mistake," Vijay said at last. "It is John; it always was John. He doesn't value the knowledge of religion, Anjali. I told you this. I told you again and again at the beginning, but you would not listen to me. I warned you because I knew he was not right for you."

"Please stay calm, Vijay," Amita Sharma said anxiously. But to no avail.

"What does your generation think of themselves?" he shouted. "Eh? Your marriage is a joke! Your generation feels like it can end a marriage whenever it wants? Get married whenever it sees fit? Is that it? Marriage is for life, not for ending when things get difficult.

"I don't know what went on between you two, but you have to go back again. A good family's daughter doesn't give out on her marriage. A good daughter fights for her marriage, no matter how hard the situation turns out to be. This is not how we raised you."

Vijay breathed heavily, trying to maintain what little composure he had left. His wife took her chance.

"What happened between the two of you?" she asked.

"He is not the person I married," Anjali said. "He is a different person now. One that I no longer understand."

"What does that even mean?" Vijay roared. "Look, Anjali, you wanted to marry this individual and we allowed it. You know he was not my first option because he does not understand our culture or customs. Only you do and we raised you in that manner.

"Look at me and your mother; still together after thirty-five years. Your mother knows I am more difficult, so we compromise. When one is furious the other doesn't talk. We love and respect one another."

"Did he beat you?" Amita said, reaching across to touch Anjali's arm.

"No."

"Then no buts, Anjali. You wanted the guy of your choice and you got one. So what is the problem here? Why do you want to leave John? A house isn't made of money; it's created by making sacrifices. You are *ardhangini,* which signifies you are his soul mate. Men will always lose their direction. That is the nature of human life. This is why God gave women to men so women can direct them on the right path.

"Women are so much stronger than men. Because they possess the strength of the patient. If a woman wants they can make a home and turn it into heaven or she can break that home. You have to decide which you want. This is your test and your struggle. Most of us know that life is a test. Don't ruin it, Anjali. Embrace it with joy. Help John. He needs you too. Love, religion and marriage have a powerful significance. Give your life for marriage." Anjali stared at the top of the table. "My blessing is with you, my daughter. Go back to him. My spirit says he needs you. I am your father. I wouldn't teach you anything wrong. Nor do I want to watch you suffer. But this is a test you must accomplish."

Anjali had listened patiently. She had known this would be the way her father would react. Her greatest worry so far as her father was concerned was that he would lose face in the community. It had been hard won to get acceptance amongst his peers when Anjali's engagement to John had been announced, but most people locally supported the Sharmas. For the marriage to break down was to invite shame from some quarters. There were still those that were against the mixed marriage and this would be their justification. From the sofa in the living room, Sachin listened in.

"I don't think I can, father. John has done some terrible things, some illegal things. I struggle daily with what I should do. I believe in *ardhangini,* you know I do, but this…"

"He was never good enough for you, Anjali. You should have married someone in our culture. Do other cultures understand the importance of the spousal relationship as we do? I always doubted your relationship, but we agreed to it because we could see how he made you happy. You must fight for your marriage to make you happy again. Are you happy now?"

"Vijay—" Amita Sharma interrupted. Her husband raised his hand to silence her.

"Well? Are you happy now?" Vijay Sharma demanded. Anjali looked at the table and gently shook her head. "Does he even understand your pain?" Again, she shook her head. Vijay Sharma leant forward and put his elbows on the table, then held his head in his hands, rubbing his eyes and pinching the bridge of his nose. Each of them in that room knew that he was thinking about family honour. Each in that room had a different opinion of its importance.

"Money can't make us happy, Anjali. I think you have forgotten that. It can only change our circumstances. You can buy anything you want: luxury, fast cars, houses, but history is our witness, money can't make happiness. It usually does the opposite."

"Father—"

"Haven't we taught you anything?" Vijay shouted, banging his fist on the table. "Have we not taught you our values? You know that marriage is sacrosanct to us. It is not the same for Western people. That is why John was never right for you, Anjali. Never."

"It is done, Father." Anjali was weary. She didn't really care what came back at her now, she just wanted it to be out there so that she could move on. "I believe in our culture and I believe in *ardhangini* as you know, but there is nothing in our teachings that say we cannot take people from different cultures, different religions, as our *ardhangini*. You know my story with John. You know how our paths crossed three times without my ever knowing his name. You know he was right."

Vijay Sharma made to say something but this time it was Anjali who raised a hand. Her father shocked into silence.

"John is not the problem, Father. His condition, *his brain* is the issue. This super intelligence of his has kept growing. He gets more intelligent every day. He is not a normal human being. Until recently I marvelled at how he kept that side of him quiet, so that it did not affect our family life.

"That's changed now. He has got to the point where he is no longer excited by making money or just doing incredible things. He has got to the point he needs to add some risk to what he is doing. He has now made mistakes and they are bad ones.

"But again, it is not John; it is his brain. He is still my *ardhangini*. I still believe we will be reunited. But for now there are very difficult times ahead. I felt I had to warn you as I think this will soon be big news. You need to be prepared."

"Prepared for what?" Vijay Sharma stated. "What can be worse than the end of your marriage?"

Anjali managed a determined smile. She realised she couldn't spend two minutes in her own parents' house, that she couldn't have peace for two minutes before she was judged. She thought the parents' house was a place to go even when the world rejected you. Parents were meant to hear their child's smallest steps, but in this she knew she was wrong.

Her father's brow was heavily creased as he tried to work out what his daughter was telling him. Amita Sharma wanted to hold her daughter, but felt she couldn't.

"Well?" Vijay Sharma demanded a response. He raised his hands in a show of frustration. "You cannot even tell me? I told you he was wrong for you and now that you discover he is, you cannot tell me why. I wish you had never met him, the shame it has brought down on our family."

"If Mum had never met Dad, then there would never have been a me." Sachin stood in the doorway, his arms by his sides. He looked at the shocked faces of his mother and his grandparents. His grandmother didn't know whether to stand and go to him or stay where she was. Anjali smiled at her son. He had made her proud in saying those words and standing up to his grandfather.

"Go and play Sachin. This is an adult conversation," the grandfather said.

Anjali realised there and then that no amount of shame could bear scrutiny to the joy Sachin had brought into all their lives. She quietly rose up and took a stride towards her son, holding out her hand for him to take. Before walking out towards the front door, she stopped and looked back at her parents.

"That is where your shame should die, Father," she said. Vijay Sharma could not look his daughter in the eye. Amita Sharma had tears streaming down her face. She rose quickly as Anjali and Sachin walked away, catching up with them at the front door.

"I don't agree with your father," she whispered, then hugged daughter and grandson as if she was never to see them again. Anjali smiled down at her mother, then kissed her gently on the cheek, coming away with a taste of saltwater on her lips. She opened the front door and stepped onto the pavement. From the kitchen came the sound of her father slamming his fists down onto the kitchen table again. It was just the once, but the lighter tinkling of disturbed crockery seemed to last longer.

Sachin stepped forward and embraced his grandmother. "I love you, Nanny," he said, realising the seriousness of the situation. Amita Sharma cried fresh tears.

I love you too," Anjali added, before taking a last look at her mother and pressing the button on the key fob to unlock the Audi's doors.

If she had looked in her rear-view mirror as she drove slowly down the tiny street, Anjali would have seen her mother remain standing outside of the humble house until the corner had been turned.

But she didn't look back. And Vijay Sharma never watched her leave.

thirty-eight

the nearest thing to an angel

She heard the doorbell the first time it rang, but it didn't quite register. The second ring brought her back into the world of the living. The television was on but she had muted it. Sachin was in his bedroom, playing a computer game. He found it easy, but addictive, as he beat the computer every time. He wanted to play against his friends; he would beat them every time as well. When he played the computer at chess, he won every time. He found it so easy to calculate the moves. Slowly Anjali got up from the kitchen table and pulled her cardigan a bit tighter around her shoulders as she made her way down the hallway towards the front door. She put her eye to the peephole and failed to recognise the man standing there.

"Who is it?"

"Gasman," came the reply. Anjali didn't see it, but the gasman had held up his identification.

"I didn't ask for you. Why are you here?"

"Reports of escaped gas in the street, madam. I need to check the valve to your supply."

I can't smell gas, Anjali thought as she looked through the peephole again. There was something vaguely familiar about the man she was looking at, but she wasn't sure what. The eyes? The voice? The door clicked open and the gasman stood before her smiling.

"The gas supply is just here," she said, pointing to a small wooden box fitted against the wall by the front door. "Give me a shout when you're done," she added as she turned and made her way back towards the kitchen.

"Anjali," the gasman said. She stopped in her tracks and looked back at the man in her hallway. Her eyes widened. *It can't be,* she thought, but he smiled at her, then began to remove his fake beard. *People wear masks when they lie.* The thought stuck in her mind.

"John…" it came out as a whisper. Anjali's head swirled as she looked at the gasman transform into her husband. "What's with the face?"

she asked, but didn't wait for an answer. She ran into the kitchen and slammed the door behind her.

Locke remained impassive in the hallway and began to pull carefully at his nose – he would need it again when he left. He wasn't surprised by Anjali's reaction, but it hurt him to think her first response was to run away from him. He placed beard and nose in the gasman's bag he was carrying and walked towards the kitchen, opening the door gently to find his wife at the table with her back to him.

He crossed the room and sat down opposite. She looked away, but not before he saw her tear-stained cheeks. He reached into his trouser pocket and pulled out a handkerchief. She waved it away and wiped her face on her cardigan instead. The gesture surprised him and left him a little unsure.

"It's good to see you," he said. "I've missed you."

"I'm surviving, no thanks to you. Your treachery has taught me to stand up for myself."

It was a sting Locke had to take. Anjali stared in a different direction; she loved him and she missed him, but her pride and morals compelled her not to show any affection. There was no smile on her face. She kept a lid on the angry voices trying to get out. Tried to show no emotion. Locke began to accept the real hurt he knew he had caused but had always played down in his own mind when he had imagined this scene previously.

"There are police outside. I had to use a disguise. This is the fourth house I've been in so far. There's no gas leak, but it's a good cover story. I'll go into a couple more after here."

"John, the day I become your habit is the day I leave. Then you shall know the meaning of life." Anjali snorted. She didn't know how else to react. She was looking for answers and yet again her husband was lying. It was clear he found it easy. The more she thought about it, the more she realised he was enjoying it.

"How's Sachin?" Locke asked, trepidation in his voice.

"Like you care!"

"But I do," Locke insisted.

"If you cared you wouldn't put us in this position," Anjali yelled. "You wouldn't throw your life away, you wouldn't throw our marriage away." Locke looked down as his wife composed herself. They had both been surprised by the outburst. "He's fine. But I don't want him to see you."

Locke nodded. "Is he here?"

"Yes."

"Then I'll try to be quiet. And brief." Anjali waited for Locke to say something of note, willing herself not to look at her husband.

"I messed up," Locke sighed. "I royally fucked up and I have never been so sorry in my life. I have lost everything because I think I have lost you. And Sachin. But I had to come back one more time to see whether we could work things out. Whether you might consider living in a distant country. It might not mean a thing to you, Anjali, but I have risked my life to come and see you and Sachin. That is surely evidence that I want you, that I want my family more than anything on this planet."

"You don't deserve happiness." Anjali spat. "Life gives you everything on a platter. I, Sachin, the riches and the genius, and love. And what about the school? The street kids?"

"A mess. A total fucking mess. I'm trying to sort it."

"How? What are you going to do? And what about Amar Rajmi? Have you sorted him? Or is he still rotting in the jail that you put him in?" Anjali's eyes blazed. "The truth is John, you saw me as someone who's an interfering little wife. Someone with a small foolish belief. Someone who believes in the unseen. You don't know the meaning of marriage, you don't know the meaning of *ardhangini*. You thought all I did was wash, clean and serve your home. *Ardhangini* means I walk in your shadow, someone who keeps you from going astray." She screamed, smashed her fists down on the kitchen table. She wanted to smash him as she cried, but striking your husband was not a custom in her world, no matter how badly he fucked up.

"It's complicated," Locke offered, thinking of the kindly man that had been the general manager of the street kids initiative, and a complete innocent in the whole sordid business. "I am trying to get him out, but it's not that easy."

"I have walked with you, when most spouses in our society distance themselves from marriage, change or circumstance," Anjali continued, as if she hadn't even heard him. "The smallest changes, unemployment or disability, and a spouse is moving away from marriage. But I stood beside you in terms of sickness and health. Did that not register in your head? You're meant to be the world's most intelligent man. You can solve anything." At last Anjali looked at her husband, her eyes ignoring the darker eyebrows, the longer hair, the bit of skin-coloured latex stuck to his cheek that had been part of the prosthetic nose.

"You are capable of anything," she spat. "Every five years, I have had to start my life over, so you have a new life. But you couldn't tell me what was happening in your head, that it's changing you. I asked you repeatedly if you were okay, but you refused to tell me. That fact is John, you liked the thrill. But you're not solving this."

"I can't do mind control on Indian prison guards." Locke smiled weakly, realising too late it was not the time to make any kind of joke.

"Then try harder. You can kill anyone. Think of conspiracy or trickery, but you can't get an innocent man out of prison. There will be times when you want to cry, but you won't be able to." She sighed and pretended to find fault with a fingernail despite its perfect manicure.

"I loved you for your innocence," she said, "not for your intelligence. At the start you weren't bright, but that never bothered me. You wanted to be intelligent and you got what you wanted. You even got the title; the world's most intelligent man. Millions of people go to the temple, to the mosque, to the church, only to put their hands on the divine, dip into the holy water, walk barefoot, keep fasting, place offerings, but you have knowledge without even trying. And you couldn't even honour it."

"We're good together," he said quietly. "I realise we've not been very together lately, and it is all my fault. I know you can't forgive me for what I have done, but there is one thing you do know; you complete me and I complete you." Locke closed his eyes. "I am asking for a final chance because we're—"

"Don't you dare fucking say it!" Anjali leapt to her feet, eyes like fire. "Don't even try to suggest it. It means everything to me. Everything! And you have trampled all over it, like some kind of selfish, uncaring monster. Like someone who is unable to respect the divine, the decision or the signs. How could you understand what love actually means? God only shows signs to those who have no faith and you are an atheist, but I never had a problem with that. There's no need for Him to show signs to people like me because we trust the invisible. Love is a shadow in our soul. A desire to love means worshipping God. *Mohabbat* means finding your destination. It means someone who fights against the storm; that is love. It's someone who fights against society for you; that is love. Worshipping someone while you overlook God is love. Looking at the diamond and recognising its sparkle, not its size.

"I recognised that in you the moment I laid my eyes on you. Before you were someone. And you have no such qualities. Saying "I love you," is easy, but fulfilment is hard. So don't you ever dare bring belief into this, or you will never see me or your son ever again. In our culture, we have names for people like you. We refer to them as educated imbeciles. Do you have any idea why? Because you have knowledge, sense, meaning, acknowledgment, but you deny the sign or the miracle that was given to you anyway. Do you understand?" Her finger was out, pointing straight at Locke. She tried to control her breathing. He had started to say the one thing that she knew would send her over the edge. *Maybe it was deliberate?* She shook the thought away. *Maybe he was telling the truth?*

Anjali sat down again, holding her head in her hands, and wept. Locke watched on and felt his own eyes well up. It was the moment he truly knew what she meant to him and he ached to reach across and hold her. He knew it would be a mistake.

She raised her gaze, again wiped her tear-streaked face on the sleeve of her cardigan and considered the man before her. *He is genuine.* The thought burned through her consciousness. She thought back to those moments when he had been lacking; pretty much the whole of the last three years. And yet she remembered him playing cricket with Sachin and could almost feel the sand between her toes as they had walked along Juhu Beach. She imagined his bright eyes and saw the terror there at this moment. She couldn't remember the last time she had really seen him smile. *He's hurting,* she thought. *He really is hurting.*

"Anjali, I'm begging you. I am begging for your forgiveness."

He came forward and tried to kiss her soft body one kiss at a time. Anjali stepped back.

"You're not the person I used to love." She turned away. The air seemed to rush from her lungs and she couldn't stop her body from shaking.

"I saw *ardhangini's* evidence," Locke said. "There's no denying it."

She took deep breaths, one after the other, trying to bring her heart rate down. Her skin grew cold and the light in the room seemed to dim a little. She was aware of Locke standing up, heard him say something, but then clarity returned. She stared back at him, at his face etched with concern, and forced her breathing to return to normal. It had come to this once and final moment.

Locke sat back down. His forehead was creased, the eyebrows, darker and bushier than normal due to his ridiculous disguise, had formed one huge mass of hair. But Anjali didn't find it funny. She found it pathetic. At the most critical moment in her marriage, she found her husband looking like a fucking idiot.

"Now you see why a wife is always looking over her husband's shoulder. It's not to interfere; it's because she wants to protect him, and to guide him. In my culture, history is our witness, men have always drifted away from his sight, committing adultery or using their wealth unwisely. But history is our witness that a man battles for love. That he can go to war over it and build a monument like the Taj Mahal to remember his loved one."

Locke was about to say something, but Anjali shut him down. She said, "I want to save you. I want to save your life and with it my life and Sachin's. He will have no life with you constantly on the run, never in one place long enough to be able to visit you, always looking over *his* shoulder in case the police are following him to try to get to you. Hell, they're already doing it if they're outside now. Wanting something and giving us a life are two different things. The best thing you can do for us is to give yourself up to the authorities."

Locke's shoulders slumped.

"You need to hand yourself in. If you do, I will fight your case, I will support you and so will our son. We need to make a case that it is not your fault. It's your condition, a condition that is going to see you collapse and suffer amnesia again. I know it's just a few days away. I will be your support there. I will tell them everything about what happens and we can tell them everything about your mental health, your risk taking, everything.

"You can give up our riches, the money, the houses. We don't need them. We just need each other. I never asked you for such wealth; I just want a normal life. You have to choose between a normal life or the one you have made for you. If you choose the wrong path, you will be alone."

Fear gripped Locke, twisting his stomach and sending ice down his spine. Anjali didn't want to but she saw the tears in John's eyes. She knew she had to continue. She knew it was the only way she could save her husband and it was the only way she could save her marriage.

"They won't understand," Locke said. "You're being naïve. All they care about is putting the blame on someone, so they can tell the media they've resolved the matter."

Anjali reached across the table to touch Locke's hand. "But we all have to go one day and face God, John. Do you not hold any fear? Our bodies will perish and turn to dust, the wealth and property, the expensive clothes, pictures, antiques become your ghosts. They will no longer exist to you. Your spirit will leave your body and only the thing you will take with you is your deeds, because there is a judgement after our death. Whether you believe it or not, John, birth, death and the future is proof there is a God. Humans can't control these things. And God forbid your sins may affect my child and put him danger."

He looked up to meet her gaze. At that moment she was the nearest thing to an angel on Earth he had ever known. He thought back to the temple. He thought back to his India. He thought once more just how badly wrong things had gone.

"John," she whispered, and held his hands across the table. "I know I may lose you in some ways, but my mind is constantly thinking about what will happen to you next. And I am constantly thinking that this is not the reason I married you. Have faith in me. Don't judge on what the outcome will be. Having fear is normal."

"I'm sorry, Anjali. I want to believe you, but I can't. The world is a cruel place, they will crucify me just like they crucified Jesus. People can't take the truth." Locke gritted his teeth and swallowed, desperate not to the let out a sob in case it looked as though he was acting. Anjali got up from her chair and walked out into the hallway. He watched her go, his thoughts confused, and heard her run up the stairs. He looked at his watch; he needed to get out fairly soon to avoid police suspicion that the gasman had been in this house for a bit too long. He forced away the idea of putting his beard or nose back on. Footsteps on the stairs signalled Anjali's return as she strode into the kitchen once again, holding a book in her hand. She threw it down on the table.

"If you have an ounce of compassion or honesty or truth left in you, John, you will read this and you will act upon it."

Locke looked at the book in front of him and realised it was a diary. He looked back up at Anjali and saw that the ragged breathing had returned, that she no longer looked quite so in control. His mouth opened but nothing came out.

"Take it," she screamed, slamming a hand down on the table. "And get out!"

Locke picked up the journal without hesitation and made his way quickly to the front door. He replaced the fake beard, but didn't bother with the nose; he'd sort that in his gasman's van. He closed the front door behind him and heard the screaming as made his way to his vehicle. He acted as nonchalantly as he could, maintaining the appearance of a utility worker rather than a lost and lonely ex-husband, which was how he truly felt.

Inside the house, Sachin stood by the kitchen door and listened to his mother's howls and watched as she smashed cups and pushed over chairs. She was unaware of his presence as the hysteria slowly passed, leaving her hunched in a ball on the floor and sobbing into her cardigan.

Sachin turned silently away.

thirty-nine
knowing i would be breaking another's heart

Reminds me of you when it's raining.
I can see your face on the moon, on the stars.
In the midst of the crowd, he makes me think of you.
Alone makes me think of you.
In my most profound mind, he reminds me of you.
Surrounded by painful thoughts, he reminds me of you.
In songs and functions, it reminds me of you.
In the dream and in the thoughts that I have, it reminds me of you.
When the wind blows, it reminds me of you.
In the warm summer and in the shade, it makes me think of you.
Your desire is part of my life.
The love that you gave me, I cannot forget.
No matter how hard I try, I can't erase your existence.
In the deepest thought, in the midst of the crowd, it reminds me of you.
Every step I take, it feels like you are here.
It was never my dream to live without you.
If I get a sign, I will return to you.
If your thoughts bring me back to you.
What should I do? Where can my heart go?
If it means stealing my heart, what would I do?
I'm sorry, I have regrets, I have complained, I'm angry with you.
I've always got love for you.

Locke stared at the journal on the sofa beside him. He had opened it briefly and was met with the headline '*The night before the escape.*' He surmised it was Anjali's innermost thoughts all the way back to when she had sought to run away from her parents and join him for a new life in London. They had been idyllic; Love's young dream, a romance through the ages, the kind of behaviour found in teenagers everywhere.

They had been young, hopelessly in love, naïve and incredibly stupid. But with the benefit of age comes hindsight and with the benefit of the world's greatest mind came a realisation that so many things could and should have happened that did not, if only so that what he was about to read had actually continued on to its own conclusion; that they would set up home in an anonymous part of the metropolis of London, Anjali working as an accountant somewhere and him trying to eke out an existence as a photographer. It could have worked. If photography didn't take off, he would take up a job in an office and they would have a steady income. They would be comfortable enough for children.

It was all so utterly and hopelessly optimistic. Nothing of the real world: how would Anjali react away from her family? How would they cope with the pressures of working for a living without the assistance of parents? Could his ideological views survive the reality of modern day living?

They never even made it onto the train. Anjali's parents had found out and she had left him in the clutches of a police officer at Manchester's Piccadilly station. In front of him now her idealised words, the story of how it happened, or didn't happen. Of what transpired before she left him and what led, ultimately, to the attack he suffered by the canal and how he had almost died.

Locke didn't want to read it, but he knew he must. He looked at his surroundings; he was in the Lodge in the grounds of the new build mansion he had designed. The new mansion was almost complete. Despite his change of fortune, the builders had still come to work daily. He was grateful for their commitment, but then he always knew that if you treat your staff above and beyond, then they would be loyal in return. He had got a message to Rob Thomas, his foreman, that they were no longer needed. He made sure there was also a kitty that Rob could divide up amongst his men for a job well done.

Sitting in the Lodge felt like hiding in plain sight, but then again, he was fairly sure the police did not put two and two together regarding Locke's two homes on the same site. He had designed the gardens in such a way as to hide the Lodge from clear view and it was unlikely anyone would know the Lodge was there unless they were looking for it. He doubted the police were.

On a whim he had bought an expensive whisky from Duty Free as he had passed through Heathrow Airport. Ordinarily he would have flown through Manchester, but a simple precaution made him feel better. He took a sip of the deep amber liquid and his head swam a little as the fiery drink hit the back of his throat.

The night before the escape.

He looked at the words again and steeled himself to be taken back to a time when love was all that mattered to him. He knew only too well how much he missed those days now.

Dear Diary,

Love is the most precious feeling we all crave for. It makes us do things we otherwise wouldn't do in everyday life. It lets us have secret encounters, to have sexual relationships or, even, to make us run away. It makes life feel easy; if others can do it, how hard can it be?

The obsession it creates makes it feel easy. I know it can be selfish, that it seems as though we don't think of others, of our families or friends, that we leave them behind, but it doesn't mean that is what we are doing. Instead, we are following our one true path.

My actions have consequences. I know that. I have considered how my actions will affect my family, but I struggle to come up with what I would recognise to be the truth. I know I am only thinking about me and about John. My parents will survive; I would tell them how I was when we had settled in London. I would tell them I was ok and that they shouldn't worry.

Our relationship makes me happy, but I knew they would not be able to see that. I tried not to think about how they would be affected.

There are times when we have to think about how our actions will affect the others in our lives. We didn't grow up out of thin air; someone has to raise us, nurture us, for us to be able to walk on our two feet, learn the language, and give us the shelter and love we need. Because of that, we become the person who raised us, who gave us their identity.

But as a child we don't really have an identity. Over time we might develop one, but most of the time we aren't sure who we are in Life. That is why we feel lost in our adolescence, but to know Life means we can recognise it. It means it feels like we can handle the obstacles which Life will throw at us. Love is Life's powerful drug and under its influence it feels like we can dispense with whatever comes our way.

But not even our parents have a guidebook; they only do what they believe is best for their child, even if we think the consequences are wrong for us. We have to accept that decision.

I try not to think why my parents only had me, why I have no siblings. My friends and neighbours, they have lots of children, lots of siblings, bigger families. Why not mine? I have often felt left out, isolated at home. It frequently feels like they only wanted one child. In reality, maybe it's different? Maybe we are not entitled to an explanation and maybe that is how Life should feel? Maybe that's how Life is normal?

Whether my parents faced obstacles that stopped them from having any more children, I don't know. It is a question I have thought about, but I am never going to ask that question. Some things are private, even from children. I have wondered about this question a lot more lately. I wondered about it the moment I decided to run away. And I decided I didn't need to give a reason to my parents.

I was thinking about that question as I packed my bag, as I stashed the money that would help provide for me on my new journey with John. Nothing had been planned, not really. We knew it was going to be London but no more than that. We were going into the unknown, but we were going together. John was to be my rock and I was to be his. I was about to risk it all for my man. Love was in the air, in my thoughts and in my heart. I was not thinking of any other person that I might hurt in the process. Was that wrong of me?

This was new territory. It was new territory as my mother, doing her usual household chores, caught me packing my bag. I didn't know she was watching at the time, but she could see I was in a rush and that I was being secretive. She didn't walk in and nor did she talk about it. I suppose she wanted to give me every chance not to do the thing I was about to do. In this culture packing your bag could mean only one thing; running away. I think she hoped I would not be able to go through with it.

The day was going slowly. We were meant to meet at Piccadilly at half one and the clock was crawling past ten. When you have planned your escape, even the hours cheat on you. I had spent most of the time in my room, but then I sat at the kitchen table. I kept looking at the clock. That was a mistake. My mother had been watching me and nothing escaped her.

"Is everything ok?" my mother asked. "Have you made plans to go somewhere else?"

I was shocked. How did she know? "No," I said. "I have no plans."

"Then why do you keep looking at the time?"

"It's just one of those days. Time isn't passing by quickly today."

"Why today, Anjali? Why now? It's just like any other day."

"No special reason, Mother," I said. I smiled at her and continued eating. Knowing I was having my last meal with her, I tried to stay calm, eat quickly, and then go back to my room.

I was on my computer, pretending to finish off a work assignment. I had my headphones in, using the music to kill time. My mother popped her head around my door several times, checking on me. I knew this because I could see her reflection in my computer screen.

Things were coming to a head. The stories I had heard, usually children ran away at night when their parents were asleep. I thought I would do the same, but then John and I agreed on a daytime train journey. I was beginning to think that was a big mistake; how was I going to get out of the house, carrying my bag, without my parents noticing? I was getting anxious.

The clock was ticking towards half past eleven. I knew I had to make my move shortly. I was to meet John at Piccadilly in two hours' time. It would take me the best part of one of those hours to get to central Manchester, so I still had time, but I could not see how I could get out without my parents noticing.

Then something remarkable happened; I heard the front door open and close. They must have gone out. I couldn't believe my luck. I decided to give it five minutes then go out after them. I had written my leaving note and I placed it neatly up against my computer screen. The house was silent. It was time.

I hoisted my bag over my shoulder and struggled down the stairs towards the front door. I was careful not to knock any pictures off the wall, or ornaments off tables. I remember taking a deep breath as I reached for the latch on the front door; I didn't think I would touch it ever again. This was me leaving home. In secret.

Then my father's voice. I nearly screamed when I realised I wasn't alone. I tried to catch my breath, to compose myself before turning around. There was no time for anything else; I had to get to Piccadilly and to John. I turned slowly, planning to laugh off any idea that I was running away with the lie I was going away with Hannah for a few days. I was going to say we were going to go walking in the Lake District.

Then I saw the gun. I was surprised then scared, stunned and shocked. My father was pointing a gun at me and my mother was by his side! My first thought, absurdly, was who had left the house if both of them were here? I don't know why the gun wasn't the first thing I was trying to solve in my head. But I remember thinking that they surely wouldn't shoot me. And they weren't going to. That was never their intention. My father turned the gun around, so the muzzle was now pointing at himself.

My head went down with instant shame. I couldn't look at their faces, realising I was running away from a man and a woman who loved me more than life itself.

"Don't be scared," my father said, softly. "I am not here to shoot you. I wouldn't let myself think like that. It's not my intention. Killing you is not my intention, nor has it ever entered my thoughts. Not only this, but I have never laid a finger on you your whole life."

I looked down at the floor. The bag on my shoulder was becoming heavy. My father went on even as I felt the tears stream down my face.

"There are few parents in the world who would want to injure their child," he said calmly, as my mother remained quiet beside him. "But there are many children in the world, who would want to offend their parents."

I couldn't look at them anymore. I kept staring down at the ground, listening to what my father had to say to me. In those circumstances I could not look into his eyes; I felt nothing but shame.

"There is something you don't know," he went on. "We struggled to conceive and your mother wanted a son. We received a girl and your mother wasn't happy. She cried for days, because she wanted a son."

I looked up. He had placed his arm around my mother who was looking sad, weeping silently.

"But I spoke to your mother and told her of the respect, pride and love a girl can give to a parent in a way that a boy can never give to his parents. That only a girl can afford you that respect. But I forgot, Anjali, the disgrace, the insult and the betrayal that a girl can give to a parent. A son would never do this to his parents."

So much was going through my mind. I was going to be late for John, but inside I was yelling, screaming, because I had put my parents in this position. Love was my path, but I hadn't seen the consequences of how it could hurt others. Was love really enough or was it worth more than my parents? I began to realise it wasn't.

"Anjali, the esteem and the honour which we have created in the last two decades within our society, will be for nothing. It is worth more than our lifetimes, but today, if you want to walk out, stamping on that honour, then go. But before you do, think about it. What is it for? A small dream he has offered you and you trust him? Do you no longer trust your parents who gave you life for twenty years, love and care?"

"Look Anjali, I am not one of those fathers who will lock you in your own home, never to see the light of day again, but if you do want to fulfil your selfish desires and aspirations then you will have to shoot me and your mother. Only then can you walk away. Only then can you be what you think of as free."

I couldn't believe what I was hearing. My father was pleading with me and it didn't feel right. He came towards me and placed the gun in my hand. I looked down at it, surprised at how heavy it was.

"Take it," he said, "if you are that desperate to run away, leaving us to answer to our society, then you might as well shoot us. It's a lot better than being insulted or taunted by our society. Come on, Anjali! Shoot us!"

I dropped the gun and my bag fell to the floor with a thud. I ran to my parents and embraced them. We were all crying. In that moment I realised that whatever route I was going to take it would have to be with their blessing; I could not let them feel as though they were at fault.

"Forgive me, Father," I said. "It wasn't my intention to hurt you. I don't need the kind of freedom where I have to hurt my father's feelings. Hurting you won't make me any happier in my new life. I love you so much that I will do what you want me to do. I will marry whoever and wherever you want me to."

They were the hardest words I had ever had to say. I loved John and I was now saying I would marry any man my father chose for me. In that moment was a clarity I hoped never to experience. But I knew I wasn't finished. John would be waiting for me, and I had to let him know in person. Anything less was dishonourable of me. I pulled from our embrace and looked at my father. He had to allow me one final thing before I granted him his wish.

"Please don't block me now, Father. Somebody is waiting for me. I assured him I would come, and if I don't go and give him a reason, no lover will ever desire another woman and the name of love will be in disgrace." I looked into his eyes, my cheeks wet with tears, my mother sobbing. "Let me fulfil my last promise and give me the permission to tell him."

"Let her go, now, Vijay," my mother said. "I have faith in our daughter. She will return and she will not put shame on our household."

"Okay," my father said, studying me closely. "I will abide by your promise and let you honour it."

And I walked away knowing I would be breaking another's heart.

*

Locke put the journal down on the sofa beside him and stared straight ahead. He had always known about the gun, but he had never heard the story retold so vividly. It slowly began to dawn on him just how much emotional pain Anjali had gone through to lose him in that first instance, trying to balance her love for him with the love of her parents. How could they ask her to kill them rather than face the shame of their community? That wasn't normal. He knew about honour killings, but this was in reverse. It somehow felt honourable and despicable at the same time. And Anjali had had to go through it.

     He thought back to when she told him she wasn't coming and his meltdown in Piccadilly station. She had been strong enough to have kept it together and he always thought that was because she didn't care. Now, with the truth about the gun fully explained, he realised what he had always known; Anjali was the strongest person he knew. And she was now channelling all of her love into their son, to be strong enough for the two of them, to plan for a future without her husband, without Sachin's father. In short, without him.

     Locke took another sip of his whisky and, for the first time since he could remember, realised he didn't know what to do.

forty

a pre-emptive strike

The woman was tall, perhaps in her forties and with straight dark hair framing a face without make-up. Anjali studied her briefly and realised she would have been very pretty, beautiful even, had she made more of an effort. The man beside her was of similar height and although he seemed to take care in his appearance with a demure tie setting off a sharp grey suit, the same could not be said of his physique. Fat pushed to get out of his tight shirt and his face had a dark pinkish hue, as if his collar was slowly throttling him.

Anjali allowed them in and showed them through to the living room. The police officers passed on the option of a cup of tea, although it was clear that the man, DC Graham Strang as he had been introduced, would have liked the option. His superior, DS Caroline Moore, had made the decision for them both. He had to make do with his officer's notepad; he was only there to take notes.

"It's about your husband, Mrs Locke," DS Moore began once the three of them were seated. Anjali remained impassive. "We've been trying to locate his whereabouts. Do you know where he is?"

Anjali shook her head. "No, I'm sorry, but I don't." And it wasn't a lie. Since Locke had been in her kitchen the day before, she had had plenty of time to mull over everything he had said, not just his begging for forgiveness, which was their affair alone, but also the fact he had said her house was being watched by the police. She had never seen anything untoward, and she made a point of not looking out of any windows in the interim should that raise suspicion about the gasman who had come to visit. But the information had focused her mind – she would be very non-committal should the police ever come, and she would be very careful not to tell any outright lies. She realised this could prove very tricky. Sachin would be the deciding factor if faced with such a situation; she would not put her husband's future above her son's.

"When did you last seen him?"

"Not for a number of weeks," Anjali said.

She had lied on just the second question, but again she was prepared for this. If they came knocking she would tell the police the truth about her and John with the sole exception of his visit the day before. "As far as I am aware he is India, where I left him."

"How do you mean 'left', Mrs Locke? Have you separated?"

Anjali sighed and looked suitably resigned to the question. "No," she said, "we have not split up. But we are on something of a break. We have not spoken since the end of May, perhaps the start of June. I can check against our flights."

"Our flights?"

"Our son, *my son,* Sachin flew back from India with me. I have not spoken to John since we landed. I had not really spoken to him much in the weeks before we left."

"Can I ask why the separation?"

"You can ask, but I don't see it's any of your business." Anjali's tone had turned acid. She didn't like being questioned by anyone. Her life was her own and no one else's. Only those with her permission had any right to know about it. This woman, already coming across as haughty and superior, had started to alienate her and would get little assistance unless Anjali wanted to give it. DC Strang shuffled in his chair, although whether through physical or mental discomfort it was hard to tell. DS Moore smiled; she had faced much harder people in her years on the force. She tried a different tack.

"You are aware of your husband's various businesses in India, are you not, Mrs Locke?"

"Of course."

"Then you will be aware that there have been a number of arrests related specifically to one of his enterprises; an initiative for street children in Delhi where children have gone missing?"

"I do, yes. And I am stunned. I knew the foreman, Amar Rajmi, personally. I cannot believe such a sweet man could have anything to do with what is being alleged."

"And what is being alleged, Mrs Locke?"

Anjali looked directly into DS Moore's eyes, and then effected a look of disbelief. "You just said that children have gone missing. Why are you asking me about things you've actually told me?"

This time DC Strang's movements were more obvious. DS Moore ignored him. She didn't like being made a fool of and Anjali Locke seemed keen to try that on.

"What else do you know about Locke Enterprises?"

"Look," Anjali sighed, "you need to rephrase that better. Depending on your viewpoint I know a lot or I only know a little. I know of the obvious the things like the school set up in my name; *The Anjali Locke High School for Girls*. It's situated in northeast Delhi, which is perhaps the poorest area of that city. It is outperforming all other schools in the area. It was founded there deliberately to show to the Indian government and to the local council that more needs to be done to help the country's poor. It helps a few hundred girls each year and I am certain of its success.

"But I'm guessing you don't want to hear that because that does not sit well with your narrative. You want to hear about the street kids initiative and the absolutely appalling allegations coming out from there. Immediately I am less able to help you. The initiative was not set up in anyone's name save for Locke Enterprises'. It was not intended to raise awareness in the same way the school was. It was John's idea to do something under the radar because he was sick of the poverty he saw every time we returned to India.

"My country is beautiful, *Miss* Moore, but it is flawed. We have indescribable wealth on one side of a street and abject poverty on the other. In the middle, orphans dart between the traffic to try to get money from passing motorists. Many die each year and many simply disappear. The initiative was meant to provide a safe haven for some of those children. I pray to God that these missing children at the initiative have not suffered the fate that some in the media are suggesting."

Anjali gathered her thoughts. And the more she thought the angrier she got. Too many people had tried to have too much to say to her recently, starting with John, but also her parents, Hannah and now the police. In all of this mess of John's making, she and Sachin were entirely innocent. DS Moore said something, but she didn't hear it and she didn't care. Her jaw clenched and she spat her words out carefully.

"So you see, Miss Moore, your question is flawed. I could spend many hours telling you what I know, but how much of it would be relevant? Do you know what you are even looking for? Do you know which part of Locke Enterprises interests you? Are you trying to get information out of me that you think will be useful in some kind of trial? If so, a trial against whom, and on what grounds?

"It seems to me, Miss Moore, that you are little more than on some kind of absurd fishing trip. I would have expected a senior officer such as yourself to have come better prepared and at the very least have a clear line of enquiry. So, to answer your first question directly, do I know where my husband is? No. If I had to speculate, I would say India, but then you seem to do quite a bit of speculating yourself, so perhaps that will be sufficient for you.

"Your other question, why the separation? John had thrown himself into his work more and more in recent months. He was becoming distant. There seemed to be little time for his family. I was already planning to head home when the street kids thing made the news. There were paparazzi all over our home in Mumbai, so I brought my son home to safety. Until you turned up, I felt as though we were safe. How ironic to say that a police officer makes me feel less safe? But I now suspect we will have the press here as well given your unnecessary and ham-fisted approach."

DS Moore opened her mouth but didn't speak. Instead her gaze turned to the door to the living room. Anjali leapt from her chair and crossed to hold Sachin in a protective embrace.

"This is my son, Sachin, Miss Moore. He is the reason your appearance here is so unwelcome."

"It's okay, Mum, I heard what the officer said. She wants to know about Dad." Sachin pulled away from his mother's protective clutches and walked across to a vacant armchair and sat down. "It looks like we're in the same boat; I want to know about my dad too. So, what can you two tell me?"

The room was silent. Sachin's intervention caught everybody off guard. Anjali worried that her son might say something they would both regret whilst DS Moore and DC Strang considered how to best approach such a direct question from a thirteen-year-old.

"I'm afraid we're not at liberty to say," DS Moore offered eventually, looking up to Anjali almost as if asking for help.

"Which settles it," Anjali stated. "If you want to question me or my son again, it will be in the presence of my lawyer. That means you will give me prior knowledge and not just turn up at the front door as you did today."

Again, DS Moore was about to say something when Anjali ignored her and carried on. "I suspect you would like to search the premises. As I have not got the time or inclination to wait for you to fool around trying to get a warrant or whatever it is you need, you have my express permission to search the house right now. I suggest you write that down Mr Strang."

DC Strang startled at the sound of his name and got back to writing in his notepad. He had not written very much since Anjali Locke had taken control of the interview.

"Well?" Anjali said. DS Moore straightened her back.

"Thank you, Mrs Locke," she said. "If you wouldn't mind waiting here while we take a quick look around?"

"I said you had my permission to search the premises. I did not say you had permission to do it without supervision. You will not enter any room in my house without me watching to make sure you don't take something you shouldn't, or worse, *plant* something you shouldn't."

DS Moore smiled. She had been spoken to by lawyers like this before, but never a suspect. She had done her homework on Anjali Locke and knew she had trained as an accountant but not worked as one in more than a decade. Bluster and bravado it maybe, but at the very least she was going to make sure that she called the shots, and she didn't care if it was necessary. As far as she was concerned the interviewee had not been fully responsive, and that took things to a different level.

"Thank you, Mrs Locke, but I will have to decline on this occasion. I will be getting a warrant for a full search of these premises and I do suggest you appoint a lawyer quickly." DS Moore rose to her feet, DC Strang took his cue and did the same. She was at least six inches taller than Anjali and enjoyed looking down at her prey. "We'll see ourselves out."

*

As Anjali watched the police officers walk down the gravel driveway towards the main road, she oddly wondered why they hadn't parked nearer the house. Only once they had turned the corner and disappeared from view did she feel she could close the door. She slumped down against the wood panelling and curled herself into a ball. *What the hell have you done, Anjali? Why did you get carried away? Did you think it a good idea to antagonise the police? Why not just answer their questions as well as you could, without incriminating yourself or John in anything?*

She fought hard not to cry. But she hated confrontation and, for some reason known only to God, she had decided to be confrontational. It was the woman, DS Moore, who had annoyed her. Not content with door stepping her home, she had refused the basic welcome into an Indian household of a cup of tea and had proceeded to ask about her marriage to John. It felt like she was being violated.

Anjali didn't know what was going to happen, so she sure as hell wasn't going to talk to a complete stranger like DS Moore. And why call her 'Miss'? She could scream at her own self-importance and the unnecessary antagonism she had displayed.

"Mum?" Anjali looked up from where she was slumped to see Sachin standing in the doorway to the living room. "What just happened?"

"Nothing much, Sacky," she said, trying to smile. She realised how ridiculous she looked and got to her feet. "They are just trying to find answers to questions that I cannot help them with."

"You seemed angry with them."

"No, no," she lied. "But sometimes you have to be firm with people, or they will walk all over you."

"So that was just a pre-emptive strike?" Anjali looked at her son, surprised at the phrase he used. "It makes sense," he continued. "You don't want to be on the back foot, so your first form of defence is attack."

"Where have you got this from?"

Sachin shrugged. "Nowhere. It just makes sense. I thought you were very good, Mummy. I didn't like that lady either. I'm so glad you didn't mention the gasman."

Anjali watched Sachin head up the stairs towards his bedroom and his console, where he could while away however many hours beating the computer at its own game, or hammering his mates across the World Wide Web. Or he might read a book, one of those medical tomes he had managed to get hold of. But his mother wasn't aware; she had too much to deal with.

As she looked at the space where her son had stood in the doorway to the living room, she suddenly felt a chill creep over and envelope her. She pulled the cardigan closer about her shoulders and shivered. But it wasn't a cold temperature that caused her skin to feel like ice; it was the realisation that she had lied. As she turned DS Moore's business card over and over in her hand, she realised for the first time that she had made herself complicit in Locke's crimes.

Her heart beat hard in her chest; she had chosen love over law.

forty-one
i always get the sense

"Mum!" The shout came from upstairs. "Mum!"

"What is it, Sacky?" Anjali shouted back from the kitchen.

"It's Dad! He's here!"

Anjali put down her newspaper and hurried upstairs, bursting through the door to her son's bedroom. She found Sachin kneeling on his bed looking out of the window into the back garden. She joined him, but couldn't see anything.

"The stumps," Sachin said. She hadn't noticed, but there were two sets of cricket stumps on the lawn creating a wicket.

"Did you not leave them there?"

"No, Mum! It's a sign."

Anjali was confused. Why the hell did Locke want to play cricket when everything was collapsing around their ears? Was this some daft realisation that his number was up, and he wanted to play with his son one last time?

"A sign of what? Where the hell is he?"

"I'm guessing he's in the shed, Mum. It's where I keep my cricket stuff."

*

The shed was situated close to the French doors at the back of the kitchen that looked out onto the back garden. It was a single-storey wooden hut about forty metres long that took up much of the left side of the garden, with the immaculate lawn spreading across to the right-hand side of the plot culminating in a hedge of tall leylandii offering privacy.

If Locke was in the shed, as Sachin was adamant and which Anjali now believed, then she realised no one could see her going in there. It meant he had chosen his movements carefully and well. His ability to deceive showed no bounds.

Anjali made a point of carrying a basket load of dirty washing with her as she made her way out to the shed, just in case someone was watching. She didn't consider it until later, but had the police known her washing machine and tumble drier were actually in the kitchen, she could have rumbled Locke's cover instantly.

She found him sitting quietly on a camping chair, her journal on his lap. He appeared to have been reading it.

"You found me," he said, smiling.

"Actually, it was Sachin. He worked out the cricket clue."

"Clever boy," Locke said nodding proudly.

"He seems to be a bit too clever, John. A bit too much of a chip off the old block."

Locke considered this. He had had the radiation treatment before Sachin had been born and before he had had his first episode. In hindsight it was always a possibility that some of what had happened to his own intelligence might be passed down to his offspring. The look in Anjali's eyes told him she didn't think that was a good thing.

"Like father like son," he said. "We always thought it might be a possibility."

"But I need my son to be like me," Anjali countered, failing to control her anger. "I need him to do meaningful things for society, for the greater good. Not selfish things like his father."

"I've been reading your dairy like you asked," Locke said, changing the subject. "I get it. I get why everything I have done has been anathema to you. And I know what I must do to make it up to you."

"And what's that? Words are cheap, John, and yours are cheaper than most right now."

"I know, and I'm sorry. But I do understand and I know there's only one way I can prove that to you. I need to come clean about everything to do with the initiative, with the bank transfers, the internet outage, everything. Only when I do that, when I have admitted everything, will you accept that you are talking to the old me. To the one in this diary."

"Yes," said Anjali.

"But how can you when I am no longer the person I was?"

"You can repent. You can't undo what you did, you can't bring back the dead, but you can change the present. This is the freedom given in every culture within each human being; a right to repentance."

Locke held up the diary, then placed it on his knee. There was a marker which he used to open it out.

"There's a particular passage I came across which I want to read to you. It was this passage amongst many others that made me realise what I needed to do."

Locke cleared his throat and began to read.

"Dear Diary,

Marriage, relationships and love are things that we all want, that we all look for, but do we know how we will react once we find them? Life is always an unknown quantity; we know the direction we're heading in, and often it feels like familiar territory. And then there is love which has such a contribution to make to our lives."

Locke looked up from the diary. "Did you know where your life was heading, Anjali?"

"I knew the risks. I was aware of the challenges. I understand that getting married or staying married is not easy. Examples exist throughout our society."

Locke went back to the book on his knee.

"Some people marry early and have regrets. They may make something of themselves, they may not."

Again he looked up. "Do you have regret marrying me?"

"I didn't," she answered truthfully. "Until I found out the truth. Deceit is the foundation of every broken marriage. That's why it is forbidden. We lose confidence in each other or in God. And we didn't make it through life."

Locke returned to the diary once more. *"Some have bigger contributions to make to their men and others less so, but whatever the proportions, it is how Life turns out."*

"I agree you have a bigger contribution towards my life," he said. "Without you, I would be lost."

"This is my culture, my customs and my obligation as a wife to support my husband. Society doesn't help, though, calling us maids or housewives when we have the knowledge of a successful marriage." She thought for a moment. "Are you going to comment on every single sentence? I'm not hearing contrition; I'm hearing you try to work your way around me again." The anger rose within her once more.

"Please," he said. "I'm not trying to be awkward. I just need to get through this my way. You know how difficult I'm finding this."

"I am now one of those millions of spouses," he said, reading from the pages, *"but instead of blind devotion and love, I keep hearing a strange question: will I be successful, or will I run a mile? How will I respond when the time comes to rescue a man's life, in this case my husband's?"*

Locke looked up at his wife. "What happened, Anjali? Why did you walk away? Why did you walk away from our marriage, away from my life?"

"I am still here," she said. "I'm still telling you to do the right thing. That's where I stand. I never left with another man or had an affair. If it was only my life I would happily give it away for you, but we have a son and I have to think about his future."

Locked paused. "I think we have reached that point, Anjali, and I think you have already proved how you would respond." She remained impassive. He looked back at the diary.

"Today was the conclusion of my first life, and the commencement of my second. I got up, had a shower, got ready, and stood in front of my God. I asked my God to help me, to give me the strength to make this marriage a successful one. Although John has me now, he has never believed in God or the power and strength He holds in us. Why would he? No portion has been given back to him; he is not blessed with an education or a career. People in society have not treated him well because they failed to see beyond his image and whether it would help them. It has created a negative image of life and people."

"This society never accepted me," Locke said, "so why would I care about community, or society, or the world? The world was already a criminal place; marriage break-ups, affairs, breaking trust, rape, domestic abuse, mental abuse. So why am I the bad guy?"

"The world is a bad place," Anjali stated. "We hear of rape, murder, terrorism, bad politics and war, but it doesn't mean we contribute to those factors. It's the citizens' contributions that makes the world a better place, not to destroy it. Amongst hundreds of bad people in our society there are millions who are good, kind and charitable. It is as though life is not worth living. It's a test for us. Can we survive among the evil ones or be a part of them? There are people who think this place is their home, their life. This is the heaven on Earth. Let them live, allow them to live and amongst those bad people you now find me."

"I didn't treat you any differently."

Locke could barely hear her as he turned back to the diary.

"They failed to see his heart, his mind, his thoughts. It was beautiful. He wanted to make the world a better place, to fill it with hope. Provide free or accessible education to low-income families. But great dreams come from great challenges. When it is time. Can it make a difference, or is it going to go in another direction? It was his choice to live here, in the UK, but it didn't mean he should feel an outsider. This is why I worry about what would happen to him if dangerous events took hold in his heart."

"I was an outsider," Locke shouted. "I will always be!"

"Oh, no you don't, John! An outsider doesn't get to find love, they're out of luck, but you did. You had someone; you had me."

"And today was like no other day. I could see his anger in his expression. He is always angry about how the world has turned out for him, how people judge an individual by looks, not by talent. They laughed at him when he was talking about dreams and changing lives. He was a joke to people. Our success starts with an idea or a dream. And if we stick to it, it becomes a reality. And I believe that he will. Guide him my Lord."

"Anger destroys a human being, John. It makes you blind to the truth." Anjali knew the text. She had reread her diaries often lately. Listening to Locke read out her innermost thoughts written down at the dawn of their marriage left her confused. They were private thoughts, but she had thrown the diary at him. What she had not realised was just how prophetic her words now seemed. Locke, she thought, didn't seem too bothered by the connection. He was showing no emotion. She wondered if his anger was growing.

"John got up," Locke continued, *"and stood by the door to the temple room of our home. I asked him why he didn't come in, but he said he*

was 'just fine' where he was. I think I had surprised him, because he had approached quietly. I knew he was there and yet my concentration and devotion were towards God. It was the same sensation I got when I was in the temple in India."

"What did you wish for in your prayer?" Locke asked.

"To give strength to my marriage."

"You didn't even know me, let alone know we were going to get married!"

"But I had a sense of a negative view of the world. I thought I might lose my husband, even though I didn't have one and I certainly didn't know it might be the guy in the background taking photographs of me. It's the same sensation I got this morning before you turned up. And the same before you appeared as a gasman. I always get the sense, John. Always." Locke eyed Anjali closely, then returned to the diary.

""This is God's home," I insisted. "No one stays on his doorstep, it's a mark of disrespect. Come in. Show your deference."

"John stepped forward.

""Do you have trust in Him? In God?" he asked.

""Don't you?" I answered back.

""No."

""You don't believe God?" I tried to sound surprised, but I knew.

""No."

""Why not?"

""We humans are only a puppet to Him," he said. "He holds all the power and the will. He plays with our emotions and whenever he requires it of us, we are just made of wood and string performing in His puppeteer play. Have you seen God?"

""No," I replied, "but the scripture says 'kun fire kun' meaning 'be and it is formed'."

""Then how do you know he exists?"

""Denying is easy, finding his replacement is hard. Out of seven billion people, find one person who claims to be god or that they can create a universe. I believe He exists, and nothing is bigger than trust or belief. Blind trust is a test for you and me. Therefore we have believers and non-believers in our society. Anyone can trust what they see. That is why people still try to prove the invisible. It's not easy to believe in the invisible. Only to discover that the answer lies before them; the Big Bang theory or the new quantum correction model based on Einstein's General Relativity Theory. This proves the universe was always there. Tomorrow, we will prove that God exists."

""The world exists based on belief?"

""I believe in the seen and the unseen. You've heard of Jesus? He was born miraculously. That is proof he exists and he even brings gifts to unbelievers, like you, to prove to society he is here. Lots of things can't be seen; the air for example, but it's still there. I love Him with all my heart, John. He gave you to me. Why don't you agree?"

""Because I never received anything back from Him. He took away anything and everything I ever wanted."

""No, John. You wanted the impossible and He gives it to you, but you misuse it. If you are going to hate anyone, hate people, hate their behaviour. Don't hate God. It's people who misuse his words. What would you do if He did give you the chance again?"

""Anything and everything," he said, "but I wouldn't allow my dream be diminished.""

"A dream rarely comes true, John," Anjali interrupted. "You had it, but you couldn't recognise it for what it was; a gift so that we could make the world a better place."

Locke ignored the comment and continued reading; ""I watched as John looked away from my God. It was as if the image was hurting his eyes.

""I too wouldn't let your dream be diminished," I whispered, looking into his eyes. "We aren't necessarily born to be husband and wife. We could just be friends, and friends tell each other their feelings. The first rule of friendship is equality. I wouldn't do anything against your will and you won't do anything that may hurt my feelings.""

"If only you had opened up," Anjali said, "I could have still helped you. I could have told you that what you were doing was wrong. I tried to guide you on the TV show, in the media, all that time I helped your recovery from amnesia. So why turn criminal?"

"I was afraid," Locke said without looking up from the diary.

""Slowly, but wisely, you would see me and I would understand you. You would understand my ancient religion and I will understand your Western upbringing. Together we can bridge the divide."

""I rose and walked over to him. My hands cupped his face and he looked back at me. "Don't be angry with Him; have faith in me. He is our divine Mother and Father and no parent would answer wrong for their children. Children maybe ungrateful to their parents, but God never turns aside from his children. The only difference is we can't see that, or see God.""

"Parents always warn their children if there is a danger," Anjali said. "They might give you a good hiding, to learn the lesson, but that doesn't mean they love you any less. My parents tried to warn me about you and I didn't listen, because you were meant to be."

""Just try to remember that whenever you feel angry at the world, just close your eyes and take a breath. Form a mental image of me, of your India, and then shout out my name: Anjali! Anjali! Anjali!"

""Why?" he whispered, still broken.

""To remind you that God gave you to me and that's a gift all of its own. Love is a gift too. Say it softly and you will visualise all your problems disappear. Be happy, John. When you are upset, God is upset too, and I am here for you."

""I tapped his shoulder and walked away slowly, thinking, God would share some light in him.""

Locke closed the diary. The silence remained between them. He pinched the bridge of his nose and looked up.

"You were right," he said, eventually. "I was angry. I had you and yet I kept focusing on the negatives. I loved you more than anything, more than my own life, and yet I was too self-absorbed and raging against the world that I could not provide for you better than I was. I wanted to make you happy, but I didn't realise you were already happy with what you had."

"But you didn't need to," Anjali replied. "I had a good job."

"I know, but that's partly the point. A husband provides for his wife, not the other way round. I could not provide for you what you deserved. And then my brain started to change and suddenly I had ability and reason and I could provide for us both. I started with the casino and, well you know the rest. But that's where my mistakes began. I thought I was doing it for you, for us. I was doing it for me; I was trying to beat the system. The thing is, I know how to beat the system. But to do that is to lose you. I will never try to do that again. All I ever do from now on is for you."

Locke put the diary down on the floor beside him. The morning sun shone brightly though the shed's windows illuminating them in gold and dust motes. Anjali wanted to hold him, but realised he needed space.

"Look at you Anjali; I loved the way you used to look in that sari. I loved that beauty about you. I'm so sorry for the hurt this has caused you." Locke gazed up at the bright blue sky through the window and seemed to find comfort in the sun's rays that warmed him. "It's my next episode in two days' time. It will happen just before six o'clock on Thursday morning. I'd be lost without you. I will be lost anyway, but to go into my episode without you there does not bear thinking about. If you are not there, then I will not be either. I've read the diary, Anjali, and I understand. I will do all you ask of me, because now I no longer understand *ardhangini;* I *believe* it."

Anjali gasped. A sob burst forth from deep within, catching her off guard. She immediately began to cry and hurried to her husband sitting on the camping chair. His tears fell freely too. It had been years in the coming, but John Locke finally understood his *ardhangini*. And she had been there all along.

"I am sorry, but I have done some unspeakable things," he sobbed. "If I had understood you better, instead of acting like no one could stop me and nothing bad could happen. I used my mind to help criminals, but I wasn't the criminal. I got the gun, but I didn't pull the trigger. I was the guru; it was my ideas, my talent, my intellect and knowledge that made things happen. It took bad men to do that, and I made it successful. I used my genius to facilitate crime.

"I should have been using my mind for the greater good and to improve peoples' lives. That's what the knowledge was for. I now understand why God didn't give me that vast knowledge, that I was better off how I was. And you fell in love with that person. You are right Anjali, having more knowledge doesn't make you who you are. What you have in your heart and your mind are what gives you your character."

Anjali hugged him to her breast, as tightly as she could. Neither wanted the moment to end and they held each other and sobbed at the realisation that now they had got back together, they were about to lose each other again with his next episode due in less than forty-eight hours.

"You must give yourself up, John, you must."

Locke made no sound. He knew she was right, but this was something he would have to face down; his fear. To give himself up was the end of his freedom. He didn't agree that his mental health could be used to his benefit. He knew they would more likely lock him up and throw away the key. That or employ him on government work.

She's still naïve, he thought. *Handing myself in is like putting myself on the cross. The public will be judge, jury and executioner.*

"I will," he said, "but allow me a final day of freedom before I do. Is that too much to ask?"

Anjali released him and stood fully upright. Locke looked small sitting on the camping chair. He looked *vulnerable*. She realised she had never seen him looking so powerless. Even in a coma he had that certain confidence good looks exude. Right now he looked feeble.

"I will," Anjali said. "Just as with our vows on our wedding day, *I will.*"

Locke stood up and no longer looked small. But he still looked vulnerable. She could see he was broken. He reached out and hugged her closely.

"One day," he whispered in her ear. Then kissed her neck and walked away.

forty-two
he needs me

Anjali stared at the wall in front of her. It was hard to tell whether it was pale green or blue, but it sported a notice board. Strikingly, there was a picture of her husband on it amongst the other loose sheets of paper pinned there.

She looked closely at the image. Locke wasn't smiling, but it was not quite a mugshot. She didn't know when or where it had been taken. It might have been the picture in his passport, but it wasn't that recent. She realised just how few lines he had in the picture compared to now. She guessed it was perhaps a decade old, and if so, then he had aged a lot in the intervening years. This surprised her as she always thought he looked after himself. She idly wondered if his criminal ways were taking their toll more than she had ever noticed. Perhaps it was guilt? Perhaps there was still an honesty inside of him that meant the body suffered while the mind plotted. She was constantly confused and conflicted whether this was the right thing to do; to hand her husband into the authorities. It was a tough decision; should she have waited for him? Would the police and wider society really understand the circumstances or assist them in any way? She was about to find out.

"Do you know where Dad is?" The question shook her from her thoughts. Sachin sat stony-faced on another of the uncomfortable plastic chairs in the dim square box of a room that served as DS Caroline Moore's office. The moment Anjali had presented herself at the police station, she was ushered through into this drab little place and briefly had the opportunity to stare down at the detective in her seat. How she loathed her, but then she was sure the feeling was mutual.

"I have an idea," she said at last. And waited. She was considering leaving by the time the door finally opened and the tall, thin make-up-less DS Moore reappeared, followed by a man in his early fifties. He took up a position behind and to the left of his colleague who took her own seat behind her desk and seemed to gather her thoughts.

"Mrs Locke, this is Detective Chief Inspector James Law," Moore began. "You said you know where your husband is?" Anjali really did despise the woman.

"No," she stated flatly. "I said I think I know where he is."

DS Moore stared down at some notes, but Anjali knew she was playing for time, or effect. It didn't matter which. "So where do you think he is?"

"I would guess that he is hiding in our new home in Sale. It's was due to be finished around now. If it's not there, then it might be the Lodge in the grounds. At least that house is furnished."

"And why are you telling us this now?" Standing against the wall, DCI Law hadn't moved. Anjali eyed him suspiciously. She regretted making the decision.

"Because he visited me yesterday."

DS Moore's eyes widened. DCI Law shuffled slightly.

"He's in the area?" he asked.

"Yes. Unless he has taken up some other residence. But I believe he is nearby."

"Why has it taken you until today to tell us this?" Law continued.

"Because he only turned up yesterday and it has taken me until now to process what he said to me and to decide that this is the correct action." Sachin looked at his mother. She caught the glance and softened her face into a gentle smile. He understood perfectly what was going on; she just wanted to reassure him.

"Where is the house?" DS Moore stated. It was a demand, not a question. Anjali willingly gave the address of the Lodge. The actual address of the new build mansion escaped her. It had been a field the last time she had seen it, listening to Locke's wild and, to her, excessive plans for the family home.

Moore left the room clutching the sheet of paper she had written the address on. DCI Law took the opportunity to take his DS's seat. He leaned forward, clasped his hands together and peered closely at Anjali.

"Mrs Locke, we have received a report today from the Metropolitan Police in London and, alongside evidence provided by the Mumbai and New Delhi police services, it seems your husband has involvement not only in what appears to have been going on in India, but also that he is, somehow, involved in the internet outage that caused all those deaths and accidents. The intelligence from London has come from an investigator hired by the major banks and others who alleges this latter series of offences. Do you know anything about that?"

Anjali had vowed, having lied to DS Moore and DC Strang a few days earlier about not having seen John, that she would answer all questions truthfully. Her husband had turned a corner, of that she had no doubt, and it meant that in giving all she knew about his affairs, which was increasingly little, she realised, would also mean that when the police finally caught up with him, Locke would admit all to purge his sins.

She knew it meant he would be in prison for a very long time. But she could cope with that. The biggest concern was Sachin. The shame of relatives didn't concern her at all. And so she told DCI Law all she could remember of how her husband had admitted to the gang murders, the initiative in India, the internet outage and anything else she could remember.

DS Moore had returned midway through the statement and stood next to her desk, her seat now occupied. She didn't seem annoyed, but then Anjali was providing the evidence that she had wanted just a few days earlier. Both officers listened with increasing amounts of barely disguised amazement.

"Look," she said, having finished all she had to say, "John will atone for his sins. I am fully convinced of that—" DCI Law raised his hand to Anjali and turned in the chair to look up at DS Moore.

"We need that house under surveillance and it has got to be very discreet. When this all comes out the spotlight will be on us, so nothing can go wrong." DS Moore nodded. "See to it and come straight back."

"Sir," Moore said, and left the room once again.

"But there is another thing," Anjali stated, annoyed the DCI had interrupted her. "He will have one of his episodes tomorrow morning."

"What kind of episode?" Law asked. He now seemed disinterested, as if he had what he wanted and anything else was irrelevant.

"He will have a kind of epileptic seizure that will require medical assistance. He will probably be placed in a coma and he will wake up without any memory." Law's brow had furrowed, deep creases forming between his eyebrows. He asked Anjali to repeat what she had just said.

"He will need help the moment it happens. I need to be there when it does."

Law leaned back in the chair, causing it to creak.

"You're telling me that as of tomorrow, he won't remember a thing?"

"As of tomorrow, he will be in a hospital with around the clock care. He will likely not wake up for a few days, or weeks, and when he does he will have no idea of what has gone on. He needs me to be with him."

"I'm sorry, Mrs Locke, but that isn't going to happen."

"It has to!" Sachin turned to look at his mother as she slowly spat the words out. "I came here today because I know the help he needs. If you were to arrest him on the spot, you will not know what is going to happen. I am here because my husband needs me to do this for him."

"He asked you to come here?"

"No, he did not. You need to listen to what I am telling you. He will collapse tomorrow morning and he will need immediate medical care." Anjali took a deep breath. "I showed up here with evidence against my husband. You know how hard that is for me. And you cannot show me even the slightest compassion?"

A smile appeared on DCI Law's face. He had heard all sorts of excuses in his near thirty-year career, but this was a good one. She did seem genuine, though. Anjali was disgusted with the way they behaved and thought back on what John had said, "They're going to crucify me."

"As you have just heard, Mrs Locke, I have told DS Moore to set up a surveillance operation on your husband's potential whereabouts. You provided the information, if you remember—"

"And you have just heard, Mr Law, that he needs me tomorrow morning. That is why I have come here today. But you can't seem to show a bit of mercy, seeing as I have helped you? You should perhaps try to listen." Anjali's voice remained calm, but the anger beneath was clear to all present. Sachin didn't like seeing his mother like this, but it made him proud that she was standing up for her husband. He missed his father and it reassured him to know his mother was looking out for him despite all the things he had apparently done.

"They couldn't care less about honesty, Mum," he said, surprising everyone in the room. "They are only concerned with the evidence. They are concerned with how to crucify someone. This is why people are afraid of telling the truth."

"I'm sorry, Mrs Locke, but I cannot allow you anywhere near the two properties you have mentioned. Your husband has been part of an ongoing investigation for some time now, and with this new information I cannot allow you to jeopardise what we are doing."

"Jeopardise? I am still trying to help you."

Law raised his hand again and sighed. "Nothing will change what has already been set in motion. You will not be seeing your husband again until we have him in custody."

"You're not listening!" Anjali leaped up, the scream shocking both Law and Sachin. The door behind her opened and DS Moore took in the change of circumstances. "You will not have him in custody; he will be in hospital. You will not be able to interview him because he will be in a coma. You will not be able to charge him because he will remember nothing!" Her voice grew louder. "He needs his wife. I am the only one who can care for him when this happens. The doctors will not understand. You will not have your trial. If you do not allow me near him, he might die.

"Speaking the truth does not give you compassion. This is the biggest mistake I have ever made. The damage has been done."

"Mrs Locke!" Law slammed his palm on the desk. "Do not shout at me. Calm down and sit down!" Anjali thought for a moment, trying to reduce her anger with deep breaths. DS Moore remained standing behind her. Just in case restraint was required. Sachin saw this and his own fists tensed, ready to leap in should either of the officers place a finger on his mother. Nobody moved for a few moments before Anjali slowly returned to her seat. Moore walked forward and took her position next to the desk.

"Surveillance units are on their way," she said.

"Good," Law replied. "If what I've just heard is true, they need to establish which property he is in as soon as possible. We're going in at dawn."

DCI Law rose from his chair and walked to the door. He opened it slightly then looked back at Anjali, then at Sachin and finally at DS Moore.

"You need to give a statement, Mrs Locke. I suggest you get a solicitor. You need to decide on someone who can look after your son. After your statement will be taken back to your home. Someone will be staying with you until after we have apprehended Mr Locke. It would be a most foolish thing to try to get involved from here on in. I trust I make myself clear."

Anjali felt the bile rise in her throat as she slowly nodded her acceptance. Locke was about to get very ill; the best thing she could do now was play dumb and appear to be doing exactly what was expected of her.

"Good," Law said, then looked at DS Moore. "Make sure you seize Mrs Locke's passport when she is taken back to her home."

The door closed behind DCI Law and DS Moore sat down in her own chair. She smiled as if she had been victorious. Anjali tensed; briefly thinking of revenge.

"So, is there someone who can look after Sachin? It should be someone very close; you might not be available for a good while yet."

*

Anjali gazed out from the hallway window. It was close to ten in the evening and she was tired. It was dark now, streetlights soaking the outside world orange. A light drizzle continued and everything in sight glistened. She thought about Sachin, now with his grandparents and terrified for his father. Their son had always been vaguely aware of his father's episodes, but it frightened Sachin when he realised just how soon the next one would be. He'd promised to be brave and not mention anything to her mother or father.

Her father Vijay had come to the police station to take custody of Sachin. He was disgusted with his daughter and told her so.

"Why didn't you seek our advice? This is a totally foolish thing you have done. It is not the way the world operates."

The words rang hollow to Anjali. She was only interested in her son. Her father shouting at her like that hadn't helped. She watched on as Vijay Sharma put an arm around Sachin and walked away. She watched as Sachin shrugged off his grandfather's arm and walked alone. She smiled at her brilliant son.

Soon afterwards she was put through an exhaustive interview that lasted several hours. The more she went on answering questions, the more she wondered why she didn't admit to Locke having visited her twice in the last few days. For some reason she clung on to that lie, not that the police seemed interested. They certainly didn't push her on it, but rather grilled her on everything else they wanted to know about. Her lawyer gave up grumbling after a while. His suggestion of a 'no comment' interview falling flat as she told the interviewing officers everything she knew. She had no idea how the police, in fact the whole legal system, would proceed once Locke had his episode. The more she thought about it, the more her comments would delay a police raid on whichever house he had chosen to hide in. That gave her a chance to get to him as she gambled that they would not arrest him before his episode. The whole interview process had taken hours and she only half-feigned weariness to wrap up things up before it got too late.

She had watched the familiar streets of Manchester blur past as she rode in the back of the police car. Her Audi was following on behind, driven by another constable. Once he had ascertained she did not have a spare key for the car, that officer had the joy of sitting in the patrol car outside the house overnight, making sure Anjali didn't try to escape by the front door.

She could see him now, and he looked like he was dozing. She wasn't thinking of sleep. Locke was a little over seven hours away from his next episode and she was going to be there, regardless of what the police had said. As if hearing her thoughts, the noise of a door quietly closing came from downstairs. It was the police officer assigned to guard Anjali in her own home. The woman was kind; nothing like DS Moore, but then maybe PC Anne Petrie was more bothered about serving people than a career-hungry ladder-climber like Caroline Moore.

It didn't really matter; Anjali had her escape planned. She had done so as she was escorted home in the police car. They wouldn't let her drive her own vehicle as she was now considered a 'flight risk'. That had riled her; did they really think she was going to leave the country without her son? She had to bite down hard when she handed over the passports, her freedom all but gone. The sound of the kettle boiling confirmed PC Petrie was making herself a hot drink.

So far Anjali reasoned she had done little wrong, but as she looked down at the Audi parked in the driveway, she felt the spare key in her hand. She listened hard for any other signs of life downstairs and glanced once more towards the police car parked across her driveway. The officer definitely looked asleep, but then again her view was blurred by the rain on the window. What made her smile was the fact there were two entrances to her driveway and the police had either not noticed or, more likely, decided she was no kind of threat so didn't bother to block the second exit. Her plan relied on getting through the second exit and onto the road before either officer had noticed she'd gone. She hoped to be able to idle slowly out, without revving the engine any more than was necessary. She would only floor the pedal if she had to.

Anjali made her way back across the hall and closed the bedroom door behind her. At her desk she began to write. The policeman, Law, had made it clear that there was going to be a dawn raid on the mansion and that almost certainly, to her mind at least, meant the police would have guns. If she succeeded in what she wanted to do, those guns might be trained on her. She looked at the sheet of paper and felt the pen strangely heavy in her hand.

This is the last will and testament of Anjali Locke...

Seeing those words on the page seemed pretentious to her, but then people wrote differently if they thought it was a legal document. Was that was legalise was? Anjali simply didn't know, but she had refrained from writing *'To whom it may concern'*.

The will was short and she hoped that wouldn't invalidate it. She didn't see why it should. There were only four instructions: two-thirds of her financial fortune to go to a charity set up in her honour to help disabled children in Greater Manchester; one third of her fortune to go to Sachin; all of her worldly goods to go to her father and mother with which to do as they pleased; and all of her saris to go to Hannah. This last she was unsure of. The relationship between them had forever broken down and that was yet another thing that saddened her deeply. But if anything was to happen to her, Anjali hoped the gesture would be taken as meant; a sign of her endearing and everlasting love for her best friend.

Finished, she folded the will into thirds and addressed it as *Last Will and Testament,* just to make sure whoever found it knew it was important. She then took a second piece of paper and realised this one would be a lot harder to write.

To my darling Sachin, she began before breathing deeply to control her emotions. It took a long time for her to write the rest of the letter.

Finished, she then lay down on her bed and watched as her ceiling flickered to the glow caused by rain sliding down her window. Downstairs PC Petrie seemed to have figured out how to turn the television on, the sound turned low, but still audible in the bedroom.

Anjali smiled and thanked God for stupid police officers. Neither had even bothered to check her bedroom. Had they done so they would have noticed the outside staircase leading down from it into the back garden. When the time was right, she would leave by that route.

Now all she had to do was wait and hope PC Petrie and her colleague had fallen asleep.

forty-three

the strange warmth of an august pre-dawn

Five forty-nine in the morning. That was the time Locke would have his episode. That was the time she needed to be by his side. It would take her a little over ten minutes to drive to the new house where she believed Locke to be. Anjali had remained awake throughout the night praying to her little shrine in the bedroom, praying for the strength to remain awake, praying for Sachin, and praying she would be able to give her guard duty the slip. But mostly she prayed for her husband knowing what he was about to go through. She asked for strength.

"Radha, Krishna, I don't know how this day is going to turn out. But I'm in need of your support. Now, this is a test for a woman. And you know I'm a lifelong contributor to my marriage. Whatever you gave me, it was a challenge for me. I've never complained about right or wrong. Because I thought it was a sign. And I will continue in my duty. Despite the fact that my life is in danger. Give John strength so that I may save him or defend him. Let the truth be brought to light. I want the truth to prevail."

She said a final prayer and rose to her feet, taking a last look at the picture of India he had taken of her all those years ago that now hung above their bed. She smiled bitterly at the irony that she was wearing the same buttercup-yellow sari now as then and to stand before her God asking for a better world and a better life. The swish of the sari sounded ridiculously loud in the silence of her bedroom but she hadn't heard PC Petrie move in a long time. She hoped the woman was fast asleep. Anjali smoothed the silk across her stomach and thought back to the day she had worn it in the temple in India, aware of Locke taking his surreptitious photographs. She marvelled at how well it still fit her, despite the years, despite the ravages of motherhood on a woman's body. If she managed to get to see him, this vision of his 'India' as they still called her when wearing this sari, then she knew it would bring him peace as he neared his latest episode.

She moved slowly across to the corner of the bedroom where the door to the outside staircase was hidden behind a room divider Locke had bought her as a Christmas present some years ago. It was beautifully ornate, depicting peacocks on a black and red Japanese-themed background. She loved it and had often got undressed behind it because she knew Locke liked to see her come back out again naked. It had been a pretext to their lovemaking on many occasions in their earlier years. She winced when she thought of what her husband had now become. She wanted to turn back time to that innocence.

After a brief glance back at her room and, specifically, the desk where her will and the letter to Sachin now lay, Anjali made her move. Almost never in use, the door to the outside gave after a heavier push and the strange warmth of an August pre-dawn rushed in to greet her. She looked again at her watch. It was time; she just needed to get her car off the driveway and she would be on her way.

*

Anjali instantly regretted her choice to wear the buttercup-yellow sari. She was lit up like a morning star even in the half light of the early dawn. Having escaped her home without seeming to alert either police officer guarding her, she had parked the Audi around the corner from the road on which the newly built mansion stood. She had crept forward to see a police car parked across the entrance to the road, blocking access to other vehicles. The police officer inside looked bored, but there was no way he wouldn't see her as she walked past.

She looked again at her watch; five thirty-eight. If she was to get to him before his episode she needed to act fast. Anjali took a deep breath and walked quickly around the corner. The police officer looked up at her and seemed initially a little surprised to see anyone, let alone a woman wearing an outfit such as hers. His hand rose to signal her to stop and she walked towards the car. The passenger side window came down and she peered in.

"Sorry, madam, but you cannot go down there."

"Oh," Anjali said, feigning surprise. "I'm just going on my normal morning walk."

The police officer shook his head. "Sorry, but not today. I'm afraid you'll have to find a different route. Police business."

Anjali looked up the street and could see an ambulance and a couple of other police cars. She reckoned there were more parked elsewhere as she could see a considerable number of shadowy figures standing behind the police cars that were blocking the mansion's driveway. At least they had taken seriously her warning about John needing medical help. She looked again at her watch; five forty. She had nine minutes if she was to make it; she could run it in less than one.

"I'm sorry, madam, but you really do need to move along from here. It's a potentially dangerous situation."

Then she heard the megaphone. "John Locke, this is the police. You are surrounded. We are armed. Come out with your hands raised."

"Madam!" the police officer opened his door.

"That's right, John, don't do anything silly. Just come out slowly and with your hands raised. Walk slowly forwards, keeping your hands raised."

Anjali saw the searchlight turn on and she knew it was being trained on her husband. He must be outside and he had to know she was there. She sprinted in the direction of the police cars. The officer behind her shouted for her to stop, but she heard Locke shout that he was epileptic, heard the megaphone bark more orders.

"John," she screamed. "John!"

She could hear the officer gaining behind her and, as she neared the ambulance, saw some figures start to move in her direction.

"He's ill! He's fucking ill!" she screeched as she sought to evade the advancing officers.

"Anjali!"

Then she felt herself pulled backwards by the sari. *Such a fucking mistake to wear it*, she thought, then screamed again. She fought with all her strength, but was no match for the officer now that he had hold of her. He was shouting at her to stop, but she continued to struggle. At least Locke knew she was there. He had shouted her name. She pulled hard once more and felt the material tear. She was suddenly free again, her struggle propelling her forwards as the two shadowy figures continued to move towards her, trying to block her route. But she had always been nimble and she sidestepped her way past both police officers as more shouts went up. She was yards from the mansion's driveway now, the light still trained on it. More orders came from the megaphone, but she didn't hear that they were aimed at her. She turned right and slowed as she took in the scene in front of her.

Locke was standing in the middle of the driveway, lit up an eerie shade of pale with the spotlight on him. The next thing she saw was a man clad in black aiming a rifle at her husband.

"Anjali!"

She ignored the armed officer and rushed straight for Locke. Shouting rose up from all angles. As she neared her husband, she saw other shadowy figures to her right; they really were surrounded as she thudded into him. They embraced. Her scent beguiling as she gasped from the sprint she had just completed. The shouting continued as she looked up into his face, into his beautiful hazel eyes and saw his smile. He smiled back and they kissed. It was the most precious moment of her life; she had her John back, if only for a moment before someone grabbed them both and pulled them apart forever. Or his episode did.

"*Ardhangini,*" Locke whispered, gazing adoringly down at his wife. His right hand went to the small of his back and he felt for the cold metal there.

"Yes!" She reached up to kiss him once more but instead felt herself being spun around. The spotlight dazzled as she found herself looking into the glare and could just make out the police cars but nothing more. He smiled maniacally.

"John?"

"Don't any of you assholes move, or I'll shoot!" Locke shouted. Then the safety catch clicked as he released it and put the barrel of the gun to Anjali's temple. "Not a single fucking one of you!" he shouted again as he started to walk both of them backwards towards the door of the house.

"What are you doing, John?" Locke's free arm was tight around Anjali's shoulders as he pulled on her, ushering her backwards. His grip was tight and the fear coursed through her. "You know this is madness. You told me you were going to give yourself up. You couldn't do it, could you? Even though you promised."

Tears stung at her eyes. At first she was confused, but realisation dawned quickly. "You've betrayed me."

"Anjali, please. Enough." Locke waved the gun in the general direction of the spotlight, then at the officers either side of them. "I fucking mean it. Don't move!"

"You're going to pass out in a minute, you need to give yourself up, not make it worse." Locke's grip tightened, making it harder for her to breathe. Anjali struggled to get free. "I mean it John, you have to stop this; I don't want it to be your last moment on Earth."

The words hit home and Locke's grip lessened. Anjali managed to twist around. She saw the gun and looked into his face. "You need to give the gun to me. You need to show them you're not a threat. Let them arrest you. I thought you said *Ardhangini?*"

"I did."

"Then why have you lied to me? You said you would give yourself up and now you're threatening me with a gun. You need to give it to me. Now."

Locke gazed down on the most beautiful woman he had ever known. "You're wearing the sari," he said. "Nice touch. But you are a fucking idiot if you told the cops the truth. They'll never understand."

"Enough, John, there's no time for this. Give me the gun so we can get you into an ambulance before you have your episode."

Locke smiled, looked at the silver gun in his hand and looked back down at Anjali. "I've got a couple of minutes yet."

"If you don't give me that gun, it will be your last ever two minutes with me."

"Until next time." He saw the slight confusion in her face. "We're joined through the ages, right? So we'll never be apart."

"That's right," Anjali smiled. "I love you, John Locke. Now give me the gun."

Five forty-seven, not that she knew it that precisely. Locke released his grip on Anjali completely and lowered the gun. Her hand was outstretched and he placed the firearm there, the barrel now pointing at his own midriff.

He closed his eyes tightly as a searing pain stabbed through his head. The episode was starting. When he opened his eyes again, the glare of the spotlight stung more than it had before, but what he saw shook him to his foundations. Anjali held the gun against her own head.

"Truth gun, John. Do you want to play?" Another pain stabbed at his eyes. He raised his hand to shield them from the light.

"What are you fucking doing?"

"Truth gun, John. You know what that means. Do you want to play?"

"I'm about to pass out. There's no time for this."

"*Ardhangini*, that's the word you used. *Ardhangini*. You know what it means. Together forever through the ages, just like you said. Do you believe it?" Locke nodded, barely perceptibly, but Anjali saw it. "You said you were going to give yourself up, but instead you pulled a gun out. Did you want to go out in some kind of blaze of glory?"

"No, I..." but the words wouldn't come.

"Remember what I said to you, John? Remember when I said I had given my life for you? Remember when I said I would die before you? I told you, John. I told you that if you lie to me, you will lose me. Remember that?"

"Yes... no..."

"You lied to me, John, now you lose me. As much as I trusted my God. This is how deeply I believed in you. For love, John. I will forget this entire world and show my loyalty even with death."

Anjali's gaze never left that of Locke's. Both were oblivious to the continuing shouting from the megaphone. Neither saw the armed police shuffling ever nearer on either side of them. Her index finger tightened on the trigger. A single tear rolled down her cheek.

"Now you lose me."

The report from the gun deafened as Anjali's head seemed to explode in front of him. Locke felt something explode within his own temple, making him scream out. An angry red mark appeared instantly in the same place as the bullet entered Anjali's head. A cloud of pink blood sprayed in every direction and he felt the wetness on his face. The flash from the muzzle imprinted on his retina as Anjali slumped before him. He screamed again as he watched, with everything seemingly happening in slow motion. Another surge of pain coursed through him like an electric current. His hands grabbed at his head trying to alleviate the agony. Anjali's body lay on the ground. Her buttercup-yellow sari stained with her freshly spilled blood, her sightless eyes still seemed be looking at him as he began to succumb to the episode. More blood oozed into the light grey bricks of the driveway where the back of Anjali's head had been blown open. In the artificial light it looked black.

But it was the eyes. As the final white-hot agony overtook him, the last thing he saw were her eyes looking back up at him. The pain at the back of his skull felt like it had been his own head that had taken the bullet. The brilliant white light behind his eyes got brighter still. He screamed again, his fingers tearing at his agony.

"Now you will lose me." The words rang out. He never knew whether he really heard them or whether they came from inside his own head.

For John Locke, the world turned black. He fell forwards onto the prone body of Anjali.

Epilogue

2018

His eyes slowly opened. The brightness of the room bringing nothing but pain. His mouth was dry and his body felt strange. He tensed a hand, tried to wiggle his toes. Nothing seemed to work as it should. Slowly voices became apparent as his vision focused. Two faces appeared above him; a woman with red raw eyes and a man with a tightly clenched jaw.

He didn't recognise them.

He couldn't discern the words the woman was saying. The man said nothing. He became aware of a siren of some kind, or an alarm, and the man and woman turned away as another figure appeared, wearing a long white coat. This man did not speak, but checked Locke's eyes, pointing a small torch directly at them, causing the pain to course through his brain. He tried to turn his head away but that caused even more agony.

Slowly he became aware of a fourth figure. He hadn't seen this one before; he hadn't moved until now. He was wearing dark blue clothing and was holding something across his midriff. As Locke looked closer he saw it was a gun; a black rifle. Nothing made sense. The man in the white coat continued to fidget and fuss around the bed.

"Who are you?"

It came out as a rasping whisper. The woman sobbed, just once, as she tried to stifle her emotions. The man ran a hand through his hair. Locke repeated the question.

"It's Mom and Dad, darling. Do you remember us?"

Locke stared at the face of the woman, desperation writ large in her expression.

"You can't be. I don't know you."

Daisy Locke sobbed again. So it *had* happened. Her son had been in a coma for weeks and now that he had come round, he was displaying signs of amnesia once again. The police officer holding the rifle shuffled slightly.

"What's he doing here?"

"It's the police, darling. They say you did some bad things."

The police officer said something Locke didn't quite hear, but he saw 'Dad' turn around at the words.

"What have I done?"

"Shush, darling," said the woman claiming to be his mother. "You need to keep your strength up."

Locke tried again to process the information. *What have I done?* It was the only thing he was really interested in. He tried to move his right hand again. Something itched at his temple. He struggled but managed to bring his arm up far enough to touch the skin. There was something there. Rough skin. A scab? He touched around the spot and winced. That too caused pain. He pulled his hand away from his temple and looked at his fingers. His forehead creased in realisation, trying to work out what was happening. He touched his temple again and again looked at his fingers. 'Mom' tried to hold his hand, but he shrugged her off. Then a sudden flash of gold. No, yellow, the colour of buttercup.

"Anjali," he said.

Daisy Locke stopped trying to clean his hand. The doctor also stopped and stared down at Locke. Joe Locke didn't move.

"What was that, darling?" Daisy asked.

"Anjali," Locke repeated. Daisy put a hand to her mouth. Joe looked at the doctor, who looked at his notes. The police officer stepped forwards.

John Locke touched the wound on his temple once more. It felt like a small hole, the pain intense. Then the throbbing started at the back of his head. He imagined a gun; a deafening report, a spray of bright pink blood.

"Anjali!"

John Locke had remembered.

2022

Sachin Locke surveyed the building in front of him. It was white; strikingly so and flared like a star in the cold sky-blue March afternoon. There were ornate carvings above the columned entrance depicting Hindu figures; Radha, Krishna, Vishnu and Brahma amongst others. To the left side of the entrance, in large gold letters were the words 'Anjali Sharma House'. To the right side of the entrance, a detail carved in bronze, but coloured gold and black, of a kneeling woman seemingly in prayer, her hands raised skywards towards her God, dark hair sculptured as if it was cascading down her back towards the ground. The artist had depicted the train of the sari in such a way as to make it look as though it was perpetually flowing, not rigid.

And in this light the effect was stunning. He had added one final detail, the effect of which was mesmerising on anyone who saw it; he had fashioned the folds of the sari in such a way as to create a human face. It was of a beautiful woman, eyes staring defiantly ahead; her own hair returning to the folds in the sari. To anyone who knew the story, it was clearly a faithful depiction of Anjali Sharma herself.

Sachin blinked away the tears that threatened and stepped forward. It had been two and a half years of struggle, of spending hours in courtrooms as lawyers banged on about how guilty his own father was of his crimes, of whether the catastrophic impact on John Locke's psyche, caused by his treatment all those years earlier was to blame, or whether it was the man himself. It had proved difficult for all concerned.

The prosecutors went for a murder charge centred on the deaths of the Roper family in Salford. They felt they could make those murders stick and leave Locke languishing in prison for the rest of his life. But then what of the internet deaths, as they had become known? The final toll was one hundred and thirteen and no one quite knew what to do there. Manslaughter? But how could you be responsible for over a hundred deaths and claim it was an accident?

Psychiatric evaluations were predictably confused. John Locke was not mad. But he had clearly done things that no ordinary human would do. The press labelled him evil, but was he really? At what point do you cross over from evil to mad? Are you evil to have murdered one person, or merely calculating? Did two murders make you more evil, or more calculating? And when did evil turn to madness?

The courts struggled with it all. Eventually John Locke was sent to a maximum security psychiatric hospital, satisfying no one. He now spent his days aiding various government organisations with whatever they sent to him and there was no doubt much of it was covered by the Official Secrets Act. Many were outraged when the news broke, but then what did you do with a genius like John Locke?

Sachin gently touched the folds of the sari manipulated into a perfect depiction of Anjali Sharma's face. The entire statue was a beautiful memorial to his mother and had attracted global attention. The paintings his father had created that went for sale in the art auction all those years ago had become world famous and one or two periodically got exhibited somewhere in the world.

The owner of his father's final painting; the seventh depiction of India, and therefore the most complete and perfect, had approached Sachin and offered to sell it to him when details of Anjali's will became common knowledge through the press. He was asking for an extortionate amount, many times more than he had paid for it all those years ago.

Sachin refused; and the greedy chancer found himself forced to sell it on the open market some months later. He never knew what Sachin Locke had done to cause his sudden fall from wealth.

The picture now hung in the hallway of the mansion John Locke had built and where Sachin now lived with his grandparents. They hadn't wanted to move, let alone live in a house that had witnessed their daughter's death, but he had insisted; said he needed to be close to his mother and if that meant living where she had died then that was what he would do. He never told his grandparents, but he wanted to live his father's dream too. Much as he tried, he could not hate his father and living in the house that he had built for his family just felt right.

His fingers left the statue and he walked through the doors into the wide atrium of the building. Indian imagery was everywhere and all of it tastefully done. It had taken almost two years to get his mother's will through probate and another eighteen months to finally see her wishes come to fruition.

The pandemic had not helped, but months of wrangling by lawyers slowed the process just as much as Covid ever had. Her fortune had been sizeable but she had left just one third to her son. It was more than anyone needed to live comfortably for the rest of their life, and Sachin understood this. The rest she had left to a charity that she had said should be called the Anjali Sharma Foundation.

She had dropped the name of Locke. And Sachin understood perfectly, whilst deciding to keep his father's name.

Well before the money was placed in trust and a group of executors put in place to oversee the use of the funds, Sachin had started to do what his mother wished. He sourced the site in central Manchester, designed the building and started to sculpt the statue. He kept that last to himself; no one knew who the genius behind the statue actually was and it led to a cult-like fascination as fans of the work tried to figure it out. His name cropped up in some conspiracy theorists' blogs and posts, but no one had anything like proof.

The building was due to open in days and already the list of people desperate for help was in the hundreds. In fact it was in danger of being overrun, but that didn't concern Sachin. He already had planned for another such venture in London. In time he saw the Anjali Sharma Foundation helping disabled children in every city in the world.

The sheer scale of that plan would see Sachin through to the end of his days, but dedicating his life to his mother's memory was all that mattered to him. Even the press seemed to like him at the moment, although he knew that once he turned eighteen scrutiny would be tighter and almost anything could be written about him. He didn't care; he knew he could manipulate events and lives and bring careers crashing down. The would-be art seller found that out to his considerable cost.

Sachin Locke took a last look around the room, at the grand hallway and reception desk down one side, the marble floors and columns and the gently winding marble staircase. Anjali Sharma had wanted the disabled children to feel that they mattered, that they were being looked after in a place where the rich and famous might go, as if it was a hotel out of the financial reach of ordinary people.

No child that her foundation was to help was going to be put aside in a rundown damp-infested concrete block in the back end of a rundown district. No. Every child the Anjali Sharma Foundation was to help was to feel their own importance the moment they came through the palatial front entrance.

Sachin Locke stepped out into the bright afternoon sunshine and delicately touched his mother's forehead in the statue he had sculpted. He touched his own forehead in the same place with the same hand. It was the point on his mother's temple where the bullet had entered. Somehow the action soothed him, as if it brought him closer to his mother. It was the only thing he couldn't really explain.

*

Almost two hundred miles away John Locke looked up from the computer he was tapping away at and placed a hand to his temple. The skin there was rough, a scar had formed and left a small depression. His little fingertip nestled perfectly within it. He pulled his hand away and looked at his fingers.

"Anjali," he said, quietly.

the end.

author's note

This story came to me as a premonition to help society and better understand marriage. My novel is dedicated to a loving marriage which I had in the past and how I used to believe and trust in it.

*

My special thanks go to Michael Thame from ghostwriterbooks.co.uk for his valuable contribution. Without his help and efforts, this book would never have been realised. And to Jem Authors Agency for their assistance in both the cover design and the publishing of this work.

There are many others out there who have helped me over the years and for whom I am eternally grateful. I am sure you know who you are.

Golam Maula

February 2022.